Praise for Davi

GW01066115

'[I]t is evident that Wishart is at home in the period.' *Sunday Times*

'Witty, engrossing and ribald . . . [*Sejanus*] misses nothing in its evocation of a bygone time and place' *Independent on Sunday*

'The Lydian Baker, a fabulous, solid gold, four-and-a-half foot statue gifted to the Delphic Oracle by King Croesus is hot stuff, and when Roman amateur sleuth Marcus Corvinus is commissioned to find it, he soon gets his fingers burned. But at least he doesn't get his head bashed in or his throat cut as happens to others who come into contact with the statue. A classical crime caper out of the top drawer.' Steve Craggs, *Northern Echo*

'Tales of treachery, betrayal and murder always make good reading, but Carnoustie author David Wishart's novels have an extra dimension – they are set in ancient Rome . . . David takes real people and weaves his novels around them . . . For while the dramatis personae have Roman names and live in Roman times, they speak in modern English which is both familiar and natural.' *Dundee Courier & Advertiser*

The Lydian Baker

David Wishart

FLAME
Hodder & Stoughton

Copyright © 1998 by David Wishart

First published in 1998 by Hodder and Stoughton
A division of Hodder Headline PLC
First published in paperback in 1999 by Hodder and Stoughton
A Flame Paperback

The right of David Wishart to be identified as the Author of
the Work has been asserted by him in accordance with the
Copyright, Designs and Patents Act 1988.

10 9 8 7 6 5 4 3 2 1

A CIP catalogue record for this title is available
from the British Library

ISBN 0 340 71529 4

Typeset by Palimpsest Book Production Limited,
Polmont, Stirlingshire
Printed and bound in Great Britain by
Clays Ltd, St Ives PLC, Bungay, Suffolk

Hodder and Stoughton
A division of Hodder Headline PLC
338 Euston Road
London NW1 3BH

For Ann Scott, mathematicist, and for Flo McPhee,
child- and dog-minder extraordinary.

Dramatis Personae ∫

CORVINUS'S HOUSEHOLD AND FAMILY

Alexis: gardener and parrot trainer.

Bathyllus: the head slave.

Lysias: the coachman.

Meton: the chef.

Nestor: a parrot.

Perilla, Rufia: Corvinus's wife.

Priscus, Titus Helvius: Corvinus's stepfather.

Volumnia: Corvinus's mother.

STAFF OF 'APHRODITE'S SCALLOP'

Antaeus: the bouncer.

Cleo
Cotile } two of the girls.

Demetriacus: the owner.

Hermippe: the manageress.

ATHENS AND THE ACADEMY

Alciphron: the Academy librarian.

Callippus: Commander of the Athenian Watch.

Dida: a public coachman.

Felix: a freedman of Gaius Caesar (Caligula).

Labrus: Corvinus's wine supplier.

Lysimachus of Cos: a doctor.

Melanthus of Abdera: an art expert and member of the Academy.

Memnon: an Ethiopian.

THE PIRAEUS

Argaius: an import-export dealer.

Bessus: a stevedore.

Chrysoulla: Argaius's wife.

Harpalus: a friend of Smaragdus.

'Prince Charming' (Glycus): a thug.

Smaragdus: Argaius's partner.

Tiny: a mentally subnormal giant.

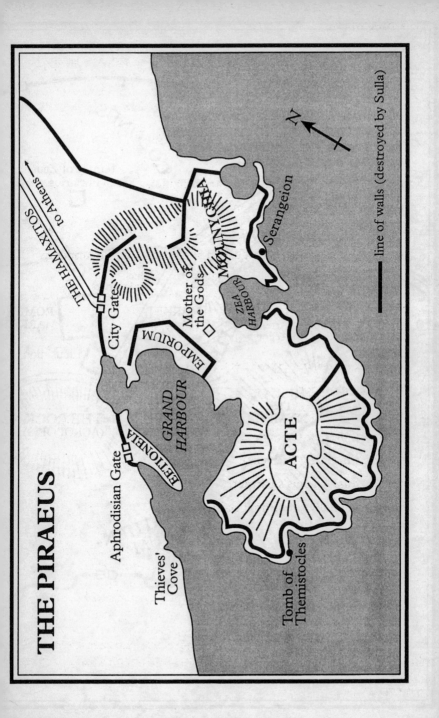

THE PIRAEUS

THE HAMAXITOS
to Athens

Aphrodisian Gate

Thieves' Cove

City Gate

EMPORIUM

GRAND HARBOUR

EETIONEIA

ACTE

Tomb of Themistocles

MUNYCHIA

Mother of the Gods

ZEA HARBOUR

Serangeion

N

—— line of walls (destroyed by Sulla)

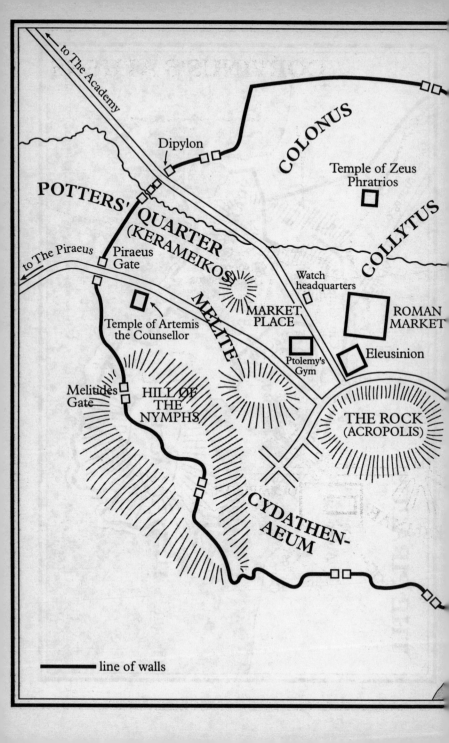

CORVINUS'S ATHENS

0 ——————— 500
metres

N

Eridanus Stream

Garden of
Theophrastos

DIOMEA

Lyceum

Corvinus's
house

Hippades
Gate

OLYMPEION

LIMNAE

ILISSOS RIVER

Purple laver . . .

I blinked and set the letter down on the table beside my wine cup. Some things – what Perilla's philosopher pals would call the Eternal Verities – never changed. They included death, pestilence and Mother's whacky recipes. In the four months we'd been back we'd piled up enough ways of cooking lentils to open an Egyptian cookshop, and some of the other stuff she recommended for a full and healthy life you couldn't put a name to even in hieroglyphs.

'Hey, Perilla,' I said. 'You any idea what purple laver is?'

The lady looked up from the book she was reading. Chrysippus's *Studies in Grammar*. That's one advantage of living in Athens, if you can call it an advantage: there're more libraries than even Perilla can shake a stick at. Serious ones, with not an Alexandrian bodice-ripper in sight. Listen hard and you can hear manuscripts crumbling all over town. Readers, too.

'It's a kind of edible seaweed, Marcus,' she said. 'Imported from Gaul, I believe.'

'Is that right, now?' Jupiter! In that case this was one recipe our chef Meton was definitely not getting his hands on. I'd enough problems with the local cuisine without letting the weird dietary habits of blue-rinsed Gauls into the act, and that bastard would slip me a batch of Mother's laver cakes just for the fun of telling me what I'd eaten and watching me go green.

'How is Volumnia?' Perilla had laid the book aside. Maybe she couldn't take the excitement.

'Thriving. She's off tomb-bashing with Priscus in Caere.' Priscus was my stepfather. The guy was well into his seventies, a good two decades older than Mother, but fit as a flea despite looking like a prune buried in sand for six months. Rooting around old tombs and collecting antiquities was his life, and although they were different as chalk and cheese she wasn't complaining. Maybe it did have something to do with what she fed the old bugger on, but even so I didn't want to know. If the gods had meant us to eat seaweed they wouldn't have invented the Baian oyster. 'Marilla's fine as well, she says. And Marcia sends her regards.'

Perilla's face softened. Our prospective daughter was still where we'd left her, on Marcia Fulvina's farm in the Alban Hills. The adoption hadn't got all the way through the courts yet but it was practically settled, and the kid's father had taken his one-way trip down the Rock for incest before the year was out. No tears there. I was only sorry I hadn't been in Rome to give him the final shove myself.

'It'll be lovely to have Marilla here,' Perilla said. 'To be a family at last.'

'Yeah. Yeah, it will.' I'd caught the tone, and it still wrenched at my gut, even after years of marriage: Perilla needed Marilla as much as she needed Perilla. It isn't easy, knowing you can't have kids of your own, and the princess was all right. I took a swallow of wine, braced myself, and picked up the letter again.

Incidentally, Marcus [Mother wrote], I have a favour to ask. Rather an unusual one. Before we left, Titus learned of a certain statue which has come up for sale and which the poor lamb is simply desperate to add to his collection. He's written his own letter which I've enclosed, so I won't go into details here, and he's also provided a note for delivery to Simon.

[Simon was our local banker. Priscus dealt with his brother in Rome.] I know very little about the piece myself, but from what Titus says it is rather special, and he'll be terribly disappointed if he doesn't get it; so do try your very best for us, my dear, because I was hoping to lure the old buffer down to the fleshpots after he's done his wretched tombs, and the last thing I want is for him to be sulking all through the holiday. Goodness knows fleshpots are no fun at all when Titus is in one of his moods, and after Caere I always find I need a break.

The Lydian Baker •

Oh, and speaking of fleshpots I don't know if you ever met
Catullina Gemella . . .

There followed a good half-page of prime Roman gossip.
Jupiter! Eat your heart out, Tullius Cicero! Maybe I should
keep Mother's correspondence to hand down to posterity as
an epistolary antidote. As well as a culinary curiosity. I sighed
and reached for the wine.

'Meton says that dinner is ready, sir.' Our major-domo Bathyllus
had oiled in on my blind side, bald scalp gleaming like Hector's
helmet.

'Namely?'

'Apple and calf's brain casserole, tripe in a honey-ginger sauce
and a fennel pottage.'

'Great.' Thank the gods for good, plain, seaweed-free cooking.
'We'll be through in a minute, little guy. Once I've finished my
pre-dinner drink.'

Bathyllus looked pointedly at the level in the jug, gave a sniff
and padded out. Bastard.

'Did Volumnia have any other news, Marcus?' Perilla said.

'Priscus wants me to agent for him. There's a statue he's got
his eye on.'

'Really?'

'Yeah.' I sank a quarter-pint of Setinian. 'You'd think the guy
would have enough junk already to last him without sending to
Athens for more.'

'Everyone needs a hobby. And at least his is harmless.'

I grinned. 'Unlike Catullina Gemella's.'

'Whose?'

'Never mind.' I reached for the second roll: Priscus's letter.
Something fell out. I picked it up and glanced at it. 'Gods!'

'What's wrong?' Perilla got up quickly and came over to stand
behind me. I was staring at the banker's draft. Harmless the old
bugger's hobby might be, but it wasn't cheap, that was for
sure. There were numbers there I didn't know existed outside
a population census.

'You think the city council's hocking Phidias's *Athene*?' I said.

'Don't be silly, Marcus.' Perilla bent down for a closer look.
Her breath caught. 'Oh. Oh, I see what you mean.'

I swallowed. Priscus might have a fair bit stashed away – apart from his tomb-bashing forays he lived pretty simply, and Mother had her own money – but he'd given Simon authority to release the price of a villa on the Janiculan, with maybe a racing yacht thrown in. No ordinary statue would cost that much. No ordinary statue even came close. So what the hell was Priscus playing at?

I opened the letter itself. Where Mother's writing sprawled across the page like the tracks of a drunken spider, Priscus's was tiny enough to give a literate ant migraine. The guy might be willing to spend several millions on a bronze wrestler or a hunk of Parian that some big-name Greek had restructured with a chisel four hundred years back, but he could squeeze more words into a square foot of paper than anyone else I knew.

> Titus Helvius Priscus gives greetings to his stepson Marcus Valerius Messalla Corvinus.
> Volumnia will have mentioned the Baker statue to you, Marcus. Tremendously exciting, and certainly, assuming it's genuine, the antiquarian find of the century. If I can acquire it I shall die a happy man. Naturally the price, great as it is, represents only a fraction of the piece's true worth, and as you'll readily appreciate I pay it gladly.

I took another mouthful of wine. 'Readily appreciate', hell! Jupiter, I'd never understand antiquarians, not if I lived to be ninety. Personally if I ever lost what few marbles I'd got and splashed out the price of a villa on a statue I'd be happy if my nearest and dearest didn't poison my gruel.

'Corvinus, hold still, please,' Perilla murmured. 'How do you expect me to read if you keep jiggling about like that?'

'Sorry, lady.' I straightened the letter and read on:

> I will not insult you by describing the Baker to you, since you will of course know of it already.

Yeah, sure I did; I carried a run-down of every work of art from Achilles' shield to the Wart's latest portrait in my head.

Describing them in painstaking detail was my favourite trick at parties.

> The obvious stumbling blocks are authenticity and prov-
> enance. My historian friends are divided over when the statue
> actually disappeared from the Delphian treasury, but the
> *terminus ante quem* can be no later than one hundred and
> thirty years ago while the *terminus post quem* is the period
> of the Phocian depredations of the Third Sacred War, dating
> back some two hundred and fifty years before that; con-
> sequently . . .

Shit. Priscus wrote even worse than he talked, and rereading didn't help much either. My head was spinning. I'd swear that half of this stuff wasn't even Latin.

'Hey, Perilla,' I said over my shoulder, 'just skim through this and explain it to me in words of one syllable, would you?'

But she wasn't behind me any longer. I looked round just in time to see her disappearing through the door in the direction of the dining-room. Yeah, well, Priscus off and running with the antiquarian bit between his teeth versus apple and calf's brain casserole on an empty stomach is no contest. I tossed the letter on to the side table, poured the last of the Setinian into my cup and followed her in the direction of the feed bag.

She wasn't in the dining-room either. Odd.

Bathyllus was doing complex things with tableware.

'Uh . . . you seen the mistress?' I asked him.

'I understand she's gone to her study for a book, sir.' The little guy had on his prim put-upon look. Or maybe it was just his hernia playing up again. 'Should I serve dinner now or would you like another pre-dinner jug while we're waiting?'

That's what I like about Bathyllus: when he wants to be sarcastic his touch is feather light. Still, he had a point. I was mildly peeved with Perilla myself. My one inflexible rule is no reading at the table; literature plays hell with good conversation, not to mention giving me heartburn.

'No, go ahead.' I stretched out on the couch and held out my hands for the slave to pour water over them. 'She'll be down again in a minute.'

A sniff. 'Very well, sir.'

She wasn't; in fact, the starters were already off and running when she came back. Sure enough, she was carrying a book-roll.

'Marcus, I've found it,' she said.

'Oh, whoopee.' I patted the couch beside me. 'But just leave it alone until we've eaten, Archimedes. Okay?'

Perilla ignored me. She lay down and held her hands out for the water, then patted them dry with a napkin and unrolled the book. 'The Baker statue was gifted to the Delphic oracle by Croesus of Lydia, six hundred years ago. Herodotus saw it at Delphi himself.'

'You don't say?' I tried to look unimpressed. Policy; give the lady an inch and she'll take a yard. 'Herodotus himself, eh? With his own little piggy eyes?' I passed her a fish pickle canapé.

'But you don't understand! Priscus is right. If the Baker's turned up it's incredible!'

I sighed. 'Perilla, it's dinner-time, I'm hungry, and frankly I couldn't care less if Priscus's hunk of marble turns out to have the nosey old globetrotting bugger's name carved across its backside in cuneiform. Now shut up and let's eat.'

'Very well.' Perilla nibbled the canapé. 'I thought you'd be interested, though. The Baker wasn't marble. Nor was it bronze. It was solid gold, four and a half feet high.'

The olive I was chewing went down the wrong way and I choked. Perilla reached over and pounded me on the back.

'You are interested, then?' she said.

Jupiter in a bucket! 'Uh, Bathyllus?' I said when I could breathe again.

'Yes, sir?'

'There's a letter on the side table next door. Just bring it through, would you?'

He left, and I turned back to Perilla. '*Solid* gold?' She nodded. 'Solid as in "solid"?' Another nod. 'And four and a half *feet*?'

'So Herodotus said, yes.'

I sat back. Yeah. Well, maybe it was incredible after all. Not that Priscus would care a toss for the monetary value; it took a philistine like me to think of that aspect. And it explained the price. Even melted down four and a half feet of solid gold is a lot of gravy.

'Okay,' I said. 'You have my undivided attention. You happen to know why this thing went missing?'

'No. But if it's reappeared, then as Priscus says it's a major find. If Melanthus confirms its authenticity, naturally.'

'And who the hell is Melanthus?'

'Marcus, didn't you *read* what Priscus wrote?'

'Not from beginning to end, no. I gave up when my brain started to hurt.'

'What brain?'

'Now listen, lady . . . !' Someone coughed: our bald-headed major-domo, mission fulfilled, complete with Priscus's letter. I grabbed it and unrolled. This time I skipped the lumpy stuff.

'I have asked a correspondent of mine at the Academy, one Melanthus of Abdera, if he would be kind enough to cast a professional eye over the statue before, Marcus, you conclude the financial formalities on my behalf.' Shit. That was all I needed. You can't move in Athens without tripping over some parboiled egghead philosopher, and the ones at the Academy are the pick of the clutch. I was getting bad feelings about this business already, find of the century or not. I carried on reading. 'Melanthus is an expert on Eastern art, and you may trust to his judgment implicitly; also, naturally, Argaius understands that any sale will depend on his approval.'

He'd lost me again. I checked above for Argaius and found him three paragraphs back. He was the seller, and according to Priscus he had an import-export business near the Serangeion. I frowned. I knew the Serangeion, in the run-down Piraeus docklands area between Zea and Mounychia harbours, and it wasn't a good address for a reputable art-dealer. Certainly not one who dealt in solid gold statues with star billing in Herodotus.

Something stank worse than the Tiber in midsummer, and it wasn't Meton's fish pickle canapés, either. I looked up. Perilla was helping herself to the fennel pottage.

'It all sounds absolutely fascinating, doesn't it, Marcus?' she said.

Perilla never ceases to amaze me. She was serious. She was

actually serious. I hated to burst the bubble, but it had to be done.

'It all sounds absolutely suspect, lady,' I said. 'Either we're talking black market here or Priscus is being sold a pup. I don't know about you, but personally I'd go for the second option.'

The spoon paused in mid-dollop. 'You think so?'

I sighed. 'Perilla, anyone with a business near the Serangeion knows more about faking ancient statues than a dog knows how to scratch. It's a con, believe me.'

'But that's terrible!' She looked stricken.

'It's the way the world works. The best favour I can do Priscus is to write back telling him to forget the whole thing, buy a hack team at the Racetrack and lose his money sensibly.'

'He'd never believe you.'

Well, she had a point there. I held out my plate for the tripe. I knew Priscus, and from the tone of his letter the guy had stars in his eyes. If I wrote back to say he'd be better throwing his cash down the nearest manhole or blowing it on wild women and fancy booze he'd ignore me and get himself another agent by return. At least I was family. And there was just an outside chance that this was on the level. The odds in favour were about the same as I'd put on a herd of flying pigs being spotted over the Acropolis, mind, but still . . .

'Marcus?'

I blinked. 'Yeah. That's me.'

'You really think this is a swindle?'

'If it isn't, lady, I'm a eunuch priest of Attis.'

'But Melanthus—'

'Perilla, I wouldn't trust one of these Academy bubbleheads to authenticate his own grandmother. They're a con artist's dream. Most of them don't have the sense to come in out of the rain, let alone spot a competent fake.'

She was silent for a moment. Then she sighed.

'Well, I suppose it does sound rather too good to be true,' she said. 'So. What can we do?'

'Go through the motions. At least until the dickering stage. After all, it can't hurt to give it a try, can it?'

Like hell it couldn't. But then, I didn't know that yet.

Next day I tossed a coin to decide who was first on the list, Melanthus or Argaius. Melanthus won. Well, best to get the bugger over with. It was just a pity he wasn't based at the Lyceum, which was just up the road, but that was the way things went. Anyway, it was a fine spring day and the long hike to the Academy would do me good.

I followed the main drag past the north side of the Acropolis to the City centre. That way I could call in on Simon and clear Priscus's bank draft, but also drop in on my wine merchant Labrus to place my order for a new consignment of Setinian. When I'd told Perilla I'd go through the motions I meant just that. Sure, I'd help Priscus out, but I had business of my own to take care of and I wasn't going to bust a gut racing round the City on what would probably turn out to be a wild-goose chase.

Athens may not be Rome but walking there has its points, and the place grows on you. The locals are less uptight about using their legs, for a start, so a well-dressed pedestrian doesn't get too many stares even if he is wearing a Roman mantle. Keep away from the squeaky-clean Acropolis where the tourists are only outnumbered by the souvenir-sellers and you'll find some parts of the city that have real character. Thieves' Market off South Square, for example, where, if you're not too fussy where the goods come from and whether the seller can produce a proper bill of sale, you can pick up anything from a second-hand bath towel to a trained python. Other things too, if you're not careful.

South Square wasn't on my route, though, even for window-shopping. I cut off to the right before the Eleusinion and headed for the Roman Market, where the expats hung out swapping dewy-eyed memories of the Tiber by moonlight and which, for just that reason, I usually avoided. Labrus's wine store was in the south-west corner, under the portico. Labrus hurried out when he saw me coming, which was par for the course: Setinian's a specialist wine east of the Ionian Sea, and ordering special shipments direct from Rome doesn't come cheap. He was a cheery, down-to-earth Miletan, and a real find; although maybe *find* wasn't the exact word because he'd come recommended by my erstwhile pal Prince Gaius. Normally I wouldn't've touched anyone who had that loopy inbred bastard's seal of approval with gloves and a ten-foot pole, but I made an exception with Labrus. The guy knew his wines, and better still he knew how to pick the ones that travelled. Give even a decent wine a two-month trip in a heaving gutbucket merchantman and nine times out of ten you're talking vinegar at the other end. I'd never had a bum consignment from Labrus yet.

'Valerius Corvinus!' He bared all three of his teeth at me in a grin: like all Miletans Labrus was addicted to honey-soaked pastries. 'A delight to see you again, lord!'

I went inside. The shop wasn't big – Labrus kept most of his stock in a warehouse behind Market Hill – but it was neat as a Vestal's boudoir, and the wine jars were well covered. Another point in Labrus's favour; some Athenian wine-dealers can be sloppy about remembering to keep their samples covered, and for me a dead fly in the tasting cup's a definite turn-off. Obviously I'd come at a good time, because there were more jars stacked against the wall than usual. This I was going to enjoy: Labrus never minded making inroads on his own stock in the cause of customer relations.

'New consignment?' I said.

'Yes, lord. Just up from the harbour this morning.' Labrus signed to one of his slaves to bring the cup. 'Rhodian whites, mostly, nothing of much interest to you, but there's a new red from Samos you may like to try.'

'Sure. Wheel it out,' I said. That was another reason I used Labrus: he didn't waste your time with stuff he knew wouldn't suit, however good it was. And even if my tastes did run on fairly fixed lines I bought the occasional Greek jar for when we had locals to dinner.

The slave came back, and Labrus poured for me. I sniffed, then sipped. Yeah, this was a good one, all right: rich in the nose, lingering on the palate with just a hint of cherries. It could almost have been Caecuban.

'Samian, you say?'

'From a single vineyard near the south coast. Five years old.'

'Uh-huh. For Samian it's not bad.' An understatement, and heresy to a Greek, but then I was Roman, and doing the buying. I pulled up the chair Labrus always keeps ready for customers with time to kill. 'Strong stuff, too.'

Labrus poured half a cup of the Samian for himself and topped it up with water. I grinned: getting a prospective customer part-plastered and keeping him company might be good for business, but a wine-dealer has to keep a clear head. Not a job I could've managed myself.

'A wine to be treated with respect, certainly,' he agreed. 'And a minor miracle. I've done business with the producer before but never had anything more than ordinary table quality, before or since. For that year, Bacchus was kind.'

I took another sip. Jupiter, it was good, all right. Better than any Samian I'd ever had, certainly, and although Samian wasn't a wine I went for all that much this one I could grow to like. I leaned back and let the glow spread through me. Maybe it was going to be a pleasant morning after all.

I left Labrus's just before noon, four cups down the jar and with the Samian singing in my head. I was feeling a lot more cheerful now about hobnobbing with Melanthus of Abdera, and not just because of the wine: we'd had our usual chat before getting down to the nitty-gritty of business, and it turned out that he was another of Labrus's customers. No bonehead, either, where wine was concerned, Labrus said, so maybe I'd been too hard on the guy. No one who knows his wines can be all that bad, even if he is a philosopher.

I called in at Simon's by the Painted Porch to clear Priscus's draft, then carried on along the Panathenaia towards the Academy. Like always, it was packed cheek by jowl as far as the Dipylon, but outside the City limits among the tombs on Academy Road the crowds and the snack-sellers' stalls melted away like magic. Wheeled traffic bound for Daphne uses the parallel carriageway, so there was only the occasional litter plus us humble pedestrians: a mixture of students, country yokels carrying poles of chickens or driving pigs, and lovers heading for the stretch of woodland between Athens and Horse Hill. It was a beautiful day, warm and rich with the smell of cypress and wild marjoram. Good walking weather. Maybe I should've brought Perilla, although that would've meant a shorter stay at Labrus's and fewer cups of the Samian: unbelievable as it may seem, hanging around wine stores and shooting the breeze isn't the lady's bag.

The Academy was bigger than I'd expected, a scatter of buildings set in the wooded grounds of an old temple complex. Forget the idea of ragged philosophers living in tubs or dickering for a handful of sprats at the fishmarket, the place smelled of old money and good taste. I hadn't been there before, unlike Perilla who'd sat in on a few highbrow public lectures, but I asked a passing student and he directed me to the library. Sure, I should've sent a skivvy to make an appointment with Melanthus before coming out all that way myself, but you can't think of everything. Luckily the guy was at work, if you can call what academics do work: halfway up a ladder with his head in a shelf-ful of books that looked like they'd been gathering dust since Socrates wet his first nappy.

Philosopher or not, Melanthus was no fool. I knew that as soon as he climbed down and fixed me with an eye you could've used for filleting anchovies.

'Ah, Corvinus, my dear fellow. Delighted to meet you.' A strong handshake. Strong, confident voice, too, and that surprised me; a lot of these guys speak like they're not too sure they exist themselves, let alone the person they're talking to. Maybe we'd get on after all. 'Helvius Priscus wrote to me that you'd be coming.'

'He did?' Common sense, sure, but with Priscus you don't take common sense for granted. 'Hey, that's great.'

'Indeed. And what's more in a letter most uncharacteristically exuberant for him.' Melanthus smiled. 'Mind you, I can appreciate the reason. For Croesus's Baker to have resurfaced after all this time is . . . well, it's remarkable, truly remarkable. I wish

I could afford to purchase it myself, but of course that would be well beyond my means. It seems that nowadays only you Romans have the money and, occasionally, the taste for such extravagances.'

Was there an edge to his voice? Maybe it was just my imagination, but I didn't think so. I'd heard this kind of stuff from Greeks before, although not always put so politely. Translated into simple Latin it meant: 'You Roman bastards are all made of money, and the only culture you'll ever have is the one you buy from us. So just be humbly grateful that we're willing to sell you it, okay?'

'Uh, yeah,' I said carefully. 'Well, if you'll forgive me for saying so, pal, not every Roman would bother to outbid you even if he could afford it. And tastes vary, even here in Athens.'

Melanthus patted me on the shoulder. 'True. That I would believe. We live in a decadent, materialistic age, Corvinus. But don't misunderstand me; I'm not vain enough to assume that everyone subscribes to my values, here or elsewhere. I suppose we must be grateful that Romans of your stepfather's stamp exist. But perhaps we can talk more comfortably in the garden.'

He led the way outside to a marble bench under a pear tree, and we sat down.

'Incidentally,' I said, 'I hear we share the same wine merchant.'

'Labrus?' He gave me a sharp look. 'Indeed? You use him too?'

'Yeah. He try you with his new batch of Samian?'

'Yes, he did, as a matter of fact. I found it pleasant enough, although a little' – he paused – 'unsubtle. Especially for a Samos wine.'

'Is that so, now?' Forget instant rapport: the guy was beginning seriously to get up my nose. I shifted tack. 'You think this Baker statue could be genuine?'

'I'm a philosopher, Corvinus. I don't venture an opinion without proof.'

'But it's possible?'

'Everything's possible. In theory, at least. I'd prefer to suspend judgment completely until I've seen it, that's all.'

'Okay. So would you like to give me some basic details?'

'Details of what?'

'Pal, you could write what I know about antiques on a busted sandal strap and still have room for the stitching. And Priscus's letter wasn't what you'd call informative. Not to someone of my level of intelligence, anyway.'

'You underrate yourself, my dear fellow.'

Jupiter with tiny bells on! 'Assume that I don't.'

That called out the smile again. 'You know, Socrates was once told that the Delphic oracle had called him the wisest man alive. He puzzled over that for a long time before deciding that what Apollo had meant was that he alone was aware of his own ignorance.'

'Is that right?' I was finding it difficult not to grind my teeth. 'Then maybe my powers of self-assessment are better than his were.'

Melanthus laughed suddenly. 'You should come here more often, Corvinus,' he said. 'You have a talent for dialectic. Very well. To answer your question. You know that the Baker was gifted to Delphi by King Croesus of Lydia some six hundred years ago? And that it was part of a larger dedication?'

'Yeah. That much I do know.'

'The temple records describe it as a solid gold figure of a woman four and a half feet high, standing erect and holding a loaf of bread and an ear of wheat.'

'Why a baker?'

'According to the story, Croesus's baker saved his life, and in gratitude he had the statue cast in her likeness. Personally I think it far more likely that the figure was of some Lydian goddess with whom the Delphians were unfamiliar, but that's immaterial.'

'Fair enough. So what happened to it?'

'No one knows; not for certain. The temple records that might have contained the information have been lost. The Phocians may have taken it when they plundered Delphi, or it might have been the Gauls seventy years later. It could even have been your Roman Sulla, although that is less likely since that would bring the disappearance almost within living memory. Essentially, though, whoever was responsible, the Baker has been missing for a very long time. What I would like to know – and a question I will certainly be asking – is how this Argaius happened to come into possession of it. And I'll expect him to have a convincing answer.'

I nodded. Patronising tone or not, at least the guy showed a healthy degree of scepticism. I'd like to hear the answer to that one myself. 'Okay. So far as it goes. But even if the answer is convincing it still doesn't mean the statue itself is genuine.'

'No. But then again I can't claim Socrates' modesty, Corvinus. Or, if you'll forgive me, your own. Where archaic statues are concerned I must admit to knowing a great deal. There are features of style and treatment that are unmistakable and which a layman, however good a craftsman he might be, wouldn't even notice, let alone be able to reproduce. Don't worry. If the Baker is a forgery – even a very skilful one – I shall certainly be able to tell. And if I have any doubt – any doubt at all – I'll advise you not to proceed with the purchase.'

Well, you couldn't say fairer than that, and the guy seemed genuine. Obnoxious, but genuine. And he certainly made me feel better about this whole business, because if – when – he blew the whistle on the deal then Priscus would take from him what he wouldn't take from me.

'So the next step is to set up a meeting with Argaius, right?' I said.

'Indeed. And, more important, a viewing. You have the man's address? He has a business near the Serangeion, I understand?'

'Yeah. I'll go down to the Piraeus tomorrow and fix something up.'

'Good.' Melanthus got to his feet. 'Then you'll be in touch.'

'Sure.' I stood up too.

'You can always reach me here.' Melanthus held out his hand. 'And now I really must get back to work. A pleasure talking to you, Valerius Corvinus.'

'Yeah. Likewise,' I lied.

I took myself out of the hallowed grounds and back to the sordid hustle and bustle of the City. I'd been impressed, sure, despite myself: the guy seemed to have his head screwed on, and I reckoned that as far as the authentication went he was the best I'd get. Still, there was something about him that didn't quite fit. And not just because he wasn't my type, either . . .

Ah, leave it. Maybe I was just allergic to academics and it was my own prejudices showing.

One of the stallholders inside the Dipylon was selling little jointed wooden monkeys that climbed a stick when you pulled on a string, and I bought one to give to Perilla. Socrates or not, I knew my intellectual limitations. Climbing monkeys just about fitted.

3

I got our coachman Lysias to drive me down to the Piraeus early next morning. The Piraeus isn't exactly one of my favourite places; in fact it depresses me like hell. You'd think that as Athens's port it'd be thriving, like Ostia, but it isn't, and hasn't been for years; oh, sure, the area around the main harbour is prosperous enough, but that's about all most foreigners fresh off the boat see before the ubiquitous cabbies or chairmen have snapped them up and whisked them off up City Road to the City itself (to Athenians born and bred Athens has always been the City; capital 'C' on the old Greek term Homer used nine hundred years back, like no other existed and time was nothing). Move out past the dockside market and the centre immediately beyond and the place is a dump. Ruins, slums, gimcrack buildings put up on the cheap by fly-by-night speculators or locals who can't afford to do the thing properly. Piles of rubble and refuse. You name it, Piraeus has it in spades. Worse, it's the fault of us Romans; barring the shoddy recent stuff that would fall down if you breathed on it too hard that's how our sterling champion of the Beautiful and Good Cornelius Sulla left it when he burned the town in a fit of aristocratic pique a hundred years back. And we wonder why after all we've done for them the provincials still don't like us.

Argaius's trading emporium was in one of the dingy streets leading down from Zea Harbour where in the old days the Athenian navy used to moor its triremes. It was a two-up, two-down building with the living accommodation over the warehouse and a stray dog pissing against the bare brick wall.

Not the sort of place, in other words, that you'd envisage as containing seriously pricey statues.

Not the sort of place you'd envisage as containing anything at all except maybe third-hand bric-à-brac and constructionally challenged used furniture. The emporium looked deserted. I tried the door. It was locked, seriously locked, and the windows either side were covered and barred.

Okay. So it was beginning to look like I wouldn't be bothering Melanthus for an authentication anyhow. I hammered on the worm-eaten panelling for five minutes just to show willing, then stepped back to look at the windows of the flat above. One of the shutters was half open, sagging from a single hinge. I was sure I saw a movement behind it, but whoever was up there obviously didn't want to know.

'Hey, Argaius!' I shouted. 'The name's Valerius Corvinus. I'm acting for Helvius Priscus in Rome. Open up, okay?'

No answer. The windows stared down at me blankly.

Shit. This didn't fit the pattern. If it was a scam I should be inside by now, being treated like royalty. There was someone in there, sure there was. So what the hell was he playing at?

I'd left Lysias with the carriage next to a cheap cookshop fifty yards further down the street. Maybe an enquiry there might help. I gave the door one final bang for luck, then set off towards it.

I was almost there when a guy who wouldn't've looked out of place down at the docks loading cabbages came out chewing on a sausage.

'You looking for Argaius?' he said. Not friendly, either; but then smiles in the Piraeus were about as rare as gold pieces.

'Yeah. That's right.' Without making it too obvious I checked the knife I keep taped against my left wrist. 'You know where he is, pal?'

The big docker took another reflective bite at the sausage. 'He just left town. Family business.'

'Is that so, now?' I gauged my distance, but Lysias was already getting down from his box and hefting the weighted stick he carried for emergencies, so I doubted if the guy would try anything. Why he might want to was another question, and an interesting question at that.

'Yeah. That's so.' His eyes never left mine.

'You know when he'll be back?'

'Uh-uh.' His jaws moved rhythmically and he spat out a lump of gristle. The stray dog pounced. 'What's it about?'

'That's my business.' I kept the tone light. 'He leave anyone behind? Someone I could talk to?'

The eyes flickered briefly towards the half-closed shutter, then away again.

'No one to leave,' he said.

Well, I couldn't call him a liar, especially when whoever was upstairs didn't want to show themselves. And short of kicking the door down and hauling them out I couldn't prove anything, either. I shrugged. 'It seems that I've had a wasted journey, then.'

'Yeah.' He didn't move. 'Shame, isn't it?'

The hell with this. I wasn't looking for trouble, and if Argaius was on the level it was up to him to make the next move; if he wasn't, then as far as I was concerned he could shove his scam where it would do the most good. I shrugged again and pitched my voice so whoever was behind the shutter would hear me. 'Okay, friend. But if Argaius comes back you tell him Valerius Corvinus wants a word with him. If he wants me he'll find me in the City. Big house on Lykaion Road, just beyond the Hippades Gate.'

The guy's eyes never shifted. 'Nice address, Roman. I'll tell him. If and when I see him.'

'You do that.' I signalled to Lysias to get back on to the box and climbed aboard the carriage. 'Thanks for your help, pal. It's been a real pleasure meeting you.'

He didn't answer, not that I expected him to. No sign from upstairs, either. I gave the order to Lysias and we set off back towards Athens.

'Corvinus, you are *not* getting involved!'

'What with?' I stretched out on the couch while Bathyllus poured me a restoring cup of Setinian.

'I don't know what with.' Perilla threw herself into a chair by the ornamental pool. 'But I don't like the feel of this. Whatever it is you are staying out of it for a change.'

'That's fine by me.' I let the nectar slip past my tonsils. 'As far as I'm concerned as from now the matter's closed, if it was ever open. Whatever the game was, Argaius obviously doesn't want to play any more. I'll write to Priscus tonight. In fact, you write the letter for me and I'll sign it.'

'Don't be silly, Marcus!'

'Perilla.' I sat up. 'This Baker business is nothing to do with me, okay? My aesthetic interest in statues is zilch, it's not my money, the whole thing smells worse than six-month-old fish sauce in a heatwave, and if Priscus wants to force the guy into conning him out of two years' income he can get on the first boat over here and do it himself. Now does that satisfy you or do I have to draw you a map?'

Perilla came over to the couch and kissed me. Grinning, I put my arms round her waist and pulled her down beside me. Yeah, well, maybe I had sounded a bit tetchy.

'It's just that I can recognise the signs,' she said quietly. 'Once you get something into your head it doesn't shift. And if past experiences are anything to go by then your personal interest or lack of it has nothing to do with anything.'

'Yeah. Well. This time it's different. Believe me, lady, the best thing that could possibly happen is that nobody will hear anything from this Argaius guy ever again. Even if the Baker is genuine, the world's lived without it for long enough and only screwballs like Priscus will care a toss if it stays lost for ever.' I kissed her ear. 'And just to show that I really couldn't care less, what would you say to an early night?'

Her lips twitched. 'Is that a proposition?' she said.

'Sure it's a proposition. What else would it be?'

'Fine.' She kissed me again. 'Just checking.'

We were halfway up the stairs when Bathyllus soft-shoed into the hall and cleared his throat. Shit. This was always happening. The little guy had as much sense of timing as a third-rate Oscan tambourinist.

'What is it now, Bathyllus?' I said wearily.

'I'm sorry to disturb you, sir . . .'

'Then don't, pal.'

'. . . but you have a visitor. From the Piraeus.'

I groaned. I knew I should've kept my mouth shut when Prince

Charming gave me the bum's rush outside the cookshop. Still, it was done and I had only myself to blame. 'Don't tell me. His name's Argaius, and he wants to talk statues, right?'

'Marcus—' Perilla began.

'Yeah, yeah, I know, lady, but—'

Bathyllus cleared his throat again. '*Her* name is Chrysoulla, sir,' he said stiffly, 'and she is an extremely upset young lady. I've asked her to wait in the porch.'

Oh, hell. The plot thickened, and with a woman, no less. I didn't even look at Perilla.

She was a honey. Small and slim, mid-twenties, hair jet black and wavy under her headscarf, face like the Praxiteles *Persephone*. Apart from the puffy eyes and smudged make-up, that is. Bathyllus was right, she was upset as hell.

'Valerius Corvinus?'

'That's me,' I said. Somebody behind me coughed. I looked over my shoulder and grinned. 'Oh, yeah. And the lady with the set jaw and the green glint in her eye is my wife Perilla.' So she'd followed me downstairs after all. Well, I supposed that was fair. With a hot little number like this hammering on our door after the lamps were lit she had a right to be curious.

Our visitor took a deep breath and bit her lip. 'You were at our house this morning.'

'You're Argaius's wife?'

She nodded. 'I didn't come to the door. I'm sorry, but there were reasons.'

'Uh-huh. You want to come in properly?' Without waiting for an answer I turned to Bathyllus. 'Bring the wine jug, little guy.'

'And some fruit juice, Bathyllus,' Perilla said firmly. 'With two cups.'

'Whatever.' I led the way into the living-room. 'Have a seat. Make yourself comfortable.'

Chrysoulla sat stiffly on the edge of the guest chair. She was nervous as a cat. I lay down on the couch and Perilla took her usual place by the pool.

'Now,' I said. 'Being a foreigner I'm not too sure about how Greeks do business, lady, but I'd bet good money they don't send their wives round to clients' houses alone after dark. Especially when they could've talked face to face the same morning. So where's Argaius?'

'I don't know.' Her hands twisted in her lap.

'The guy outside the cookshop told me he was out of town on family business. That isn't true?'

A pause. 'No.'

'Marcus, stop it!' Perilla was looking frosty as hell. 'This isn't an interrogation. Or it shouldn't be one.' She turned to Chrysoulla and said gently: 'Your husband's disappeared, hasn't he? When did it happen?'

'Last night, ma'am. He said he had to meet someone. About the Baker.'

I opened my mouth to speak, but Perilla shot me a look before turning back to the girl.

'Did he say who?'

'No. He never tells me nothing—' She stopped and then said carefully, '*Anything*. About the business. He just said he had a meeting with a buyer. On Mounychia.'

Uh-oh. This I didn't like the sound of. Mounychia was the old quarry area to the north-east of Zea Harbour, and what few buildings there were in that quarter were shanties or slums. No one who had enough cash to be interested in the Baker would live on Mounychia, so it had to be an assignation. A clandestine assignation. And that stank like dead oysters in July.

'He didn't come back?' Perilla said.

The girl shook her head. 'No. And it's been a whole day now.'

Bathyllus padded in with the wine and fruit juice. Chrysoulla took a token sip and laid the cup down.

'There's no chance that he's simply been delayed?' Perilla asked. 'Or that he's gone on somewhere else?'

'He said it'd only take a couple of hours, ma'am. A preliminary meeting.' Chrysoulla stumbled over the phrase. 'Anyway, he would've sent a message. But that's not why I'm worried.'

'No?'

'Just before midnight someone knocked on the downstairs door. We keep it barred at night, even when we're both in. I thought it was Argaius, but it wasn't.'

I set down my wine cup. 'Don't tell me. The guy I met in the street today, outside the cookshop. Right?'

She swallowed. 'Yes, lord.'

'You know him?'

'I'd never seen him before. He didn't do anything, he just told me that if I wanted to see my husband again I should stay at home and not answer the door to no one till he said different.'

'So why come and see me now?'

'Because I'm scared, lord,' she said simply. 'And because there's no one I can go to.'

'What about family? Friends?' That was Perilla.

'Argaius hasn't any family, ma'am, not living, anyway. And mine are in Crete. As for friends we've none that could help. And the law won't be interested because' – she hesitated – 'well, they just wouldn't be, that's all.' She looked at me. 'I hoped that a Roman like the lord here would have . . . might be able to . . .' Her shoulders began to shake.

Uh-oh. There went the interview.

'Marcus,' Perilla said, 'take your wine into the dining-room, please.'

'Uh, yeah. Yeah, okay.' I sidled out quickly.

Not unwillingly, though: I needed the chance to think.

4

I parked my superfluous carcass on the dining-room couch. What the hell was going on here? Sure, the basic scenario was obvious: Argaius had been suckered into a phoney business assignation on Mounychia by Prince Charming or his boss, probably the latter because Prince Charming hadn't exactly struck me as the artistic type. The 'why' was obvious, too: whoever had snatched the guy had done it to get his hands on the Baker without going through the tedious process of actually buying it. I didn't know much about Greek business etiquette, but I'd bet that wasn't normal practice. Which meant that someone out there wanted Priscus's statue pretty badly. Badly enough to put themselves outside the law to get it.

A straightforward assessment of the situation, right? Only from the angle I'd been coming from so far it made as much sense as an oyster running for consul. If this was a scam like I'd been assuming then lifting Argaius was crazy. The corollary of *that* was that maybe the statue was genuine after all, and Prince Charming's boss knew it. On the other hand, bubblehead Chrysoulla had let slip that if Argaius wasn't exactly crooked he was the next thing to it, certainly the kind of citizen whose disappearance the authorities wouldn't bend over backwards to investigate. So the guy had form, and guys with form who offer to sell rich punters long-lost solid gold statues with Herodotean pedigrees for large amounts of gravy rate pretty low on anyone's credibility scale. On the *other* other hand, even if by some miracle Argaius was playing straight then how the hell had a small-time Piraeus crook got his hands on a seriously missing six-hundred-year-old art treasure in the first place?

Conversely, the whole deal might still be phoney as a land-lord's tears, and whoever had kidnapped Argaius was just a mad, misguided, gormless enthusiast like Priscus with all the common sense and social conscience of a walnut . . .

My brain was beginning to hurt. I poured out a full cup of Setinian and downed it in one. What did it matter, anyway? Perilla had had a point: I'd no personal interest in this, and just thinking about spending that much on a statue, solid gold or not, genuine or not, brought me out in hives. The best thing I could do was send Chrysoulla down to Watch headquarters with a note for the commander asking as a favour if he'd look into the matter and then write to Priscus saying the deal had fallen through. And if that meant screwing up Mother's sex life for the next few months then tough cheese. She'd just have to spend her time in Baiae taking cold baths and learning to crochet.

I was getting up to give our uninvited guest the polite brush-off when Perilla appeared in the doorway.

'She's all right now, Marcus,' she said. 'It's safe to come back through.'

'Uh, fine, lady.' I picked up the wine jug. 'Just give me five minutes in the study first, okay?'

'To do what?'

'To write a letter for her to show Callippus.' Callippus was the City Watch Commander.

Perilla was frowning. 'Wouldn't it be better if you went in person?'

'What for? She's a big girl, she can manage these things on her own, and the guy won't eat her.'

'Yes, but you could explain matters yourself in more detail, couldn't you?'

Jupiter! I thought I was being crystal clear here, but obviously something wasn't getting through. Maybe I was more tired than I'd thought. 'Perilla,' I said, 'listen. For once I'm going to take your advice, okay? I'm going to drop this thing like a hot brick, right now.'

'But, Marcus, dear, you can't do that!'

I stared at her. 'Run that past me again, would you? I must've missed something.'

'The poor girl is in a terrible state. You heard what she said about having no one to go to for help. And whatever you put in your letter you know perfectly well that Callippus is not going to take any action whatsoever.'

'Maybe not, but that's up to him. Argaius is a crook, after all. Chrysoulla practically admitted it.'

'That has nothing to do with it. He's Chrysoulla's husband and he has gone missing under very suspicious circumstances. If the authorities won't take action then someone ought to.'

'Not me, lady.'

'Very well, Corvinus.' Her jaw set. 'Then I most certainly will.'

Oh, shit. Double shit. I knew that tone. There was a flash of green on the wall as our friendly household gecko streaked for cover.

'Perilla,' I said slowly. 'Are you serious about this?' She didn't even bother to answer. 'Only let's just get things straight here and now so's there's no comeback later. You actually want me to start digging the dirt on this Baker scam after all?'

'I want you to find the girl's husband for her, yes.'

'Don't fudge, lady. Just answer the question.'

'Marcus . . .'

'Uh-uh.' I was beginning to enjoy myself. Perilla was caught, and it wasn't often I got the chance to see her squirm. 'I'm happy either way. Just give me a straight yes or no.'

'Corvinus, I will kill you for this. I swear.'

'No swearing. Besides, Chrysoulla may be a bubblehead, but she's a stunner. And I never could resist stunners who ask me to do something for them. As you know yourself from experience.' I was grinning, and although she didn't say anything Perilla's lips twitched. 'So. Put up or shut up. Is it yes or no, lady?'

'Marcus Valerius Corvinus, you are an absolute rat.'

'Admitted. Yes or no?'

She bent forward and kissed me slowly. 'Yes,' she said.

'Okay. So let's do it.'

Chrysoulla was dabbing her nose with a napkin. She looked like a small and very sexy dormouse.

'I'm sorry, lord,' she said.

'Hey, that's all right.' I poured myself another cup of Setinian and lay down on the couch. This time Perilla lay down beside me. 'You mind answering a few more questions?'

That got me a guarded look. 'What sort of questions?'

'Nothing complicated. If we're going to help then we need some information. First off, what exactly do you know about the Baker?'

'Nothing. I told you, Argaius doesn't talk to me about work.'

'You know what it is?'

'Of course.' She seemed proud of herself. 'A solid gold statue, from the old days. Argaius says it's over five hundred years old.'

'Have you seen it? Do you know where it is?'

'No, lord.'

'Which question's that an answer to, lady?'

She hesitated, frowning. I reckoned we were working at the limit of the lady's linguistic and intellectual capacities here.

'Both,' she said at last.

Well, I hadn't expected anything else. If Argaius hadn't discussed the ordinary day-to-day stuff over their breakfast porridge he was hardly likely to have told her where he'd cached their key to a fortune. And the odds on the statue being in the Piraeus flat doubling as a towel rack weren't worth quoting.

'So you can't tell us anything?' I said. 'Nothing at all? Like where your husband got it from, for example?'

Her brow cleared. 'Oh, I know that! It's a family heirloom.'

I sighed. Yeah. Sure. And I was a pygmy with a grass skirt and a bone through my nose. A four-and-a-half-foot solid gold statue handed down the family line like Aunt Calliste's Corinthian vase I just wouldn't swallow. Still, Argaius had had to tell her something, no doubt, and even Chrysoulla wouldn't believe the old chestnut of the Baker having fallen off the back of a delivery cart.

'Okay, let's change tack,' I said. 'What about this guy your husband was going to meet in Mounychia?'

'I told you, lord. He just said a man. A "potential customer".' The careful phrasing again, like she was quoting. Probably she was.

'Had he mentioned anyone before? Anyone who was interested in the Baker?'

'Oh, yes.' She brightened again. 'A man in Rome. Very rich, but a bit' – she spun a finger against her temple – 'you know.'

'Yeah, I know.' I sighed again: it was as good a description of Priscus as I could've given. 'Forget him. That's the guy I'm agenting for. Anyone else? Someone more local, maybe?'

'No. At least, no one I know. But then Argaius—'

'Didn't talk to you about the business. Yeah. I've gathered that.' I elbowed Perilla in the ribs. 'You got any questions, Aristotle?'

'Only one,' Perilla said. 'For you, Corvinus, actually. How did your cookshop friend know you'd be coming round to Argaius's this morning?'

I opened my mouth to answer – and then closed it again. Fair point. Of course, it could've been coincidence, but still . . . Especially since our star informant here didn't know of any other punters in the running. It was worth thinking about, anyway. And while we were on the subject of our star informant . . .

'Hey, Bathyllus!' I shouted. The little guy wasn't actually in the room, but I knew professional pride would've kept him within yelling distance. Sure enough he padded in before the echoes had faded.

'Yes, sir.'

'Make up a spare bed,' I said. 'Our guest here's sleeping over.'

Bathyllus looked at Perilla, eyebrows raised. She nodded.

'Oh, no, lord!' The dormouse was looking shocked. 'I couldn't! It wouldn't be proper!'

'Look, lady,' I said. 'Go home now and if your pal with the sausage finds out where you've been you're in trouble up to your earrings. Besides, if this whole thing's a mare's nest and Argaius has been out on the tiles the guy can do a little worrying on his own account.' I'd've laid out good money that wherever the hell Argaius was he wasn't tomcatting, but there was no point in making things worse for her than they were already. 'First thing tomorrow morning we go down to City Watch headquarters and have a word with the boss. After that we take things as they come. Agreed?'

'Very well, lord. Thank you.'

'Don't mention it. Go with Bathyllus, okay?'

She left, still sniffing.

From the looks of things, I had a busy day ahead. An early night still seemed a good idea. I ran a hand down Perilla's arm.

'Bed, lady?' I said.

'Bed.' She smiled.

Ah, well. Better late than never.

5

The main headquarters of the City Watch are off the north side of the market-place, behind Herm Porch. Sure, the City and the Piraeus are separate jurisdictions, but Callippus was a friend of mine, or at least a good acquaintance, and to get Chrysoulla any sort of attention at all would need a favour, even if it did come second-hand. In this instance I didn't mind asking: unusually for a Greek, Callippus had a genuine soft spot for Romans. He even spoke decent Latin, and he liked the chance to practise.

He was reading over some papers on his desk when we walked in. I was glad to see he smiled when he recognised me; with officials that doesn't happen too often.

'Valerius Corvinus!' He put the papers to one side. 'You're far from home this morning.'

'Yeah.' We shook hands Roman-style, and I switched to Greek: Chrysoulla wouldn't understand the Latin. 'It's business, I'm afraid.'

'Really?' He looked at Chrysoulla. 'Nothing serious, I hope?'

'You and me both, pal. This lady's name is Chrysoulla.' I thought his eyebrows lifted, but I may've been mistaken. Evil-minded bastard. 'Her husband's gone missing.'

'Indeed?' He reached for a notepad and stylus. 'Which district?'

'Not in the City. The Piraeus. Zea Harbour area, or possibly Mounychia. I was hoping you might give me a note for the guy in charge down there.'

'Not a problem.' Still, I noticed he'd laid down the stylus: in Athens, like in Rome and everywhere else I've ever heard of, the City Watch is overstretched, and they've got enough on their own patch to keep them busy without worrying about anyone else's. The Piraeus guy could take his own notes. Also, although Callippus was too polite to say so, missing persons below City Magistrate level aren't the concern of Watch chiefs. We were filling in time here, although I appreciated that he was taking the trouble to go through the motions.

'Your husband's name?' Callippus turned his attention to Chrysoulla.

'Argaius, lord.' She sounded nervous as hell: probably like most Piraeans her contacts with Watch officials hadn't been exactly friendly up to now. 'We've an import-export business near the Shrine of Hyakinthos, behind the Serangeion.'

Nerves or not, she'd said it with a shy pride that I found pretty touching, especially since I'd seen the place myself, but Callippus grunted and lowered his eyes. Callippus knew the Serangeion district and what 'import-export' was a euphemism for as well as I did.

'And he's been missing since when?'

I saw that he'd picked up the pen again; not because he was interested, I knew, but because he'd noticed that she'd noticed he wasn't taking notes. I had a lot of time for Callippus: Athens might claim to have invented democracy but as far as putting the lower orders in their place is concerned some of these guys from the old aristocratic families could've given the Tarquins lessons.

'Since the night before last.' Chrysoulla's hands twisted together in her lap. 'He went out just before sunset.'

'Physical description?'

'What he looked like, you mean? Taller than me, but not much. Thirty. Dark curly hair.'

'Distinguishing marks?' Callippus waited; nothing came. 'Scars? Blemishes? Birthmarks? Anything like that.'

'Oh.' She blinked. 'Yes, I'm sorry. He had a long scar on his wrist. Under the thumb. From a dog bite.'

Callippus looked up at her, his broad face expressionless. 'And which wrist would that be, now?'

'The left one.'

'I see.' Callippus laid the stylus down. 'Lady Chrysoulla, would you mind if I stepped outside with Valerius Corvinus for a moment?'

Uh-oh.

'No. Of course not.' Her eyes were wide and scared.

'Corvinus?' Callippus got up. I followed him outside and he closed the door carefully behind us and moved away from it. His face was grave.

'He's dead, right?' I said quietly.

He nodded. 'Very. The description matches, and the scar's a clincher. We'll need a formal identification, of course. You can do that?'

'No. I never met the guy.'

'That' – Callippus's mouth twisted – 'is a pity.'

'Yeah? Why so?'

'He's a mess, Corvinus; badly beaten, throat cut from ear to ear. I'd rather his wife didn't see him.' Jupiter! 'Is there anyone else we could ask? Anyone at all?'

I swallowed. 'No. Not that I know of. Where did you find him?'

'Practically on our doorstep. On the Founders' plinth, with his back against the Ptolemy statue. My lads thought he was drunk and had jumped the barrier, got stuck and gone to sleep.'

'This was two nights ago?'

'No. First thing this morning.' He hesitated. 'The body's next door, as it happens.'

'You want to tell her?'

'Unless you'd care to do it.'

'No way. You're the professional, pal.'

'You think that makes it any easier?'

Maybe not, but I took the coward's way out all the same. I stayed where I was while Callippus went back into his office and told Chrysoulla she could see her husband now.

After Chrysoulla had identified Argaius we left her in charge of a motherly cleaner while I took a look at the corpse myself. Callippus was right: the poor bastard was no sight for anyone, never mind his wife. Whoever had beaten him up before slitting his throat had done a thorough job.

'Was there any blood?' I asked.

Callippus shook his head. 'Not by the plinth. Not any-where else in the market either, in the quantities that must've

been involved. By the looks of things they used a crowbar.'

'Uh-huh.' I felt sick. 'So he was killed first, then dumped.'
Callippus said nothing. 'But why the hell murder him in the
Piraeus and then bring the corpse five miles to Athens? And
why leave it in the market?'

'You're assuming he was killed where he disappeared. He
could've been brought to the City alive.'

'Sure. But both Athens and the Piraeus are full of places
where he might not be found for days. Maybe never. That
doesn't answer my second question.'

'No. But it might explain these.' Callippus pointed to four
livid bruises on the corpse's wrists and ankles. 'Rope burns.
He was tied, although when my lads found him the ropes had
already been removed.'

'Uh-huh.' So. Rope marks. Signs of a thorough and systematic
beating. The obvious inference was that the killer had been
persuading Argaius to talk. No prizes what about, either.

'Corvinus.' Callippus's voice was quiet, almost apologetic. 'I've
been careful so far not to ask you where you come into this.
Maybe you'd better explain now.'

Well, that was fair. I told him all I knew, including what
Chrysoulla had let slip about her husband's business activities
and my own meeting with Prince Charming. He took down the
guy's description without a word.

'It doesn't ring any immediate bells,' he said. 'You could
be right and the killing's a one-off, amateur stuff. On the
other hand, running illegal antiquities, genuine or fake, is
a profitable business locally. My guess is your friend had
stepped on someone's toes. Someone a lot bigger than he
was.'

I nodded. 'Yeah. Yeah, that makes sense, I suppose.'

'It would explain where the body was dumped, too.'

'Is that right, now? You like to explain why, pal?'

'The Founders' plinth is used for notices; very official, very
public. If Argaius was in the trade, or trying to break into it,
then leaving his body there would act as a warning.'

Uh-huh. That was an angle I hadn't thought of. There wasn't
much organised crime in Athens but as Callippus said the

antiquities trade pulled in the cream. And these guys didn't
encourage competition.

'You think that's the answer?' I said.

Callippus shrugged. 'Maybe. I'm guessing, of course, but it's
an educated guess. In any case we'll look into the matter. For
what it's worth.' He closed his pad. 'You've seen enough?'

'Sure.' I frowned at Argaius, lying there on his wooden table
like a big broken doll. 'One more thing. What about the funeral
arrangements?'

'Those are up to his wife, naturally. Once the body is identified
it's released to the next of kin automatically.'

'You know of anyone who'll take them on for her? A local
undertaker, maybe?'

'Of course. Lots of them. Cleiton in Knifemakers' Alley,
Euphorbus at Three Springs . . .'

'Send someone round to Cleiton's. Middle-of-the-road job,
nothing too cheap, whatever he does most of. Get him to send
the bill to me. And find a lawyer who handles property sales in
the Piraeus.'

Callippus looked at me curiously. 'You . . . ah . . . you're sure
you've told me everything about this business, Corvinus?'

'Yeah.' I had. 'Why?'

'And this Chrysoulla. She's a friend of yours?'

'In a way. You got a problem, pal?'

'No. Just curious.'

Sure. I'd bet he was. A nice guy, Callippus, but over-suspicious
and a mind like a sewer. Still, I suppose that went with the job.

I took Chrysoulla back home with me: I didn't want to risk
another death and she wouldn't want to go to the Piraeus house
now in any case. Which meant I had one more arrangement to
make. While Perilla was settling her down in the guest room I
sent Bathyllus to the nearest shipping agent's to book a passage
on the first boat to Crete. I could get an address from her before
she left, in case the Baker was on the level and she suddenly
found herself an heiress. Not that that was likely, mind. Jupiter,
what a mess!

When Perilla came back into the sitting-room I was drowning
my sorrows in the jar of Samian Labrus had sent me. It was

prime stuff, all right, pure liquid gold: that over-civilised bastard Melanthus might be able to hold his own at the sharp end of a Socratic *elenchos*, but as far as appreciating good wine was concerned the guy was whistling through his aristocratic ears.

'How's Chrysoulla?' I asked, making space on the couch.

'Sleeping, thank goodness. I gave her some poppy juice.' Perilla squeezed in beside me. 'So what exactly does Callippus think happened?'

I told her. When I got to the part about the Founders' plinth and Callippus's theory of a gangland killing she frowned.

'You're sure Callippus said that Argaius's body was found under the Ptolemy statue, Marcus? The *Ptolemy* statue?'

'Yeah. As far as I can remember. So what?'

'Maybe nothing.' She slipped off the couch. 'But if so then it may be significant. Let me just check a reference. I'll be back in a moment.'

While she took herself off to her study I took a reflective swallow of wine. Jupiter knew what bee the lady had in her intellectual bonnet now. The Founders were the Founders: statues of the eponymous ancestors of the twelve Athenian tribes, plus the two honorary members who had been added later for services rendered to the state, Attalus of Pergamon and the Egyptian King Ptolemy. So much I knew, for what it was worth. Obviously Perilla knew a bit more; but knowing Perilla she'd got hold of an angle that I hadn't thought of. And *that* might be interesting.

She was back in five minutes with a book-scroll, and she was grinning like the cat who got the cream.

'You find something?' I said.

'I think so.' She lay back down beside me. 'It may be coincidence, of course, but Ptolemy had one of his brothers executed for treason. I'll give you one guess as to which.'

Jupiter! 'Come on, Perilla! You're the bookworm of the family! It's been a long day and I'm tired.'

'Very well. The brother's name was Argaius.'

Everything went very still. I sat back, the hairs on my neck prickling. Score one for the bookworms. Coincidences happen, sure they do; but I'd bet this wasn't the time. Real life just ain't that neat.

So. Forget coincidence; and forget the gangland angle. Top-notch criminals have better things to do than indulge in esoteric historical puns when they choose where to dump their victims.

The only problem was, what the hell did it mean?

6

I spent the following morning thinking about what the next move should be. Scratch throwing in the towel, that wasn't the Roman way. I couldn't walk away from this, not until I knew for absolute certain that I was out of the game. Also if Mother ever found out she'd kill me.

So. The obvious place to start was the cookshop where I'd had my run-in with Prince Charming. Cookshop owners as a rule may have all the social graces of a seriously constipated scorpion, but in districts like Zea where only one family in twenty cooks its own dinner they tend to know who's who locally. Argaius might not tell his wife much about his business, but I'd bet a used boil plaster to a gold piece the guy behind the counter would be able to give me chapter and verse. Not that I was looking forward to asking, mind.

Ten miles there and back, plus the distance across town, was too far to walk, so I whistled up Lysias and took the coach. It was late afternoon before I arrived.

Even as cookshops go, this was something special: the smell of old fat and frying dogmeat hit me before I'd even reached the door. I took a deep breath and went inside. Maybe I'd been too optimistic; the place wasn't exactly doing a roaring trade, in fact there was only one other customer, a huge guy with the build of a wrestler and a head like a pear small side up. Big jowls, tiny skull and a trail of spit down the side of his mouth. That figured: only an idiot would choose to eat in a place like this. Not that the guy was eating. He gave me an empty-eyed grin and went back to feeding his dog bits of sausage. I wondered about cannibalism.

The owner was behind the counter, chopping a tired-looking lettuce he was using to garnish the meatballs. So the place still kept some culinary pretensions. He took a long look at my Roman mantle, turned away and spat carefully into the corner. Forget constipated scorpions. As far as friendliness went this guy wouldn't've measured up to an asp with a migraine.

'Hi,' I said. 'Nice day, isn't it?'

No answer. Ah, well. I brought out a silver piece and held it up. Silver and cookshop owners were just made for each other.

'You serve wine, pal?' I said.

'Sure.' He set the knife down. 'What kind you want?'

'I'm not fussy. Just make it the best you've got.'

Smiler fetched an earthenware cup from a shelf, gave it a wipe with a rag and poured from a chipped jug. I tasted the result. Jupiter! This was the *best*? What wasn't sediment was pure vinegar. Probably used for pickling cockroaches.

'Who do you buy from?' I said, wiping my mouth. 'Peleus?'

Peleus means 'Mud-man' in Greek. The guy wasn't amused.

'You don't like it, Roman, don't drink it.'

Yeah, well, he had a point. I pushed the cup away but left the silver piece on the counter. 'You know a guy called Argaius? Import-export business, two doors down?'

'Maybe.' I laid a second silver piece next to the first. His eyes narrowed. 'Yeah, I know Argaius.'

'He work alone?'

The guy looked pointedly at the two coins. Wordlessly, I added a third.

'No. He has a partner.'

Hey! Maybe we were on to something here after all. I took out a fourth coin but kept it between the tips of my fingers.

'Is that so, now?' I said slowly. 'You care to give me the guy's name?'

He sucked on a tooth and eyed the fourth drach. I'd got him, sure I had: four silver pieces probably represented a good day's takings, probably more.

'This just curiosity, Roman,' he said at last, 'or have you got a reason for asking?'

'We have some unfinished business, Argaius and me. Only he seems to have left town suddenly. A partner could help.'

'Uh-huh.' The guy looked like he wanted to spit again, but this time he didn't: we were obviously getting somewhere, relationship-wise. I had the impression that he thought Argaius had swindled me somewhere along the line and he wasn't particularly surprised. Not particularly interested, either: smartass Romans were fair game in Zea. Anyone was. All of which was fine with me. 'Okay. Argaius's partner's name is Smaragdus. He boards at the third house along on the left after the Mother of the Gods.'

Bull's-eye! 'Gee, thanks, chum.' I put the fourth coin down and gave him my best smile. 'You've been very helpful.'

That got me a grunt. He swept the coins into his palm, threw them into a drawer and picked up his lettuce knife.

Just as I was turning to leave the pear-headed guy came up behind me and gibbered something. It wasn't Greek, and I'd've bet it wasn't any other language known to man either: there was spittle drooling out of one side of his mouth, and his eyes were shifting about like someone had cut the cords that fastened them in. The hairs on the back of my neck lifted. Insanity I can't take, and this guy was clearly not just two tiles short of a roof, he couldn't even have mustered the joists.

'Fuck off, Tiny,' Smiler said. Not nastily, but like it was part of an ongoing conversation. Maybe it was.

The big guy held out a hand like a ham. He was still holding the dog. It was fat as a ball of lard.

'I said fuck off.' Smiler turned away and banged a skillet down on the stove. 'One for free I don't mind. The next you pay for.'

The hand never wavered. It was clear what the guy wanted. I reached into my purse and pulled out a few copper coins.

'That's okay, pal,' I said. 'Have it on me.'

Smiler glanced round, shrugged, pulled a sausage from the string above his head and handed it over. The big guy gave me a gibber and went back with the sausage to his table while Smiler scooped up the coins.

'Don't encourage him,' he grunted. 'That bastard's always on the scrounge.'

'It's my money, friend,' I said equably. 'One more thing before I go. You had a customer a couple of days back.' I described Prince Charming. 'He come in here much?'

'Nah.' The guy picked up the rag he'd wiped my cup out with and moved it back and forward along the greasy countertop. Maybe getting rid of the idiot at the soft Roman's expense had put him in a talkative mood. 'First time. Never seen him before.'

'You're sure?'

He set the cloth down and turned his back. Talkative mood, nothing. Ah, well. It had been worth a try. And I had my lead; or at least I hoped I did. I gave the idiot a wave and set off for the Mother of the Gods.

It wasn't far: a big sprawling place that'd seen better days but was still hanging on into the modern world, like the Mother herself. The third house along was a seedy tenement, maybe a rooming house but more probably a brothel. Not a prosperous brothel, either, from the look and smell of the entrance, but that was par for the district. I told Lysias to wait, climbed the stairs and knocked on the door of the first-floor flat.

The old woman who answered had three teeth. She could've kept a fair-sized cheap cosmetics factory going single-handed.

'Yeah?' she mouthed.

Jupiter, she was ugly! I took a step back, but she closed the gap.

'Uh . . . I'm sorry to disturb you, mother,' I said, 'but I'm looking for a guy called Smaragdus.'

That got me a twenty-candelabra glare. 'Top floor. And less of the mother, dearie.'

'Right. Right.' I backed away again: wine I enjoy, but not second-hand; and not mixed with raw onion, either. 'Sorry.'

'You won't find him, though.' She flashed her brown teeth at me. 'The bugger's out. He's been out for days. I'm giving him to the end of the month and then he can pick his stuff up in the street.'

Oh, shit, here we go again. Was nothing simple? 'You know where he's gone, maybe?'

The door behind her opened further and two girls sidled out. One was big, blonde and busty, the other was a rake-thin negress. They wore skimpy, grease-stained tunics and their eyes were glass-hard.

'No. But then maybe I can find out, lord.' The old woman's grin widened. 'Why don't you come in meantime? My daughters'll amuse you while I'm gone. Isn't that right, girls?'

The fake blonde – I could see the black roots under the dye – gave me a slow smile.

'Sure,' she said. 'We'd enjoy the company.'

'Uh . . . maybe some other time, okay?' I took out a silver piece and slipped it down the top of her tunic. She giggled and caught it halfway down. 'Today I'm in a hurry, sister. Just point me in the right direction.'

'Harpalus would know,' the negress said. The blonde looked at her and gave another giggle. 'Why don't you try Harpalus?'

'Yeah. I might just do that.' I pulled out another coin. This was getting expensive. 'You know where I can find him, bright eyes?'

She glanced down at her piggy bank. Ah, well. In it went.

'You sure you don't want to stay?' she said.

'No, I'll settle for Harpalus, thanks.'

The blonde giggled again and leaned over to whisper something in the negress's ear. The second girl shook her chime-bar earrings and laughed.

'Okay, Roman,' she said. 'If that's your fancy. But he'll be at work just now. In the bird shop, two doors down.'

I turned to go. The blonde's voice caught me as I reached the stairs.

'Watch yourself, dear,' she shouted. 'The bastard charges over the odds. Particularly for Romans.'

7

The bird shop was one of these sad grey places smelling of dank feathers, old blood and bird droppings that you get near temples and that double as religious suppliers and on-the-claw delicatessens. Under the awning, cages packed with pigeons, thrushes and ortolans hung waiting for punters to make their choice and either take it off live to the Mother of the Gods or have its neck wrung there and then for the stewpot or the griddle. There was only one splash of colour. On a perch next to the door was a red and green parrot.

Yeah. Unusual, right? Parrots are strictly high-class merchandise: you see them preening themselves outside the chichi shops around the market-place, tricked out with ribbons and bells like Corinthian prostitutes and being cooed over by fluffy matrons with more bangles than brains. Only this one looked more like something that had staggered home pissed out of his skull after a wild all-night party and been woken by the neighbours' dog an hour later.

In other words he looked familiar. Hauntingly familiar. If he hadn't been so obviously a bird I'd almost have sworn that . . .

I went over for a closer look. Jupiter, I was right! All the feathered bastard needed was a broad-striped mantle and he'd be the spit and image of my Uncle Cotta. No exaggeration: literal truth. It was weird.

'Hey, Cotta.' I stroked his back. 'How's it going, pal?'

The parrot hunched his shoulders, opened a jaundiced, red-flecked eye and fixed me with a glare like I was a cockroach he'd found among the lupin seeds in his feed tray.

'Bugger off, sunshine!' he said.

He meant it, too, I could tell.

Yeah, sure enough, Cotta to the life. I chucked him under the beak, nearly losing a finger for my trouble, and went inside. There was someone ahead of me, an old woman buying a pair of doves to go. I waited until she'd finished then walked up to the counter.

After what the girls at the rooming house had said, or at least implied, the guy behind it had to be Harpalus. Maybe he saw himself as one of the gilded butterflies of the City porches, but he just looked sad as the birds he sold. He was no kid, for one thing: twenty-five if he was a day, thin-haired and balding already, with a broad coarse-pored face and the hands of a navvy. Forget the 'gilded' as well: the face that turned towards me wasn't so much made up as seriously enamelled. It brightened, though, when he saw me. Thinking of the big blonde's parting shot about Romans, I didn't know whether to take that as a compliment or not.

'Yes, lord.' He smiled. Bad teeth, too: it seemed like the poor guy had nothing going for him at all. 'And what can I do for you?'

'Uh . . . that parrot outside. He for sale?' Shit. I hadn't meant to say that, it just came out. Still, as an opening it was as good as any, and you don't come across a psittacine version of Cotta every day.

'Nestor?' The guy looked surprised. 'Sure. Fifteen drachmas.'

Ouch! And *Nestor*? Jupiter in spangles! 'Ten.'

'He's worth fifteen, lord. And in the City you'd pay thirty.'

'True enough, pal, but not for a bird with his colourful turn of phrase. That's no delicate toy for the Beautiful and Good you've got there.'

He glanced at the door. I could almost hear him mentally weighing twelve silver pieces in the hand against one very foul-mouthed bird on the porch. Avarice – or maybe it was pragmatism – won out.

'Okay,' he said. 'We'll call it twelve. And I'll throw in the perch.'

'Deal.' I took out my much-slimmed-down purse. 'Your name Harpalus, by the way?'

He paused. 'What if it is?'

'You're Smaragdus's friend?'

'We know each other, yes,' he said cautiously.

'You know where I can find him?'

'Maybe.' He wasn't smiling now. If anything he looked nervous. 'What's your business with Smaragdus, lord?'

I reached into the purse and brought out a shiny half gold piece. 'I need to talk to him urgently. About a certain article he and his partner are handling. His ex-partner, rather. I was hoping you might be able to help. If you can then Nestor's price has just gone up and there's no need to tell your boss by how much.'

His eyes fixed on the coin and he wet his lips. Forget nervous; for some reason – and I'd've given a lot to know what it was – he looked scared as hell.

'You're from Eutyches, aren't you?' His voice had sunk to a whisper.

I kept my face straight. 'Maybe.'

'Uh-huh.' He swallowed. 'Very well. I'm not making any promises, lord, but I'll pass your message on. How can I get in touch with you?'

'You can't, sunshine.' I wasn't going to give him my name; no way. Not after that little exchange. 'I'll call back tomorrow. Same time. Okay?'

'Okay.'

I passed the gold over. This time I didn't regret it, because he'd told me a lot. For a start, that he – and so Smaragdus – knew about the Baker. Second, when I'd given him a time limit he hadn't blinked, so if he could deliver the message to Smaragdus and come back with an answer inside a day then Smaragdus couldn't be far away. Last, he'd handed me another piece to the puzzle, even though I couldn't place it. Who the hell was this Eutyches? Somebody important and, from the guy's reaction, none too chancy.

Interesting, right? And definitely food for further thought. I gave the subdued Harpalus a brief nod and went out to collect my purchase.

I walked back to the carriage carrying Nestor on his perch like a legion's eagle, with the bastard glaring at me and trying to take my ear off the whole way. I was having serious qualms of conscience here: when she heard our new pet's language Perilla would kill me. Also just thinking about having a dead ringer for Uncle Cotta permanently in residence gave me hives. Maybe I should hand him straight over to Meton and be done with it: roast parrot with a nut and sunflower-seed stuffing had a sort of ring to it . . .

There were a couple of snot-nosed lads hanging around the carriage, kicking the wheels and bad-mouthing Lysias. They took to their heels when they saw me coming, but I called the elder one over. He came, eventually, and stood glowering at me.

'Hey, sonny.' I hunkered down to his level: no point in intimidating the poor kid. 'You want to make yourself an easy drach?'

The eight-year-old looked me up and down with eyes that belonged to a hard-boiled city-square huckster. He turned away and spat neatly into the gutter.

'Doing what?' he said. The tone suggested he thought he knew already, and the price was just about to take a hike. Jupiter! So much for innocence!

'The guy at the bird shop. You know him?'

'Harpalus?' The kid sniggered. 'Sure.'

'If he goes out I want to know where to. And I don't want him to know I know. Get me?'

'I get you.' He looked at his brother, who was about three years younger, waist-high, and at the taciturn, nose-picking stage. 'We work together, lord. Fixed rates. Three drachs each, up front.'

Gods alive! What did they teach kids nowadays? For six drachs I could buy half a parrot. 'Deal. One now, two later. Fair?'

He considered, then held out a grubby mitt. 'Two now, two later. Otherwise you can go screw.'

I sighed and handed over the silver. At this rate I'd have to be paying a visit to my banker soon. Maybe I should start making a list of expenses and charge them to Priscus's bill. 'Okay. You know the cookshop near the Shrine of Hyakinthos? Behind the Serangeion?'

'I'll find it.'

'Good. When you have something for me leave a message there for Marcus Porcius Cato and collect from the owner. You got that?'

'That your name? Cato?' The kid might not know his Roman history, but he could spot a lie a mile off. I grinned.

'It'll do,' I said: the tight-fisted old so-and-so would be spinning in his urn. 'Just make sure Harpalus doesn't spot you.'

'Harpalus? Harpalus couldn't find his own arse with both hands, lord.'

I winced. Well, I could see now where the parrot got his vocabulary from. It was obviously par for the local course. 'Okay. Don't forget. Marcus Porcius Cato, the Hyakinthos cookshop.'

'Marcus Porcius Cato, the Hyakinthos cookshop,' he repeated, and gave me a look like I was capable of dribbling into my bedtime gruel. 'You've got it, lord.'

I straightened up, and the two kids ran off. Probably on their way to liberate the lead from the Mother of the Gods' roof. Yeah, well, it kept them off the streets, and if they didn't break their necks in the process they'd probably end up millionaires. I shoved Nestor into the carriage and told Lysias to head back to Zea. Then, after I'd squared arrangements with my pal at the cookshop – another two drachs' worth – he turned the carriage in the direction of the City Gate and home.

The next bit I wasn't looking forward to. This was going to be tricky. And I don't mean Smaragdus, either.

Perilla was in the garden, picking flowers. When she saw Nestor she beamed. Good start.

'How beautiful, Marcus! A parrot! Wherever did you get him?'

'Bugger off, sunsh—'

Oh, hell! I grabbed at his beak, just in time. Luckily Perilla didn't seem to have heard, or maybe she just didn't believe her ears.

'Uh . . . a shop in the Piraeus,' I said. 'His name's Nestor.'

'But he's an absolute darling!'

The absolute darling was trying to bite through my finger.

Enough was enough. I put my mouth next to the feathered bastard's head.

'Listen, pal,' I hissed. 'Cut it out. One word out of place in front of the lady and you're cat's-meat. Understand?'

The biting stopped. Carefully I let go. Nestor shuffled sideways along the perch, glaring at me. Perilla stroked his breast-feathers and he arched a claw in sexual ecstasy.

'He's lovely!' she said. 'What does he eat? Besides fingers, that is.'

Jupiter! I should've thought of that and had Harpalus throw some birdseed in with the deal. Well, no doubt Meton could rustle something up temporarily.

'Nuts. Sunflower seeds.' I caught the evil glint of an eye. 'Spare ribs. Hamsters . . .'

'Surely not.' Perilla frowned. 'Parrots are vegetarians.' She turned to Nestor and ruffled his feathers again. 'You don't eat meat, do you, darling?'

'Drop your pants, lady.'

This time my hand was years too late. Perilla pulled back like she'd been stung.

'Marcus, what did that bird just say?'

I had him by the beak again, and I swear I could feel the bastard grin. 'It's . . . uh . . . just one of his standard phrases, Perilla. He comes from a deprived background. A few days in a more refined environment and he'll be a changed bird. I promise you.'

The frown didn't shift. 'Corvinus, I have enough on my hands training you. I have no intention of taking on a parrot in addition.'

'Fu—'

'Sorry, lady, my hand slipped. He'll be okay, honestly. Just give him time.'

'Very well. He has a month.' Perilla was staring at him. 'You know, Marcus, this may sound silly but if you imagine him wearing a broad-striped mantle he'd be the spit and image of—'

I gave a yell of agony. Nestor had finally got a proper bite in, and it felt like being mugged by a set of nutcrackers. Which I suppose was what it was, really.

'Cadmus is an onanist!'

Right. That was the last straw. I didn't mind the swearing, personally, but when a parrot started using words I didn't know it was time for drastic action.

'Bathyllus!'

'Yes, sir.' The little guy oiled up out of nowhere.

'Here.' I handed him Nestor on his perch. 'Take this bit of crow's-meat up an alleyway and kick some civilisation into him, will you? I don't want to see the bastard again until his language is dining-room standard.'

'Like your own, sir.' Bathyllus sniffed. 'Certainly. Alexis the gardener has a way with animals. I'll give the bird to him.'

'You do that, little guy. And tell Alexis he has a month. After that one blue phrase and we fricassée the bugger.'

'Alexis or the parrot, sir?'

'Don't try to be funny, pal. It's been a long hard day and I haven't the mental energy.'

'Very well, sir. Apropos, Meton says that dinner is almost ready.'

'Great. What is it tonight?'

'Mussel forcemeat sausage, baked eel with egg sauce and a purée of green vegetables, sir. The chef is feeling nautical.'

'Eels are freshwater.'

'Piscatorial, then. Will that be all?'

'Yeah.' I stopped myself. 'No. What happened to the wine? You know the standing orders when the master's out.'

'It was waiting for you, sir, beside the pool.'

Shit. I'd walked right past it. And after a hard day back and forth to the Piraeus with nothing but the Hyakinthos wineshop in the middle I needed a drink badly. 'Okay, my mistake. Go fetch, sunshine.'

'Certainly, sir.' He padded back inside.

Perilla set the flowers in a vase on the stone table and sat down on the bench. I sat beside her and draped an arm round her shoulders.

'How's Chrysoulla?' I said.

'The funeral was this afternoon. She wanted to go straight home afterwards, to get things ready.'

I nodded. Her ship wouldn't be sailing for a couple of days yet, and it would've been better and safer if she'd stayed, but that was her decision. Maybe she had a friend or two somewhere in the Piraeus after all. I hoped so.

'So, Marcus.' Perilla kissed me. 'How was your day? Apart from the parrot.'

'Not bad.' I gave the edited highlights. 'It sounds like this Smaragdus is lying low somewhere and using his pal Harpalus as a go-between with potential customers.'

'That would seem very sensible, under the circumstances. Considering his partner has been murdered.'

'Yeah.' I frowned. 'A propos of which, Harpalus assumed that I'd been sent by a guy called Eutyches.'

'A rival bidder, perhaps?'

'Could be.' Bathyllus reappeared with the wine jug and a full cup. I took a long swallow. 'Only if so then why didn't Priscus mention him in his letter?'

'Is that so strange? A seller is under no obligation to provide a list of bidders, surely.'

'Maybe not, lady. But I got the distinct impression this was a one-horse race. So if Eutyches is a customer then what kind of customer is he? New or old? Bona fide or the type who goes to business meetings on Mounychia with a crowbar under his mantle?'

'Oh, Marcus!' Perilla's eyes widened. 'You think he was the one who killed Argaius?'

'It's a working hypothesis. We know Argaius went to meet someone on Mounychia, and up to now Eutyches is the only game in town. Another thing. When Harpalus thought I was representing him the guy was jittery as a cat on a seesaw. Whoever the bastard is, customer or not, one gets you ten he's no paragon of respectability.'

'But if Smaragdus even suspected that this Eutyches was responsible for his partner's death then surely he'd have nothing to do with him?'

I shrugged. 'Not necessarily. To guys like Argaius and Smaragdus a customer's a customer. We're not shopping in the Porches now.'

'Marcus, this is all beginning to sound horribly risky.'

'You're telling me something I don't know?'

'Of course not. What I am saying is that perhaps you should leave this thing alone after all.'

'That won't get Priscus his Baker, lady. And I don't see why the old guy shouldn't have it, if he's willing to pay good Roman silver in exchange. Assuming it's genuine, of course.'

'You think it is?'

I hesitated. 'Perilla, I don't know any more. Maybe. However unlikely it seems. Because if it isn't then a lot of people are putting in a hell of a lot of effort for nothing.'

'Yes. That's true.' Perilla looked thoughtful. 'So what happens now?'

'Simple. Tomorrow, one way or another, I talk to Smaragdus. See the statue, get Priscus's pal Melanthus's opinion. After that we take it from there.'

'And Eutyches?'

'Eutyches is Smaragdus's problem. And maybe Callippus's.'

'No silly heroics, Corvinus? Promise?'

'Sure.' I kissed her. 'Now. You want to watch me waste away or should we scare up some dinner?'

She got up. 'Dinner.'

We went in for the eels.

8

I took the long hike down to the Piraeus again the next morning. This was getting monotonous; maybe I'd do better renting a flat somewhere and moving lock, stock and barrel for the duration.

I checked at the cookshop and found that my kids had come up trumps. An hour after I'd left, Harpalus had put up the shutters and headed in the rough direction of Acte, the high ground at the end of the Piraeus peninsula. It seemed that Smaragdus – if the guy he'd visited was Smaragdus – had a beach hut on the coast a few hundred yards to the north of Themistocles' Tomb. Bull's-eye. I took the carriage as close as I could then told Lysias to wait and walked the rest.

I spotted the hut right away, lying in the middle of a small cove at the head of a sandy beach. Jupiter knew why it was there; maybe some misanthrope had built it years back when places like that were fashionable, or it could've been some sort of club-house of the more disreputable kind that needed privacy. Now it was the usual blend of solidity and squalor that you saw all over town: a good stone base with a cheap modern superstructure and whatever would keep the rain off for a roof; in this case an old sail over a framework of planks. The place looked deserted, but there was a boat drawn up in the shallows opposite.

I checked the knife against my wrist and went on over. Before I could knock, a guy came out holding a length of two-by-four like he meant to use it. I stepped back and spread my hands to show they were empty.

'You're Smaragdus?' I said.

'Who wants him?' Not the friendly type, that was sure. But if I was right he had reason.

'My name's Corvinus. Marcus Valerius Corvinus. Your pal Harpalus probably said I was coming.'

'That's right.' His eyes were still wary. 'He didn't give a name, though.'

'He didn't get one.' I looked pointedly at the makeshift club. 'Uh . . . you want to put that down now we've been properly introduced, friend?'

'Not just yet.' He hadn't left the shadow of the doorway, either. 'So. You're Helvius Priscus's agent? The son-in-law who lives in the City.'

'Stepson,' I said.

'Stepson.' He didn't smile, but he did lower the two-by-four. 'Sorry. My mistake.'

'No problem.' 'Mistake', nothing: it had been intentional, and he'd just checked me out; Smaragdus was no fool. What did surprise me, though, was that he spoke a good educated Greek. I'd never talked to Argaius, but I'd met Chrysoulla, and Cretan or not she was strictly Piraeus docklands bubblehead. This guy was another matter. 'Who's Eutyches, by the way?'

If I'd thought the direct question might catch him off guard I was disappointed. His eyes flickered, but he took his time answering.

'Just another customer.'

'A "prospective customer"?'

'Of course. Like your stepfather. You see, I believe in keeping my options open, Corvinus. Do you have any objections?'

'None at all. It's good business practice.'

'Exactly.' He stood aside. 'Come in. I'm sorry for the brusqueness of the welcome. I wasn't expecting you until later, and with Harpalus.'

'Uh . . . you mind if we stay out here?' Just the thought of going inside that pile of rubble gave me claustrophobia, and I wouldn't have trusted it not to fall down on top of us. Also, outside I could see any trouble coming before it arrived.

He shrugged and sat down with his back to the hut wall. 'Suit yourself.'

I settled down against a convenient rock. 'So,' I said. 'Where's the Baker?'

'Safe.'

'Can I see it?'

'Naturally. After we've talked.'

I nodded; well, that was something, anyway. At least I was still in the game. 'Fair enough. But no quick sales, right? I'm no expert, and I'll want it looked at professionally before I put in a bid.'

'By Melanthus of Abdera. Of course. That was understood from the beginning. Call this a preliminary viewing.'

'And Eutyches? Does he get one of these as well, or has he had it already?'

'Any arrangement involving Eutyches is my business, Corvinus. And I won't discuss one potential customer's affairs with another. It isn't ethical.'

Jupiter! You'd think we were in one of the fancy South Porch law offices here! The guy was too cocky for my liking. He needed shaking up.

'Speaking of ethics,' I said, 'one thing's bugged me from the start. Since I got Priscus's letter, in fact. If the Baker's legitimately yours and this is all above board then why the hole-in-corner stuff?'

'I'm sorry.' His eyes flickered. 'I don't follow.'

'Then try harder, pal. You could've lodged the statue with the City authorities and saved yourselves a headache. Not to mention a murder. You'd've had to pay commission, sure, but with what you'd be making off the deal you could afford it. So what stopped you?'

He took his time answering; not that he was rattled – a smart cookie like Smaragdus would've expected the question – but like he was wondering how best to explain two times two to an idiot.

'Athenian officials are funny people, Corvinus,' he said at last. 'They like proper documentation. A provenance guarantee, past ownership history, everything cut, dried and legal. You know the sort of thing.'

'Sure I do. And it sounds like a reasonable attitude to me. In fact, I'd go along with it one hundred per cent, and so would my stepfather.'

'I see.' He paused. 'Then I may as well admit to you now that I haven't got any documentation for the Baker whatsoever.'

Well, he was frank enough, I'd give him that. 'Is that so, now?'

'That is so.'

'In that case you mind telling me what you have got? Besides the statue itself, of course.'

'Not at all. I have a story.'

I laughed. Well, I'd give the guy full marks for nerve, anyway. Con merchants weren't usually so up front, or so obvious. 'Then it'll have to be some story, pal. Because if the statue's hot then whether it's genuine or not we won't touch it with a ten-foot pole.'

'Oh, the Baker isn't stolen. At least, Argaius and I didn't do the stealing.'

'Hey, great! That makes all the difference.' I made to get up. Obviously I was wasting my time here: Priscus wouldn't okay any deal made along these lines, I knew that now. Obsessive the guy might be, but he was down-the-line straight. 'Thanks for the offer, but no thanks. I'll see you around.'

'Wait a moment.' Smaragdus hadn't moved. 'Listen to the story, at least. Have you ever heard of the Tolosan treasure?'

'No.'

'How about Brennus?'

'Brennus I know. He was the Gaul who invaded Greece and plundered Delphi.' Slowly, I sat down again: scam or not, this sounded interesting. 'About three hundred years back, right?'

'Correct. When the southern Greek states rallied and drove him out Brennus took the Delphic treasures north. On the way the Gauls ran foul of the Thessalians and Brennus was killed; but some of his men got back home, and they took the best of the treasures with them. Including Croesus's Lydian dedications.'

'You're going in the wrong direction, pal,' I said. 'Gaul's west of here. And it's a long way from the Piraeus.'

'There's more.' Smaragdus didn't bat an eyelid. 'That's only the first part of the story. The second involves a Roman, Quintus Servilius Caepio. You've heard of him?'

I was getting seriously interested now. 'You have the ball, friend. You run with it.'

'Caepio was one of your provincial governors about a century back. He fought a war against a tribe called the Tectosages in southern Gaul. He took their main town, a place called Tolosa. When he sacked it he found a treasure cache in one of the local temples. The cache was part of Brennus's Delphic spoils, and it included the Baker.'

'Carry on.'

'Caepio packed the treasure up and sent it to Marseilles with the rest of the booty from the war for trans-shipment to Rome. Or at least that was what he said he'd done with it.'

Yeah. This was beginning to make sense; in fact, knowing the way governors' minds work, I could've written the next part myself. 'And you're saying he didn't, right?'

'The treasure never arrived. Even your Roman Senate was suspicious. When Caepio botched his next season's campaign and lost an important battle they took the opportunity to deprive him of his command and had him accused of expropriation. The case never came off because Caepio fled to Smyrna, where he died a pauper.'

'Is that so, now?' I tried to sound more unimpressed than I felt. The whole thing might be pure moonshine, sure, but the names rang true and it felt real. Too real for fudging. 'So what had happened to the gold?'

'The official story stops there, Corvinus. But you see the implications, of course.'

'Sure.' If the guy had died broke they were obvious. In the days before Augustus was around to put the screws on, profiteering governors who managed to squirrel their loot away abroad were set up for life, even if the Roman Senate did kick them out of Italy. And rich exiles don't die paupers. 'Caepio went to Smyrna. His treasure didn't.'

'Right.' Smaragdus paused. 'So now we come to the part of the story you have to take on trust, because it isn't in the records and with Argaius dead I'm the only person who knows it. What had happened was that Caepio had packed the Tolosan treasure – including the Baker – in sealed crates and sent it privately to Asia on board a Greek-owned merchantman. The ship was the *Amphitrite*, her captain was a man called Polybus and the mate and co-owner was Phrixus. Polybus was Argaius's great-great-grandfather. Phrixus was mine.'

I sat back. It worked, sure it did. If the guy was shooting

a line it was one of the best I'd ever heard. 'And your great-great-grandpas pirated Caepio's crates for him, right?'

'Yes.' Smaragdus nodded. 'Not that that was the original intention. They didn't know what they were carrying until the *Amphitrite* ran into a storm off Sicily, when the crates broke loose and one split open.'

'Whereupon temptation proved too much. And they'd know that when he found out Caepio would be in no position to squeal.' Yeah; I'd go for this. It was beautiful. And, like Smaragdus said, far enough back to make the moral aspects academic now. To Romans, at least. I doubted that even Priscus would object too much, not with something like the Baker at stake. 'Carry on, pal. This is fascinating.'

'The *Amphitrite* was Piraeus-based. Polybus and Phrixus sailed back here and put in to the east of the town at a spot called Thieves' Cove.' Yeah. Plausible again: I knew Thieves' Cove, a small bay two or three miles up from the harbour. Ever since the Piraeus has been in existence it's been a popular place for smugglers: Greek skippers don't like paying port dues any more than Roman ones do. 'Then they and their crew hid the treasure in a cave. The agreement was that everyone would have a share.'

'Very democratic.' I was ahead of him again. 'Only Polybus and Phrixus had other ideas, right?'

Smaragdus hesitated; maybe the guy even blushed a little. 'I'm not defending them, Corvinus. I'm simply telling you what happened.'

'Yeah.' Well, that was fair enough: you couldn't choose your family. We had a skeleton or two in our own cupboard that I'd hesitate to blow the dust off in front of strangers, and some of the old Valerii Messallae had been guilty of things a hell of a lot worse than theft and murder. 'Sorry. Carry on, friend.'

'As you say, Polybus and Phrixus had other ideas. Once the treasure was safely hidden they knifed the other three men, stove in one of the *Amphitrite*'s planks and scuttled her. When they got back to the Piraeus they claimed they'd been shipwrecked on the last stretch.'

'Losing Caepio's crates and their own crew in the process.' Yeah. 'So the guys ended up with an excuse for not delivering

the goods and the treasure split two ways instead of five. Neat.'
I grinned. 'There's only one problem.'

'Oh?' He gave me a sharp look. 'And what's that?'

'A crate or two of gold bullion is a lot of gravy, pal, and
splashing gravy around gets you noticed. Especially if you claim
to have just lost a cargo belonging to a Roman governor.'

'Polybus and Phrixus weren't fools, Corvinus. They knew if
they suddenly started spending money – a lot of money – the
authorities would become suspicious. So they agreed to draw
on the treasure bit by bit, as and when necessary. Nothing
too much, but enough to allow them to live comfortably. You
understand?'

'Yeah.' I nodded slowly: Chrysoulla's claim that the Baker
was a family heirloom was beginning to look more plausible
than I'd thought. 'In effect what they'd got was a private bank
in the hills, right?'

'Exactly. Only they were family men, and the bank was to
be a family bank. Sensibly used, there was enough gold to last
for generations.'

'Uh-huh. So how come it didn't?' That much was obvious:
I'd seen Argaius's house, and I'd seen where Smaragdus hung
out. They weren't what you'd expect of guys whose families had
had a century's access to their own gold mine, careful or not.

'Simple.' Smaragdus smiled. 'Because about twenty years later
something happened that ruined everything.'

Twenty years. I frowned. History wasn't my strong point,
especially Greek history. Twenty years from a hundred would
just about bring us up to . . .

I'd got it now. 'The Sullan siege.'

He nodded. 'The Sullan siege. Twenty years after Polybus and
Phrixus had hidden the gold Mithridates of Pontus declared war
on Rome, Greece supported him, and your man Sulla was sent
out. The Piraeus was besieged. As a result, Polybus and Phrixus
were cut off from the treasure. They'd told their sons where the
cave was, but *their* sons were too young yet to be trusted. The
siege brought plague, and Phrixus, his son and Polybus's son
died. Polybus was executed later in the reprisals.'

Again, it fitted: the guy had all the answers, that I had to
admit. The Sullan siege and its aftermath had practically killed

the Piraeus. Like I said, a hundred years later it still hadn't
recovered.

'Unlucky. And no one had thought to leave a map, right?'

'No. Or if so it was lost when Sulla's army burned the town.
The two eldest grandsons – our grandfathers – knew of the cave's
existence, but they didn't know where it was. They searched the
coast around Thieves' Cove for years without success. The two
families have been looking for the treasure ever since.'

The jigsaw in my head came together. 'And then you found
it.'

'We found it. Or part of it, anyway. Two months ago we
discovered a cave that had been closed off by a rock-fall. We
cleared the entrance and' – he spread his hands – 'there was
the Baker.'

'Only the Baker? What about the rest of the treasure?'

'Most of it was gone, where I don't know, nor did my
grandfather or Argaius's. Perhaps Polybus and Phrixus had
moved it elsewhere for safety without passing the information
on; perhaps that part of the family history was lost. Oh, there are
a few bits and pieces, but the Baker's the plum.' He looked me in
the eye. 'And it's genuine. No tricks, Corvinus, believe me.'

Okay. I was convinced, I admitted it. 'I believe you,' I said. 'So.
End of story. You've got a customer, pal. A potential customer,
anyway. You want to show me this cave of yours now?'

Smaragdus got to his feet. 'Yes. Of course. Why not? The
boat's ready and waiting.'

9

The boat . . .

Boats and me have never got on, especially small ones, and in a bad light you could've mistaken Smaragdus's for a corn-skip. I cast my best nautical eye over it and decided that the odds on Poseidon scuttling us before we got halfway were too high for comfort. And that even if he didn't, I'd be wishing he would. It was time for some negotiation.

'Uh . . . we're headed for Thieves' Cove, right?' I said.

'Not quite.' Smaragdus frowned. 'To one of the bays close by.'

'Whatever. Then I'll tell you what, pal. You carry on over in this sow-sickener here; me and Lysias'll take the carriage round the main harbour and meet you there, okay?'

'No deal, Corvinus.' The frown deepened. 'That would take twice as long, you'd have to walk from the Town Gate and even then without my help you'd never find the place. The wind's perfect, too.'

Bugger. Yeah, well, the guy was right, certainly about the distance involved, and as far as winds were concerned I was prepared to take his word on trust. Mind you, of the four elements wind wasn't exactly the one that was worrying me. Also, we were close enough to the boat now for me to get a good hard look at what I'd be letting myself in for, and the sight wasn't exactly cheering: beached or not, you could've washed your smalls in the spillage, if it had been cleaner. I didn't think all these little pinholes in the planking had been put there for decoration, either.

'Okay, pal. You're the boss.' I swallowed and sent up a

quick prayer to Neptune. 'You . . . ah . . . you're sure this gutbucket's safe?'

He gave me a look like I'd just cast aspersions on his grandmother.

'The *Alcyone*? Of course she is. I've had her for years.'

That I'd believe. I didn't know much about changes in boat design, but if he'd told me Polybus and Phrixus had towed this particular specimen behind them all the way from Marseilles I wouldn't have blinked. In fact, scratch that: the thing looked like it could've dated back to Deucalion's flood.

'Yeah,' I said. 'Yeah, I can see you have. That's just my problem.'

Taking a boat trip on the Gulf voluntarily was one thing; coming back the same way was something else. I might be stupid, but I wasn't crazy. While Smaragdus bailed the *Alcyone* out and got her afloat I went round to where I'd left the carriage and told Lysias to meet me at the Aphrodisian Gate. When I got back Smaragdus was already aboard.

'Hurry up,' he said. 'There's nothing to be nervous about.'

'Sure there isn't.' I waded out and pulled myself over the side. The boat bucked like a frightened horse. I wished I had a cup of wine to keep Poseidon sweet, but it looked like I'd just have to hope that the old guy was in a good mood and had a soft spot for Romans. 'Only I just had breakfast and I'd like to keep it that way, you know?'

'You're not a sailor, then?' He was grinning.

'Full marks for observation, pal.' I got myself settled. 'You win the nuts.'

'Relax. I told you, you're perfectly safe. I do this all the time.'

He swung the yard round and took the steering oar. The wind caught the sail and we heeled over on our beam. Greece shifted . . .

'Gods!' I sat down quickly and grabbed for the side. 'Uh . . . maybe I should warn you now. I swim like a brick.'

'There's a coincidence. That makes two of us.'

Now he told me. Oh, great; perfect, in fact. That was all I needed. We could hold hands on the way down.

I shut up and started to pray in earnest.

The *Alcyone* took off like a swallow: well, at least he'd been right about the wind. I'd thought we'd hug the coast, but he set the oar straight and we went barrelling out into open water. It was choppy as hell, and I couldn't see the bottom. Maybe that was just as well.

'Nice weather for a sail, isn't it?'

The bastard was needling me intentionally, but at that precise moment I had other things on my mind. Like what was happening just south of my ribcage.

'Uh, yeah,' I said. 'Yeah, beautiful.' Jupiter! This was . . . I gulped. 'Hey, Smaragdus, you think maybe we could . . .'

Too late. I'd hardly got the last word out before my stomach gave up the unequal struggle and I lost my breakfast to the fish.

I wasn't feeling all that hot an hour later when we finally reached the far side of the gulf, either. Happy the farmer who knows not the sea. Still, I had to hand it to Smaragdus, the guy knew what he was doing; he brought us into the cove sweet as a nut and pulled the *Alcyone* up on to the beach while I lay in the pointed end and sweated.

'We're there,' he said. 'Now we walk.'

'Fine, fine.' I tried standing up, but my legs felt like they'd been filleted and there was a taste in my mouth like something had died there. If that was sailing then I'd take a five-star hangover any time. 'Just give me a minute, okay?'

Smaragdus laughed. Sadistic bastard. I climbed out, eventually. Sand and pebbles underfoot had never felt so good. I took a deep breath and opened my gummy eyes.

'So where's this cave?' I said.

'That way.' He pointed inland. 'Not far, about a quarter of a mile.'

A quarter of a mile. Great. The ground was heaving. If I'd ever wondered why Poseidon is both the sea and the earthquake god I had my answer. 'You – uh – say you do this often, pal?'

'Often enough, in fine weather. You Romans never have made good sailors.'

'No arguments there, Agrippa.' I scooped up a palmful of

water, rinsed the birdshit from my mouth and eyes and took a few more deep breaths. Things were starting to look a bit better. Meaning the hills weren't jumping around so much any more. 'Okay. So let's go.'

He led the way up a goat-track along the edge of the cove and into the scrub beyond. The ground began to rise steeply.

'You're telling me these two guys – Polybus and Phrixus – carried the treasure all this way?' I was gasping already; the after-effects of the seasickness.

'Obviously.'

'That amount of bullion would've weighed a ton, friend. Literally.'

'I told you.' Smaragdus hadn't broken stride. 'They had help, and they did it in stages. Besides, they had to. The caves in Thieves' Cove were used by smugglers. Choosing one of them would have been too risky.'

That made sense. All the same, I wouldn't've liked to do it myself even at my best. It couldn't have been easy. Some places even a goat would've had problems.

And speaking of goats . . .

I was beginning to notice certain things; like the marks on exposed parts of the path. Goats might have feet, but even the Greek variety didn't wear hobnailed sandals.

'Hey, Smaragdus,' I said.

He turned back. 'Yes?'

'I thought we were out in the sticks here. This path used much?'

'Not that I know of. We're a long way from the road.'

'Yeah. Yeah, that's what I thought.' I was getting a bad feeling about this: the marks looked recent.

'We're almost there now.' Smaragdus nodded towards a small cliff. 'That's the place up ahead.'

I looked. Jupiter. If that was Polybus's hidey-hole I wasn't surprised it had stayed lost for so long. The 'cave' wasn't so much a cave as a wide split at the base of the cliff, screened by bushes and half buried in rubble; the remains of the rock-fall Smaragdus had mentioned, no doubt. Before that had been cleared away the place wouldn't have merited a second glance.

Smaragdus produced a lamp and a tinder-box from the satchel he was carrying.

'It doesn't go all that far back,' he said, 'but it's much deeper than it looks. We'll need light.'

'Fine.' While he got the lamp going I examined the ground in front of the entrance. There were more sandal prints and a deep dent. A very deep dent, like something heavy had rested there . . .

Smaragdus held out the lamp. 'After you, Corvinus.'

'You're the host, pal. You go ahead.'

We clambered over the tumble of rocks and into the cleft itself. There was more room inside once we'd passed the entrance; plenty of room.

Too much room, in fact.

Polybus's cave was bare. As in 'empty'.

Yeah, well, I couldn't say I was exactly surprised. And it had all been a little too good to be true. Sure, Smaragdus hadn't been spinning me a yarn: there'd been something here all right, that was obvious, something heavy that had left deep-scored rowels in the earth of the cave floor where it had been dragged towards the entrance.

Smaragdus's mouth was hanging open like someone had cut the cords.

'It was here!' he said. 'I swear it was!'

'Okay, pal.' I sighed. 'I believe you. But it's gone now and there's nothing we can do about it. Let's get into the open air.'

We clambered out.

'Corvinus, I swear to you . . .' Smaragdus was still looking like someone had slugged him with a blackjack.

'Yeah, I know.' I pointed to the dent in the ground and the sandal prints. 'You can see the marks where they pulled it out and took it down to the cove.' Jupiter! The thing must've weighed a ton! But then how heavy *is* a four-and-a-half-foot-high solid gold statue?

'But who did it? No one else knew, only me and Argaius.'

I hesitated. 'This Eutyches guy. You brought him here?'

'No. No, I've never met him. Nor had Argaius, as far as I know.'

'Uh-huh. How about Argaius himself? Would he have moved the Baker for any reason?'

Smaragdus was still in shock. 'No. It was safe enough here. And he couldn't have done it alone, anyway.'

True enough; even as an outside chance it was unlikely. Besides, the answer was obvious. I thought of the smashed-up doll with the gashed throat on Callippus's table. You don't kill the golden goose until it's laid its egg, and a severed throat is pretty final in anyone's book. Whoever had killed Argaius already had what he wanted.

There was only one candidate, too.

'So,' I said. 'This Eutyches. What exactly do you know about him?'

'Nothing.' Smaragdus raised his head. The guy looked sick. 'I swear, nothing, only the name. Argaius handled the business side on his own. That's how the partnership worked.'

'What about that final meeting? In Mounychia?'

'He told me about it, certainly, but I wasn't involved. It didn't need both of us. And like I said I left the business arrangements to him. He was better at them than I was.'

'Uh-huh.' Not good enough, though, that much was obvious. Well, like I'd said there was nothing to be done about it now: the bastard already had his statue and I might as well go home and take up embroidery. 'You want to report this to the Watch?'

'There isn't much point, is there?'

That came out bitter as hell. Yeah, well, the guy was right. Callippus would go through the motions, sure, but there wasn't a whole lot he could do. Or, considering the circumstances, even want to do. I said nothing.

'I'm sorry about this, Corvinus. Really sorry.'

'Yeah, that makes two of us, pal. Three, counting Priscus.' The old guy would take it hard; when he'd written that letter he'd thought the deal was in the bag. Mother would be pretty peeved as well. I'd write to them tonight.

'You don't want to change your mind? About going back in the *Alcyone*?' Smaragdus tried a grin. The effect was ghastly.

'No.' In my present mood that would've put the lid on. 'No, I'll walk. Lysias will be waiting. Thanks all the same.'

'Fine.'

He hadn't moved, and he still looked grey as death; but there was nothing I could do for him, not now. I gave a half-hearted wave and started off up the hill in the direction of town.

10

When I got to the Aphrodisian Gate there was still no sign of Lysias with the carriage. Hell. The end to a perfect day. I parked myself outside a handy cookshop with a good view of the gate and ordered up a jug of Chian. After walking across what felt like half of rural Attica I could've murdered a plate of bean stew to go with it, but I took one look at the waiter leaning against the door jamb and digging the wax from his ears with the blunt end of a snail-spoon and decided to forgo the pleasure. Pissed off and starving I might be, but I wasn't that desperate.

Besides, I think best on an empty stomach and a full wine jug. Food's a distraction.

So. What had we got here? What had happened was clear enough: Eutyches, whoever he was, had suckered Argaius into a bogus meeting on Mounychia, bundled him up, taken him somewhere quiet and persuaded him with the help of Prince Charming and a crowbar to reveal the whereabouts of the Baker. Having got the information he wanted he'd slit the guy's throat, dumped him at the Founders' and raided the honey-pot, leaving me sitting on my hands and looking like ten different kinds of fool just when I'd been congratulating myself on tracking down Argaius's partner . . .

Yeah. Smart work, right? The question was, what was I going to do now? I couldn't give up; no way. Sure, I'd lost the statue, but I still had a lead or two, and now I had a personal axe to grind. No one likes to be made a mug of, and just the thought of the sneer on Prince Charming's face had me reaching for the razor. When I did find Eutyches – and find him I would – the guy was catfood.

Okay. So let's start from the other end and think with my brain instead of my backside this time. Just what did I know about Eutyches? Sure, the name was common enough to fit a good slice of the City population, but I could narrow the field a lot more because my Eutyches would have to satisfy certain criteria. First of all, he needed to be, if not rich, at least pretty well-heeled: to hook Argaius and establish his street cred he'd've needed to put up a show of wealth at least, and hired help like Prince Charming, plus the tame muscle he'd need to shift the Baker, wouldn't come cheap. Slaves, plural, cost money, even if they are just bullion-shifters. And freemen who had to be squared would rate even higher.

Yeah. So. Let's call the guy 'comfortably off' at worst. From a cultured background, what's more: if Perilla was right, and his choice of Ptolemy's statue as the dumping place for Argaius's corpse was deliberate, then the guy was a prime culture vulture, someone who was up to indulging himself with chichi historical puns that were way beyond the average punter. Second, unless his only concern was the Baker's meltdown value – which was a possibility, but I doubted it somehow – he had at least an educated layman's interest in art. Scratch that: given he was prepared to go to any lengths to get what he wanted, Eutyches had to be a full-fledged antiquities nut in the same league as Priscus, only without Priscus's scruples.

He had to be capable of murder, too. Second-hand murder, at any rate. That went without saying.

I picked up my wine cup and took a thoughtful swallow. I'd have to remember this place: otocathartic waiters or not, their Chian wasn't bad, especially with nothing to soak it up. I was feeling brighter already.

Fair enough. I'd got myself a profile, and it hung together. A Eutyches who fitted as narrow a description as that shouldn't be all that difficult to trace; in fact, a word to Bathyllus might do it, because even in the short time we'd been here he'd built up a knowledge of the Athenian social register that almost equalled his shit-hot mastery of the Roman one . . .

Only asking Bathyllus who Eutyches was wouldn't do a blind bit of good because the guy didn't exist; I'd bet a used boil plaster to a double consignment of Setinian on that right now. He couldn't exist, because neither Smaragdus nor, by implication, Argaius knew anything about him, and they should have done. Sure they should: as decent-living, hard-working professional con men they'd carry a list of possible marks in their heads. A rich antiquities buff like Eutyches would stick out like Priapus in a lettuce bed. Neither of the partners had ever seen the bastard face to face, either, barring, perhaps, Argaius's final – and fatal – interview on Mounychia. That was significant too.

The explanation was simple: if I was right, and the description did fit, then Eutyches wasn't the guy's real name at all.

Okay. Now we were getting somewhere. If 'Eutyches' was an assumed name the field was wide open again. So who did I already know who was comfortably off but not filthy rich enough to do things honestly; well read and cultured, with certain show-off tendencies; an art freak on Priscan lines; who knew that the Baker had come on to the market; and finally who was someone strong-minded enough – potentially, at least, in my opinion – to contemplate murder as a means to an end?

Correct. I took a smug mouthful of the Chian.

One got you ten that Eutyches was my oenophilic pal Melanthus.

The old brain wasn't working too badly after all, and I was feeling pretty pleased with myself: I could fit a name to Eutyches and I'd a jug of wine in front of me that was well on the good side of drinkable. No sign of Lysias yet, but I wasn't complaining: there aren't many pleasures that measure up to sitting in front of a cookshop by a busy street looking at life go by. I watched an argument between a porter and a customer who reckoned the guy had delivered his basket of fish in a poorer condition than they'd started out, and picked up a few choice words to add to my Greek vocabulary. Then there was a real honey of a girl with a figure that even from what I could see of it under her mantle wouldn't've looked out of place on a sculptor's model. And finally, just when Lysias drove up and parked in the carriage rank next to the gate, there was a big, flashy Ethiopian on a mule.

You don't see many Ethiopians even in Athens, let alone out here in the sticks. He wasn't a slave, either, or at least he wasn't dressed like one. And like I say he was big: you could see the muscles straining against the seams of his tunic, which was one of the snazziest I'd seen in a long while: canary yellow with a red stripe up the side and a broad belt studded with gilt nails and scraps of coloured glass that winked in the afternoon sunlight.

The guy wasn't in any hurry, that was for sure. He'd stopped by the horse trough beside the gate and dismounted to water the mule. Now he was looking in my direction, or rather in the direction of the cookshop. I thought for a moment he'd come over, but he seemed to change his mind and just sat down on the edge of the trough and communed with nature while the mule took on water one end and got rid of it the other.

Lysias turned the carriage and gave me a wave. Okay. End of floorshow, time to go home. I left a silver piece on the table and walked over to the rank. The Ethiopian's eyes followed me. It was unnerving, like being ogled by two hardboiled eggs smothered in octopus ink. Yeah, well, maybe a Roman in this part of the Piraeus was as rare a sight to him as an Ethiopian was to me. I gave him a nod as I passed but he didn't respond.

'Okay, Lysias,' I said, climbing aboard the carriage. 'Take it away.'

We were halfway to the Hamaxitos when the hairs at the nape of my neck started to crawl. That doesn't happen often, but when it does I listen. On a sudden hunch, I opened the flap at the back of the carriage and looked out. Sure enough, the Ethiopian was behind us. And that was strange, if you like, because when I'd first seen him the guy had been headed the other way, out of town towards Echelidae . . .

Okay, it might be coincidence; certainly it wasn't worth making a fuss over. Maybe he'd suddenly remembered he'd left the stewpot on at home or had a premonition he'd be mugged by a visually challenged bear with a down on loud tunics; or maybe he'd just decided that Athens couldn't get along without him after all. Whatever his reasons, they were his own business, and probably as innocent as a virgin's dreams.

Still, it didn't explain the twitching of my neck hairs. And some of those virgins' dreams can be pretty hot stuff. I'd be willing to lay a substantial bet that the flashy bastard was a tail.

The question was, whose was he, and why?

I closed the flap and settled down to think.

11

When I finally got back, Perilla was in the sitting-room. Happy was something the lady wasn't.

'Corvinus, where on earth have you been?' she said. 'Meton's livid! Dinner's been ready for hours!'

Uh-oh. That sounded bad. Hell hath no fury like an angry chef's, and Meton took his duties seriously. By his code of conduct, coming in late for dinner was tantamount to giving the Germans free passage across the Rhine and letting them have a complimentary crack at Gaul. Well, it was too late to do anything about that now.

'I'm sorry,' I said. 'Things took longer than I'd thought.'

'Did you find Smaragdus?'

'Yeah, I found him. For what it was worth.' I told her what had happened. She listened in silence.

'You're sure the statue was there?' she said at last.

'I'd bet good money. And apropos of that, I know who took it. Our tame art expert from the Academy.'

'Melanthus?' Perilla stared at me, her eyes wide. 'But, Marcus . . . !'

'Excuse me, sir.' Bathyllus had oozed in. 'Dinner is served. As of two hours ago.'

I considered telling him to stick his canapés where he wouldn't find them for a month, but that would just have played into the bastard's hands. Instead, I kept my face straight. Bathyllus hates that.

'You care to divulge the menu, little guy?'

'Certainly, sir. Overdone chicken dumplings, slightly warm peas vinaigrette and a wilted endive salad.'

'Yum. Sounds great. I'm starving. Serve it up.'

Bathyllus hovered, fizzing quietly.

'Meton says he admits no responsibility,' he said finally.

'Good, good.' I poured myself a drink from the jug which I'd brought in from the hall. 'Tell him better late than never, okay?'

'I'm sure that will be a great comfort to him, sir.'

Weak. I grinned: game to me for a change. 'How's our new pet, by the way?'

'Alexis is doing his best, sir, but it's an uphill struggle. The bird's vocabulary is irrevocably tainted.' A disapproving sniff: if the super-straight Bathyllus had his way Nestor would be burger.

'Early days, pal, early days.'

'If you say so, sir.'

We went through to the dining-room and lay down on the couch.

'Marcus,' Perilla said, settling herself. 'Just how serious are you about Melanthus being responsible?'

'Deadly.' I took a swallow of wine. 'He fits. Or have you got a better candidate?'

'But Melanthus of Abdera is a respected member of the Academy. A distinguished philosopher . . .'

'He's also an art nut, lady. One who'd prefer not to see a national treasure like the Baker fall into profane Roman clutches.'

'That's nonsense!'

I shook my head. 'Uh-uh. He told me that himself. Oh, he was polite enough and he didn't labour the point, but it came across loud and clear. And he fits the bill in other ways.'

'You mean he's capable of torture and murder? Corvinus, really!'

I sighed. 'Perilla, you've never met the guy. I have, and he's no shrinking violet. Jupiter, even Priscus might be capable of beating someone to death with an Etruscan grammar if they got between him and his mania.'

'Now you're being facetious. And that is in very bad taste.'

'Yeah, well, maybe not Priscus. But Melanthus is a tough

cookie, and being a philosopher doesn't mean he's immune to everyday human frailty.'

She sniffed. 'How interesting, Corvinus. I had no idea that your definition of everyday human frailty embraced theft, torture and murder.'

Jupiter on a seesaw! Women! 'Listen, lady—'

'Dinner, sir.' Bathyllus trundled in with a loaded tray and set the dishes in front of us with a crisp efficiency that radiated disapproval. 'The kitchen staff wish me to say they hope you enjoy your meal.'

Bastards. Every last one of them. I poked tentatively at the dumplings with my knife. For once the little guy hadn't been exaggerating; you could've used the things for slingshot. Hell. I reached for the olives.

'This accusation of yours.' Perilla was helping herself to peas. 'You are basing it on firm evidence, I take it?'

'Sure.' I refilled my wine cup. 'Melanthus has known about Argaius and the Baker from the start. Unless he's a crypto-millionaire, which I doubt, he was in no position to put in a counter-bid. If he wanted the statue then he had to steal it. Melanthus is our boy. QED.'

'Corvinus, I'm sorry.' Perilla frowned at the peas, tried one and put down her spoon. 'Perhaps you misheard. I asked if you had any evidence. What you've just given me is theory. And half-baked theory at that.'

'Is that right, now?'

'That is right.' She pushed the plate away. 'Even if one does accept your unwarrantable assumption that the man is morally capable of theft and murder.'

'Okay, Aristotle. Suppose you tell me what's wrong with the theory? As a theory?'

'Very well.' She held up a finger. 'One. Your stepfather had heard about the statue in Rome, so the fact of its existence can hardly be a close secret. Other aficionados besides Priscus and Melanthus must have known about it for months. Allied to this, two' – she bent down a second finger – 'Melanthus had plenty of time to put his plan into operation, and the longer he left it the greater the likelihood was of the Baker being sold out of his reach. To postpone things until you were actually on the point of establishing contact with both him and Argaius would show incredible foolishness.'

'Maybe. He could've been working himself up to it, lady. I never said he was a natural criminal. He just wants the Baker.'

'True. But you did say that he was a strong-minded man. There is, at least, a partial inconsistency there which needs explaining.'

Yeah, well, she had a point. Certainly one to think about.

'Three. Melanthus is well known in Athens. If he introduced himself to Argaius as the fictitious Eutyches don't you think the man would be just a little suspicious?'

I was on firmer ground here. I shook my head. 'No. Argaius never met Eutyches, nor did Smaragdus. Any negotiations were carried out through an intermediary. And if Melanthus was planning a double-cross he'd know a personal meeting need never happen.'

'Hmm.' I'd scored, I could see that by the way she absently reached for a dumpling. 'All right. Accepted. With reservations.' Jupiter! Well, the lady's nothing if not a fighter. 'Lastly. If you were the only other person interested in the Baker Melanthus wouldn't have had to steal it.'

I blinked. 'Uh . . . run that past me again, will you?'

Perilla prodded the dumpling with her spoon. It didn't give an inch. She put it back in the dish with a sigh. 'Priscus asked Melanthus to authenticate the statue, Corvinus. To prevent the sale all he would have to do is say it was a fake.'

Yeah, I hadn't thought of that. Still, as an answer it wasn't good enough. Not by a long chalk.

'Wait a minute,' I said. 'Sure, if Melanthus didn't give the go-ahead our particular deal might be off but he still wouldn't end up with the statue himself. And Argaius would've smelled a rat if his customer's tame art expert gave it the thumbs down one minute and then offered to take it off his hands the next. Also, he'd still have to raise the necessary cash, and even if Argaius was willing to drop his price rather than look for another customer gold statues that size don't come cheap. If Melanthus is Eutyches then he had to steal the Baker, lady, because even acting through an intermediary he'd no other option.'

A long pause. Got her! Well, maybe it was hunger.

'Corvinus,' she said finally, 'I apologise.'

'Hey!' I grinned: apologies from Perilla were about as common as July blizzards. 'You mean you think I'm right?'

'No. But your theory is at least tenable. On present evidence at least. I'm sorry I was so dismissive.'

'Uh-huh.' I kissed her. 'It's worth a bit of digging, sure. Maybe tomorrow would be a good time to pay the Academy another visit. Rattle the guy's cage a little, see which way he jumps.'

Perilla set down her spoon.

'Marcus, be careful,' she said softly.

I grinned. 'I thought you weren't convinced.'

'Perhaps not. But if you are right then the man can't be quite sane. And he's already killed once.'

'I'll be careful. I guarantee it.' My stomach rumbled. Perilla frowned and set down her spoon.

'Oh, this is ridiculous!' she snapped. 'Do you think Meton has any eggs?'

'Uh, yeah.' I was investigating the endive salad. Whatever endives were supposed to look like, these ones didn't. 'Yeah, I should think so. Why?'

'Good.' She got up. 'Then he can make us an omelette.'

Gods alive! I watched her go admiringly. Forget Melanthus: facing Meton unarmed on his home ground and ordering up an à la carte omelette takes real courage.

She got it, too. I just hoped it was an omen.

12

Next day I took the carriage out to the Academy. No prior appointment this time either: if Melanthus was our man then I didn't mean to give the bastard a chance to think up a story or, worse, to make tracks for the tall timber. I'd thought about calling in at Callippus's office and sharing my suspicions with him, but I decided against it. Like Perilla had said, I'd no real evidence, and there was just an outside chance that I was doing the guy an injustice. Also, crook though he might conceivably be, Melanthus was a respected member of the academic community. Callippus would listen, sure, but all I could reasonably expect from him in the end was a request for proof and the polite brush-off when I couldn't deliver.

I left Lysias waiting by the carriage outside the precinct gates and went inside on foot. I felt uncomfortable: these places where high-powered intellectuals hang out always make me nervous, and I can never shake off the feeling that any minute some clever bastard with a brain the size of a pumpkin is going to jump out on me and start asking me questions about where I stood on the issues of life, the soul and divine purpose. It didn't happen, although I passed by some conversations that would've made even Priscus sound like a monosyllabic barfly. Education may be a wonderful thing, but that doesn't mean it's good for you.

The library was packed to the door. I looked for Melanthus but he wasn't around. Shit. Well, the Academy was a big place. Maybe he was lecturing, or had a tutorial group or whatever the hell he did when he wasn't shifting large amounts of bullion from A to B. Somebody would know, anyway.

I picked on an old guy stumbling out with an armful of books. Probably a Peripatetic who'd lost his way.

'Excuse me, sir,' I said politely.

'Yes?' Grey eyes peered myopically at me from under ratty eyebrows.

'Do you know Melanthus of Abdera at all?'

'Of course.' One of the books rolled off the pile. He made a senile grab for it and three more fell. I picked them up and stashed them under his armpits. 'Thank you, young man.' He turned to go.

Jupiter! The entire Platonic legacy to choose from and I had to land myself with this one! I tried again. 'Then do you happen to know where he is at present?'

'Philosophically?'

He meant it, too. I didn't believe this. 'Uh, no. No, physically.'

'Mmm. That is more difficult.' He scratched the chin under his beard. Five other books tottered. 'Have you tried the fine arts section?'

'And where would that be?'

'By the main reading desks.'

Yeah. I'd looked there first. It was where I'd found him the previous time. 'No, he isn't there. Not that I could see, at any rate.' I was getting the hang of this philosophy stuff now.

'Then I'm afraid I can't help you.'

Hell. 'Is there anyone he's particularly friendly with, sir? A colleague, perhaps?'

'You could try Alciphron. He's the head librarian. The desk right at the back. Now if you'll excuse me, young man . . .' He tottered off.

Back to the reading-room. I tiptoed through the silence as quietly as I could manage: one sandal-squeak out of place here and these guys stare you to death. Sure enough I spotted a big desk at the end with another serious beard parked behind it, making about the fiftieth I'd seen so far. If there was a hell for barbers it was probably modelled pretty closely on the Academy. I went over.

'Excuse me, sir,' I said, 'but is your name Alciphron?'

The beard was taking notes from a scroll. He held up his left hand and kept on writing. I waited until he'd put the pen down, then gave him the big smile.

'It is.' He didn't smile back. Maybe it was my aftershave. 'What can I do for you?'

'I'm looking for—'

'Quietly, please!'

'Melanthus of Abdera.'

He paused, then said carefully: 'He isn't in today.'

'Ah. You know where he might be?'

The guy looked at me, then down at his scroll. My eyes followed. I was expecting Greek, but the thing was covered in squiggly lines like an ink-stained spider had thrown a fit all over it and finally slit its wrists at the bottom. He sighed and rolled it up.

'Perhaps we'd better talk elsewhere,' he said. 'You are Valerius Corvinus, aren't you? The Baker fellow, Priscus's stepson?'

'Uh, yeah. Yeah, that's me.' A horrible thought struck me. 'The guy isn't dead, is he?'

That got me a sharp stare: very sharp indeed. 'Good God, man, of course not! Why on earth should Melanthus be dead?'

There was no answer to that; not one that would make sense, anyway. It was just that I'd had suspects corpse on me before, and I didn't want to add to the list.

'No reason, friend,' I said. 'Forget I asked.'

'He's working at home.' Alciphron stood up. He was a lot smaller than I'd expected, the top of his head barely reaching my chin, but he had the build of a boxer. The nose, too. Powerful arms, thick chest, strangler's hands and wrists. 'He often works at home.'

'You feel like giving me an address, maybe?'

He hesitated. 'Of course. But let's go outside first, shall we?'

'Sure. If you like.' I frowned. Something was wrong here: the guy was nervous as a cat and acting like he had beans to spill, although I couldn't see why.

He led the way to the exit, and I followed. It was good to get into the open air; just being next to all these books had been giving me a headache. A dry throat, too. I could've murdered a cup of wine, but Academicians don't go in for fripperies like booze, not when they're working, anyway: according to cutting-edge philosophical theory it throws the soul's balance out of kilter or something. In any case the nearest wineshop was back at the Dipylon Gate.

'Now.' Alciphron indicated a bench. At least there were plenty of these around: unlike wineshops, benches are philosophically correct. The Academy grounds are full of them. 'First of all Melanthus's address. He has a house in Melite, near the Temple of Artemis the Counsellor. It's easy to find, but should you get lost then anyone will direct you.'

Yeah, well, that was one thing settled, and a visit there wouldn't take me all that far out of my way: Melite was just the other side of the Potters' Quarter, between the Hill of Ares and the Hill of the Nymphs.

'You could've told me that inside,' I said.

'True.' Alciphron's thick eyebrows twitched. 'But if you noticed I did say "first of all".'

Uh-huh. Beans was right. 'You mean you wanted to talk to me.'

'Yes. I'm afraid I did.' A frown, and a hesitation. 'Valerius Corvinus, this is difficult for me. Morally difficult.'

'So try to force yourself, pal.'

'I have a great deal of respect for Melanthus of Abdera both as a scholar and a friend. He has a right to govern his own affairs as any freeborn man has, without interference from me or from anyone else.' He paused. 'However, recently I have become more than a little worried about . . . well, about his state of mind. In respect of the arrangement he has with your stepfather. And in respect of this . . . Baker statue.'

I sat back and tried to keep the interest out of my face.

'Is that so, now?' I said.

'The thing has become an obsession with him. I use the word advisedly.'

'You care to elaborate, maybe?'

'You must see how Melanthus views this business, Corvinus. Art is his life. For a treasure like Croesus's Baker, believed lost for three hundred years, suddenly to reappear is something very special to him. Uniquely so. And – forgive me – to see it pass into the hands of a private collector who is moreover not a Greek . . . you understand?'

'Sure I understand.' I felt smug as hell. It's not often you get theories confirmed so dramatically. I was just sorry Perilla wasn't there to listen so I could crow properly. 'He wants the statue himself.'

'Yes. He would be ashamed to admit it in so many words, of course, perhaps even to himself, but that is my firm belief. So when I learned that the seller had been found dead . . . not that I think for one moment that Melanthus could be involved, that is completely impossible.' I nodded. 'Still, it is disquieting, is it not?'

'Yeah.' Jupiter! Disquieting it might be to Alciphron, but I was having a hard time keeping the grin off my face. Got the bastard! 'You know that the statue has disappeared?'

Again that sharp stare. Alciphron was no fool, either.

'No, young man,' he said. 'That I did not know.'

'Argaius – the guy who was murdered – had it squirrelled away in a cave near Thieves' Cove. His partner took me there. Only someone else had got to it first.' Alciphron said nothing. I paused. 'You . . . uh . . . happen to know if Melanthus has a slave or a freedman or an acquaintance of some kind who looks like a docker?' I described Prince Charming.

'No.' The word was spoken carefully: he hadn't missed the implications of the question. 'But then I don't know much about his life outwith the Academy itself. An acquaintance is most unlikely, not a man such as you describe, certainly. And Melanthus has very few slaves. Like most of us, he may be comfortably off but he is not rich. Not by Roman standards, at least.'

Did I detect the barest sniff? Jupiter, these Greek academics were all the same. Scratch one and you got an inverted snob. Yeah, well, it'd been worth a try.

'Is there anything else you can tell me, sir?' I said. 'Anything at all?'

Alciphron hesitated. 'Nothing. Except that Melanthus is not by nature a thief, Corvinus, let alone a killer. Quite the contrary. On that I would stake my reputation. I've known him for fifteen years, and he is a man of strong and unbending principles. He has his weaknesses, as do we all; but I firmly believe they would not lead him to murder.'

'You're sure? Not even for the Baker?'

That got me a hesitation. 'You are perhaps familiar with Heraclitus's declaration that unity is achieved in any organism only through a balance of the opposites contained within its nature?'

'Uh . . . well . . .'

'That declaration may be relevant here, I'm afraid. I hope and pray that it is not, but Heraclitus's view is quite a valid one in respect of the human psyche. A month ago I would have answered your question with a categorical "no", but now . . . well, I can only hope that in this case the rule does not apply and that my friend is still the man he was.'

Uh-huh. Interesting, right? And in more ways than one. Food for thought, certainly. I thanked the guy and went back to Lysias and the coach.

I'd have to remember that crack about Heraclitus, too. One-liners like that are worth their weight in gold at parties.

13

Alciphron had been right about Melanthus not being rich: the house by the Temple of Artemis was middle-bracket standard but no more, a two-storey building round a small central courtyard. I knocked at the door and an elderly slave opened it.

'The master at home?' I asked.

The slave shook his head. 'No, lord. I'm afraid not.'

Hell. 'So when do you expect him back?'

'That I couldn't say.' He hesitated. 'Was your business urgent?'

'The name's Valerius Corvinus. He was doing a favour for my stepfather. Authenticating a statue. Perhaps there's someone else I could talk to? One of the family, maybe?'

'The master isn't married, lord. He lives alone.' Another hesitation. 'But if you'd like to come in I'm sure Timon would be pleased to help if he can.'

'Timon?'

'Our head slave, lord.'

'Oh, right. Yeah, sure. Thanks.' I stepped past him into the hall.

'If you'd care to wait a moment I'll fetch him for you.'

The slave padded off and I sat down on a convenient chair and looked around the room. If he didn't have money, Melanthus had taste, although by my standards it was pretty highbrow. There weren't many ornaments visible but having met the guy they were what I'd have expected: an antique bronze head of a bearded god that was either an original or a good copy, a small statuette of a man with almond-shaped eyes carrying a ram on his shoulders and a black-figure pottery mixing bowl that had been broken and carefully glued back together again. Weird, but maybe the thing had some sentimental value. The chair I was sitting in was old, too. I couldn't place it, but the decoration wasn't Greek or Egyptian. Carian, maybe, or from somewhere even further away. All I knew was that it was uncomfortable as hell.

'Valerius Corvinus.' The man had come from the inner part of the house. 'Welcome. I'm Timon, sir.'

Gods alive! He was speaking Latin: good Latin, at that! If the door slave hadn't said he was the major-domo I would've taken him for Melanthus's secretary, or even a colleague, even allowing for the slave's tunic. We were moving in high intellectual circles here. I made to stand up but he waved me down.

'No, please. Be comfortable. I've told them to bring you some wine. You wanted to see the master, I understand?'

'Yeah. Yeah, that's right. When do you expect him back?'

'He didn't say, sir. Perhaps he's gone directly to the Academy.'

'No, I've just come from there. I got the address from Alciphron. Although if Melanthus isn't long gone I may've passed him on the road.'

Timon hesitated. 'That's possible, sir,' he said. 'Although not likely. The master spent the night away.'

My interest sharpened. 'Yeah? Whereabouts?'

'Again he didn't say.' I noticed that a cagey tone had crept into the major-domo's voice.

'This happen often, pal?'

A pause that said very clearly that it was none of my business. Nevertheless, he gave me an answer.

'Quite often, sir. Once or twice a month, perhaps.'

'Without giving you any details?'

'It isn't my place to ask.' Timon's lips set. A fair point; although if he'd been Bathyllus he would've found out anyway, for his own satisfaction. Knowing where the master is, even when he'd rather keep it a secret, is a point of honour with head slaves. There again, for all I knew philosophers' households were run differently from ordinary people's. From what I'd seen of this menage I'd believe it.

The wine came, in a plain pottery cup that looked antique, foreign and very fragile. It was good stuff, top-of-the-range

Rhodian, ten years old at least. Maybe I'd misjudged the guy after all. Even so, a paid-up member of the Academy who knew his wines well enough to take that amount of trouble over choosing and serving them, let alone pay Labrus's hefty prices for what were part of life's very physical pleasures, was unusual. Very unusual . . .

Which, taken along with what Timon had just told me, suggested another interesting possibility. Maybe being single Melanthus had other unphilosophical tastes. Ones that would explain regular overnight stays, for example.

'You . . . uh . . . remember what time he left exactly, pal?' I asked.

Another pause. Sure, I was pushing it, but I had to get all I could now, even if Timon did put me down as a Roman boor.

'An hour or so before sunset, sir,' he said at last.

'That's his usual time? For these expeditions?'

'More or less.' The guy was looking distinctly peeved, and the pauses between question and answer were getting longer. 'Although "expeditions" is not a word I would use myself.'

'Yeah? And what word would you use?' That got no answer; this time I'd pushed too far. I tried another tack. 'You mind if I have a word with your coachman? I really do have to see Melanthus pretty urgently. Maybe the coachman can tell me where he went.'

'I'm sorry, sir, but that's impossible.' I could hear the relief in the guy's voice. 'We haven't got one, sir. Nor litter slaves. The household is a very small one.'

Bugger. 'You mean he went on foot?'

'No. Not necessarily. If he were going any distance he would normally hire a coach or a litter from the public rank at the Piraeus Gate.'

'I see.' I sipped my wine. That complicated matters, as Timon knew, and it also explained the major-domo's sudden cheeriness. 'You have no idea where he went? None at all?'

'That, sir, I'm afraid I can't say.'

Sure he couldn't. But I appreciated the intentional ambiguity of the answer all the same. Even Bathyllus couldn't have done it better.

*   *   *

I left Melanthus's place and set out along Piraeus Road for the coach rank by the City Gate, my brain buzzing all the way.

Okay, so we had three possible scenarios here. First was that Perilla was right and the whole thing was a mare's nest, in which case Melanthus's disappearance was pure coincidence. In support of that, Timon had said that the guy was in the habit of slipping off for the night regularly without telling anyone where he was going, and this could simply be one of those times. I could guess why: academic high-flyer or not, Melanthus hadn't struck me particularly as the unworldly type. There was good red blood there, he was in the prime of life, and Athens offered plenty of opportunities for the confirmed bachelor to let his hair down in private. Beard. Whatever. And although the academic community was pretty tolerant about individual freedom he might not like it to get around that he spent his free time pressing the sheets with a bit of female company. That would explain Timon's reticence: sure, he was an upmarket slave, but for any slave, upmarket or not, not to make it an issue of personal pride to know what his master was doing every hour of the day and night wasn't natural. If Melanthus was in the habit of visiting one of the City whorehouses or comforting someone else's lonely wife his major-domo would know about it. Sure he would. And, like Timon had implied, it was no business of mine, and there was an end of it.

Second scenario: I was right, and Melanthus was the phantom Eutyches and guilty as hell. In that case he'd got the Baker and was lying low somewhere until the heat died down. Certainly what Alciphron had told me about the guy being obsessed supported that idea, and it made all sorts of sense because like I said Melanthus fitted the bill perfectly. Furthermore, he was no fool, and as such he wouldn't take me for one either. If, as I suspected, he'd planted our flashy Ethiopian pal from the Aphrodisian Gate on me as a tail he'd know I'd been asking questions, and it wouldn't take a top-notch philosopher to put two and two together and come up with the conclusion that he'd been rumbled. He might have decided that brazening things out wasn't an option and having got what he was after it was time to fade into the woodwork, at least for the time being. Not, perhaps, the action of a sane man, because that would be tantamount to a confession; but then I didn't think Melanthus was sane, not where the Baker was concerned, anyway. And Heraclitus would back me up on that.

The third scenario I didn't like even to think about. We'd already had a guy in this business who'd gone out one evening and hadn't come back, and I hoped the score hadn't just doubled. If it had, then the theory was screwed: Melanthus wasn't Eutyches at all, he was as innocent as a new-born babe of both the murder and the theft, and we were back where we started. But that just didn't sit right. Melanthus had something cooking, I'd take my oath on it even without what Alciphron had told me: the guy had form for all sorts of reasons. The itch in the back of my neck told me that, and the itch wasn't often wrong.

Then there was Alciphron himself. I wondered about Alciphron . . .

Ah, leave it. The first job was to find where Melanthus had disappeared to. And if I was very lucky and willing to invest a silver piece or two one of the coachmen or litter teams at the gate would be able to tell me.

The rank was on the other side of the street, just outside the gate itself. I turned round before crossing to check that I wouldn't be mown down by some would-be charioteer chicken-carrier behind with his deliveries . . .

And froze.

About twenty paces behind me was the Ethiopian. It was the same guy, I was sure of that: there aren't many six-foot-tall soot-black negroes in the City, and I'd bet precious few of them had a penchant for loud tunics hung with flashy paste jewellery.

This time I wasn't giving the bastard the benefit of the doubt, because there wasn't any. I went straight for him.

The guy saw me coming. Quick as lightning, he swerved down an alleyway between two pork butchers' shops. I put on a burst of speed and went after him . . .

. . . slap into the side of a porter's mule which panicked and stood on my foot. Hard.

I doubled up in agony. When I'd stopped hopping around and pushed past the mule and its cursing driver the Ethiopian was gone. Long gone, and in that part of the Potters' Quarter you can lose yourself in the crowd like water into sand. Especially if you've got two good feet to the other guy's one. Hell. So much for that idea, and now he knew I was on to him he'd be more careful. I gave my crushed toes a rub and hobbled back to the main drag.

Ah, well. You win some, you lose some. And the guy I really wanted at this precise moment was Melanthus. There were half a dozen coachmen in soiled tunics hanging around the gate touting for custom. I picked out the sharpest-looking.

'Coach, lord?' he said.

'Uh-uh. Not today, friend.' I took out my purse and hefted it so the coins jingled. 'What I'm after is information.'

'Is that right?' He eyed the purse. 'And what sort of information would that be, now?'

'I want to trace a fare. He took a coach or a litter from here yesterday just before sunset.' I described Melanthus. 'You know him?'

The coachman rubbed his jaw. 'He come here often?'

'Yeah. Or so I've been told.'

'Then I might've seen him around. He's not one of my regulars, though. Where was he headed, lord? Do you know?'

'No. That's what I want to find out.'

He nodded, and turned. 'Hey, Stichus!'

'Yeah.' Another man ambled over; a brother, from the facial resemblance, only this one's nose had been broken at some point and no one had bothered to reset it.

'Gentleman here's looking for one of the regulars.' The first guy repeated my description. 'Ring any bells with you?'

'Sounds like one of Dida's.' Broken-nose turned to me. 'Was he here last night, lord, around sunset?'

'Yeah. Yeah, he was.' Hey, great! I looked at the crowd of tunics. 'Which one's Dida?'

'You're out of luck. Dida hasn't been around today.' The cabby glanced at his brother. 'Am I right?'

Stichus nodded. 'He hasn't been in, lord. I've been here since first light and I'd've seen him. He's your man all the same.' He scratched at a wart. 'I saw him set out last night with your friend myself.'

'Which direction?'

'In. Towards town.'

'You know where this Dida lives?'

The two brothers looked at each other. The cabby answered for both.

'No, lord.'

Ah, well, I'd just have to be patient. 'Never mind. Look, my name's Valerius Corvinus, right? I live in Diomea, about a quarter-mile beyond the Hippades Gate. Next time you see this Dida you tell him from me I'd like a word.'

'Hippades Gate's right the other side of town, lord,' Stichus pointed out. 'That's a long way to go just for a talk.'

'I'll make it worth his while.' They looked sceptical. 'Really worth his while. Okay?'

'Okay.' It was grudging, sure, but they'd deliver the message. And I couldn't hang around the gate for ever.

I pulled out my purse and gave them a tetradrach each. 'Here. Thanks for your help.'

'You're welcome, lord.' Well, that'd put the smile back on their faces, anyway. Eight drachs wasn't bad for two minutes' work, but it was money well spent: I hoped now they'd tell Dida that whatever he was after the Roman was no piker.

I was turning to go when another thought struck me.

'Maybe I will take your coach after all, pal,' I said to the first brother. Nothing like keeping your informants sweet, and in any case I'd sent Lysias back home. It was a good day for walking.

'Sure.' The smile widened. 'Lyceum Road, right?'

I shook my head. 'The Piraeus. Tomb of Themistocles. Oh, and one more thing.'

'Yeah?'

'Keep your eyes peeled for a big black guy in a fancy tunic following us. If he's there I want to know.'

Once was enough. The next time I saw that Ethiopian bastard I'd make sure we talked.

14 ∫

I left my tame coachman waiting at the roadside and walked down to Smaragdus's beach hut. Now I'd got a name and a face for Eutyches, potentially at least, it might help to have another talk with the guy in the hope that they'd jog a hidden memory or two; certainly it was worth a try, and I wasn't doing anything else that day anyway.

The hut looked deserted, but the *Alcyone* was pulled up on the sand and the door was ajar. I knocked. No answer. Well, maybe he'd slipped out for a cup of wine somewhere. Still, it was just as well to check. I went inside.

There were no windows, and the only light came through the cracks in the wall and the spaces between the roof joists and their sailcloth cover. Even so, I could see that the hut was completely empty except for a truckle bed and a cheap folding table with a loaf of bread and a water pitcher. As my eyes adjusted to the gloom I noticed that one of the knife-edged slivers of light shining in through the gaps lay across a bundle on the bed.

A large bundle . . .

Oh, shit. I took the two steps between door and bed. My hand met cloth . . .

Only cloth: a pile of tunics, underclothes and a cheap woollen cloak, all gathered together in a blanket ready for tying with the length of rope that lay on the bare mattress next to them. I took a deep breath. False alarm. Still, clearly wherever Smaragdus was he'd decided to pack up and leave.

Yeah, well, that made sense, I supposed. With the Baker gone he'd nothing else to fear from Eutyches – if he ever had – and even his room over the brothel would be luxury compared to this dump. Trouble was, when he went back there he'd know that that was all there'd ever be. And he might not have even that if the old harpy who owned the place had already pitched whatever he'd left behind him into the street. Jupiter! I felt sorry as hell for Smaragdus. The guy couldn't be looking forward to the future all that much.

Okay, but just where was he now? Forget the cup of wine: there wasn't a wineshop or a shop of any kind this side of Acte, the *Alcyone* was there in the shallows and from the looks of things he'd interrupted his packing at its final stage. Left his door open, too, although who would take the trouble to filch a pile of suspect laundry out here in the sticks I didn't know. I looked around, but there were no other clues.

Except that the bread on the table was hard as a rock and the water in the pitcher had five dead flies floating in it . . .

Uh-oh. The hairs at the nape of my neck lifted. I left the hut and cast an eye over the beach.

I noticed the footprints straight off. I would've seen them before, if I'd been looking, but now they shouted at me. There were two sets, heading in the other direction from the one I'd come in. The first started towards the *Alcyone*, then doubled back towards the rocks and the high ground at the far end of the cove; the second cut straight across and met them at an angle. Both sets were running footsteps, with lots of sand kicked up. I followed them until they disappeared among the tangle of rocks that led to the small promontory.

Then I saw the crows squabbling over something that lay underneath the promontory itself, and I knew I needn't look for Smaragdus any further.

Forget futures; the guy didn't have one, not any more. He was lying at the base of a scree, his head at an angle and his skull wedged against a boulder. The crows took off as I came closer, but they didn't go far. Probably too full, because from what I could see they'd had at least one good meal off him. Them and about a dozen others. I only knew it was Smaragdus because he was wearing the same tunic he'd had on the last time I'd seen him. Anyway who else could it have been?

I turned away and was sick on to the sand. Then I took another look at the footprints.

Okay. So what had happened? Smaragdus had had a visitor, that was clear. He'd seen or heard them coming and made a run for it, towards his boat first of all before he realised running that way wasn't going to help. At that point he'd changed his mind, or maybe he'd just panicked. Anyway, he'd bolted towards the cove's far end. He'd reached the scree enough ahead of the other guy to climb a fair way, probably as far as the point fifteen or twenty feet up where the angle steepened and the scree became a proper cliff. There he'd lost his grip and fallen badly among the rocks, breaking his neck and staving in his skull.

Okay as far as it went; but it begged one major question. If Smaragdus had had all that time in hand why hadn't he taken to the water and swum round the promontory itself? That would've increased the distance between him and whoever was chasing him, and I knew that beyond the headland there was another stretch of beach that gave access to the landward side. Given a decent start he could've got away easily. Or comparatively easily. And it certainly beat trying to climb the cliff.

The answer was obvious; he'd given me it himself on the boat. Smaragdus couldn't swim, and the water beyond the headland was a good ten feet deep. It was either climb or drown, and at least the first way he had a chance.

Well, I couldn't leave the poor bastard for the crows to finish. What was left of him to finish, anyway. But I didn't fancy carrying that grisly patchwork of flesh and bone back to the hut, either, even wrapped in his cloak. I found a piece of driftwood by the shoreline and dug a shallow pit next to the corpse. Then I pushed it in, shovelled on the sand and piled rocks on top. That would do him for now, and at least he'd had the scattering of earth that would keep his ghost happy.

Once Smaragdus was safely underground I sat back on my heels to think. What the hell was going on? Eutyches – Melanthus? – had no reason to want Smaragdus dead because he had the Baker already. Even if Smaragdus's death was an accident, which it had been from the looks of things, it still didn't make sense. Whoever had chased him obviously wanted to talk to the guy pretty badly; and equally Smaragdus hadn't wanted a meeting. To avoid it, he'd been desperate enough to try a climb that not even a monkey would consider.

So what did that give us? Smaragdus was no fool. He'd recognised his visitor's intentions well in advance and decided right away that his only chance was to run. The visitor wasn't a stranger, then – unless he was doing something obvious like waving a knife around – and he wasn't a friend, either, for the same reason. That didn't leave much. But then why run in the first place? Smaragdus had known himself that the game was played out and that he'd nothing more to lose. He'd even been packing up his things when he was interrupted.

Unless of course the visitor *had* been waving a knife and the intention was to kill the guy. But then we were back to the original question. With the Baker gone, Smaragdus was no further use to anyone. Who would want him dead, and why?

Ah, hell, I was going around in circles. None of this made sense. All I could do for the poor bastard now was to see Harpalus, tell him his pal was dead and leave him to arrange a proper funeral; and after that drive back to Athens and twiddle my thumbs until Dida contacted me.

All in all, not a very successful day. Maybe I should take up woodturning.

I stood up and walked back towards Stichus's coach.

Harpalus recognised me straight off.

'Lord,' he said firmly, 'we do not exchange parrots.'

I had some smartass comeback ready but I didn't use it. If I was right and they'd been fond of each other then this just wasn't the time.

'I'm not here about Nestor, Harpalus,' I said.

Maybe it was something in my face, or my voice, but he got the message right away.

'Smaragdus?'

'Yeah. I'm sorry, but he's dead.' I was watching him closely. He was shocked, sure he was; but unless I missed my guess he wasn't all that surprised. And that was interesting. 'I found him near the beach hut.'

The guy had sat down hard on a bench behind the counter. Forget the superannuated butterfly, now he just looked old.

'How did it happen?' His voice was a whisper.

'An accident.' I hesitated. 'Probably an accident. He fell.'

'Is that all?'

I knew what he meant. 'No. He was being chased at the time.'

'By you?' There was no accusation in the voice. It was just a straight question.

'No. Not by me. He was dead when I found him.'

'How long dead?'

'A day, max.'

I'd kept that intentionally vague, but he pounced on it like a dog on a rabbit.

'You saw him yesterday, didn't you? He took you to the Baker.'

I hesitated again. 'Not exactly.'

'What do you mean?'

'He took me to where the Baker had been. Only it wasn't there any longer.'

He nodded, but he kept his eyes low where I couldn't see them clearly. None the less, I saw them flash: that nugget of information hadn't come as a surprise either. Harpalus knew more than he was telling. I shelved that for later.

'No, it wasn't,' he said. 'But then you'd know all about that already, wouldn't you?'

That caught me off balance. 'And how do you make that out, pal?'

'Because you told me you came from Eutyches.'

'Wrong,' I said; but I said it gently. I didn't want to hassle the guy more than was necessary. The news of Smaragdus's death might not have surprised him, but his shock was real. And his grief. 'You told me that yourself, Harpalus. Or I let you assume it. I don't even know for sure who Eutyches is. Just for the record, my name's Valerius Corvinus. I'm representing my stepfather Helvius Priscus back in Rome.'

His eyes came up. 'You're not Eutyches's man? You swear it?'

'Sure.'

'And Smaragdus knew?'

'Sure he knew. He knew as soon as he saw me.'

'Well, that makes sense, I suppose.' He shook his head slowly. 'It was my fault. I didn't describe you to him, you see. I just said you were a Roman. And then of course you found him yourself. That was smart.' He looked up. 'I suppose you followed me? Or had me followed?'

'Something like that, yeah.'

'It doesn't matter now.' He stood up. 'Where is he? Did you leave him in the hut?'

'No. I dug a shallow grave. You'll find him under a pile of rocks near the far headland.'

'Thank you for that, anyway.'

'So who's Eutyches?' I said gently.

He'd been expecting the question, because the shrug was casual. 'I don't know. Honestly. I only know the name. Smaragdus said if he got in touch with me I should pass the message on without giving him any more information. Which is what I did. Or at least what I thought I'd done.'

'Okay.' I let that go for now. 'Does the name Melanthus ring a bell at all?'

'Melanthus of Abdera? The Academician?'

I kept my face straight. 'You know him?'

'I've seen him. Many times, in fact.' He gave a small smile. 'I used to hang around the Academy in my younger days, Corvinus. Not altogether as a student.'

'Would Argaius have known him too?'

'No. Not Argaius.' A twist of the lips. 'He wasn't the scholarly type.'

'How about Smaragdus?'

'Yes. Smaragdus would have known Melanthus. By name and by sight. He had an interest in philosophy. Just because we live out here in the sticks doesn't mean we're dead from the neck up.'

Uh-huh. Well, that was something I hadn't expected, but it didn't matter: in fact, if anything it confirmed the theory that Eutyches and Melanthus were one and the same, because 'Eutyches' had been careful to work through an intermediary. Besides, I'd been listening for the signs of a lie, and Harpalus's voice hadn't changed. Either he was a good actor or putting the two names together genuinely didn't mean anything to him.

'So why should Smaragdus go into hiding in the first place?' I asked.

'I should have thought that was obvious. He was frightened. His partner had just been murdered.'

'Sure. By Eutyches. But in that case why should he tell you he was open to messages?'

That got me another shrug. 'Perhaps Eutyches didn't murder Argaius after all. Anyway, he was a customer, full stop. People like us, Corvinus, we've got to live in any way we can. Sometimes that means taking risks, giving people the benefit of the doubt even when no doubt exists and taking out whatever insurance is possible. We can't afford your fat-cat moral scruples.'

He was right, of course. I'd used the same argument myself with Perilla, although without the bitterness. To Smaragdus, selling the Baker would've meant the difference between a life of luxury and no life at all, and money has no smell when you don't have much.

'Fair enough,' I said. 'But then Smaragdus knew he had another customer lined up. Me. Or my stepfather, rather. So why leave the suspect channel open when the alternative was there?'

'Look, Roman.' Harpalus turned away. 'Just go, will you? My friend's dead, I've got arrangements to make, and I don't feel like answering any more stupid questions, right? I'm grateful for what you did, but now just leave both of us in peace.'

Yeah, well. He had a point. I left.

There was still no sign of Dida when we got back to the Piraeus Gate, so I had Stichus take me home. All the way something was bugging me. When I'd told him the Baker wasn't in the cave any more, Harpalus had accepted the fact like he'd known it all along.

The question was, if he hadn't seen Smaragdus since I'd left him, then just how did he know?

15

It had been a long wireless day, which would've pleased Perilla – she always complained I drank too much, Jupiter knew why – but played hell with the cerebral juices. I had Bathyllus pour me a cup of Setinian as I pulled off my grimy mantle, drained it at a gulp and held the cup out for more. Thank the gods for home comforts.

'The mistress around?' I asked.

'Yes, sir. She's in the garden with Alexis and Nestor.' A sniff.

'Yeah?' Now that was news. If Perilla was taking a proprietorial interest in my latest acquisition we'd have a docile, clean-mouthed citizen on our hands in no time. Look at me, for example. 'Tell me more, Bathyllus.'

'I understand Alexis is putting on some sort of demonstration, sir.' Sniff number two, this time full affronted-Bathyllus power. 'Although personally if I may say so I think the bird would serve a more useful and decorative purpose as a stuffed centrepiece for the dining table.'

Ouch. Well, Bathyllus never did have much time for anarchists, even feathered ones. I took the cup and jug through to the garden.

I was just in time; the show was about to start. Alexis was setting Nestor's perch complete with glaring star performer centre-stage, just where the evening sun showed his rugged profile to the best advantage.

Perilla was sitting on a wicker chair in what would've been the broad-striper row. She turned round and gave me a smile. I planted a smacker on top of it.

'Marcus! You're back! Did you have a good day?'

'Not exactly.' I had a quick mental image of what the crows had left, and the slither as it went into the hole I'd dug. 'It'll keep. Tell you later, lady.'

'Fine. Alexis has been working wonders.' She turned. 'Haven't you, Alexis?'

The kid grinned and ducked his head. I had a lot of time for Alexis. He was one of my smartest slaves, and the only reason he was stuck with the garden was that he'd asked for the job himself: gardening for Greeks is respectable, seemingly, and not just for the bought help, either; even my pal Heraclitus had arranged to be buried in a pile of horse manure. Which showed if nothing else that grade-A philosopher or not at least the guy had had a sense of humour.

'I've been training him solid since you got him, sir,' Alexis said. 'He's a changed bird.'

'Is that so, now?' I looked at Nestor on his perch. He didn't look changed to me: still Cotta to the life, disreputable as hell and with a gleam in his eye that suggested he was just playing along for now and waiting to let rip. 'Okay. So let's see what he can do.'

Alexis held up a dried fig. 'Come on, then, Nestor,' he said. '"Sing, Goddess, the wrath . . ."'

I grinned. Homer. Oh, Jupiter! This I just had to see!

The black eye fixed itself on the fig and the beak twitched malevolently.

'"Sing, Goddess, the wrath . . ."' Alexis prompted again. 'Come on, you mouldy lump of cat's meat!'

Nestor lifted a claw and reached for the fig. Alexis moved it back. A spasm of pure disgust passed over the parrot's face, the claw was lowered and the beak opened . . .

'"Sing, Goddess, the wrath of Peleus's son Achilles."'

Perilla clapped her hands. 'Alexis, that's marvellous! Isn't it marvellous, Marcus?'

'Amazing,' I said. I meant it, too; I was impressed. A bit lacking in expression, sure, but for a bird it wasn't bad. His accent was better than mine for a start. 'You going to coach him through all twenty-four books, pal?'

'He's a quick learner,' Alexis said proudly. 'Why not?' He held out the fig. Nestor took it carefully, bolted it down and gave a shudder of pleasure.

'Fuck it!' he said happily.

There was a long and terrible silence.

'Changed bird, right?' I said at last, trying to keep my face straight.

'I'm sorry, sir.' Alexis was beetroot red. 'He forgets himself sometimes.'

'Not your fault, pal. Put it down to experience.'

'One month, Corvinus.' Perilla had got to her feet and was giving Nestor her best chilling stare as Alexis lugged him off in ignominy towards the servants' quarters. 'That is all.'

'Yeah.' I was still trying not to laugh. 'Somehow I don't think Homer's his bag.'

'Perhaps not. But language like that we can do without.'

'Come on, Perilla!' I said. 'He's a parrot! He doesn't understand what he's saying.'

'You honestly believe that?'

Good question. I kissed her instead of answering. 'Leave it. What time's dinner?'

The lady was still bristling, and I got the backlash. 'Not now. Meton insisted on waiting until you got back. It's grilled fish, and he didn't want it to spoil.'

'Fine.' I sighed; what with subversive parrots, touchy chefs and linguistically sensitive wives my domestic life was currently a mess. 'Okay. So let's just have a plate of olives and cheese out here until Meton gets his finger out. I'm starved. Bathyllus?'

'Yes, sir.' The little guy oiled up. 'Olives and cheese, sir. And one extracted digit. Certainly, sir.'

'Don't push it, pal.' I turned to Perilla. 'You want a fruit juice?' She nodded. 'One fruit juice, little guy. And easy on the sarcasm.'

Bathyllus left in high dudgeon. You can add a sarky major-domo to the above. Ah, well, at least I wouldn't die of boredom.

'So did you talk to Melanthus?' Perilla sat down on the bench under the oleander. I joined her and pulled up a foot-stool. My legs were stiff. I'd been doing too much travelling around in coaches these past few days, and I was missing the exercise.

'No, I didn't talk to Melanthus.' I poured a fresh cup of wine and put my free arm round her shoulders. 'Because Melanthus has disappeared. And Smaragdus is dead.'

'What?' She turned to stare at me. 'Oh, Marcus!'

'Not murdered. At least, not quite.' I told her the whole story, glossing over the grisly part. 'So we're stuck again,' I finished. 'Unless this guy Dida can help.'

Bathyllus came out with the fruit juice and snacks on a folding table. I started in on the cheese.

'Actually' – Perilla sipped her fruit juice – 'I'm beginning to think you're right about Melanthus. He sounds horribly like Marius.'

I nodded: yeah, I'd made that comparison myself. Our prospective adopted daughter's father had been an obsessive art freak too, and the two were a type. Sextus Marius had been red-blooded, a man's man, clever, sophisticated, cultured. Sane in every respect but the one that mattered; and there the guy was a thorough-going, five-star, gold-plated nut. The world was well rid of him.

'All the same,' I said, 'I wonder about Alciphron. He seemed just a bit too keen to slag off his colleague. And whether it fits in or not the only evidence for Melanthus's obsession comes from him.'

'True.' Perilla hesitated. 'On the other hand the academic world is rather . . . uncompromising.'

'You mean bitchy?' I grinned.

She ducked her head and smiled. 'Yes, I suppose that is what I do mean. The criticism can get quite personal at times.'

'Yeah. Well, maybe it's nothing and I'm maligning the guy.' I sipped my wine. 'Forget it. Anyway, we're stymied as far as Melanthus goes at present until this Dida character shows up. But what's really bugging me is how Smaragdus fits in. Him and his pal Harpalus.'

'In what way?'

I shrugged. 'I'm not sure. But there's something out of kilter in that direction. Too many things don't add up.'

'Such as what?'

'For a start, Smaragdus moved out to his beach hut because he was afraid what had happened to Argaius would happen to him, right?'

'Yes.'

'Only when I talked to the guy's landlady she said he'd disappeared – I quote – "days ago". She was giving him until the end of the month before pitching his smalls out into the street and putting the "To Let" sign up. Sure, she might have been exaggerating because she wasn't exactly the soft-hearted motherly type, but if she wasn't then Smaragdus must've done a runner before his partner was chopped, not after.' I paused. 'Strange, right?'

'Yes.' Perilla nodded thoughtfully. 'Yes, that is strange. Very.'

I emptied my wine cup and refilled it. 'Then we come to Harpalus. The news that Smaragdus was dead rocked him, sure, but it didn't come as any surprise. It was as if he knew something like that was on the cards. And yet with the Baker gone it shouldn't have been. Eutyches had no reason to give Smaragdus any grief because Argaius had spilled the beans over where the statue was stashed and he had it already; furthermore, if Melanthus is Eutyches then it makes even less sense because the guy's obsession starts and ends with the Baker. I'd go along with Alciphron there, one hundred per cent: Melanthus may be capable of murder, but he wouldn't kill for the fun of it.'

'But Melanthus didn't kill Smaragdus. You said his death was an accident. Besides, he had an accomplice.'

'Prince Charming. Right. Still, Melanthus would've had to give the order to hassle the guy. That's what I can't make out. What did Melanthus stand to gain?'

'Unless your Prince Charming was acting without orders.'

'Why should he do that?'

'I don't know. But it's possible.'

'Anything's possible, lady.' I took a swallow of wine. 'Probable is where things get tricky. And probable it isn't.'

'Very well. Leave it for now. Go on.'

'The other screwy thing about Harpalus was that he knew the Baker had disappeared. If I was the last person besides his visitor to see Smaragdus alive then he shouldn't have known, because even Smaragdus didn't know until he took me to the cave.'

'Harpalus could have talked to him between your visit and his death.'

'That doesn't leave all that much time. Smaragdus had been

dead for quite a while. Take my word for it.' We'd still got dinner coming, and I didn't want to mention the crows. 'And if Harpalus had been over to the beach hut he would've found the body himself.'

'Maybe he did. Maybe Harpalus was the second visitor. Or led the man to him.'

'Uh-uh.' I shook my head. 'No way. Whoever he was, Smaragdus's visitor wasn't Harpalus, or the guy wouldn't have run. Sure, again it's possible, but I'd bet good money Harpalus didn't know his pal was dead before I told him. He isn't the murdering type, especially where Smaragdus was concerned, not even at second-hand. And if he'd found Smaragdus dead he would've buried him or taken him home. No, we've only got two probable scenarios here. First, that Harpalus knew where the cave was and had checked it out personally after we'd been there, and second that someone told him the Baker was gone before Smaragdus died.'

'But that assumes he was a lot more involved than you thought he was.'

'Sure it does. And that's interesting, because I got the impression from Smaragdus that only he and Argaius knew where the statue was hidden. Sure, he might've shared the secret with Harpalus, but I doubt it. Not intentionally, anyway.'

'You mean Harpalus could have followed the partners on one of their visits? Without Smaragdus's knowledge?'

'Yeah. It's one explanation, anyway. And if so then knowing where the Baker was stashed he could've gone there any time between Melanthus's visit to the cave and this morning and found the cupboard bare. That way he wouldn't have to know anything about Smaragdus's death.'

'But why would he bother, Marcus?'

I shrugged. 'Search me, lady. It's only a theory.'

'Unless he was in league with Melanthus, of course. That would explain everything.'

'Uh-uh.' I shook my head again. 'That won't wash either. Sure, it sounds good, but I can't see Harpalus in a lovers' double-cross. He's straight, by his lights. Or that was my impression, anyway.'

'Mmm.' Perilla sipped her fruit juice.

'In any case, what it doesn't explain is what went on at the beach house when Smaragdus had his accident. The guy knew he was in trouble, sure he did, or he wouldn't have been so desperate to get away. So what trouble was he in?'

'You say he knew Melanthus by sight. Perhaps if he saw him coming and recognised him he put two and two together.'

'That still doesn't make sense, Perilla. We keep coming back to the fact that Melanthus – or Eutyches, anyway – already had the statue. He was home and dry, Smaragdus was out in the cold and there was no reason for Melanthus to talk to him. Unless . . .' I stopped.

'Marcus? What's wrong?'

Oh, Jupiter! Jupiter best and greatest! There was only one *unless* that I could see, but that was a beaut. And it explained everything: why Smaragdus had left his digs before Argaius had died, how Harpalus had known the Baker was gone, and what had happened at the beach hut.

'Marcus?' Perilla tugged at my sleeve.

I glanced up at the sun. Hell. It was too late, now, for another trip to the Piraeus, and anyway if I stood Meton up again the guy would poison the soufflé. It would have to be tomorrow, early. 'Uh . . . sorry, lady. I was wool-gathering.'

'Nonsense. You've thought of something, haven't you?'

'Yeah.' I took a contented swallow of wine. 'I know now why Smaragdus was hiding out at the beach hut. And why Melanthus needed to talk to him.'

16

I stopped off at the Piraeus Gate coach rank in case Dida had turned up, but there was still no sign of him. Hell. This looked bad. Sure, it might be coincidence, but I reckoned that with Melanthus and his coachman both going missing at the same time a bit of paranoia was justified. However, there was nothing else I could do but repeat the promise to make it worth the guy's while to contact me and then head on down the Hamaxitos to the Piraeus and Harpalus's bird shop.

Behind the counter was a fat guy with dandruffy hair and a guano-specked tunic. Obviously the owner in person. So where was Harpalus? Forget simple paranoia. The way people were disappearing I must've had every god in the pantheon lined up against me.

'Good morning, lord.' The fat guy smiled greasily. 'How can I help you?'

'Harpalus around?' I said.

The smile faded to nothing. 'He's out. Private business.'

'Is that so?' I leaned on the counter between two disapproving cages of pigeons. Great. Even the stock was glaring at me. 'You happen to know where he's gone?'

'You're the Roman, right? The one who bought the parrot?'

'Nestor? Sure.'

'How's he settling in?'

The tone suggested that the guy knew all about Nestor's sunny disposition and couldn't have wished him a better home. Up yours, pal, I thought, and gave him my best smile.

'Very well, as it happens,' I said. 'In fact, he's one of the family already. Marvellous with children, and my white-haired old grandmother simply dotes on him. They talk together for hours.'

The guy gave me a stare like he wasn't sure whether I was serious or not. I smiled back and waited.

'Harpalus is burning that fancy friend of his,' he said at last. 'Over at the graveyard outside the City Gate.'

Yeah, I should've thought of the funeral. Harpalus would've collected Smaragdus yesterday evening and arranged the burning for today. Not that there was much left of Smaragdus to burn.

'The little bugger left me a note. Pinned it to the door.' The owner was glaring at me like he thought it was my fault. 'You can tell him from me he needn't bother coming back.'

'Sure. I'll do that, pal.' I paused. 'By the way, I can see now where the parrot gets his temperament from. And given the choice between the two of you I'd take him any time.'

That got me a grunt. I waved and left.

Okay, so it was back the way I'd come, up the Hamaxitos: the tombs lined the main road to town, and I'd probably passed him without noticing. I got into the carriage and gave Lysias his new orders.

A thread of smoke led me to the scrap of waste ground set well back from the road where the poorer Piraeans burned their dead. The funeral was over by the time I arrived. What there was of it. From the size of the ash-heap the pyre had been the cheapest going, and I'd have bet Harpalus was the only mourner. When I got out of the carriage he was washing the bones and stowing them in a plain clay urn. The undertaker and his men had already left.

'Hey, Harpalus,' I said.

He glanced up, then carried on with what he was doing.

'Leave me alone, Roman,' he said.

'I'm sorry.' I was. 'But we've got to talk.'

'You may have to. I don't.' He put the lid on the urn with a bang.

This was no time for indulging my finer feelings. 'Look, pal,' I said. 'It's either me or Eutyches's bunch. And that you wouldn't enjoy at all.'

'Just forget it.' He left the wine jar where it was and picked up the urn. 'Let me go.'

'Uh-uh.' I shook my head. 'You've got some explaining to do first. Like where you and Smaragdus stashed the Baker.'

He stared. 'You're mad. Eutyches already has the statue.'

'Oh, no he doesn't. He's still looking for it. Which is why Smaragdus died. And believe me, pal, you're next on his list.'

He must've been expecting that because his eyes didn't flicker.

'Corvinus, I haven't the slightest idea where the Baker is. Now you can believe me or not, but just get the hell out of my life.'

Yeah, well, it might be the truth at that; but if Harpalus genuinely didn't know then Smaragdus had. I'd bet my entire wine cellar to a pickled mushroom on that.

'You won't have a life for me to get out of unless we talk now.' I pointed to the urn. 'That's all you'll get from Eutyches, friend. And if you're on the level about not knowing then with nothing to trade it's a certainty.'

'You think I care?' I'd shaken him, though. Maybe he was telling the truth.

'Maybe so, maybe not. But you've got two options, and two only. One is to walk away from me in which case you're as dead as Smaragdus. The other is to go for a drive down to the harbour and let me arrange a passage for you on the first ship out to anywhere. Your choice. Only make it now.'

When he still didn't speak I turned and walked off in the direction of the road. I'd gone about five steps before he said quietly: 'Very well, Corvinus. You win.'

I waited for him to catch me up. When we got to the carriage I held the door open.

'Right,' I said. 'We can have our talk on the way. Climb aboard.'

'So. Smaragdus had got greedy and was pulling a fast one on his partner.' I stretched my legs out as we bumped along the Hamaxitos towards the Town Gate.

Harpalus nodded wearily. He'd set the urn on the seat beside him and was cradling it in the crook of his arm. 'I told him it was a mistake, but he wouldn't listen. And while Argaius was conducting the negotiations he went to the cave and moved the treasure elsewhere.'

'Just like that? He must've had help. He couldn't've managed the Baker on his own.'

A shrug. 'I don't know anything about help. I wasn't involved.'

'Come on, Harpalus!' I shifted irritably. 'You expect me to believe that?'

'It's the truth, and like I said, you can accept it or not. The idea was his. He didn't want me to know, either where the original cave was or where he'd moved the statue to. He said the less I knew about it the safer it was for both of us.'

'But when he moved the gold he was willing to trust a third party?' Jupiter, that made no sense at all! 'Who did he use?'

'I don't know that either.' He glanced at my expression. 'I'm not lying. I was to be the go-between. With the customer.'

'Eutyches?'

'Whoever. I only knew *his* cut-off.'

'A big guy?' I described Prince Charming. Harpalus nodded. 'You know his name?'

'No. He never told me. And I only knew Eutyches's from Smaragdus. Just the name, no more. In case he got in touch.'

Something was bugging me here; a question I should've asked long ago but hadn't because others had crowded it out. Maybe now was the time. 'Smaragdus and his partner had two customers. Eutyches and my stepfather. We've always been up front, Eutyches hasn't. So why should Smaragdus go for Eutyches?'

'You've said it yourself: you were up front. Eutyches didn't care who sold him the statue, or how things were arranged, so long as he got it. You might be different, you'd ask questions, and he couldn't take the risk.'

Yeah. That fitted. And if Melanthus was Eutyches then it would be an added fillip to have put a Roman out of the running. 'So. After Smaragdus moved the treasure he hid out in his beach hut. Only at that point he wasn't hiding from Eutyches; he was hiding from Argaius.'

'Yes. Until the new deal with Eutyches could be arranged and the money paid over. Then he and I would just disappear.' Harpalus's hand stroked the urn. 'Alexandria. Pergamum.

Somewhere big. We'd have enough money to live like kings. Eutyches didn't know about the hut either, of course. Smaragdus wanted it that way, especially after Argaius died. Like I say, as far as Eutyches was concerned I was to be the know-nothing middleman who'd bring the two together when I was satisfied everything was okay.'

Uh-huh. 'So if you usually dealt with Prince Charming why assume that I'd come in his place?'

'Because I thought we'd gone beyond the cut-off stage. You could even be Eutyches in person, for all I knew.'

'But Smaragdus . . .' I stopped. I'd been about to say that Smaragdus would know I wasn't Eutyches, but of course the two had never met. So until I'd mentioned my name, Smaragdus wouldn't've known who the hell I was, only that I'd made the approach through Harpalus. Which explained why he'd come out with a piece of two-by-four in his hand: I'd broken the rules; worse, it meant all his careful arrangements were screwed up from there on in. Only then, of course, he'd realised that he'd made a mistake and I didn't come from Eutyches at all.

'Smaragdus what?' Harpalus said.

'Forget it, it doesn't matter. So Eutyches didn't know the statue had been moved?'

'No. There was no reason to tell him. And of course it was Argaius's bad luck that when Eutyches tried to cut corners he only knew the original location. I was sorry about that. So was Smaragdus. He never meant his partner to be hurt. Not physically, anyway.'

Yeah. The sob stuff aside, bad luck was putting it mildly: when he found the cave empty Melanthus must've been fit to be tied, and it had sealed Argaius's death warrant. 'You took a hell of a risk carrying on with Eutyches, didn't you, pal?' I said. 'Especially after Argaius was murdered.'

Harpalus shrugged. 'What could we do? I told you, Corvinus, people like us have to work things out as best we can. Life's a risk; you have to trust someone, even if you don't trust them. If you see what I mean.'

You have to trust someone. Sure. Only the poor boobs had to choose Melanthus, and now one of them was a handful of ashes while the other was running for his life with nothing to show for it but the clothes he stood up in. Well, that was the way things worked, I supposed. I glanced out of the carriage window. We were almost at the square before the shrine of Zeus the Saviour. Not far now to Market Quay and the boats.

'So to recap,' I said. 'Smaragdus was camped out at the beach hut waiting for Eutyches to make contact through you. At which point I turn up and Smaragdus puts on his innocent act by taking me to the original cave.' A thought tugged at me, and I frowned: there was something screwy here . . . Ah, leave it. 'Only I'd been followed by Prince Charming, or maybe you had earlier, and Eutyches knew where Smaragdus was holed up after all. All he had to do was have his strongarm boy sit tight until Smaragdus got back and then repeat the tactics he'd used with Argaius. Smaragdus was no fool. He started packing; not to go back to his old room like I'd thought, but to get the hell out to another bolthole. Because if I'd managed to find out where he was then Eutyches could as well.'

Harpalus nodded. 'We had a fallback location, a cave on Acte. I'd wanted to use it all along, but Smaragdus said no. He said if he couldn't live like a proper human being at least he wasn't going to live like an animal. The beach hut was bad enough.'

'Right. So knowing his hidey-hole wasn't so safe any more he'd be watching out this time. Or maybe Prince Charming didn't care how much noise he made and Smaragdus heard him coming. Anyway, he spotted him, guessed what he wanted and made a break for it in the only direction possible. The guy chased him, and the rest we know.'

'Yes.' Harpalus was staring out the window at the bulk of the Shrine of Zeus. I could smell the stink now of the mud at the edge of the Grand Harbour, and see the tops of the masts. 'That was probably how it happened. It certainly makes sense. But we were so close. So close!'

Even knowing what I knew, I could still feel sorry for him. Whatever you thought of Smaragdus, Harpalus was no criminal. And I even had some sympathy left over for Smaragdus.

'One thing it doesn't explain,' I said. 'The Ethiopian.'

Harpalus turned in surprise. 'Who?'

I'd been half talking to myself. 'You wouldn't know him. A big black guy who's been tailing me.' I frowned. 'Unless of course Eutyches had two henchmen waiting. One stayed behind to deal with Smaragdus, the other followed Lysias and the carriage round to the Aphrodisian Gate hoping to pick up the trail from that end.' Yeah, it made sense. As far as Melanthus knew, Smaragdus could've taken me to the real cave (there was that itch again! Shit!) and so I'd know where the Baker was stashed. Only that didn't work: by Melanthus's reckoning if Smaragdus had shown me the Baker he wouldn't have left me, however much he trusted me; and by this time the statue might be packed up and on its way to Rome. That had nothing to do with the problem of the Ethiopian, mind, but still . . .

Ah, all this thinking was giving me a headache. Besides, we were almost at the gate in the precinct wall round Market Quay. I put my head through the window and told Lysias to drive up to the harbourmaster's office.

Harpalus was in luck: winds permitting, there was a boat sailing next day for Rhodes. I didn't have the full passage money on me, but I was able to put down a decent deposit with the captain and promise to send a slave round with the balance as soon as I got home; luckily a Roman purple-striper's word is money in the bank. Not that it cost much: guys like Harpalus don't travel in the deckhouse, and the captain needed a part-time skivvy.

'You want me to take care of that for you?' I indicated the urn.

'No.' Harpalus shook his head. 'He may as well be buried in Rhodes as anywhere else.'

'Yeah. Well.' I held out my hand. 'Good luck, pal. I'm sorry things didn't work out.'

'Not your fault. I'm only sorry Smaragdus didn't stick to the original arrangement with Argaius. Half would've been better than this.' He stroked the urn. 'And I don't believe in curses, Corvinus, but that statue's caused nothing but trouble and death since they found it. I wish it had stayed lost.'

'Uh-huh.' I slipped him the last two tetradrachs in my purse.

'You'll need some food for the trip. Get what you need here. I wouldn't go home again if I were you.'

A shrug. 'Why should I want to go home?'

There was no answer to that. I left him on the quay and went back to where Lysias was waiting with the carriage.

17

Perilla was out at a public lecture in one of the Porches: on what, I just didn't want to know. I went through to the study and took Harpalus's passage money out of the strongbox.

Bathyllus had followed me in with the obligatory wine jug.

'Hey, little guy, tell Alexis I want to see him right away, okay?' I said.

'Yes, sir.' He poured and handed me the cup. 'With or without the parrot, sir?'

'Without. This is business.' I let the wine trickle past my tonsils. Beautiful. 'Oh, incidentally, tell Meton we'll be eating later than usual, when the mistress gets back.' Best to get these things clear: since the omelette affair relations with Meton had been uncomfortable as a high priest in a strip club.

'Very well, sir.' Bathyllus hesitated. 'About tonight's dinner. Meton has a suggestion.'

'Yeah?' I was interested: touchy at times though he might be, unlike Mother's cook Meton was a culinary artist, and so to be encouraged.

'Yes, sir. He has a recipe for braised flamingo which he says he could adapt, if you so wish. He seemed quite keen to try it.'

'Yum! Sounds great!' I paused. 'Hang on, sunshine. As you were. "Adapt"? Adapt to what?' Silence. The penny dropped. 'Oh, Jupiter! Go away, Bathyllus. And make it clear to Meton that parrots are off the menu. Permanently. You get that?'

'Yes, sir. Just passing the message on, sir. But the bird did bite him this morning.'

'Is that right?' I grinned: maybe Nestor was showing signs of improvement after all. A certain selectivity, at least. 'Give the bastard my condolences.'

'Certainly, sir. I'm sure he'll be very gratified.' Bathyllus sniffed and closed the door carefully behind him.

Business. I bagged Harpalus's passage money and locked the safe. Well, at least by this time tomorrow he'd be on his way to Rhodes. I was glad of that: when I'd warned him he was in danger of ending up in an urn I hadn't been exaggerating, and I didn't want any more corpses on my conscience. Anyway, the guy deserved a break.

Someone knocked on the door. Alexis. I gave him the money and his instructions.

'So how's Nestor's training going?' I said.

'Not bad, sir.'

'That wasn't the impression I got, pal.'

'He's a quick learner. It's just that he can be' – he hesitated – 'difficult.'

I grinned. Difficult. Yeah, well, that was one word. 'I hear he bit Meton.'

'Only slightly, sir. And it wasn't altogether Nestor's fault.'

'That so?'

'Meton was trying to force-feed him almond ginger stuffing, sir. The ginger was all right but Nestor's not very fond of almonds.'

'I see.' Almond ginger stuffing, eh? Jupiter! There ain't nothing more single-minded than an experimental chef. Still, for Nestor it could've been worse: he was lucky Meton's a top-end man. 'Maybe you'd better keep the bird out of the kitchen from now on, okay?'

'Yes, sir.'

There was another knock on the door. Bathyllus this time.

'Don't tell me,' I said. 'Nestor's making ornithological history by screwing the kitchen maid.'

'No, sir.' He had on his disapproving look. 'You have a visitor, sir. A carriage driver. He says you wanted to see him personally.'

Hey! Dida! 'Sure! Show him in!' I turned to Alexis. 'You know what you're doing?'

'Of course.' He held up the bag. 'I give this to the captain of the *Thetis* at Piraeus, with your compliments, and bring back a receipt.'

'Right. Hang on.' I opened the desk and took out a second, smaller purse. 'See Harpalus gets this, will you? Give it to him direct if you can, otherwise leave it with the harbourmaster.'

Alexis nodded, tucked the purse into his belt and left just as Bathyllus came back.

'The carriage driver, sir,' he said.

'Great. Go polish the spoons.'

Bathyllus exited with a sniff. I turned to Dida.

Polycleitus material he wasn't: a little runt of a guy as wide as he was long with brown teeth and a rheumy left eye. No wonder Bathyllus had practically ushered him in with a pole.

'Stichus down the Piraeus Gate rank said you wanted to talk to me, lord,' he said. 'About one of my regulars.'

'Yeah.' I lay down on the reading couch and waved him into a chair. 'Melanthus of Abdera.'

He shook his head. 'The name wouldn't mean anything. Big florid man, middle-aged, neat beard, going grey. Good talker.'

'That's him,' I said. I reached for the wine jug. 'You want some, by the way?'

He looked surprised. 'Sure. If you're offering.'

I poured two cups and handed him one. He sipped.

'Good stuff,' he said. 'Italian?'

I raised my eyebrows. 'Yeah. Setinian.'

'Thought so. From Latium, near the Pomptine Marshes, right?'

My eyebrows went up a notch or two more. 'Uh . . . yeah. Right.'

He sipped again. 'Don't see it much here. They use a different grape. Not better, just different. Puts people off.'

Well, it just shows you can't go by appearances. I was beginning to like this guy. 'You know your wines, pal,' I said.

'Some of them. I'm from Kyrenia originally. Father was a wine-shipper before he went bust. He had a few Roman customers.' He set the cup on the table. 'I'd've come before, lord, but this eye laid me up. I didn't get the message until this morning.'

'That's okay.' I took a swig from my own cup. 'So. Only one question, but that's the big one. You took Melanthus somewhere three nights ago. Where was it?'

'Simple. Where I usually take him. Aphrodite's Scallop.' I must've looked blank, because he grinned. 'You married, lord?'

'Yeah. Yeah, I'm married. So what?'

'That explains it. A bachelor wouldn't need telling. The Scallop's a brothel near Ptolemy's Gym. Very select, and pricey as hell, but you get what you pay for. Or so they tell me.'

'You say it's where you usually take the guy?'

'Sure. Twice a month, maybe three times.'

Uh-huh. That squared with what Timon had said. 'And this has been going on for how long?'

'Four years. Maybe five. Ever since the place started up, in fact.'

So. My first scenario had been right after all, and Melanthus had been doing a bit of innocent tomcatting. Hell. There went the theory. Still, it didn't explain why the guy had disappeared. And Melanthus was too good a bet to give up on that easy.

'You pick him up when he's finished?' I said.

'Sometimes. Mostly, though, he stays the night. Like I say, the Scallop's upmarket. They don't throw their customers out in the street until they want to go.'

'But this time he stayed?'

'That I can't tell you, lord. All I know is he didn't tell me to wait.'

I drummed my fingers on the edge of the couch. It would probably turn out to be a wild-goose chase, but at present it was the only lead I'd got. And, like I say, tomcat or not, Melanthus was still my number one suspect. 'You bring your coach with you, pal?'

'Sure. I had a lucky fare to Dionysus Theatre.'

'Fine.' I stood up, opened the desk and took out my remaining petty cash. What there was of it: this business was costing me an arm and a leg. It would have to be the safe again for Dida. I unlocked it and handed him a gold piece. 'Here. Thanks.'

His jaw dropped. 'That's too generous, lord.'

'Part of it takes me to the Scallop and back. Fair?'

That got me a brown-toothed grin. 'Sure. More than fair.'

'Okay.' I opened the study door. Bathyllus was dusting the bronzes, but carefully out of earshot. Not that he'd dream of listening at keyholes, anyway. Eavesdropping was outwith

Bathyllus's moral code. 'Hey, little guy!' I said. 'Bring my mantle, will you?'

'You're going out, sir?' Bathyllus cast a jaundiced eye over Dida.

'Yeah. You have a problem with that?'

'Of course not, sir.' A careful sniff: no fighting in front of the lower classes. 'What about dinner?'

'We agreed late, right? I should be back.'

'And the mistress? What should I tell her?'

Shit. Perilla. She'd be back long before I was, and she'd want to know where I'd gone. Saying I'd taken a public coach to an upmarket city cathouse was not an option. Or not one I cared to contemplate, anyway. 'Uh . . . just tell her it's business, Bathyllus. She'll understand.'

'Business.' You could've used Bathyllus's tone to pickle radishes. 'Very well, sir. Have a nice time.'

Bastard! Perspicacious bastard! I collected the mantle myself, and we left.

18

Aphrodite's Scallop was in a side street just short of the Hill of Ares: a good district, although we weren't in its best part, and, like Dida had said, definitely upmarket. Jupiter knew what a brothel was doing there in the first place, mind, because like with most cities Athenian brothels tended to cluster round the main gates or in the less salubrious districts. The neighbours were either more than usually tolerant or the place catered for a very select clientele.

Probably the latter: right from the first view the Scallop had class written all over it. It was the biggest and neatest of a row of old two-storey courtyard houses sharp as a new set of pins. Above the freshly whitewashed outer walls trees poked, and I could hear the sound of birds and splashing water.

We pulled up in front of the door. It was shut. Yeah, well, maybe we were a bit early: the sun wasn't properly down yet and the torch-cressets along the wall were still empty.

'You want to wait?' I said to Dida as I got out.

'Take your time, lord. I'll be in the alley round the corner. Go ahead, knock. The Scallop never closes.'

I walked over to the door. It could've belonged to an ordinary private house, except that there was a discreet plaque cemented into the embrasure with a relief of the naked goddess on her shell. Tasteful stuff. Good quality artwork, too, not all hips and boobs and horse-face like you usually get outside these places. No graffiti phalluses or crude comments scrawled by drunken punters, either. If first impressions were anything to go by it didn't surprise me that Melanthus was a regular here. Pre-Perilla, I'd've used it myself. I might have been tempted still, if I didn't know the lady would skin me for it when she found out. Not if. When.

I lifted the heavy dolphin door-knocker and let it drop.

No spyhole. Only, when the door opened, a guy so big he could've doubled for Hercules; a full head taller than I was, twice the width, and most of it hard muscle. Obviously the bouncer, and as such a man deserving of respect.

'Uh . . . the boss around, pal?' I said.

He stood aside, and the air shifted around him. 'Come in, sir. Welcome.'

Tasteful was right: the hall was light, airy and decorated with pictures: not murals, proper paintings on boards like you get in the Porches, hanging from the moulded cornice. No smut, either, even tasteful smut. The nearest they came to that was a six-by-four of Achilles hiding among the women, and there wasn't an unclad nipple in sight. One bronze centre-stage, a beauty, of Venus braiding her hair: I was no expert, but it looked old, and original. Chips of sandalwood were smouldering in an alcove on an incense burner that Priscus would've gone into ecstasies over.

Classy. More than classy; the place had style. However, I wasn't here to gape. Or for anything else other than business, unfortunately. I tried the big guy again.

'The name's Marcus Valerius Corvinus,' I said. 'I was hoping to talk to the boss.'

'I'm afraid he isn't here at present, sir.' Jupiter! Cathouse bouncer or not, the guy could give Bathyllus lessons in buttling any day! 'However, the Lady Hermippe will be arriving shortly.'

'The Lady Hermippe?'

'She runs the house in his absence, sir.' He paused. 'Could I enquire what your business is exactly?'

Polite enough, sure, but an order all the same, and there was no way of getting round it. Not with a guy this size doing the asking.

'I was hoping to trace one of your clients.' I used my best patrician vowels. 'He was here a few nights ago and he . . . ah . . . seems to have disappeared.'

The guy's expression didn't change but I had the distinct feeling that little speech, patrician vowels or not, had gone down like a slug in a salad. Well, I wasn't surprised: brothel customers tend to insist on privacy. Also however delicately I'd phrased that last bit it was bound to seem like I thought they were running a catmeat factory in the basement and Melanthus had just gone through the mincer.

'I doubt very much if that will be possible.'

Perfectly polite, but final as a slammed door. I noticed the lack of the 'sir', too. Still, I couldn't afford to back down. I tried again.

'The gentleman's an associate of mine. Melanthus of Abdera. And like I say it's business.'

He was looking at me like I'd just crawled out of the woodwork, and I felt my ribs constrict. 'Bouncer' was the operative word for this guy: he could punt me off all four walls like a football if he wanted to without breaking sweat, and both of us knew it. That doesn't make for an easy relationship.

'Very well,' he said. 'When the Lady Hermippe arrives I'll tell her you're here. But you do understand the decision rests with her.' Another pause. 'And that there will be no further discussion of the matter. Absolutely none. You understand?'

'Yeah.' I swallowed. 'Yeah, thanks.'

'Meanwhile perhaps you wouldn't mind waiting in the salon. Cotile will look after you.'

He turned away, and I saw the girl.

She'd come out of the door next to the Achilles painting. Small, dark-haired, dark-eyed, with curves under her silk mantle that would've made Pythagoras give up geometry.

'Uh . . . no problem, friend,' I said. 'None at all.'

'Follow me, sir.' The girl smiled at me. 'In here.'

My eyes widened: she'd spoken Latin, not Greek. Good accent, too. I stepped past her into the room and got a whiff of her perfume on the way. Low-key, Alexandrian, and, costwise, the olfactory equivalent of a villa on the Janiculan. I was beginning to have a healthy respect for the Scallop's standards.

The salon was a big room opening on to the courtyard garden, complete with dining couches and a beaut of a table that had a polish on it that would've reduced Bathyllus to tears. The place was probably used for dinner parties and discreet private functions. I don't mean orgies or bachelor club nights, either;

in my experience these little get-togethers tend to leave traces even the best housekeepers can't get rid of. Like teethmarks in the furniture and gravy on the ceiling, for example.

I took the couch with the best view of the flower-beds and ornamental fountains. Jupiter! This place must've cost a bomb!

'Would you like some wine, sir?' the girl said. There was a silver jug and matching set of cups on the table.

'Yeah. Thanks.' All this and wine too. Maybe I'd died and not noticed it.

'I'm Cotile.' She smiled and poured. The silk sleeve of her tunic slid up her arm and my heart lurched. This was going to be tricky.

'You speak Latin very well,' I said.

'I'm only half Greek.' She brought me the cup then sat demurely on the couch opposite. 'I was born in Tarentum, and my father was Italian. Cotile's just an adopted name. My real one's Pigrina.'

'Uh-huh.' I sipped the wine: Chian, pure nectar, ten years old at least. 'Good decision.'

'Changing my name?' She giggled. 'The clients expect it. And the Lady Hermippe said Cotile described me perfectly.'

Chatterbox. Well, even on this short acquaintance I'd believe it: you don't often meet someone who tells you their life history inside two minutes. Maybe I'd struck even luckier than I'd thought. It was worth a try, anyway.

'You've been here long?' I said.

'No. About a year.'

Long enough. 'You know a guy called Melanthus?'

'I'm afraid we don't ask names unless they're offered, sir.' That came out prim as a dowager's put-down. 'It's one of the house rules.'

'Big guy. Philosopher type, comes here regularly. And forget the "sir". My name's Corvinus.'

'Corvinus. Perhaps, then. If it's the man I'm thinking of, yes, I've seen him, although we've never gone together.'

'Uh, yeah. Right.' I took a swig of the Chian. If she'd been a painted hag, or even a bit less like someone's kid sister, I wouldn't even have blinked. As it was I was almost blushing. 'The problem is, Cotile, the guy's disappeared. I'm trying to trace him, and I need all the help I can get. You understand?'

'Disappeared?' Her beautiful eyes widened.

'The coachman who brought me says he dropped him here three nights ago, just before sunset. That was the last anyone saw of him.'

'Is he a middle-aged man? Interested in sculpture? Old sculpture?'

'Yeah.' My pulse quickened. 'Yeah, that's Melanthus.'

She bit her lip and glanced towards the door. Her voice dropped to hardly more than a whisper. 'I really shouldn't talk about one client to another, Corvinus. That's another house rule.'

Yeah. It would be! 'Sweetheart, this is business, right? And it's important. There'll be no hassle, I promise you. Cross my heart.'

She hesitated; another glance at the door. 'Three nights ago, you said?'

I nodded.

'All right. He's one of Anthe's. Or mostly Anthe. Usually when he arrives late he stays the night. Only Anthe said the last time he was here he didn't.'

'Is that so?' Jupiter! Maybe it hadn't been a wasted trip after all! 'He give her a reason?'

'No. And Anthe wouldn't ask, of course, because that's—'

'Another house rule.' Bugger!

She nodded. 'She was upset because he's one of her nicest. And he seemed worried about something.' A frown. 'No, not worried. What's the word? Preoccupied?'

'It'll do, sister. It'll do very well.' Gods! 'Can I talk to this Anthe by any chance?'

'She left for Corinth yesterday. With another of her regulars. They won't be back for a month. But I don't think she could've told you any more anyway.'

'How long did he stay? You know that?'

'Not long. Only enough to . . .' She made a gesture with her fingers that no kid sister I'd ever met would use. 'You know.'

'Yeah. And then he left the building?'

'Anthe wouldn't know that, Corvinus. Unless of course—'

Behind us, the door opened, and Cotile clammed up tighter

than an oyster. Hell, there went the interview, right at the interesting stage. We both turned round.

It was my pal the friendly giant, and he didn't look pleased.

'The Lady Hermippe will see you now, sir, if you'd care to follow me.'

'Yeah. Sure.' I drained my cup and got to my feet. 'Thanks for the company, Cotile. See you again some time maybe.'

'I look forward to it.' The primness was back, and she looked sexy as hell. Jupiter, I was tempted! But like I say Perilla would kill me.

'This way, sir.'

We went upstairs. The staircase was polished cedarwood, and there were pricey busts in alcoves all the way up. On the landing above a corridor with doors all along it led off to the right. On the left was a single door. The big guy tapped and opened it.

I could've been in any top-notch executive's office in the City, only there was a woman sitting behind the desk. I thought for a moment it was the old empress back from the dead, and the hairs stirred on my neck, but the Lady Hermippe was about forty years younger. She was a looker, too, and that was something even her best friends – if she had any – couldn't've said about Livia.

'Valerius Corvinus.' Hermippe indicated the chair in front of the desk. 'Pleased to meet you. I'm sorry to have kept you waiting. Do have a seat. That will be all, Antaeus.'

Antaeus. Jupiter! The big guy nodded and left, closing the door behind him.

At least the chair was solid, unlike Livia's bit of ancient Egyptian ivory. No smell of camphor, either. No smell at all. Hermippe obviously didn't have the traditional madam's love of either strong perfume or strong drink. We were still up at the top end of the profession here.

I sat. Not a creak.

'Now.' She rested her elbows on the polished desk top and steepled her fingers: executive was right, there was no nonsense about this lady. 'I understand from Antaeus you wish to contact a client of ours.'

'Yeah.' I crossed my legs and tried to look nonchalant. 'That's right. A business associate by the name of Melanthus of Abdera.'

'The Academician.' She nodded. 'We don't encourage names

here, of course, but I do know the gentleman you mean. How-ever, I'm afraid I can't help you, Corvinus.'

'Can't or won't, lady?' I was perfectly polite, but I had to get this clear.

She smiled. 'Under different circumstances it would be won't, because as I'm sure you realise a house like ours is committed to discretion absolutely. However in this instance I can say with perfect sincerity that I genuinely cannot help you, even if I wanted to.'

'He was here three nights ago.'

'Yes, he was. But he left shortly after he arrived. Where he went then I really do not know. Nor is it any of my business.'

Yeah. Well, that squared with what Cotile had told me. And from her tone of voice there wasn't any point in prolonging the conversation. I stood up. 'Okay. It was just a thought. Thanks for giving me your time.'

She stood up too. Definitely no Livia: she was almost as tall as I was, and stacked. 'Not at all. I do hope you manage to find him, and that this all ends . . . happily. You know what I mean. Melanthus would be a great loss to Athens, Corvinus. To the whole civilised world.'

'Uh-huh.' That was a matter of opinion. 'Well, thanks again.'

'Don't mention it.' She walked me to the door and opened it. Good posture, good figure. I'd imagine she'd been one of the girls herself in her younger days, and popular as hell. 'Antaeus will show you out. Unless of course . . .' She gestured delicately down the corridor.

'No. No, that's okay.' Bacchus in rompers! More temptation I didn't need! 'I'm sorry to have troubled you.'

Antaeus was waiting in the hall, but there was no sign of Cotile. I was glad of that: seeing her again might've proved one temptation too many.

'Goodnight, sir.' The giant held the front door open. 'And good luck with your search.'

'Yeah. Yeah, thanks.'

The door closed behind me. Well, that was that. Something was itching, though, and it had nothing to do with dark eyes and Alexandrian perfume.

That *unless*. Not Hermippe's. Cotile's . . .

Whatever Hermippe had told me there might be more unpleasant digs for a guy who wanted to disappear to hole up in than Aphrodite's Scallop. And it was a big place . . .

Ah, leave it. Back home for a bath, a chaste dinner and a not-necessarily-chaste early night. Dida would be waiting in the alley round the corner with the carriage.

Only he wasn't. And a split second after I realised that he wasn't someone smacked me from behind with the Parthenon and the lights went out all over Athens.

19

I woke in the dark with a head that felt like all the Cyclopses under Etna were working overtime between my ears. Gods! I hadn't had a hangover like this since I was seventeen and learned not to mix my drinks.

Only it was no hangover. I discovered that when I tried to stretch. My hands and ankles were tied and I was lying on stone. Smooth stone. A floor. I bumped backwards. Mistake. The wall was barely two feet behind me, and I found it the hard way with the back of my head. The guys with the sledgehammers went into overdrive.

Well, at least I could sit up now. Although maybe on reflection that wasn't such a good idea . . .

Luckily my stomach was empty and I only retched: nasty personal smells at this point I could do without. Jupiter, that had been a belt! I leaned back cautiously and my scalp touched cold stone a good three inches before it should've done. The feeling wasn't pleasant.

I sat just breathing for five minutes until the dizziness passed and I could think straight again.

Okay. So. Status report.

The first part was obvious: whoever had slugged me had been outside the Scallop waiting. Or even inside the Scallop waiting. And they wanted me alive: a knife between the ribs would've been just as easy as a blackjack, and the fact that I was lying here – wherever the hell 'here' was – trussed like a chicken instead of stiff and cold on the floor of the alley suggested that Corvinus was still a valuable property.

So the next question was why? Killing me I could understand.

As far as Eutyches was concerned – and this had to be Eutyches's work – I was a serious inconvenience that wouldn't go away, and a knife in the ribs made every kind of sense. If Eutyches was Melanthus then the guy might just conceivably have had scruples, but leaving me tied up only postponed the problem. Unless the idea was that I just starved to death, of course. Apropos of which, maybe postponing dinner hadn't been such a hot idea after all.

Dinner. Perilla.

I groaned. Shit, she wouldn't know where I was! Or where I'd been, anyway: I'd just told Bathyllus I was going out with Dida. Well, there wasn't anything I could do about that now. The lady would just have to worry.

The pain in my head had settled down to a steady throbbing, but I tried to ignore it. Okay. Melanthus wanted me alive. So why? It wasn't as if I had information he needed, like Argaius or Smaragdus. Sure, if I'd known where the Baker was stashed it might've been different, but . . .

I stopped as the obvious answer hit me. Oh, Jupiter! Jupiter best and greatest!

Melanthus thought I knew! Or at least he was covering the possibility. Whether he honestly thought I was in on the secret or not was immaterial: as far as he was concerned I was the only game left in town.

The problem was, this particular game was about as viable as a cat in a winepress. I remembered Argaius's smashed-up corpse at Watch headquarters and swallowed.

Somewhere above me a door opened, spilling in lamplight. I looked up, squinting.

'So you're back with us, Corvinus?' said the guy with the lamp at the top of the stairs. 'That's good. Now we can start.'

I couldn't see the face but I recognised the voice. Sure I did. The guy was Prince Charming. If this was trouble, then it was trouble in spades. I swallowed. My throat felt like a sand-tray.

'Fair enough, pal,' I said. 'But you think I could have some water first?' A cup of neat Setinian would've been better, but that was pushing it. And whatever he had in mind it wasn't a drinks party.

'Maybe later.' He came down the steps. 'If you co-operate.'

'Co-operation's my middle name, friend. Especially when I'm tied up in a cellar with a lump on my head and a homicidal maniac swinging a crowbar.'

'You noticed?' He laid it against the wall and set the lamp down beside it.

I hadn't: it'd been a joke. But I did now. Trouble in spades was right; this could be bye-bye Corvinus.

'That what did for Argaius?' I said.

'Sure. The throat-cutting was an extra.' He was grinning. 'The boss gave me a free hand.'

'Speaking of free hands . . .' I shifted and brought mine out as far as I could from behind my back.

He shook his head slowly. 'No chance. None at all. You stay as you are.'

Yeah, well. It'd been worth a try. Not that I could've taken him anyway, the condition I was in. 'So killing him wasn't altogether your boss's idea?' I said.

He was quiet for a long time. Then he said softly: 'No, Corvinus. No, it wasn't. The boss doesn't like needless deaths, or even needless violence. Me, I'm different.'

Uh-huh. 'What about Smaragdus? You kill him too?'

'He fell and broke his own neck. I would've done, sure, once I'd got the truth out of him, one way or another. Like that fancy-boy of his at the docks.'

Oh, hell. 'You killed Harpalus?'

'Yeah.' A chuckle. 'Surprised, Corvinus? Don't be. You were followed all the way from the City Gate. Easy as shelling eggs. He didn't know nothing about nothing, mind, you can be sure of that if you weren't before. He would've told me if he did. Believe me.'

'I believe you.' I felt cold. Well, I'd tried my best for the poor sucker. It just hadn't been good enough, that was all.

'Good.' He leaned his shoulder comfortably against the wall. 'Believe me some more. The boss wants to know where Smaragdus hid the Baker. Very badly indeed. So how about telling me? Maybe I'll get a crisis of conscience and let you live.'

Yeah. And pigs might fly. Still, I'd been right: Eutyches did think I might know where the statue was. Maybe I could use that. 'Melanthus won't want me dead,' I said carefully. 'Don't push your luck, friend.'

Another pause. A long one.

'How did you work that out?' he said at last.

'That Eutyches is Melanthus? Easy. There's this thing called a brain, pal. You use it to think with.'

His hand smashed suddenly across my face. Pain exploded through my skull as my head hit the wall.

'Don't get smart, Roman!' he said.

'That's just it.' My tongue probed a molar. Loosened, but at least it was still there. 'Roman. I'm a Roman citizen. The purple-striper variety, what's more. You know what that means, pal?'

'Sure.' I'd rattled him, though. Thinking obviously wasn't Prince Charming's strong point.

'I'll spell it out anyway. Kill me and they'll track you down and nail you to a couple of planks. There isn't a hole deep enough or a ship fast enough for you to escape that. And your boss knows it. He also knows that unless he's a Roman citizen himself – which he isn't – he'll be right up there on a cross of his own beside you. Understand?'

'They'll have to find your body first.'

'You think that would matter? If I've disappeared that would be enough. You're dead meat, friend. This time you believe me.'

He passed a hand over his mouth. I'd got to him, sure I had.

'Okay,' he said. 'So maybe I won't kill you after all. Maybe. If you lead us to the Baker.'

I let out my breath slowly and hoped he hadn't noticed. 'Get me some water and we'll talk.'

He straightened up and moved towards the stairs. I hoped he'd leave the lamp and give me the chance to burn through the ropes, but even Prince Charming wasn't that stupid. He took the crowbar as well. 'Don't move, right?'

'I'm not going anywhere.'

'Fucking right you're not!' Another chuckle; well, at least the bastard had a sense of humour. He went back up the steps and closed the door, leaving me in darkness.

So. Melanthus was Eutyches, that was definite. Not that I could use the information now. And I wasn't conning myself: I may've bought a bit of time, but that was all. When Melanthus realised I didn't know where the Baker was I was cooked, purple-striper or not. The guy was mad, that was plain, and I doubted that even the threat of crucifixion would stop him killing me.

I sat back and tried to hold down the panic. There wasn't much else I could do: this looked about as bad as it could get, and optimism doesn't go a long way when you're tied up in the dark without a bargaining chip to your name. I was finished, and I knew it.

What seemed hours later, Prince Charming came back with the lamp. He was carrying a water jug.

'You still thirsty, Roman?' he said, holding it up.

'Sure.' He didn't move. 'You want to help me, maybe, or should I just look and dream?'

He grinned, put the lip of the jug to my mouth and tilted. Water flowed down my chest and I gulped. Nectar! All it needed was a couple of pints of Setinian in it to make it perfect.

'Okay.' He took the jug away. 'That's it. All the niceness you get. Now where's the Baker?'

'You think I'd tell that to you?' I coughed. 'Tell your boss to come himself.'

That fazed him. His eyes shifted. 'Look. Stop fucking around, Corvinus. We had a deal. Tell me where the Baker is and you go free. Once we've got it, naturally. You have my word.'

'Yeah? Oh, whoopee.'

I thought he'd hit me again, but he didn't. 'We've got no quarrel with you. Once we have the statue I'll drop the word to your pals where to find you.'

'No deals, friend. Or not with you. Fetch Melanthus.'

He sat back on his heels, thinking. Or doing what passed for thinking.

'Okay,' he said at last. 'You've got it. But whatever the boss says, if you're lying what happened to Argaius will seem like a picnic. Crucifixion or no crucifixion.'

I swallowed. Well, maybe while he was gone I could hump myself up to the top of the stairs and do a Smaragdus off the top. There was a clear drop of ten feet on to the flags, I could see that. Better than what he'd have in mind, certainly. Unless I could get my hands free somehow, of course . . .

Dream on, Corvinus! 'Just do it. I want to see Melanthus,' I said.

He reached forward suddenly, gripped the front of my tunic, and pulled me on to my face. I gasped with the pain.

'Relax, Roman.' He chuckled. 'I only want to make sure your hands are still tied before I go. Not that it matters. The door's three inches thick and it has a bolt. You're as safe here as back home in the Mamertine.'

Uh-huh. It looked like the stairs after all, then. A pity Perilla would never know. And it wasn't something I was particularly looking forward to myself.

He picked up the lamp and left me to it. The door slammed and I heard the sound of a heavy bolt slip into place. So. That was that, then.

I gave him ten minutes or thereabouts to get clear. Then I turned over and started to crawl towards the stairs.

20

I made it eventually and got my back to the first step. Then I stopped. Shit, I couldn't do this. If I was headed for the death mask then fine, but crowbar or not I couldn't die without a fight. Maybe I'd get lucky and take Prince Charming or Melanthus with me.

Only to fight I needed my hands free.

Okay. I lifted myself up the riser of the step and felt the top edge. It was worn smooth in the middle, but further over my fingers found a ragged line of chipped stone. Yeah, that might do the job. If I had the time before PC came back. If I didn't, then . . .

The hell with speculation. I set the rope between my wrists across the line and began to move it back and forward. I'd hardly started when from above came the sound of the bolt being pulled. Sweet holy Jupiter! Prince Charming couldn't have brought Melanthus already, surely?

Unless, of course, I was back in the Scallop and the guy had been there all along . . .

I hunched down under the shadow of the step. Maybe if they didn't see me straight off I could trip whoever came down first. It wouldn't do much good, but I'd at least have the satisfaction of hurting one of the bastards. I might even provoke Prince Charming into killing me outright, which the way things were going would be a plus.

The door opened. I couldn't see what was going on now but I did notice the light in the cellar hadn't changed much, and that didn't make sense. They'd have had a lamp, sure they would. Probably a couple of torches. If this was to be an interview they'd want light.

Someone started down the steps. I tensed.

'Valerius Corvinus?'

A man's voice, pitched low. Not PC's, and not Melanthus's. In fact, no voice I recognised at all.

'Corvinus? You down there?'

A pause, while he waited for an answer. Ah, hell. Things couldn't get much worse anyway. I raised my head.

'Who wants him?' I said cautiously.

The guy let out a breath. I could see his silhouette against the doorway, and nothing else in the blackness but the whites of his eyes.

The large whites of his eyes.

Search as you will, there ain't nothing blacker than an Ethiopian down a midnight cellar.

'You mind telling me who you are, pal?' I struggled to my feet. 'And what the hell you're doing here?'

He didn't answer. Instead he came quickly down the steps, spun me round, tied a gag between my teeth, put a bag over my head and hoisted me over his shoulder like a sack of turnips. Shit. Maybe it was something I'd said. And obviously I'd been wrong about things not getting worse. At least before the bastard arrived I could speak, see and breathe . . .

Being upside down with my ribs crushed wasn't doing marvels for my headache, either.

I'd had enough. Being kidnapped twice in one night is once too many. I kicked out hard as I could manage and felt him stagger. Only for a moment. Then he righted himself.

'Okay, Roman,' he growled. 'We can do it two ways. This is one, and you'll like the second even less. Still, it's your decision. You want to co-operate or carry on making things difficult?'

Put like that, I didn't have much choice. I grunted into my gag and went limp. We started up the stairs.

Ears were all I'd got left, and I was listening hard when we got to the top and through the door. The Ethiopian's nailed sandals clicked on stone or tile for a good twenty strides, then he stopped and reached forward. There was the sound of a door opening and I felt cold air around me. A few steps later he swung me round and set me down on a flat wooden surface at chest level. The surface gave, and I heard the jingle of harness. So. We were going on somewhere by mule-cart. I felt cloth pulled over, covering me completely. Yeah, well, at least wherever it was I'd do the trip in comfort. And anything would be better than the cellar with only Prince Charming to look forward to.

The cart started up with a jerk, banging my already aching ribs against the floorboards, and the pain almost made me bite through the gag. Okay, so I'd been wrong about the comfort; but at least I was alive. If you can call being bounced across Athens in a mule-cart with your head in a mouldy flour sack living. And bruised ribs or not now was the chance for some constructive thinking before Big Black Hercules up front hauled the rug off again and we were in for yet another round of fun and excitement. Besides, I didn't have anything better to do at present.

The cellar could've been part of the Scallop, sure: the hallway had had a pricey marble floor, I remembered, and the door hadn't creaked when Hercules had opened it. Well-oiled hinges; that fitted the Scallop too. It was a shame about the bag. A whiff of sandalwood would've proved things beyond doubt, but all I could smell was weevily flour. On the other hand, we hadn't stopped on the way, and if Hercules had had no business being in the Scallop – which was a reasonable assumption – he'd've wanted to check the coast was clear before tiptoeing across an open hallway with a body slung over his shoulder. Even brothel customers with their minds on frank carnality tend to notice things like that, and if Antaeus had been around he wouldn't have made more than a yard.

Shelve the problem of location for now, then. A more important question was what the hell was going on here? The guy must've tailed me and waited his chance, that was obvious, but this was no last-minute rescue. The cart and the bag argued forward planning. I was being taken somewhere else, which meant someone besides Melanthus and his tame gorilla wanted Corvinus for a sunbeam and Hercules was working for him. So who was Hercules's boss? Who else besides my Academician pal would be interested enough in the Baker to want to talk to me?

I was still puzzling that out when the cart stopped. I felt the cloth being yanked away.

'You still awake, Roman?' Jupiter! For a pointless question that absolutely took the nuts, but I nodded anyway. 'That's good. Just lie quiet and you won't get hurt.'

Yeah. The trip so far had been a real bed of roses, hadn't it? I would've groaned but before I could summon up the energy he hauled me out and hefted me over his shoulder again. This was getting monotonous. Now I knew how a side of beef felt on its way to the butcher's.

When he finally dumped me it was on stone, and he didn't do it gently. I heard the sound of a knocker.

Things went very quiet. Somewhere very close a door opened. Then the bag was suddenly jerked away and I was blinking at a face staring down at me in the light from the streetside cresset.

'Sir?'

Bathyllus had never looked so beautiful.

'But, Marcus, where on earth were you?' Perilla dabbed with a damp cloth at the egg-sized bruise on the back of my head.

I winced. 'Jupiter, lady, be careful! That hurts!'

'Then it serves you right! We've had a terrible night! Bathyllus was frantic!'

'Would you believe listening to a recitation of Pindar's "Pythian Odes" at the local glee club?'

The cloth came down again. Hard. I winced a bit more.

'Lady, please . . . !'

'Don't you "lady" me, Corvinus!' Perilla snapped. 'And stop joking! I've been worried sick!'

Worried sick or not, peeved or not, there was no way I was going to tell her I'd been belted from behind coming out of a brothel. Some things Perilla just wouldn't understand, and tonight I didn't need the hassle.

'I was following a lead,' I said. 'I got jumped by muggers. End of story.'

'Very well.' From the tone she didn't believe it, but to be fair not even my saintly old grandmother would've believed it, and I could run rings round her when I was five. Still, she obviously didn't want to press the matter either, for which I was duly grateful. 'So who brought you back?'

'You tell me, Perilla. You were the one who took delivery.'

Bathyllus had come in with a tray. Thank the gods for well-trained staff. I grabbed the cup of Setinian and drank it down. The wine hit my empty stomach like a velvet club.

'We didn't see either, sir,' Bathyllus said. 'The man had already gone.'

'Uh-huh.' Understandable: I'd thought my Ethiopian pal might be the shy, retiring type from the way he'd dumped me. Well, whoever Hercules was he could wait because my head felt big as a melon and some bugger was trying to squeeze my ribs until they met in the middle. 'Are the baths hot, little guy?'

'They should be, sir. They were on earlier. I'll check.'

'You do that.'

He left. Perilla was still frowning, which was bad news. 'Corvinus,' she said, 'you were bound and gagged and your purse was intact. I'm sorry, but that does *not* sound like muggers to me.'

I sighed. So I wasn't off the hook after all.

'Look, Perilla,' I said, 'I've been through one interrogation this evening and I don't need another, okay?'

'Interrogation?'

Oops. So much for stonewalling. Well, I was never very good at it anyway, especially where Perilla was concerned. 'Okay,' I said. 'You've got me. Scratch the muggers. I was right, Melanthus is the guy we want. I've just had a talk with his right-hand man. He thinks I know where the Baker is.'

'Tell me,' she said simply.

So I told her; not about the Scallop, just what happened afterwards. She was quiet for a long time. The frown was gone now. Now she only looked upset, which was worse.

'Oh, Marcus!' She tried a hug, but I yelped and she let go. 'Can't you leave this alone? Please? Priscus wouldn't want you to get hurt, and if the statue's gone it doesn't matter.'

'Sure it matters.' I massaged my bruised ribs. 'And the statue hasn't gone. It's still out there wherever Smaragdus left it.'

'Then at least talk to Callippus. This is a matter for the Watch. If Melanthus is the killer then it's his job to track him down, not yours.'

True. And Callippus probably had more brains than to get himself sapped and end up breathing weevils, what was more.

'Yeah. Yeah, okay,' I said. 'I'll do it tomorrow. Today, rather.' The light was already filtering through from the courtyard garden: dawn, or near enough. 'Whatever. Go to bed, Perilla. I'll have a quick bath and come right up.'

'You're sure you're all right now?'

'Comparatively. Anyone ever tell you first-aid's not your strong point, lady?'

She kissed me and left. I filled my wine cup and drank slowly. My brain was beginning to turn over again. Hercules. I was missing something, sure I was, but what? The guy had had me cold, ripe for the sweating. Why risk his own life just to bring me home? Who was he working for, and how did he fit in?

It made no sense. None at all.

'The furnace was out but I've ordered it to be stoked up again, sir.' Bathyllus was back. 'The baths will be ready shortly.'

'That's fine, Bathyllus.' I stood up. Holy gods, I was getting too old for this sort of thing. It felt like every bone in my body had been taken out and put back the wrong way round. 'You go off to bed too, okay?'

'Yes, sir. Goodnight, sir.' He padded off.

Okay. Bath first, then bed. Tomorrow – today – I'd have a word with Callippus.

21 ∫

I knocked and went in to Callippus's office. He was at his desk reading through a sheaf of reports. What with a split lip, multiple bruises and too little sleep I can't have looked my usual stylish self, because when he saw me his eyes widened and he set them aside.

'What the hell happened to you, Corvinus?'

'I was slugged, tied up in a cellar and carted halfway across the city by a crazy Ethiopian.' I pulled up a chair and sat down. 'So how was your evening?'

He was still staring. 'Would this have something to do with the Baker?'

Jupiter! Fast as a speeding snail! Maybe he'd woken up too early.

'Sure,' I said. 'The gorilla who kidnapped me was under the impression I might know where it had got to.'

'I see.' He reached for a wax tablet and pen. 'Would you like to give me the full details, please?'

So we were being official here. I started to tell him, and when I got to Prince Charming he held up a hand.

'This Prince Charming of yours.' Not a smile: the guy takes his job seriously, and he doesn't approve of nicknames for villains. 'He's the same man who met you outside Argaius's place?'

'Yeah.'

'Then he's the one who killed Argaius.'

'Sure. He admitted as much.'

'He *admitted* it?' Callippus sat back. 'Corvinus, you do realise, don't you, that you're very lucky to be alive?'

'Yeah, I realise that.' I did: if things had gone any different

147 •

this time it would've been me lying beaten to a pulp on that table next door. Assuming I was ever found, of course. 'You still don't know who he is?'

'No. I've had the description you gave me circulated, but he's not one of the usual local toughs. We're still looking. Carry on, please.'

I decided not to mention Melanthus, not yet, not until I'd softened him up first; knowing Callippus, that bit was going to be tricky. Instead I told him what PC had said about Smaragdus and Harpalus.

He nodded. 'That squares with my own information. My colleague in the Piraeus reported that the body of Argaius's partner had been delivered to a local undertaker two nights ago under very suspicious circumstances; and that a man whose description matches that of the person who delivered it was found dead last night in an alleyway near the docks. Badly beaten and with his throat cut.' He indicated the reports on his desk. 'I only got that part of the story a few minutes ago.'

'Uh-huh.' So Prince Charming had been telling the truth when he said he'd got Harpalus. Well, I'd been expecting to hear that the poor bastard was dead sooner or later, but it didn't make the news any more pleasant. Or me feel less guilty. PC would've caught up with him eventually, sure, but that wasn't much of a consolation. 'By the way, you haven't come across an Ethiopian, have you? A big guy with a penchant for flashy jewellery and bright tunics?'

'No. He was involved in your kidnapping?'

'In a manner of speaking, although I was wrong about him. He doesn't work for Eutyches at all.'

Callippus's head lifted. 'Eutyches?'

Uh-oh; we'd got on to sensitive ground at last. I'd forgotten that Callippus didn't know anything about Eutyches. Still, I couldn't fudge this; he'd just have to take it on the chin.

'Prince Charming's boss. The man behind this whole business.'

I had Callippus's full attention now. 'You know him? Who he is, I mean?'

'In a way. The name's a pseudonym.' I paused. 'Eutyches is Melanthus of Abdera.'

Callippus put down his pen slowly. 'The Academician? Corvinus, I don't mean to be rude, but that's absolute nonsense.'

I shook my head. 'No, it isn't. That was another thing Prince Charming admitted.'

'He actually told you?'

'I'd worked it out already. But he confirmed it.'

Callippus was silent for a long time, and I got the idea he was weighing me up. Finally he said: 'You know, do you, that his head slave has reported Melanthus of Abdera as missing?'

'Yeah, I knew that. The fact that he'd disappeared, anyway. So Timon reported it, did he?' That was significant: it showed that although an overnight stay wouldn't worry the guy unduly, anything more prolonged was unusual. Which was fair enough. Even philosophers leave messages with the help when they go on extended junkets.

'He informed me personally, yesterday afternoon. We were treating the case as kidnapping.' Callippus hesitated. 'Or perhaps as something worse.'

'Forget it. Melanthus is our villain. He wants the Baker, and he's willing to kill for it. Has killed for it. Now that things are hotting up the bastard's gone to ground.'

'I don't like this, Corvinus.' Callippus was frowning. 'I don't like it one bit. Melanthus of Abdera is a highly respected member of the academic community. A distinguished philosopher and scholar.'

I sighed. 'Sure he is. I never said there was anything wrong with his brain, friend. Not in that sense. But where the Baker's concerned he isn't rational. If you want more proof go over to the Academy and talk to Alciphron the librarian.'

Callippus still didn't look happy, but I could see he was more than half convinced.

'You're sure about this?' he said. 'Absolutely sure?'

'Cast iron, swear on my grandmother's hoary old curls.' I paused. 'Also, for what it's worth, I've an idea where the guy's hiding.'

'And where is that exactly?'

'The brothel where I was hit. Aphrodite's Scallop.'

Callippus's eyebrows came down. 'Corvinus, as I've already said, Melanthus of Abdera is a respected academic. He would not patronise a brothel. Not even one as exclusive as the Scallop.'

Jupiter! I didn't believe this! Talk about warped values! The guy might be willing to accept that Melanthus was a murderer, but not that he'd set foot inside a cathouse. Well, maybe Athenian Watch officers were less jaundiced and more narrow-minded than the Roman variety; or maybe it was just further proof if I needed it that Greeks just didn't think like us.

'I hate to disillusion you,' I said, 'but the guy's a regular customer. He's been getting his rocks off at the Scallop for years.'

'The truth of that remains to be seen.' The City's Watch Commander was staring down his aristocratic nose at me like an outraged dowager. 'But even if you're right, why should he choose a brothel to hide in?'

I grinned. 'Callippus . . .'

'Granted, of course, that he had any reason to hide in the first place.'

Hell's teeth; we were back to square one. I was losing him, and I didn't want to do that. I should've known that using the jokey, all-lads-together approach was a mistake with someone like Callippus. He was even more married than I was, with three kids and a wife who'd have his guts for sandal straps if she even suspected him of stepping out of line. More, he liked it that way: Watch Commander or not, Callippus came from a long line of no-nonsense tub-thumping moralists and sometimes it showed. I moved on to slightly safer ground.

'You know the Scallop?' I said. 'Apart from just the name?'

'Not personally, no.'

Ouch! Maybe I should go away and come back later when the dust had settled. 'Fine, fine. Keep your wig on, pal, I meant professionally.'

'Not professionally either. There is no conceivable reason why I should.'

'Uh-huh.' I tried to keep my voice neutral. 'Who's the owner?'

'A local businessman by the name of Demetriacus. Although he employs someone else to manage the place, as I understand.'

'Yeah. I met her. A lady called Hermippe.'

'Possibly. I really don't know. As I said, to my certain knowledge neither the Scallop nor its management has ever had dealings with the Watch. On any level. A fact which makes your theory even more unlikely.'

Well, that made sense, I supposed: from what I'd seen of it, the place was squeaky-clean, and if Melanthus was typical of the clientele I couldn't see the local Watch officers being called in to break up fights over girls or handling complaints from neighbours disturbed by late-night punters singing dirty songs under their windows.

'You say this Demetriacus is a local businessman?' I said.

'Very much so. One with wide commercial interests, of which the Scallop is only a minor part.'

'Is that so, now?' The back of my neck was prickling. 'Commercial interests, eh? Such as what, for example?'

'The usual range. Shipping. Trading. Property . . .'

'Black market statues?'

'Corvinus!' That came out with a snap: I'd obviously pushed Callippus one step too far this time. 'That's enough! First you accuse Melanthus of Abdera of murder, now with absolutely no justification whatsoever you cast aspersions on Demetriacus. I told you, as far as the Watch is concerned neither he nor his business interests offer in any way a cause for suspicion. Incomer or not, he's a model of respectability.'

This time I couldn't help grinning: Callippus was an okay guy in many ways, but he came from an old City family, and like in Rome old City families had ingrained prejudices that went back to Deucalion's flood. Some of them raised their ugly heads with monotonous regularity, however fair-minded the scion of a noble race was, or tried to be, and incomers were one of the biggies. Demetriacus's forebears could've come to Athens with Orestes, but as far as the top Five Hundred were concerned he was still a pushy foreigner. Being autochthonous has its drawbacks.

'Uh-huh,' I said. 'That being the case, he wouldn't object if we asked to look the place over, right?'

'What?' Callippus's head came up like I'd just dropped a rotten egg under his nose.

I shrugged. 'It's a reasonable question, under the circumstances.'

'Corvinus, I've been very patient with you, but please understand this. I'll help you to the best of my ability in tracking down your assailant, certainly, but I will not harass private citizens simply on your say-so. Apart from the fact that you were attacked outside its doors the Scallop has provided no justification whatsoever for an official search.'

'Even though it was the last place Melanthus was seen?'

'Was it? Are you sure of that?'

I was feeling a little tetchy myself now. 'Sure I'm sure. Like I said, he spent some time with one of the girls.'

'Perhaps. But did he actually disappear while he was on the premises?'

'No, the girl I talked to said he left early, but—'

Callippus interrupted me. 'Let's get this clear, please. First of all, what proof do you actually have that the man in question was Melanthus?'

Jupiter! Bureaucrats! I counted to ten before answering. 'Hermippe admitted as much when I talked to her, pal. And I'd already got a positive identification from another girl.'

'Corvinus. Marcus.' Callippus sighed. 'If you tell me that as a friend then I must believe you; but if you want me to take this up officially then I have to be sure of my ground. And that means collecting information myself, not at second-hand.' Yeah, well, that was fair. 'However, you were told that after he had finished his . . . business Melanthus left the building to go elsewhere. Correct?'

'Sure, but he could have—'

He held up a hand. 'I'm not interested in speculation. Yes or no?'

'Uh . . . yeah. Yeah, that's right.'

'Very well. In that case we're certainly justified in interviewing the Scallop's owner, if only to get his permission to question his staff. As far as anything further goes I can and will ask, but I will not insist. And if Demetriacus refuses then that will be the end of it. For the moment, at least. Critias!'

The door opened and the clerk came in. 'Yes, sir.'

Callippus scribbled down a note and handed it to him. 'Have

this delivered to Demetriacus son of Demetrius. His house, I think, is near the Diochares Gate, but you can find that out for yourself. And the messenger is to wait for a reply.'

The clerk nodded and left.

I didn't believe my ears. 'You're giving him advance warning that we're coming?'

'Of course.'

'Oh, great! Smart thinking, pal!' I was really angry now. 'Do want to find Melanthus or not? Because if he's at the Scallop he sure as hell won't be after Demetriacus gets that note!'

'Now listen to me, Corvinus.' Callippus put the pen down carefully. 'I'm being very patient with you, but as Commander of the Watch there are certain rules I must follow, and I will not bend them for anyone. Demetriacus is in no way under suspicion. I have only your word for it – backed by no evidence whatsoever – that Melanthus of Abdera is a criminal and that he is concealed in one of Demetriacus's properties. These are very grave charges involving two prominent Athenian citizens. As far as I am concerned, Melanthus is simply missing. I've indulged you to the extent of asking Demetriacus to meet us at the Scallop so that I can talk to his staff in his presence, but that is as far as I will go. Do you understand?'

There was nothing more to say. I stood up. 'Okay. Thanks for your help.'

'Don't mention it.' He turned back to his reports. 'I'll let you know when a meeting has been arranged.'

'Fine,' I said.

I didn't slam the door as I left; but it took all the willpower I'd got.

I was fuming as I left the building. Sure, Callippus was within his rights to let this Demetriacus guy know we were coming, but it made the whole thing a useless exercise. Worse, it was counterproductive. What I wanted was to go through the place like a dose of salts, and if Melanthus was there catch him with his metaphorical pants down. Preferably his literal pants, too, just to show Callippus how silly his notions of academic disinterest in fleshly pleasures were. Demetriacus needn't be personally involved in the Baker business, but that was no reason to tempt fate. And if the guy was bent then tipping him off was crazy.

So what could I do?

While I was thinking that one out I made the trip across town to the Piraeus Gate to ask Dida why he hadn't been waiting in the alley as per instructions. I thought maybe I'd have to hang around until he came back to the rank, but he was shooting the breeze with a few of his pals over a skin of wine and a loaf. He gave me a wave and I went over.

'You want a carriage this morning, lord?' he said.

I shook my head. 'No thanks, friend. When I pay good money for a return trip I don't expect to walk.'

I must still have looked angry, because the other guys, scenting trouble, did a fast disappearing act. Dida just looked puzzled.

'I'm sorry, lord,' he said. 'I don't understand.'

'Last night at the Scallop you said you'd wait. You didn't. You care to tell me why?'

'Because you told me you'd changed your mind.'

'*I* told you?' Now it was my turn to look puzzled.

'Not you personally, lord. Of course not. But you sent a messenger out.'

Uh-huh. This was beginning to make sense. 'A big, squat guy, built like a docker, right?'

Dida's face cleared, and he grinned. 'Yeah. That's the one. I don't blame you, either. The Scallop's some place.'

I nodded. So. Prince Charming had sent Dida packing while I was talking to Cotile. Hermippe. Whoever. That was interesting.

'You say I sent this guy out,' I said. 'He came from inside, then?'

'Maybe. Maybe not; I was in the alley, remember. All I know is he told me he came from you.'

Yeah, well, it'd been worth a try. And the story rang true. If Dida was on the level – and I didn't have any reason to think that he wasn't – Prince Charming wouldn't want him hanging around when he sapped me.

Dida was inspecting my war wounds. He frowned.

'You've been in a fight, lord?'

'Yeah. You could say that. With your pal the messenger.'

I could see that one going in: the guy was no fool.

'So you didn't send him after all,' he said.

'No, I didn't send him. You were suckered, chum. We both were.'

He nodded glumly and passed over the wineskin in silence. I drank.

'Good stuff,' I said. It was: an honest swigging red with plenty of body and a kick like a mule.

'My cousin makes it. He's got a farm out by Brauron, and he knows vines.'

I passed the skin back. 'Brauron's local. I thought you said you were from Kyrenia.'

'Yeah. But I moved. So did my cousin.' He paused. 'If it's any help, the man who delivered your message was Cypriot too. Probably a Paphian, from his accent.'

'Is that so, now?' Interesting: my Greek's pretty fluent by now, but I still can't place accents very well. 'Thanks, pal. That may be useful.'

'He hasn't been in Athens long either. Unless he's slow to change. Hick accents tend to get you laughed at in the City.'

'Uh-huh.' I took out a silver piece. 'Here. That's for the information. And by way of an apology.'

He shook his head. 'Put it back, lord. You already paid me. And I don't like letting a customer down, especially if he gets rolled as a result.'

'Fair enough.' I turned to go. 'I'll see you around. Thanks for the wine.'

'Don't mention it.'

Well, that was one problem solved. I walked away, still thinking about Melanthus, the Scallop and Callippus's note to Demetriacus. If I waited for Callippus we might as well not bother with a search at all. The question was, how the hell could I get to search the place before Melanthus found out what I was up to?

I'd got about five yards before the answer hit me.

Obvious, right? Too obvious. But it was the only way.

I turned back.

'You forget something?' Dida looked up in surprise.

'Uh . . . would the Scallop be open this early?' I said.

He grinned. 'I told you before, lord. It never closes.'

'Fine.' Gods alive, what was I doing? Perilla would kill me! 'You've got yourself a fare.'

In the interests of research, you understand. Purely in the interests of research.

I had my second thoughts on the way, and they had nothing to do with Perilla or moral rectitude. If the Scallop was bent then I could be making a big mistake here. On the other hand, paying customers don't need an archon's warrant to hang their mantle up in a cathouse lobby, and once I was in I was in. It was a gamble, sure, but then there's nothing wrong with gambling if the odds are right.

'Okay, pal,' I said to Dida as I climbed out of the coach. 'Get it straight this time. You wait here until I come out, and you don't budge for nobody. I don't care if Zeus himself comes down from Olympus with half the pantheon and a dozen naked female flute players to tell you different, you spit in his eye and call the Watch. Understood?'

Dida grinned down at me. 'Understood, lord.'

'Good.' I knocked at the door.

It was opened by Antaeus. He didn't look fazed when he saw me, which was a good sign, but then I'd already decided that Antaeus was a pretty cool customer.

'Valerius Corvinus,' he said. 'How nice to see you again. Welcome.'

I went in and he closed the door behind me.

'The Lady Hermippe around?' I said.

He paused. 'That depends on why you want to see her, sir.'

'No sweat. This visit's social.' I tipped him the ghost of a wink. 'You get me?'

He nodded; the smile came back. 'Of course, sir. In that case if you'd care to wait in the salon I'll fetch her at once. I think you know the way.'

'That's okay. This time I'll just stay here and look at the pictures.'

'As you please.' He made for the stairs.

I let him get to the landing and out of sight, then tried the three other doors off the lobby. Two of them were locked, but the third gave out on to a passageway. Sure, it might lead to the cellars but I couldn't risk a foray down it, not yet. I shelved that for later. I was examining the Achilles painting when Hermippe came down.

'That a real Panainos?' I said.

She smiled. 'You have an eye for art, Valerius Corvinus. Rare in a Roman.'

'Not me, lady. I just know someone who does.'

'Then she taught you well. No, it isn't a Panainos, but it was done by one of his pupils and the style is almost identical. Beautiful, isn't it?'

'It's okay, yeah.'

'Shall we go into the salon? It's more comfortable.'

'Sure.' She led the way. No Cotile, not this time: the room was empty.

'Now.' She sat on a chair and waved me to a couch. 'Antaeus tells me this is a private visit. I'm delighted. It's always a pleasure to add to our clientele, and to welcome new friends personally. Do help yourself to wine, by the way.'

I did. 'You like some, lady?' I said.

'No, thank you. Wine isn't one of my weaknesses.'

Jupiter! If this was a cathouse then it wasn't like any I'd ever been in, and it was making me nervous as hell. Any minute now she'd start passing round the almond cakes and ask how my mother was doing. 'Uh . . . you are open for business, aren't you?' I said. 'I mean . . .'

'Of course.' Another smile. 'But I must know your preferences. I find that a relaxed chat on the first visit resolves all sorts of problems in advance. What exactly are your interests?'

'Uh . . .'

'We have quite a range of girls free at the moment, especially at this time of day. Cleo, perhaps? She's from Palmyra, Persian-trained, very skilled. Then there's Thalia, an Alexandrian, or if your tastes run to the more exotic I can offer you a Nubian girl, although . . .'

'How about the one I saw yesterday? Cotile?' Research; strictly research.

She hesitated. 'I'm afraid Cotile isn't available. Not for the next two or three days, anyway. Another time, perhaps.'

Ah, well. Maybe that was for the best. 'You like to recommend a girl yourself, maybe?'

'Certainly. I'd be honoured, if that's what you wish.' She gave me a summing look. 'Cleo, I think. Antaeus will show you to her room.' She reached into the fold of her mantle and took out a small bell. 'Incidentally, and I hope you'll forgive me mentioning the subject, but some of our guests prefer a monthly payment. It's quite up to you, but I would recommend it.'

'Uh, no.' I could just see Perilla's face when the bill hit the mat. I fumbled for my purse. Jupiter! That was a new one since my day! I wasn't used to moving in such civilised circles! 'No, I'll pay now.'

'That will be quite acceptable. And naturally there will be a reduction for the first visit.'

She named a sum that had me reeling. Jupiter's balls on a string! No wonder the place had original paintings on the walls! Still, I managed to pay up without seeming too boorish. At least I hoped I didn't.

Hermippe stood up. 'No need to take your wine with you, Valerius Corvinus. Cleo will have a tray of her own.' She rang the bell and the giant squeezed through the door. 'Antaeus, take this gentleman up to Cleo's room, please.' The guy bowed and stepped aside. 'I do hope you enjoy your time here, Corvinus. And that you'll favour us again soon.'

'Yeah. Yeah, thanks.'

'This way, sir.' Antaeus led me up the stairs. 'You didn't find the friend you were looking for, incidentally?'

'Melanthus? No. Not yet.'

'A pity. Still, I've no doubt you will in time. Cleo's is the last door on the right, sir. Stay as long as you wish, naturally, and tell her if there is anything else you require in the way of food or drink.'

I'd been looking at the doors as we passed. Each of them had a small plaque with a girl's name written on. All except one, the one at the end of the corridor, beyond Cleo's. That one had no plaque at all.

Antaeus knocked at the last door on the right, then went back downstairs without a word. I went in alone.

Jupiter!

23 ∫

It felt like I'd just stepped across the River Orontes and into the Parthian king's palace. The sharp corners of the room and the ceiling were hidden with spreads of blue and yellow silk, making a tent, and the air was heavy with perfume and spices. The girl lay on a divan lit by a single standing candelabrum. She sat up with a whisper of silk on bare flesh. Her almond eyes were ringed with black cosmetic.

Sticking with the research idea was going to be difficult. I could tell that already.

'Uh . . . you're Cleo?' I said.

'Yes, lord.' She stretched, and the bells at her ankles rang gently. 'Come in, please. Make yourself at home. Would you like some wine?'

'Yeah.' My throat was dry already. 'Yeah, that'd be good.'

The jug and cups were sitting on a low table by the bed. She reached over to pour, and the thin silk blouse moulded itself around her nipples.

'Your mantle, lord.' She smiled. 'You'd be more comfortable without it, I think.'

'No, that's okay.' She was right, though: the room was warm, and there was a small brazier giving off a scent that cut through the other perfumes and set the back of my nose tingling. 'I'll keep it on for now.'

'As you wish.' She held out the cup. 'Here. Some honeyed figs? From Damascus. Very good. You're hungry?'

'No, I'm fine.' I took the wine cup and sipped.

'Then lie down. Relax. There's no hurry.'

Jupiter best and greatest! Maybe I'd've been better with Cotile

161 •

after all, time of the month or not; at least I had past acquaintance to fall back on. Hermippe was right, Cleo was a real honey: smooth skin white as cream, dark hair done up in the Parthian style, breasts shining through the thinnest of silk coverings.

I lay down on the divan. Her fingers touched my forehead, light as feathers.

'You're Roman, lord?'

'Yeah.'

'I haven't met a Roman before. Not properly.' The fingers found the bruise at the back of my head. I winced. 'You're hurt?'

'It's nothing. Just a bump.'

'Not just a bump. Put the wine cup down and turn round a little, please. Let me reach your neck. There, that's better.'

Jupiter and all the gods, that was good! Her fingers worked their way down slowly to the top of my spine, rubbing gently.

'The doctors do this in Parthia, lord,' she said. 'It's a very old skill which relaxes the muscles. You feel it working?'

Sure I did. I was almost purring. As a masseuse back in Rome she could've made a fortune. 'Yeah. Yeah, that's great. Fantastic.'

'Good. You have a strong neck, but the muscles are bunched and knotted. Something is worrying you.'

'Maybe.'

'It's not important. Or not now. Relax.'

I found myself drifting. Relax. I hadn't felt this relaxed for years. Certainly not recently. Certainly not since . . .

Since . . .

Oh, hell! I was falling asleep! I shook my head and sat up.

'Lord?'

'It's okay,' I said. It had to be done now, or never. A pity. Personally at that moment I'd have opted for never, and the hell with Priscus, Melanthus and the Baker, but I knew I'd regret it later. 'Cleo, you mind if we talk for a minute?'

'Of course not, lord. We can do whatever you like.' We were face to face. Her eyes were wide and luminous and her breasts with their gilded nipples beneath the transparent silk were brushing the folds of my mantle. Jupiter! Maybe this hadn't been such a good idea at that. And whatever was burning on that brazier was doing funny things to my brain. Pleasant as hell, sure, but that wasn't the point . . .

I shook my head to clear it. 'I'm looking for a guy called Melanthus, Cleo. A regular. He usually goes with Anthe. You know him?'

She considered. 'No, lord. I haven't been here long. And we're strictly forbidden to—'

'Discuss one customer with another. Yeah. Yeah, I know. One of the house rules. But this is important.' I described him. 'You seen him around, maybe? Outside working hours, as it were? In the building?'

'No, lord.'

Well, it had been worth a try. Back to the original plan. I took out my purse and found the remaining gold piece. 'Okay. I'm going to slip out for a while. Say nothing and this is yours. That seem reasonable?'

'The Lady Hermippe . . .'

'I won't tell, I swear. I've gone down to have a word with the coachman, that's all. Cleo, this is important!'

A pause. 'Yes, I know,' she said. 'Cotile said he'd disappeared. The man you were asking about.'

'Yeah. Yeah, that's right. Only he may still be here, and I've got to check. You understand?'

She nodded; not the world's greatest brain, but with a body like that who needs brains? 'Very well, lord. It's not really permitted, but . . .'

I slipped her the coin and got to my feet. Gods alive! I just hoped that if Perilla ever found out about this she'd appreciate the sacrifice I was making. Not that she ever would find out . . .

'Uh . . . what is that stuff you're burning, by the way?' I said.

'The upper leaves of the *qef* plant, lord.'

'The which?'

She smiled. 'It hasn't a name in Greek. They burn it in Parthia and inhale the smoke. It brings good dreams.'

'Is that right?' Well, maybe it was the *qef* or Cleo's massage, or probably a combination of the two, but I felt really good, almost like I was flying. 'You stay here, okay?'

• David Wishart

'Of course.' She half sat on the divan and drew her beautiful legs under her. I took one last look. Gods, I must be crazy!

Crazy or not, it had to be done. I listened for a moment at the closed door, then opened it and slipped outside.

There was no one around. It was lucky we were at the end of the corridor and I only had one direction to worry about. I put my ear to the unmarked door next to Cleo's. Nothing. I turned the handle . . .

Then I heard the sound of voices from downstairs: men's voices. I froze, ready to dive back into Cleo's room, but whoever it was must have crossed the hall and gone into one of the downstairs rooms because I heard a door close and then silence. I turned the knob again.

The door opened on to a broom closet. Hell. Talk about anticlimax. Well, if Antaeus caught me I could always say I'd had this uncontrollable urge to sweep the corridor. So. That left downstairs, which was a complete bummer. Added to which I didn't know where Antaeus parked himself when he wasn't doing his perfect butler act. On the other hand, there had been those voices, and although I hadn't heard them at all clearly I was pretty sure neither of them belonged to the jolly giant. It was just possible one of them was Melanthus's; but if so then I sure as hell wasn't going to find out shaking in my sandals up here.

I walked along the corridor as quietly as I could without sneaking: if Antaeus did come up I could tell him what I'd told Cleo, that I wanted a word with Dida outside.

The middle door on the right was marked for Anthe. I stopped. Cotile had said she'd gone to Corinth, which meant the room should be empty. And if Melanthus was hiding out in the Scallop then an empty room was well worth checking.

I listened, then tried the door. It was open. I pushed.

Anthe obviously had a thing about dried flower arrangements: the room was full of them, but otherwise it was uncluttered. The bed was made up. I went in and closed the door behind me. Then I checked the dressing-table and the clothes chest. Lots of perfumes and cosmetics, but nothing else, and the only clothes in the chest were women's ones. What there was of them; Anthe was clearly the direct type. Well, it'd been worth a try. If Melanthus was here I doubted if he'd taken that much trouble over his cover; or if he had then I didn't want to know. Downstairs it had to be.

I stopped outside Hermippe's office at the top of the stairs. No sign of Antaeus. Hopefully he was off somewhere polishing his diphthongs. I could hear the voices again, muffled this time. They weren't coming from the salon but from behind one of the doors I'd tried earlier. Cautiously, I came down and put my ear to the panel . . .

'Can I help you, sir?'

I spun round. Shit! Antaeus! The guy must have woollen feet!

'Uh . . . I just wanted a word with my coachman, friend,' I said. It didn't sound convincing even to me. 'He's waiting outside.'

'Indeed.'

'Yeah. So if you'll just excuse me . . .'

He didn't move. It was like finding that a stone wall had suddenly decided to get between you and where you wanted to be.

'Perhaps, Valerius Corvinus,' he said, 'if you're so interested in overhearing private conversations you would care to join in.'

'Uh, no, that's okay. I think I'll just . . .'

He reached over and took a grip of my arm. Gently enough, but it would've been easier to get out of a vice. With his other hand he knocked at the door. The voices stopped.

Antaeus opened the door and guided me inside.

The place was another office, like Hermippe's, but plusher, almost a sitting-room, with two or three life-size bronzes and veneered marble panelling round the walls. Behind the desk was a little wizened guy, his bald head sticking up from an expensive-looking mantle with enough purple and gold thread on it to fit out a triumphal procession. As I came in the man sitting opposite with his back to me turned round . . .

I shook Antaeus's hand off. He stepped back and did a good imitation of a piece of decorative furniture.

'Well, well,' I said.

24

'What are you doing here, Corvinus?' Callippus asked. The guy wasn't too pleased, and it showed.

'I could ask you the same question, pal,' I said.

'I'm interviewing Demetriacus, of course. As I told you I would.'

'Fine.' I kept my voice level. 'Only somehow I got the impression you'd let me know when it happened.'

'That was my intention, although I don't recall extending a formal invitation.' Now he sounded peeved as hell. 'In any case, there wasn't time.'

'Fortunately the situation seems to have remedied itself, Commander,' the baldy in the fancy mantle said drily. 'Please sit down, Valerius Corvinus. Antaeus, a chair for our other guest.' I sat. Callippus didn't look at me. 'The fault was partly mine, I'm afraid. Naturally I came straight here as soon as Callippus's messenger arrived. I don't have the privilege of knowing Melanthus of Abdera personally, but I have heard of him, and the Scallop's reputation is very important to me. Accordingly if he has disappeared then I view it as a duty to help the authorities in every way I can.'

Uh-huh. Quite the little speech. I'd decided the moment I came in that I didn't like Demetriacus. With his round hairless head poking up from the starched edge of the mantle he could've passed for a shaved monkey: a very smart monkey who spoke careful, well-structured Greek. Too careful and well structured for my liking: something about it rang phoney, and I've never trusted guys who balance their clauses.

'Yeah. Yeah, sure,' I said. 'Very public-spirited of you.'

'Corvinus, if you insist on being present then I insist on civility!' Callippus snapped. 'This gentleman has left his sickbed to come here!'

'No, no, that's all right,' Demetriacus said. 'I can understand your friend's suspicions, especially since, as you tell me, he was attacked himself last night in our side alley. With no long-term ill effects, I hope?' He gave me a tight smile.

'I'm okay,' I said. 'Only . . .'

'Leave it!' Callippus muttered. Jupiter, the guy was annoyed. Seriously annoyed. Still, he was right, and I was here on sufferance. Putting backs up at this juncture wasn't going to get me anywhere.

Demetriacus had turned to Antaeus. 'Ask the Lady Hermippe to join us, please,' he said. 'And bring wine and a glass of boiled milk.' I must've let my shudder show, because he smiled at me again. 'The commander wasn't exaggerating, Corvinus. Or only by a little. No wine for me at present, I'm afraid, and an invalid's diet.' Antaeus bowed and left. 'Now. Callippus has told me that Melanthus was here the evening of his disappearance. I can't confirm this personally but Hermippe can no doubt tell you one way or the other. However, he also says that the gentleman left the premises not long after he arrived.'

'Melanthus left the girl's room, sure,' I said. 'Whether he left the premises is another matter.'

'True.' The smooth pink face didn't change. 'That's a fair distinction, although again Hermippe should be able to tell us for certain whether or not it's valid in this instance.' He paused. 'Can I assume that you think it is? That Melanthus didn't leave the Scallop early after all?'

'It's a possibility. Yeah.'

Callippus stirred. 'Corvinus . . .'

'That's all right, Commander.' I still had Demetriacus's full attention. 'Let your friend speak his mind. Yes, again you're quite correct. It is certainly a possibility, in theory at least. And the logical implication underlying it is that you believe the disappearance took place here. That Melanthus had in fact been murdered.'

Well, that was direct enough. Callippus glared at me, although he didn't speak. 'No, I don't think that,' I said carefully. 'Or rather I don't think the guy's dead. I think he disappeared voluntarily.'

Demetriacus's eyes widened. 'Really? Why on earth should he want to do that?'

The hell with this. If he could be direct then so could I, and I was tired of fencing anyway.

'Because the guy's a crook,' I said. 'He was after a gold statue that my stepfather was trying to buy from a man called Argaius. He'd arranged Argaius's murder and he knew I suspected him of it. And I think as a consequence he's hiding out somewhere in this building.'

I'd been expecting Callippus to butt in. Now he did.

'Corvinus, that's enough! More than enough!' He turned to Demetriacus. 'Before we go any further, sir, can I say that this is not the official view or anything near it. Melanthus is—'

The door opened, and Antaeus reappeared with Hermippe in tow. She stopped and stared at me.

'Valerius Corvinus?' she said. 'I thought you were with Cleo.'

'Uh . . . yeah.' I glanced at Callippus. His lips were set tight, and he looked like someone had just inserted a very long poker up his rectum. 'I just . . . ah . . . slipped downstairs for a moment.'

'Sit down, Hermippe.' Demetriacus indicated the other guest chair. 'Valerius Corvinus is a friend of the Lord Callippus here. The City Watch Commander. He's asking about Melanthus of Abdera who is, I think, a client of ours?'

His voice held a question. Hermippe paused before answering.

'Yes, sir,' she said at last. 'A regular client of several years' standing.'

'I'll fetch the wine and milk now, sir.' Antaeus made a move towards the door.

'Wait a moment. Antaeus.' Demetriacus held up a hand. 'Perhaps you can help us here yourself. The Lord Corvinus has suggested that Melanthus may not have left the house that evening. He did, didn't he?'

Antaeus frowned and looked at Hermippe.

'Of course he did,' she said. 'Shortly after sunset. Antaeus was otherwise engaged, but I saw him leave personally.'

'You're certain?'

Her back straightened. 'Absolutely certain, sir.'

'Thank you.' Demetriacus turned back to Callippus. 'There's your answer, Commander. Naturally if you don't believe us you're quite at liberty to search. We have no clients at the moment who might find that inconvenient. Or do we, Hermippe?'

'Only Valerius Corvinus himself.' Her voice was dry. 'And I take it he would have no objection.' Callippus didn't look at me, but his lips set even tighter. Jupiter! How the guy could be a Watch commander and still subscribe to the moral code of a sixty-year-old Vestal beat me.

'Fine.' Demetriacus was smiling. 'Then please feel free to look round, gentlemen, as much as you wish.'

'Great, that's—' I began.

'A search won't be necessary, sir.' Callippus stood up. 'And I don't think we need trouble you any further. My thanks for your help. And my apologies for the inconvenience. Come on, Corvinus.' He paused. 'Unless you have other commitments, of course.'

Snide bastard. I didn't move. 'There is one thing, Demetriacus,' I said. 'You mind if I have a look at your cellar before we go?'

Demetriacus frowned. 'The cellar? I don't understand.'

'Put it down to Roman idiosyncrasy. I have this thing about cellars.' Callippus had his mouth open to object but I talked through him. 'It won't take a minute.'

'Take as long as you please. Antaeus?'

The big guy moved forward. 'This way, Valerius Corvinus.'

I'd heard more cheerful invitations, but I'd got what I wanted. 'You coming, Callippus?' I said.

'No.' He was looking grim. 'I think you can make a fool of yourself perfectly well without my help. You've done a fine job of it so far, anyway.'

And screw you, too, pal, I thought. Well, this looked like the end of a beautiful friendship, but it was the only chance I was going to get and if I was right it would be a clincher. 'Okay. I'll see you outside.'

Callippus grunted. I got up, nodded to Demetriacus, and followed the now-not-so-jolly giant across the hall and down the corridor next to the Achilles painting.

Everything fitted: the distance, the sound of our footsteps.

Everything. Sure enough, when we got to the kitchen there was the door. This time it was open.

'Would you care to go down, sir?' Antaeus said. There was an edge to his voice that I didn't like more than half. No, I didn't want to go down, not a second time, not with the Last of the Titans here waiting up above ready to tie me into a neat bow when I came back up, but I needed confirmation. Then it would be a case of fighting my way to Callippus if necessary, showing him that I had the facts to back the theory, and nailing Demetriacus's lying hide to his fancy front door. That I'd enjoy.

'Sure,' I said, surreptitiously checking that my knife was where it should be in its wrist sheath. 'You got a lamp, pal? Or should I just break my neck and save you the trouble?'

He didn't say anything. Crossing to a cupboard in the corner of the kitchen, he took down a pottery oil lamp and lit it with a spill from the charcoal stove. I took the lamp and went down the stone steps.

The cellar was full of wine jars. Very full. If it was a cosmetic job, whoever had done it had had divine help. He'd even managed a few convincing spider webs and a layer of dirt, dust and grime. Not to mention a dead mouse or two.

Bugger.

'Have you seen enough, sir?' Antaeus said when I came back up. Polite, but sarky as hell underneath. I handed him the lamp without a word and went outside to face Callippus.

Okay. So I was wrong. Wherever I'd had my talk with Prince Charming, it hadn't been the Scallop. Sure, Melanthus could still be hiding out there and Demetriacus could've been bluffing from start to finish: Hermippe had been lying when she said he'd left, I was certain of that; you get the feel for lies when you've heard them often enough. The question was why? Her boss had wanted her to bail him out, sure he had; I'd noticed the loaded question, and she'd done it nobly. Out of loyalty, or something else? Or was I just fantasising again; Demetriacus was the upstanding public-spirited citizen he pretended to be and the Scallop was the only honest cathouse between here and the Pillars of Hercules?

Callippus had gone, but Dida was there waiting. He was grinning from ear to ear.

'Your friend the Watch Commander left a message for you, lord,' he said. 'He suggests that if you have any other half-baked theories you drop them down a very deep hole. He also said that he'll be grateful if you stay out of his hair completely for the next decade or so. Preferably in Corinth.'

'Uh, yeah. Yeah, got it. Message delivered.' Jupiter!

'That's a paraphrase. His actual words weren't so polite.'

Uh-huh. That I'd believe. 'Just take me home, Dida, okay?'

I got into the coach, feeling drained. Well, you win some, you lose some, and this wasn't even close to a draw. It had been worth a try, though, and I'd still bet a hatful of rubies to a smoked sardine that Melanthus was holed up inside somewhere. Maybe behind one of the doors I hadn't opened, or in a room the other side of the courtyard. Or maybe there was another cellar that the big guy hadn't shown me. The problem now was I was stymied. I doubted that Demetriacus would let me over the threshold now legitimately, and with Antaeus straining at the leash to see how far I'd bounce if he got to throw me out, short of a full-frontal attack with a cohort of Praetorians at my back I didn't have a hope in hell of getting in any other way. Checkmate. For now, at least.

So. I had to approach the problem from another angle. There were two possibilities, and both of them were total bummers. One was to track down Prince Charming and/or the Ethiopian, the other was to concentrate on the statue itself. I hadn't had much luck so far with the first, and from Callippus's message I got the distinct impression that he wouldn't bust a gut to help me in future. So, bummer or not, it had to be the second.

Harpalus might not have been involved with moving the Baker, but someone must have been. Tomorrow I'd go back down to the Piraeus and have a word with the owner of the Zea cookshop. He'd given me Smaragdus's name; maybe he could give me another if I asked nicely. Not that I was looking forward to asking: the guy hadn't exactly fallen over himself to be helpful last time around, and I doubted if he'd sweetened any. Also, his wine stank.

I looked out of the carriage window. We were coming up to the major intersection beyond the Rock, heading for the Hippades

Gate. There was a cluster of shops there where I could pick up a conscience present for Perilla.

'Hey, Dida!' I shouted.

'Yeah?'

'Pull in here. I'll walk the rest.'

The carriage stopped and I got out. A thought struck me. 'By the way,' I said. 'That bastard who snatched me. The Paphian. You think you can find him?' Public coach drivers go everywhere. And their grapevine may not be as hot as the slaves' version, but they've got contacts.

'I can try, lord. I'll spread the word around, anyway.'

'You do that. The Ethiopian as well. The guy in the loud tunic. Top rates.'

'Understood.' A grin. 'I'll be in touch. If and when.'

Well, it was a long shot, but it was as good as I could manage at present. I watched the coach head back towards Piraeus Gate.

There was a flower-seller on the corner, but I gave him a miss: flowers always made Perilla suspicious. I grinned to myself. Jupiter! An innocent half-hour in the Scallop and I was acting like any other tomcatting husband in the City! In the end, I went into a scent shop and chose a small bottle of top-of-the-range perfume that cost an arm and a leg. I asked the shopkeeper if he had any *qef*, but he'd never heard of the stuff. Shame.

I looked around on the off-chance, but there was no sign of the Ethiopian. That was one guy I wanted a word with.

Okay, call it a day. And not one of my best, either. I tucked the perfume bottle into a fold of my mantle and went home.

When I walked into the cookshop the owner was arranging rissoles on a platter. The place was empty.

'Hey, friend,' I said. 'Remember me?'

'Sure.' He straightened and scowled. 'The wine expert.'

'Don't let it rankle, pal.' There was a stool beside the counter. I sat on it. 'We can't all be born with palates.'

He was looking at my bruised face. 'You have an argument with someone?'

'Just a minor disagreement.'

'Smaragdus?' His mouth split into a grin. On that mug it was as out of place as a gorilla in a barbershop. 'Never knew the bastard had it in him.'

'Not with Smaragdus.'

'Pity.' He set the last rissole on top of the pile. A circling fly moved in for the kill. 'So. What'll it be?'

I took out my purse slowly. 'I was hoping you could help me a bit more over names. What's yours, by the way, while we're on the subject?'

'Euphrastus.' Sweet gods! His parents must've had some sense of humour! 'And this is a cookshop, friend. You sit down, you eat. I've got a living to make.'

'Uh-huh.' I cast an eye over the contents of the counter. What I could see of them under the flies and the layer of grease. 'You have anything there that didn't go woof once and wag its tail?'

'Not a lot.' Well, I'd asked and he'd told me. 'How about beans?'

'Beans are fine.'

He lifted the lid of a casserole on the stove, ladled a grey mess on to a plate and added a chunk of bread and a spoon. 'Wine?'

'No wine. Definitely no wine.'

'Suit yourself.' He put the plate in front of me and licked sauce off his thumb. 'Enjoy.'

Not the word I would've used. I tasted the glop and pushed it away. If Pythagoras was right the souls that'd gone into the pot would've done better to have stayed in the queue. 'Okay, pal. Now the information.'

'About Argaius? You're wasting your time, Roman. There's nothing more I can tell you. The guy's dead and his wife's left town.' He leered. 'Shame. That's one widow I wouldn't mind comforting.'

'Not about Argaius. About Smaragdus.'

'You didn't find him at Mamma Glypho's?'

'He's moved.' If the guy hadn't heard that Smaragdus was dead I wasn't going to tell him. He might get jittery. Certainly the price would go up. 'His friend Harpalus is gone too.'

'Uh-huh.' Euphrastus indicated the plate between us. 'You going to eat that, by the way, or let it go to waste?'

'I'll pay for it, if that's what you mean. Otherwise I'll pass.'

'Fine. I was just going to eat myself anyway.' He dunked the bread in the bean mash and took a soggy bite. My stomach turned. 'So Glypho finally threw the bugger out, right? I'm not surprised. A guy like that, he's bad for trade.'

I tried not to watch as he shovelled down the beans like there was no tomorrow. Well, at least I couldn't say he didn't have the courage of his own culinary convictions.

'Did Smaragdus have any other business associates besides Argaius?'

'Sure.' He licked a stray scrap of sauce from the spoon handle. 'What else would you expect? Doing deals with people was his job.'

'Can you give me names?'

'Go down to the harbour, pal. Anyone you see there, put him on the list. Smaragdus has dealings with half the Piraeus.'

That was discouraging, but I hadn't come all this way just to give up. 'Regulars, Euphrastus. We're talking regulars.'

He reached a leisurely finger to the back of his mouth, pulled out a lump of grit the size of a cobble, inspected it and flicked it to one side. It landed in the tray of rissoles. 'Regulars I wouldn't know. And unlike some other nosey bastards I don't care.'

Well, it'd been worth a try. I could always drop by the harbour like he suggested and ask around. Meanwhile there was another tack I might try.

'Okay. So what about the other end? People who worked for him? If Smaragdus had a job that involved rough work, heavy lifting, say, who would he go to?'

'He'd hire any help he needed at the Emporium, same as anyone else. There's always plenty of cheap muscle around on the quayside. Or he'd just use Tiny.'

'Tiny?'

'Big guy.' Euphrastus tapped his temple. 'Soft in the head. You met him already. He was in last time you were here with that dog of his.'

Oh, yes, I remembered Tiny! I might be on to something here. 'You happen to know where I can find him?'

That got me a long considering stare. 'Maybe.'

I sighed and undid the purse.

Zea Harbour wasn't much used these days, and hadn't been for a long, long time, not since Athens gave up any pretence of being a naval power and the government shipyards were left to rot. Most of the traffic was local: small-time shippers cutting costs on dues levied at the main dock on the other side of town or fishermen landing their catch. The old trireme sheds were still standing, but most of them were empty and locked up. Waiting for better days, maybe, like the rest of the Piraeus. The whole place had a shabby, grey look to it that made me feel depressed as hell.

At the quayside closest to me there were three boats moored, one of them a coastal tub. Guys in grimy tunics were unloading what looked like sacks of cement and iron scrap into a cart while the shipmaster chewed on an apple and watched. I went over.

He tossed the core away when he saw me coming.

'Yes, lord? You're looking for a boat?' he said.

'Not today, pal. But I am interested in the help.'

The eager look vanished. 'These men are already hired. Try the Emporium.'

'I'm interested in one guy in particular. A big guy, simple in the head. Name of Tiny.'

'Is that right?' He gave me a long stare, then shrugged and shouted: 'Bessus!'

One of the men loading the cart dumped his bag of cement and came over, wiping his hands on his tunic.

'Someone here looking for Tiny,' the master said, and walked off to check his bilges.

I turned to the new guy. 'I was told he works here sometimes,' I said.

'That's right.'

'You know where I can find him?'

The man shook his head. 'I know him, lord, sure, but he isn't one of ours. Not a regular. He comes and goes. You want him special?'

'I think he might've done a job for a friend of mine. I wanted to check, that's all.'

'Uh-huh.' He looked doubtful. 'Who would this friend be, now?'

'A guy called Smaragdus.'

'Smaragdus?' His face split into a grin. 'Sure, I know Smaragdus. Then it's likely, lord, although I can't say for certain. Tiny's choosy who he works for, but he has a soft spot for Smaragdus.'

'Choosy?'

He hesitated. 'You've met him, lord? Tiny, I mean?'

'Yeah. Once.'

'Then you'll know how he is.' He must've seen the look on my face. 'Oh, he's harmless. Tiny wouldn't hurt a fly. But he has his likes and dislikes, and you can't budge him. Smaragdus is one of the likes.'

Uh-huh. That fitted. 'How is he as a worker?'

'Like I say, it depends. When he works he works.' He nodded at the cement bags. 'I've seen him carry four of these, two beneath each arm, without breaking sweat. Keep it up, too.'

'Then maybe I should hire him instead of you, Bessus.' The master was back, and obviously I'd used up any goodwill there was going from that quarter. 'That cart isn't going to load itself.'

'Yeah. Yeah, right,' I said. 'No problem, friend. One minute more, okay?' The guy frowned, but there wasn't much he could do without telling me straight just to piss off. He drifted off again, and I took out a four-drach piece from my purse.

'My name's Valerius Corvinus,' I said. 'I've got a house in the City, on the Lyceum Road past Hippades Gate. If and when Tiny shows up bring him round and I'll match this with another. Deal?'

Bessus shook his head. 'Save your money, lord,' he said. 'Nobody takes Tiny nowhere he doesn't want to go. And I'll tell you now that he won't.'

Uh-huh. Well, at least he was honest. 'Do your best, okay?' I handed him the coin and waved to the shipmaster. 'Thanks for your patience, friend.'

The guy gave me a sour nod. I walked back towards the harbour gates where I'd left Lysias with the coach.

Four cement bags at a go and a shine for Smaragdus, right? Maybe I'd hit lucky after all.

26

I spent the afternoon pottering around the City centre, doing all the little jobs I hadn't had time for these past few days. Like visiting my banker Simon, for example, and screwing some of Priscus's money out of him for expenses. I didn't mind helping the old guy out, but when it came to being beaten up on his account the free ride was over. When I got back Perilla was in the atrium. She didn't look happy. I kissed her, but that didn't seem to help much.

'Problems, lady?' I said.

She threw aside the book she hadn't been reading. I could almost see the steam leaking out from above her earrings.

'Marcus, this is hopeless! You really will have to get rid of that damned bird!'

Oh, hell. Not Nestor again. I knew now how Orestes felt when he couldn't shake the Furies. I took off my mantle and tossed it on to a chair. 'What's he done this time?'

She was up and pacing the room. 'I don't mind so much for myself, but when it comes to insulting my friends I draw the line.'

Uh-oh. 'Uh . . . we talking general here, Perilla, or have you someone particular in mind?'

'The latter.' She sat down, finally, on the couch next to me. 'And "particular" is exactly the right word. Euelpida.'

'Ah.' I saw the problem. Euelpida was one of Perilla's more strait-laced cronies, the wife of a top Lyceum scholar and a mean mind herself. Nestor couldn't have made a better – or a worse – choice. It was eerie. 'Euelpida, eh?'

'She called round earlier for a chat,' Perilla said coldly, 'and we went out to the garden.' The 'chat' would've been heavy stuff: I was glad I'd missed it. 'It never occurred to me, of course, that Alexis might have Nestor there. He usually keeps him in his room.'

'And the bastard disgraced himself in front of Euelpida, right?'

'At some length. And in very pungent terms.'

'You . . . uh . . . remember what he said, by any chance?' I was really interested: Nestor's range of vocabulary was doing wonders for my Greek.

'Not in detail, Marcus, no.' Sure. Like hell she didn't. Understood it, too: there were red spots high on the lady's cheekbones. 'And I certainly wouldn't repeat it to you if I did.'

Pity; but then I hadn't really expected her to. Some aspects of foreign language learning Perilla doesn't encourage. I lay back and cradled my wine cup. Bathyllus had left the tray out in the hall for me as usual, although there was no sign of the little guy himself. Hardly surprising. When Perilla was in a mood like this even spiders kept a low profile.

'Okay,' I said. 'I'll talk to Alexis later. Maybe we can work something out.'

'You had better. That bird is a liability, Corvinus. A corrupting influence.'

'You think Euelpida is open to corruption?' I gave her my best leer. 'Does Aristoboulus know?' Aristoboulus was Euelpida's husband, a long streak of a guy like an asparagus shoot soaked in vinegar.

'Don't be silly!'

'Yeah, well, you could be right.' I put my arm round her shoulders. 'But speaking of corrupting influences . . .'

'Now you're trying to fudge the issue!'

'Lady, I never fudge issues.' I nuzzled her ear. 'And I'm sure in Euelpida's case Aristoboulus would welcome some constructive corruption. The poor boob could do with a bit of domestic excitement.'

The sides of Perilla's mouth began to twitch; I was getting through to her at last. 'I suppose,' she said slowly, 'that in retrospect the situation does have its amusing side.'

'That's more than can be said for Euelpida.' I kissed her properly and felt the first small giggle break through. 'What did she say? After Nestor did his stuff, that is?'

'Nothing.' Perilla bit her lip. The lady was still holding on gamely to her Roman matron pose, but the cracks were definitely beginning to show. 'She just ran back inside.'

I stared at her. 'Euelpida? Run?' Jupiter! That I would've loved to see. As far as likelihood went, it ranked with the Academy doing a conga through the market-place with Alciphron on spoons.

'Like a hare!' The Roman matron pose finally collapsed, taking Perilla with it. 'Oh, and Marcus, she squeaked! It was so dreadfully embarrassing!'

'Yeah.' I kissed her again. 'Say what you will about Euelpida, the kid's no squeaker.'

'Corvinus, stop it, please!' Perilla was hugging her ribs. 'I've been trying to hold this in all day! It's not funny!'

'Is everything all right, sir? Madam?' I hadn't noticed Bathyllus sidling in. The little guy had evidently decided it was safe to break cover. He was radiating disapproval so hard he glowed.

'Yeah, we're fine, Bathyllus. At least, I am.' I was patting Perilla on the back while she choked into my tunic. 'Behave yourself, lady, you're upsetting the staff.'

'Meton says dinner will be served shortly.' Bristle, bristle: Bathyllus didn't even look at Perilla. 'If you're both ready, of course.'

'Whenever he likes. Oh, and tell Alexis to keep his pal with the beak under wraps when we have guests in future, right?'

'Yes, sir.' He left. I could hear his sniff all the way to the kitchen.

Perilla had finally come up for air. She was bright red, but at least she could breathe now. We settled down on the couch with my arm comfortably round her shoulders.

'I think you've just seriously undermined the empire, lady,' I said. 'Sleep with a knife under your pillow tonight.'

'Nonsense.' She kissed me. 'Anyway, I feel better for that. How was your day?'

'Pretty good, for a change.' I told her about Tiny. 'One gets you ten Smaragdus used him to shift the Baker, and in that case he knows where it's stashed. My only problem now is tracking him down.'

'And getting him to tell you.' Perilla frowned. 'From what you say about this man I don't think you can count on that, Marcus.'

Yeah. I'd made that jump myself. With the best will in the world, the guy was still an idiot. Even if I did find him there was no guarantee I could even make him understand what I wanted. Still, with Smaragdus dead he was the only lead we'd got to the Baker, and without him we could wait another hundred years before it surfaced again. If it ever did.

There was another reason for finding Tiny, too: if I didn't, then sooner or later the opposition would. And when he got the guy into that damned cellar of his, wherever it was, I couldn't see Prince Charming asking nicely.

'So.' Perilla snuggled down. 'What are your immediate plans?'

I filled my cup one-armed. 'We wait, lady. There's nothing else we can do. I've got half Athens and the Piraeus on the payroll, and barring some sort of break we'll just have to hope they come through.'

Someone coughed. Bathyllus.

'I'm sorry to disturb you, sir. Madam. Meton reports a crisis. Dinner will be delayed.'

I sighed. A crisis in Meton's book was anything from a full-scale Parthian invasion with four legions massacred to the sauce curdling, in that ascending order. 'Okay, little guy. Just top up the wine jug and we'll sit it out in here.'

'Very well, sir.'

Perilla stayed quiet until he'd oozed off to the kitchen. Then she said: 'Of course, Marcus, if you're not too concerned about the wine we could always look for a suitable knife.'

'Knife?'

'To put under the pillow.'

Uh-huh. I know when I'm being propositioned. We went upstairs.

We made love slowly while the crisis in the kitchen was resolved. When we'd finished Perilla nestled into the hollow of my shoulder.

'I never asked you,' she said. 'Why the perfume?'

'What perfume's that, lady?'

'The bottle you brought me yesterday. What was it for?'

'Uh . . . nothing in particular. It just seemed a good idea at the time.'

'Really?' I felt her smile. 'I thought it might be an indication of guilt or something.'

Oh, Jupiter! 'Guilt?'

'I did say "or something".' She reached up and kissed me. 'Not that I'm prying, you understand. I'm just curious.'

'Yeah.'

A pause.

'Euelpida was saying that Aristoboulus has taken to staying out late. Some sort of work party at the Lyceum, or so he told her. She was quite concerned.'

'Is that so, now? And what did you say?'

'I told her not to be a fool.'

I laughed and planted a smacker on top of her grin. 'You want to get dressed, lady? Or should we scandalise Bathyllus some more and go as we are?'

'I'll get dressed, thank you. If you'll let me up.'

I did, eventually. When we got downstairs the crisis was unresolved and there was a woman waiting for me in the hall. 'Woman', not 'lady': Bathyllus is a complete snob over things like that. Sometimes I despair.

'She give a name, little guy?' I said.

'No, sir.' A sniff. 'But she said you'd know her when you saw her.'

'Yeah? What's she like?' I stood still while he helped me into my mantle.

'Young. Quite good-looking, sir. In a common sort of way. Oh, and she speaks Latin.'

I almost dropped a fold. Shit. Cotile; it had to be Cotile. What the hell was she doing here?

Perilla was looking at me. I swallowed. 'Uh . . . you want to join us, lady?' I said.

She shook her head and smiled. 'No.'

'Fine.' I turned to the hovering Bathyllus. 'I'll be in the study, Bathyllus. Bring a few lamps and show the lady in.'

It was Cotile, all right. She was nervous as hell.

'Valerius Corvinus,' she said, 'I had to come. I'm sorry.'

'That's okay. No problem.' I pulled up the desk chair and sat her in it. 'You want some wine?'

'No. No, thank you.'

'Have some anyway.' I poured two cups from the jug Bathyllus had left, put one into her hand and took the other over to the reading couch. 'How did you find me?'

'It wasn't difficult. There aren't many purple-stripers in Athens.' We were speaking Latin, and she used the idiomatic word. 'And I'm . . . off at present.'

'Hermippe let you leave the Scallop?'

'We aren't prisoners. Although we're usually expected to ask permission.'

'Did you?'

She hesitated. 'No. No, I didn't.'

Uh-huh. 'You know I talked to Demetriacus yesterday?'

'Yes. Cleo told me. That's why I'm here.' She gulped at her wine. 'You haven't found your friend?'

'Melanthus? No, not yet.' I paused. 'You know where he is?'

'No.' She looked at me in astonishment. 'Why should I?'

'I just assumed . . .'

'I told you. I don't know anything about him. Or no more than I've already said.'

'He's not in the building? Hiding out?'

'I don't know. He could be, I suppose. Hermippe and Demetriacus have their own private quarters in a separate part of the house. We girls aren't allowed in there.'

Uh-huh. Now that was an interesting tidbit; and I wondered if that was 'quarters' singular or 'quarters' plural. If Demetriacus and his manageress were an item it might explain a lot.

'Okay,' I said. 'So why did you come?'

'To tell you what I was going to say when Antaeus interrupted us.' She hesitated. 'When Melanthus left Anthe she thought he might have gone down for a chat with Demetriacus.'

'He what?' I sat back.

'Anthe doesn't know for certain, of course. But he often did. They were good friends.' She must've noticed the expression on my face because her eyes widened. 'Demetriacus didn't mention it?'

'No. No, he didn't.' Mention it, hell: he'd specifically said he didn't know the guy. If Cotile was right he was lying through his teeth. 'You say they were friends?'

'Demetriacus is interested in philosophy. And he wants very badly to be an Athenian gentleman.'

I nodded slowly. That figured: it would explain the careful Greek, for a start. 'An *Athenian* gentleman? You mean he isn't from Athens originally?' Callippus had said he was an incomer, of course, but like I said that meant next to nothing. The word was a technical term, and always had been.

'No. He's a Cypriot. From Paphos.'

I stared at her. Oh, Jupiter! Jupiter best and greatest! 'Demetriacus is a Paphian?'

'Of course. That's why he chose the Scallop's name, for the Paphos connection. He came here about ten years ago and bought the house from Melanthus.'

'Wait a minute.' My brain was spinning. 'Melanthus used to own the Scallop?'

Cotile nodded. 'Anthe didn't know the man's name, but yes. He inherited the property from an uncle. He told Anthe the first time he was with her that the room they were in used to be the old man's study. He found the changes she'd made quite . . . amusing.' She paused. 'Corvinus, I hope I've done right coming here. Only Anthe is fond of Melanthus. She'd want me to help find him.'

'Yeah. Yeah, sure.' I sipped my wine uncomfortably. 'You won't get into trouble over this, will you?'

'If I'm asked I'll say I was visiting one of our old girls. She's married to an oil-shipper and she lives not far from here. She'll cover for me if necessary.'

'Fine.' I took a gold piece out of my purse. 'This is . . .'

'No. No money.' Cotile got up. 'I hope it helps, that's all.'

I saw her out.

I hope it helps.

Jupiter!

27

I sent Cotile back in the carriage and went into the dining-room where dinner was, finally, being served. Perilla had already started.

'Well, Corvinus?' she said. 'Has your girlfriend gone?'

'Uh . . . yeah.' I settled down beside her and held up my cup for Bathyllus to fill. The little guy was still quietly bristling: Bathyllus has standards, and he expects you to keep to them. Good-looking young women turning up unescorted and soliciting private interviews with the master during the hours of darkness come within the Prohibited category. 'Lysias is driving her back to the Scallop.'

'The Scallop?'

'Aphrodite's Scallop.' I helped myself to kidney beans in fennel. 'It's a . . . er . . . property near Ptolemy's Gym.'

'"Property"?'

'Lady, you're beginning to sound like Nestor. Cut it out, okay? You know very well what I mean.'

She ducked her head and kissed me. 'Yes, Marcus, of course I do. I'm sorry. What did the girl have to say?'

'Her name's Cotile.' I gave her the background, minus some of the physical description and without mentioning Cleo at all: honesty in a marriage is one thing, but you can take it too far. Even so, Bathyllus left in the huff halfway through.

'So you think this Demetriacus is involved with Melanthus?' Perilla dipped a chicken wing in the almond sauce.

'To the eyeballs. And why should he be so careful to deny a connection if there wasn't something fishy going on?'

'He could simply be distancing himself from Melanthus's

disappearance. You said he was anxious to preserve his reputation and the reputation of his brothel. And if Melanthus
did leave early that evening then their relationship is irrelevant.'

'He didn't.'

'Marcus, you don't know that! Hermippe stated categorically
that he did.'

'Hermippe was lying. Demetriacus as good as told her to.'

'And you think Melanthus is still there?'

'Where else would he be?' I chewed on a liver meatball. 'The
Scallop's perfect for him. Cotile said Demetriacus has a private
suite which the rest of the staff aren't allowed into and which,
of course, Demetriacus doesn't normally use because he's got a
house of his own. Melanthus would know about that, plus all
the other ins and outs of the place. And I'd give my eye teeth to
see inside it because one gets you ten that's where the bastard's
hiding.'

'Corvinus.' Perilla set the chicken wing down. 'You cannot
break into a private house. Certainly not on the grounds of
mere suspicion.'

'I don't have to. Callippus'll listen to me now if for no other
reason than the original bill of sale for the Scallop has to be on
record. Which will prove that Demetriacus was lying when he
said he didn't know Melanthus. And if he lied about that he
could be lying about everything else.'

Perilla sighed. 'Not necessarily; as I said, he might simply be
concerned for his reputation.'

'Okay.' I emptied my wine cup and refilled it. 'Let's theorise
and see where it takes us. Starting four years back, which is as
long as the Scallop's been in operation. Melanthus is a respected
philosopher, but he's no ivory-tower academic: he's got an itch in
his pants and he likes to scratch it, only discreetly and in civilised
surroundings. So when he inherits his uncle's house he sells it
to Demetriacus. Or maybe he doesn't sell it. Maybe the two of
them go into partnership and set up a cathouse that Melanthus
can patronise in the long term without worrying about stories
going the rounds. Sound reasonable?'

'Reasonable, yes. Convincing, no.'

'Come on, lady! It would work. And I've been inside the

place, remember. It's got style, and you don't buy that, not easily. Whoever planned the decor was no cut-price hack from the Potters' Quarter.'

'Really, Corvinus?' Perilla smiled sweetly. 'And since when have you been an expert on art?'

I ignored her. 'Melanthus is sitting pretty. He's got the house of his dreams stacked with high-class art and high-class whores, and because he has a deal with the owner he can use it as often as he likes. That's another thing: the guy may be comfortably off, but a visit to the Scallop costs an arm and a leg. Twice a month or more regular would bankrupt him in a year. Whereas if he were a partner he'd actually be making on the deal.'

'Unless he was taking his share in kind, of course.'

I almost dropped the wine cup. 'Lady, I'm shocked. Sometimes I wonder about the level of your moral education.'

She grinned. 'Just an observation, and not an unnatural one. You'll also have noticed, by the way, that I haven't asked you how you come to know about the Scallop's charges.'

'Uh . . . yeah.' I reached for the wine jug. 'Yeah. Fair point. Now. Demetriacus. What does he get out of the arrangement? According to—'

'I mean, is there an itemised price list? Or perhaps a general service charge? Or do you simply—'

'Jupiter, lady!' The Setinian splashed over my hand. 'Cut that out right now! This is serious!'

'I'm sorry, Marcus.' She sipped her fruit juice. 'Of course it is. You were saying. Demetriacus.'

'Right.' I finished pouring and took a swallow. 'According to Cotile the guy's got social ambitions. He's a hick from Paphos who wants to shine in high society, and knowing Melanthus is the best thing that's ever happened to him. Demetriacus might have money, but he's got no culture . . .'

'Why on earth shouldn't he be cultured just because he's an immigrant? And Melanthus isn't a proper Athenian himself. He's an Asian Greek.'

I sighed. 'Perilla, you know how things work here. Demetriacus is in trade; he peddles olive oil and bodies for a living. So ipso facto, money or not, as far as the cream are concerned he's an intellectual pygmy. And if he does happen genuinely to know his Aristotle from his Epicurus he's an upstart poser educated beyond his station and gets snubbed anyway. Whichever way he plays it, he loses hands down. Except for one way.'

'And that is?'

'The same method Ptolemy used when he built his gym. Or any other rich outsider you like to name these past three hundred years who wants to be persona grata on the Rock. He becomes a *euergetes*. You know what that means?'

'Corvinus, my Greek is better than yours. Of course I know. A public benefactor.'

'Right. So he goes to his pal Melanthus and asks him how best to do it, because Melanthus knows the ropes. And Melanthus tells him.'

'Tells him what?'

'He tells him about the Baker.'

There was a long silence while Perilla thoughtfully shelled a quail's egg and dipped it in fish sauce.

'Marcus, that's quite ingenious,' she said at last. 'I'm impressed.'

I took a smug swallow of Setinian. 'It's a marriage made in heaven, lady. Demetriacus has the money, Melanthus has the know-how. The perfect partnership. From Melanthus's side, the statue stays in Greece where it belongs, safe from the grasp of filthy materialistic Romans like poor old Priscus. Meanwhile, Demetriacus gets the kudos of having discovered a lost Greek treasure and gifted it to his adopted city. Where they might have sneered if he'd just built them yet another flashy porch to hang their pictures in, the Athenian culture vultures lap the guy up and ask him to dinner.'

'Fine,' Perilla said. 'But there is just one small problem.'

'Yeah? And what's that?'

'Demetriacus didn't buy the statue. If what you're suggesting is correct then he would have openly bid against Priscus and acquired it legitimately.'

'He probably started off that way, sure. The two partners invented a single fictitious bidder called Eutyches . . .'

'Why should they do that, Marcus? If the transaction was intended to be above board then it wouldn't be necessary, surely.'

'How the hell should I know, lady?' I said. 'Maybe Melanthus was embarrassed about two-timing my stepfather. Or maybe they just wanted the gift to be a surprise.'

'Oh.' Perilla shelled another quail's egg. 'Oh, I see.'

Uh-oh. I hated it when she went demure on me. It meant I'd gone out on a limb somewhere and she had the saw ready and waiting.

'You got a problem with that?' I said.

'No. I was just making another silly observation. Ignore it, please. Carry on.'

'Okay.' I gave her a suspicious look, but she was dipping the egg. 'So. They approach Argaius. Only then Demetriacus – or maybe it was Melanthus – has a better idea. Five-foot solid gold statues don't come cheap, and even Demetriacus is no Ptolemy. Both guys have expensive lifestyles to support, and a legitimate purchase would knock a hole in their savings you could sail a trireme through. Especially when there's no material return on the investment. So they decide to cut the corner. "Eutyches" invites Argaius to a meeting on Mounychia and Demetriacus has his Paphian sidekick Prince Charming lift the guy on the way in the hopes of persuading him to let the statue go for the asking. Only by that time Argaius's partner Smaragdus has pulled his double-cross, the Baker is missing again and our pair of public benefactors are in the sewer up to their eyeballs. Worse, a nosey Roman bastard called Valerius Corvinus is raising hell with the local militia and as a result half the partnership is a prime candidate for official scrutiny. Melanthus goes to ground at the Scallop while his pal runs round in circles trying to pick up the pieces.' I paused. 'How am I doing, Aristotle?'

'Very well,' Perilla said. 'There is just one small thing that puzzles me, though.'

'Sure. Spit it out.'

'A legitimately bought gift to the city I could understand; but don't you think the Athenian authorities would be a little apprehensive about accepting a statue obviously acquired by skulduggery?'

'Uh . . .' Damn, 'Maybe. Put like that, I suppose . . .'

'Not to mention subsequent murder, kidnapping, grievous bodily harm . . .'

'Perilla . . .'

'Just a suggestion, Marcus.'

'Yeah. Yeah, thanks. Point taken.'

Perilla leaned over and kissed me. 'Eat your dinner, Corvinus,' she said. 'It'll all work out eventually.'

I bit savagely into a chicken leg. Ah, hell. She was right, of course. About the skulduggery angle, anyway. The Athenian governing class might turn a blind eye in public, sure, if it meant getting the Baker, but privately was another matter, and the private aspect was what Demetriacus was interested in. When the news got around the City's Beautiful and Good that the guy was a crook he'd've been lucky to find an invitation to the opening of the latest sewer branch line hitting his doormat, let alone a ticket for the archon's birthday bash. Still, I was on the right track, I knew I was. And whatever his reasons the bastard had been lying; Perilla couldn't get past that.

Nailing him for it, however, was another matter. I couldn't do that alone; I hadn't the authority.

Next day I'd have to go round and make my peace with Callippus.

28

He had company when I arrived. Well, maybe that was all to the good: at least he'd have to throw me out politely.

'Corvinus.' Not a smile. Callippus was evidently still gravely peeved. 'I was just going to send for you. Take a seat, please.'

Uh-oh. So it was rap-over-the-knuckles time right enough. I pulled up a chair.

'Hey, pal,' I said. 'I'm sorry about landing you in it the other day, but—'

'This is Beryllus. He's an officer from the Melitides Gate station.' The other guy – he was standing – gave me a nod. 'There've been developments. The Melitides lads have found a body.'

A cold finger touched my spine. Oh, no! Not Cotile! I shouldn't've let her go back, especially in my carriage. These things get noticed.

'Luckily Melanthus of Abdera's description was passed out to all the stations in the City.' Callippus still looked serious as hell. 'Melitides were able to identify him and get in touch right away.'

My brain went numb. Sweet gods. Dear, sweet gods. It was impossible.

'Melanthus?' I said. 'The corpse was Melanthus's?'

'We're fairly certain of that, sir.' Beryllus turned to me. 'Although it had been lying for some time. Naturally we're contacting his household for confirmation.'

'He was found by a courting couple late yesterday evening under some bushes on the Hill of the Nymphs.' Callippus was looking at the wall a foot past my left ear.

Oh, shit! Oh, Jupiter best and greatest! I shook my head to clear it. 'How long did you say he'd been there?'

'Three or four days, sir, at least, from the condition of the body. It's a pretty out-of-the-way spot.' Beryllus's lips twisted into a grin. 'Hence the courting couple.'

'And this is the fifth day since Melanthus of Abdera disappeared.' Callippus stood up. 'Very well, Beryllus. You can go. Keep me informed.' The guy nodded and went out. Callippus waited until the door closed behind him. 'Corvinus, I ought to lock you up and throw the key away. If I could, I would, believe me.'

I was still in shock. 'Hey, come on, pal! Just because—'

'You've taken considerable pains to besmirch the name of one of Athens's most prominent citizens while all the time that citizen has been lying murdered under a bush at the edge of town. You've wasted official senior Watch time on fruitless wild-goose chases in the course of which you've done your best on no grounds whatsoever to throw suspicion on other innocent citizens. You've behaved throughout in a boorish, high-handed and completely irresponsible manner which personally I find totally reprehensible. And you have the gall to come back this morning and off-handedly apologise for "landing me in it".'

'Uh . . . yeah.' Well, he had a point: maybe I had screwed things up a little in places.

'Exactly. That response sums you up, Corvinus.' He sat down and pulled a pile of reports towards him. 'Now I have work to do even if you haven't. As far as I'm concerned the case is closed. Melanthus of Abdera was attacked and killed by footpads and his body dumped. Can I say, however, that had we not, on your advice, wasted time and effort in trying to trace the living man we might have found the body before and had a chance of bringing his killers to justice. As it is, that is about as likely as your own chances of setting foot in this office again so long as I am Watch Commander. Now good-day to you. Please ask my clerk to step in as you leave.'

I didn't move: I was getting pretty angry myself now.

'Okay,' I said. 'Sure. After you've explained one or two things. First. What the hell was Melanthus doing on the Hill of the Nymphs? Like you say, it's on the edge of town, and if he was jumped on his way home from the Scallop, pal, then he was going in the wrong fucking direction.'

'That was only where the body was found.' Callippus was glaring at me. 'He could have been killed anywhere. And, Valerius Corvinus, I will not have gutter language used in this station!'

'Yeah, okay. I'm sorry.' I swallowed hard. 'But just answer me this. You say Melanthus was killed by footpads. How many Athens muggers do you know who'll take the trouble to drag a corpse half across town after they've had the guy's purse off him?' I saw his eyes shift. 'His purse was missing, wasn't it?'

'That's beside the point!'

'You mean you don't know? Jupiter, Callippus, I thought you were supposed to be the professional here!'

'*That* is—'

'And one more thing. I'd bet a rotten sardine to the whole of the City treasury that the guy's throat was cut!'

His hand slammed down on the desk between us. 'Now that is enough! I will not have my professional standards brought into question by anyone, least of all a Roman dilettante like yourself!'

'If it's necessary then someone has to do it, pal! And calling names won't get you off the hook either. I'm right about the cause of death, aren't I?'

He took a deep breath: angry Callippus might be, but even angry the guy was fair.

'Very well,' he said at last. 'Yes, Melanthus of Abdera did die from a severed throat. Which is not uncommon in these cases. And no, I do not know whether his purse was missing. But now that you've been so kind as to point out to me the gap in my knowledge, Corvinus, I will remedy it forth-with.'

'You do that, sunshine. And while you're about it you might send someone down to the records office and check a bill of sale.'

That stopped him. 'What bill of sale?'

'A property transfer, dated about four years back. Between Melanthus of Abdera and your friend Demetriacus.'

There was a long silence. 'For the Scallop?' he said at last.

'For the Scallop. The house used to belong to Melanthus. He inherited it from his uncle, and he sold it to Demetriacus.'

'You're sure of this?'

'Sure I'm sure.' Now was no time for fudging. 'There's a firm connection, Callippus.'

I'd got him. Sure I had. 'But Demetriacus said he didn't know Melanthus.'

'He was lying. They've been bosom buddies ever since the Scallop started.'

'Corvinus, if this is another of your half-baked suppositions . . .'

'Just check, okay? That's all I'm asking.'

He gave me a level stare. Then he got up and opened the door. 'Critias!'

The clerk came in. He gave me a nervous look: the party walls in these government offices are pretty thin.

'Go round to Property Records,' Callippus told him. 'You're looking for a deed of sale to a house near Ptolemy's Gymnasium, date about four years ago, seller Melanthus of Abdera, buyer Demetriacus son of Demetrius. I want to know at once if and when you find it.' He looked at me. 'Especially if you don't. You've got that?'

The clerk had been scribbling the details down on his notepad. 'Yes, sir.'

'Do it now.' The guy left and Callippus closed the door gently behind him. 'Corvinus,' he said, 'I swear that this is the last time I listen to you, you understand? And if by any chance Critias doesn't find that deed . . .'

He left the sentence hanging, but the sense was clear. Sure it was. I just hoped Cotile had her facts right.

'He will,' I said. 'And if he does you'll have another talk with Demetriacus?'

'Perhaps.'

'Jupiter on wheels, Callippus!'

'Very well. Yes.' He held up his hand. 'But I do it alone.'

'Oh, come on, pal! I've just given you the information!'

'For which I'm grateful. If, that is, it proves to have any substance. Even so this is official Watch business, and as an ordinary citizen – an *honorary* ordinary citizen – you have no rights in the matter.'

'Okay.' I swallowed; no point in pushing the guy too far. 'Point taken. I'm asking you as a favour to let me tag along. And I give you my solemn word this time there'll be no hassle.'

'Corvinus . . .'

'You want to bring in a portable altar? Or should I take a quick trip down to the Temple of Zeus Herkeios and bring back a notarised statement?'

His lips twisted; like I say, deep down Callippus was an okay guy. 'No. No, that won't be necessary.' He paused. 'I have your word?'

'Absolutely.'

'All right.' He moved the reports back to the side of his desk. 'Now. How did you come by this information of yours?'

'Cotile told me.'

'I thought Hermippe said you were with . . . Cleo, wasn't it?'

'Don't be prissy, Callippus! Cotile was the first girl I talked to. While I was waiting to speak to Hermippe that first visit to the Scallop. Cotile came round to my place off her own bat last night, and since then I've been doing some thinking.'

'As a result of which you've decided Demetriacus is guilty after all?'

'Uh . . . well . . .'

He sighed. 'Come on, Corvinus! If I'm going to interview the man I need all the ammunition I can get. Even if it does derive from half-baked supposition.'

I grinned. 'Okay. Although I may have to modify the original theory a little now.'

'Modify away.'

'Right.' I settled back in my chair. 'I think Demetriacus and Melanthus were partners. Demetriacus wanted to break into society and Melanthus suggested the best way to do it was to buy the Baker and present it to the city. Only Demetriacus had other ideas. He cut the corner and had his pal Prince Charming kidnap Argaius.' I paused. 'Prince Charming's a Paphian, by the way. Did I tell you I'd found that out?'

'No.' Callippus was frowning. 'No, you didn't.'

'My tame coachman pal Dida recognised the accent. And Demetriacus is from Paphos too. Cotile told me last night.'

'That I did know, and I take the point. Most definitely I do.' He steepled his fingers. 'Go on, please.'

'Okay. So much for the original theory. Now we come to the modification. I thought Melanthus was still in on the scam and was hiding out in the Scallop. Obviously I was wrong, but not by much. Let's say he was a more moral character than I gave him credit for. He'd genuinely expected Demetriacus to do an honest deal with Argaius, and when the guy was murdered he put two and two together. He went to the Scallop and faced Demetriacus out, maybe even threatened to denounce him to the authorities.'

'And Demetriacus had him killed.' Callippus nodded. 'It makes sense, Corvinus. Especially since this Melanthus of Abdera is much closer to the man I knew, by repute at least, than the one in your last version. He was an enthusiast, certainly, but he was most definitely not a murderer. Nor would he condone murder.'

'Yeah. That's what Alciphron told me.'

'Demetriacus, now . . . well, I'm afraid I wasn't strictly honest with you over Demetriacus.'

My pulse quickened. 'Is that so?'

'Don't mistake me, I told you no lies. He's done nothing illegal, or nothing that I'm aware of, at least, and as far as the Watch is concerned he's a respectable businessman. But certain friends of mine – friends in business themselves – have mentioned him once or twice. Off the record, of course.' I nodded. These 'off the record' confidences were the reason why someone like Callippus was Watch Commander. He moved in the right circles to pick up inside information that otherwise would never be made public. 'Oddly enough, "cutting corners" is a phrase which crops up rather frequently in these conversations. It explains his success, of course. And Demetriacus is very successful.'

'Yeah. Yeah, I'd believe that,' I said. 'So the guy's a grey area. Respectable enough on the surface, but not averse to the occasional bit of sharp practice within the law.'

'Exactly.' Callippus sat back. 'Your "within the law" being the operative – and cautionary – phrase. So. Judgment suspended. We wait for Critias. And if he finds your deed then I talk to our friend Demetriacus again.' He cleared his throat. 'Meanwhile, perhaps you'd care to tell me about Cleo.'

'Who?'

'Cleo. The girl you left to join our last conversation.'

'Uh . . . yeah.' I hesitated. 'What about her?'

'Oh, come now, Corvinus! Even we soundly married men can do with a little light relief on occasion.'

Priapus on stilts! I'd never have believed it, but there you were: seemingly Aristoboulus wasn't the only guy who had dreams of kicking over the traces. Even Callippus had his human side after all.

Mind you, I'd met his wife.

29

Critias came back with the news that the deed was there, and I breathed again: sure, I hadn't doubted Cotile for a second, but there was just the chance that, if he and Demetriacus had set the Scallop up together, Melanthus had kept the ownership in his own name. So now I had my first bit of hard evidence linking the two.

'So we make another appointment?' I said to Callippus.

'No.'

'What?' I didn't believe this. 'Look, pal . . . !'

'No appointment, Corvinus.' He had a determined look on his face that I hadn't seen before. 'This time we go straight round to the house. I don't like being lied to. And the man has questions to answer.'

'Hey! Great!' I stood up.

'Wait a moment. My questions, not yours. Remember that. I have your word.'

'Sure.' It would be difficult, but if that was the deal I could hack it. 'I've got Lysias outside. I'll give you a lift.'

'That won't be necessary. This is an official investigation and we'll take an official carriage.'

Gods! Talk about pernickety! Still, if the niceties of protocol were all that important to him it was fine with me. I shrugged.

He didn't speak on the way, and I kept my mouth shut. Good practice. Besides, I wanted to keep him sweet. In his present mood Callippus was touchy as a sackful of vipers.

Demetriacus had a modest little mansion outside the Diochares Gate, backing on to Theophrastus Gardens. Successful was right:

he'd even got the Eridanus River flowing through his grounds. A slave led us through the portico to the garden beyond. I took a quick look round and nodded to myself. It fitted: the place was chock-full of statues and ornamental urns big enough to take an oak tree. There was money here by the barrowload, sure, but unlike at the Scallop it didn't whisper, it shouted. Demetriacus had chosen this particular decor himself, without Melanthus's help, and it showed.

He was in a lounger, reading. Serious stuff, I noticed from the label on the roll: Apollonius of Perga's *Conics*. Poetry I can hack, but mathematics is the pits. He set the book aside. For a split second, when he saw us, the guy looked fazed, but he covered it well.

'Commander. Valerius Corvinus. Delighted to see you,' he said. 'Alcis, some wine for our guests.'

The slave bowed and left. I indicated the cup of milk on the table beside him. 'Still having problems, right?'

Callippus shot me a glance. Yeah, well, it had slipped out. Covertly, I held out my hand, palm down, in apology, and he nodded.

'Still having problems, Corvinus.' Demetriacus smiled. He was wearing a plain tunic this morning, but he still looked like a shaved monkey. 'Never be an invalid, young man. It's the most boring thing in life.'

'I'm sorry to disturb you again, sir,' Callippus said. 'Especially since I assured you there would be no more questions. However, there have been fresh developments.'

'Really?' Demetriacus indicated the two chairs opposite. 'Whatever the reason, you're most welcome. Have a seat, please.'

We sat down. 'First of all,' Callippus said, 'we've found Melanthus of Abdera's body.'

If he'd expected to catch the guy out – and I was sure he had – then it didn't work. Demetriacus's face didn't change.

'But that's dreadful,' he said.

'Yes. My colleagues discovered it yesterday evening, on the Hill of the Nymphs. His throat had been cut.'

'Ah.' Demetriacus picked up the cup and took a sip of milk. 'Robbers, I suppose? The Hill of the Nymphs is quite a wild region.'

'Not robbers, sir. At least, we don't think so.' Callippus's eyes went towards me. 'Melanthus was killed elsewhere and his body hidden under some bushes. It was only found by accident.'

'I see.' Demetriacus set the cup down. 'And what does this have to do with me?'

'I wondered if perhaps you'd care to change your statement.' Callippus's voice was neutral. 'About not knowing the deceased. Truth's always helpful, sir, and every piece of information in an enquiry such as this is important.'

'You're accusing me of killing the man?' That came sharp: milk-drinker the guy might be, but underneath he was hard as an Ostian bruiser.

Callippus blinked: like most Athenians he wasn't used to such straight talking. 'No. Of course not.'

'Then why come here?'

'I learned today' – Callippus was still being ponderously official – 'that you purchased your property near Ptolemy's Gymnasium, now called Aphrodite's Scallop, from Melanthus of Abdera. The records office has confirmed this.'

'I see.' The cold eyes rested on me. 'And who would your informant be, may I ask?'

I stared back. Callippus's own eyes didn't move.

'That I'm not at liberty to say, sir, and it's not important. However, the fact of the transaction itself is beyond dispute.'

The slave came back with the wine. Demetriacus waited until he had poured and left. He was still looking at me even when he talked to Callippus. 'Very well. Yes, I knew Melanthus, and yes, he sold me the Scallop.'

'And you have been close friends ever since?'

He paused. 'Yes.'

'Would you mind explaining why you claimed at our last talk that you'd never met the man?'

Demetriacus sighed. 'Watch Commander, I have spent my whole life avoiding irrelevant complications. If I had told you I knew Melanthus – that he was a friend, indeed – I would have been subjected to precisely the pointless interrogation I'm facing now. I may not look it, but I am an extremely busy man, and I have too much on my mind at any one time to bother with trifles.'

'Trifles like murder?'

'Melanthus of Abdera was a friend and an entertaining companion, but he was . . . peripheral.' He frowned. 'If I may use the word of such a first-rate scholar. I'm sorry he's dead, but since I have no idea whatsoever of how he came to be so I feel no pangs of conscience at having lied to you about our relationship.'

'So he didn't visit you in your office at the Scallop the night he died?'

Demetriacus looked at him sharply. 'Who told you that?'

'Did he?'

'Watch Commander, I'm sorry, but I think you had better go. I have a very important business meeting this morning, and I need to relax.'

'You decline to answer?'

'The question has no meaning for me.'

'Very well, sir.' Callippus stood up. I followed him. 'One last thing. I was wondering if you knew a compatriot of yours from Paphos.' He repeated the description of Prince Charming that I'd given him.

Demetriacus pulled himself to his feet. His face was still impassive, but his eyes were narrow slits.

'Alcis!'

The slave came running.

'These gentlemen are just leaving.' He gave me a poisonous look. 'See them to the gate, please.'

Callippus was hard-faced as we got back into the carriage. 'I enjoyed that,' he said.

'Yeah. I could see.'

'My congratulations, by the way. You're a man of your word.'

'It was no sweat. You were doing okay without me, pal.'

The coachman started up, and we rattled along the road to the Diochares Gate. 'Can I drop you?' Callippus said. 'We can cut across to Lyceum Road once we're inside the City boundaries.'

'No, it's okay. Perilla wants some things in town, and Lysias will be waiting. Also, I'd like to talk.'

'Yes. So I imagine.' Even so he was quiet for a good two minutes. Then he said: 'Demetriacus knows your Prince Charming.'

'Yeah.' I'd seen the flash myself, when Callippus had asked his question. 'He didn't like the suggestion he'd talked to Melanthus that night, either.'

'No.' A pause. 'You think he's guilty? That he killed him?'

'Sure. Or had it done, rather. Don't you?'

Callippus nodded slowly. 'There's steel there, Corvinus, under the surface. Not too far under, either. And I wouldn't like to cross him.' He glanced at me. 'Like he thinks you've done.'

'You noticed that?'

'I noticed. And I think that, in the immediate future, you should be very careful. Very careful indeed.'

A cold finger touched my spine. Yeah. I'd go along with that. And I'd already met the guy's hit man. Next time it might be a different story. 'So what do we do?'

'Zeus alone knows.' Callippus sighed. 'We've got no proof, and we're not likely to get any. Demetriacus knows that. Dig, I suppose, and see what comes up. But I'm not hopeful.'

Right. That was the problem. Demetriacus was our villain, sure he was: pinning it on the guy was another matter. 'Unless I can find Prince Charming,' I said.

'If the man's in the City or the Piraeus he's keeping his head well down.'

'Yeah. But sooner or later the bastard's got to come up for air.'

Callippus looked at me. 'Maybe so,' he said. 'But if he does then my advice to you is to watch your back.'

I nodded. I meant to, very carefully indeed. Whatever else we'd achieved today, I knew I'd just made myself an enemy.

∫

30

I did Perilla's shopping – a peace offering for the outraged
Euelpida and a bag of raisins for Nestor – and then went round
to the Eleusinion where I'd arranged for Lysias to pick me up.
He was there already, chewing on a plaited bread ring bought
from one of the hucksters on the steps. I gave the guy his orders,
climbed into the carriage and settled against the cushions to think
while we rattled on our merry homeward way.

Okay. So how far had our little tête-à-tête with Demetriacus
actually taken us? We knew that Demetriacus was 'Eutyches',
or the surviving half of him, anyway. On the other hand, like
Callippus had said, just knowing didn't help us much without
proof, and getting that was going to be a real pain in the
rectum because the guy was smart. Too smart to make any
sudden panicky moves, certainly, and now he knew we knew
his connection with Prince Charming he'd be careful to keep him
under close wraps as well. Maybe even get him out of Athens, if
he hadn't done that already . . .

I ran that last bit past myself again. No, Demetriacus wouldn't
send Prince Charming away. Nothing to do with using him to
settle scores with me; on sober reflection I reckoned that after
our visit I was safer from PC's attentions than I had been for
quite some while, because if Corvinus were found face up in
the morning dew at this stage of the game then Callippus would
come down on his boss like a ton of marble slabs. Which would
be the end of Demetriacus. I hadn't been kidding when I'd talked
in the cellar about crucifixion. That's one thing about the Roman
governing classes; when one of their own gets chopped, even a
neverwuzzer like me, they don't stop to take prisoners.

So Prince Charming was still around somewhere, and he'd stay that way until Demetriacus had the Baker. Forget the theory that he wanted it to buy entrance into the Athens top Five Hundred; that was impractical now even if he'd ever considered it. I doubted if he had, seriously, although he might well have used it as a ploy to hook Melanthus: like Callippus had said, he was a businessman first and last, and there were plenty of rich punters in Asia who'd be glad to give it a place in one of their fancy dining-rooms with no questions asked. Selling it wouldn't be a problem. The tricky part, from his point of view, was finding it; and to do that he'd have to go through Tiny.

Tiny was the key. If Demetriacus didn't know about him already then we might just win out after all. If he did, then . . .

That was what was worrying me. This thing had developed into a race in the dark. I'd just have to keep going and hope I was still ahead.

Perilla was upstairs in her own study, where she goes sometimes when she's got serious reading or writing to do and doesn't want to waste part of her brain fielding half-assed comments from me. Sure enough, when I went in she had a book-roll in her hand that you could've used to stun a rhino.

'Oh, you're back, Marcus.' She kissed me. 'Did you get Euelpida's present?'

'Yeah.' I handed her the ivory plaque I'd picked up in one of the specialist shops on the Panathenaia. 'Look and marvel, lady.'

She looked, and giggled. 'Marcus, I can't give her this! She'd never forgive me!'

'What's wrong with it? I thought Artemis fleeing from Alphaeus was pretty apt.'

'Yes, but . . .'

'You should've seen some of the others. At least the guy's in proportion.'

That finally got me a grin. 'Corvinus, you're hopeless! I should have gone myself.'

'Too late now.' I brought out the bag of raisins. 'These are for Nestor. If we're very lucky the bastard'll choke on the pips.'

Perilla marked her place in the roll with a slip of paper and set it aside. 'How did your interview with Callippus go? Is he still angry?'

'No. He was okay. Latterly, anyway.' I hesitated. 'And he's found Melanthus. The guy's been dead for days.'

'Oh.' Perilla went very still. 'Oh, dear.'

'Yeah. But at least it clears the ground, and we've got our villain for sure this time.' I told her about the interview with Demetriacus. 'Now all we need is proof.'

'Callippus is reopening the case?'

'He's got no choice.' I sat down on the edge of her couch. 'He'll have backing, too, because Melanthus had important friends. And with luck Demetriacus will slip up somewhere.'

'You think that's possible?'

'Anything's possible.' I told her my latest theory. 'Now Callippus believes he's guilty he won't let go.'

'But, Marcus—'

There was a knock on the door. I turned round. 'Yeah?'

'I'm sorry, sir.' Bathyllus's voice. 'A visitor.'

'Come in, little guy. We're decent. What visitor?'

Bathyllus stuck his head round the door. 'He's waiting in the street, sir. With his carriage.'

'His carriage?'

'It's that public coach driver, sir.' Bathyllus sniffed. 'He says he has news for you. Something about finding a man you're looking for.'

Holy gods! Dida had found Prince Charming! I looked at Perilla. She'd gone very pale.

'Marcus, be careful.' She touched my arm. 'Please.'

'Yeah. Yeah, I'll be careful.' I kissed her. 'Maybe things are breaking after all. I'll see you later, lady.'

Dida was grinning.

'Your slave tell you?' he said. 'We've got him, lord.'

'Great! Good work!'

'One of the lads had a fare to Colonus and he spotted him going into a house near the Shrine of Hera. I can take you there now, if you want.'

'Sure.' I was getting in to the carriage when a thought struck me. 'Hold on, Dida. I'll be back in a moment.'

Bathyllus was hovering in the hall, making sure I didn't get mugged by the working classes for my sandals. 'Hey, little guy,' I said. 'These two bruisers we use for lugging oil jars. They around?'

'Yes, sir. They'll be in the kitchen, I expect.'

'Dust them down and bring them outside. And roust out a couple of decent clubs.'

'Clubs, sir?' His eyebrows went up to where his hairline would've been, if he'd had one.

'Clubs.' If I was going to pay a visit to Prince Charming I wanted some insurance, and these two were the best policy I could get. 'Preferably with nails in.'

A sniff. 'Clubs with nails in, sir. Certainly, sir. I'll search the broom closets.'

Supercilious bastard. I went back out to Dida.

'Slight delay,' I said. 'We're taking on passengers. Now where did you say our Paphian pal was stashed?'

Dida frowned. 'It's not him, lord. It's the other.'

'The other?' For a moment, I was fazed. Then I remembered. Of course: I'd asked Dida to look out for two men. 'You mean the Ethiopian?'

'Sure. And before you ask, it's definitely a home address because the guy went straight in.'

'Uh-huh. Nice going, friend.' Well, one out of two wasn't bad. And I'd like a few words with Hercules, certainly.

'You wanted us, master?'

The insurance policy had turned up, grinning and fingering very serious damage limitation clauses. Evidently broom closets were more interesting places than I'd thought.

'Sure, boys.' I jerked my head towards the carriage. 'In you get. We're going for a ride.' I doubted now that they'd be necessary – if the Ethiopian had wanted to put a permanent crease in my skull he could've done it the last time we'd met – but they looked so happy I didn't have the heart to send them back.

I made sure I had my knife in its wrist sheath, though. Some things you don't take for granted.

The property near the Shrine of Hera was pretty upmarket, even for Colonus, which is out in the suburbs and one of the places the rich and good choose to build. Not in Demetriacus's league, of course, but a good solid detached house in a prosperous street, with a walled garden and a freshly whitewashed front. We pulled up outside.

'Wait here, Dida,' I said, getting out. 'You boys come with me. And no unauthorised moves. We don't want to annoy the neighbours. Clear?'

'Clear, master,' the spokesman said. The guy looked disappointed, but they'd had their trip out and I couldn't be expected to provide all the entertainment.

Okay. So here went nothing. I lifted the heavy bronze knocker and let it fall.

The door was opened by a slave dressed in a smart blue tunic. His eyes widened when he saw the Heavenly Twins, but he bowed and stepped back into the lobby. I was impressed: I could've been paying a courtesy call on some grey-haired ex-archon. For that matter, maybe I was.

'Come in, lord,' the slave murmured. 'The master is expecting you.'

'Uh . . . he is?' That was news to me, unless the guy was an augur.

'Yes, lord. If your name is Marcus Valerius Corvinus. He has been for several days now, I understand.'

I blinked: somebody was crazy here, and I didn't think it was me. I waved the twins in ahead and stepped over the threshold.

'You . . . uh . . . mind telling me your master's name?' I said. 'Just for the record?'

The door slave's eyebrows rose several notches; well, from his point of view I suppose it did sound a pretty stupid question for an expected visitor to ask, but I was beyond caring.

'Eutyches, lord,' he said.

My jaw almost hit the fancy marble floor. *'Who?'*

'Eutyches.' He turned. 'He's in the garden at present. If you'd care to follow me, please.'

I went in a dream. The slave led me through the portico into a walled garden at the back, where a little guy in a bright yellow tunic was sitting in the shade of a pear tree communing with nature. When he saw me coming he got up smiling and came towards me, his hand held out, and a huge chunk of the puzzle fell gently into place.

Eutyches. Shit. Of course he was. How could I have been so stupid?

31

'Felix,' I said.

'How marvellous to see you again, sir.' He was beaming as we shook hands. 'You're looking terribly well. And Lamprus sends his best regards.'

I turned to my two bodyguards. 'Okay, boys, holiday's over, I won't be needing you now. You can go back to the carriage and twiddle your thumbs.' They gave me a reproachful look and trooped back inside. 'Felix, you bastard, I've made a total mess of this business. Do you want to kick me round the garden, or should I do it myself?'

'Oh, not a total mess, sir,' Felix said brightly. 'We can't function with one hundred per cent efficiency all the time. And you're here now. That's what matters.'

'Yeah.' I had the feeling that that added up to something less than a compliment, but I didn't have the energy to work out the whys and wherefores. Also I deserved all the insults the guy could throw at me.

We'd been followed out by a wine slave holding an ornate silver jug. Wordlessly, he poured out a cup and set it and the jug on the table beside me. At a nod from Felix he bowed and left.

I pulled up a chair. 'How's your boss, pal? Still waiting for the call and buffing up his winged sandals?'

Felix's smile faded. 'Prince Gaius is very well, Corvinus; but as I think I told you last time we met certain jokes are in poor and very dangerous taste. Very dangerous taste indeed.'

Yeah. I did remember that, now he came to mention it; but that was long ago, in another country, and besides the guy wasn't there to hear me bad-mouth him. Or at least I hoped he wasn't. I picked up the wine cup and took a swig . . .

The wine slipped past my tonsils like velvet, giving them a warm hug and a kiss in passing.

'You like it?' Felix was smiling again, at my expression this time. 'Imperial Caecuban, from the master's own store. He gave me a jar before I left Rome and told me that if our paths did happen to cross I was to welcome you properly.'

'Uh-huh.' Well, maybe Gaius wasn't all that bad after all. He might be a dangerous, loopy, overbred bastard who suffered from delusions of grandeur, but he had style. I sat back and sipped contentedly. 'So. What have you been doing with yourself since we put the skids under Sejanus?'

'Consolidating, sir. The emperor is failing fast. It can't be long before the master succeeds him.' That was all he knew: I reckoned it at about a month short of five years, give or take a few days, but I'd given the Wart my promise and I kept my mouth firmly shut. Where imperial secrets were concerned you didn't mess around, especially with this one. 'However, Prince Gaius sent me over here on a purely private matter.'

'To bid against me for Priscus's statue.'

'Quite, sir.'

'I should've guessed it was you from the name you chose. Eutyches is just the Greek version of Felix. Both names mean "Lucky". That was intentional, wasn't it?'

'Of course. If I may say so, sir, you really should have spotted that long ago. Mind you, it's not an uncommon name.'

'Uh-huh. Nevertheless. Did I mention the kicking?'

'You did, sir.'

'Fine.' I took another sip of the Caecuban. 'The name aside. Those snazzy tunics your Ethiopian pal wears. I was supposed to pick up on them as well, right?'

'Memnon does tend to favour a more conservative style. He was quite difficult to persuade.'

'Yeah. I see.' Jupiter, I'd been thick! Still, it was no use crying now. I'd had my chance, and I'd muffed it. 'You mind telling me why you bothered in the first place?'

He smiled. 'A little game, sir. Rather a childish one, I admit, although I did hope you'd catch on to it. For obvious reasons when he sent me out on this business the master insisted on anonymity, but I thought since you were to be our competitor I'd give you a fighting chance all the same. And, naturally, myself an opportunity to renew an acquaintance which I found most stimulating.'

'Yeah. Sure.' I wasn't impressed: where Felix is concerned I'm immune to flattery. 'So when Argaius was murdered and your line to the Baker went cold you put a tail on me in the hope that I'd find it for you.'

'I have always had the utmost confidence in your detective ability, Valerius Corvinus,' Felix said primly. 'You know that. It was simply a matter of time. But you're wrong in one respect. Argaius's murder didn't affect me at all, not in the business sense. I had no dealings with Argaius whatsoever. In fact I never even met him.'

I'd been picking up the wine jug to refill my cup. Now I put it down like it was made of glass. Everything went very still.

'Run that one past me again, would you?' I said carefully.

'Of course. As far as Prince Gaius and I were concerned the seller was Smaragdus. He wrote directly to the master in his own name and without mentioning a partner. I'd assumed you knew that.'

'Felix.' The back of my neck was prickling like hell. 'Let's get this clear. Smaragdus told me that Argaius handled the business side of things; that he – Smaragdus – wasn't involved; and that he – still Smaragdus – had never met you.'

Another smile; broader this time. 'Then I'm afraid, sir, that he was lying.'

'Jupiter!' I rubbed my forehead: my brain was starting to hurt. Sure, it was possible, if you looked at it from the other side: I'd never met Argaius myself, and the only evidence of the arrangement between the partners had come from Smaragdus. If what Felix said was true – and I didn't see why it shouldn't be – the guy had been planning his swindle from the beginning. But *that* meant . . .

'Corvinus? Sir?' Felix was peering at me with a worried expression on his face. 'Are you all right?'

'No,' I said. 'All right, pal, is the last thing I am. Look, I need to talk this through. Stop me if I go off beam, okay?'

'Very well.'

I took another swallow of the Caecuban first: I'd need all the help I could get here.

'First off, Smaragdus writes to your boss claiming to own the Baker and offering to sell it, yes?'

Felix nodded. 'Correct.'

'At the same time he already knows – because Argaius is acting up front – that his partner has another deal cooking with me. However, he doesn't let on to him that he has a second customer in line. Gaius is private and personal, and he keeps him strictly under wraps.'

'That I wouldn't know. But certainly Smaragdus represented himself as the statue's sole owner. Its *sole* owner. It wasn't until—'

I held up my hand. 'Wait. Let's take things bit by bit, because I haven't got them straight myself yet and they're complicated, okay?'

'Very well.' Felix was leaning back in his chair, his fingers steepled. 'Go on, sir. Oh, you can't believe how much I'm enjoying this!'

'Bully for you, chum. Okay. Smaragdus has plans, private plans: he'll sell the Baker to Gaius behind Argaius's back with the intention of slipping off with the cash as soon as the deal goes through. Only then he thinks of a refinement. He'll move the Baker to another hiding place and pretend . . .' I stopped. 'No. That doesn't make sense.'

'What doesn't make sense?'

'I was going to say he'd pretend to Argaius that the statue had been stolen and so buy himself some extra time. But that wouldn't work now.' I scowled. 'Shit!'

'Why not, sir? Surely as you say it would give him some leeway with his partner; and as far as bringing me to the statue was concerned one cave was as good as another.'

One cave was as good as another. That was the second time that point had come up. There was something . . .

'Corvinus?' Felix was looking faintly puzzled. 'Didn't you hear what I said? The fact that Smaragdus had moved the statue to a different hiding place wouldn't register with anyone but Argaius. However, if Smaragdus wanted to pretend it had been stolen then naturally moving it was essential.'

'Yeah,' I said slowly. 'That was my original theory. But at the time I thought Argaius was dealing with you.'

'So?'

'Come on, Felix! Smaragdus had you set up as the villain. If Argaius didn't know you existed then he wouldn't have anyone to point the finger at.'

Felix stared; I could see him working that one out. Then he said softly: 'You're right. Of course you are. Oh, well done, sir!'

'Argaius wasn't stupid. Only he and Smaragdus knew the location of the cave. If Smaragdus had come to him and told him someone had robbed the pantry he would've put two and two together pretty fast. And yet we know that Smaragdus shifted the Baker before Argaius's death because otherwise his killer would've found it. So my question is, why did Smaragdus do it?'

'Perhaps as a safeguard. He knew Argaius was dealing with you. The deal could have been formalised at any time, and Argaius would have got in first.'

'Yeah, that's a possibility. But if so the guy was running one hell of a risk. All it would take was for Argaius to arrive and find the cupboard bare for the excrement really to hit the shovel.' I frowned: the answer was there, if I could only get it. *One cave would be as good as another* . . . 'Ah, leave it for now. Maybe it'll come. You want to tell me more from your side, pal?'

'There isn't much more to tell.' Felix topped up my wine cup. 'I discovered – completely by accident – that Smaragdus normally worked with a partner. Naturally I was concerned, as I knew Prince Gaius would be, that the transaction was above board and this partner's rights were not in any way being infringed.'

I grinned. 'Sure you were concerned!' I liked Felix, but that didn't blind me to the fact that the guy's ethical code had more holes in it than a cabbage-strainer; while Gaius wouldn't know what an ethic was if one jumped up and bit him. 'But you also wanted to make certain there'd be no comeback later if it turned out Smaragdus hadn't the sole right to sell.'

'There was that aspect of the matter too, of course.' Felix

looked pained and virtuous. 'In any case, having learned of
Argaius's existence I sent Memnon to him to arrange a meeting.'

Uh-huh. Memnon being my Ethiopian pal. This was all beginning to make sense.

'Just that?' I said. 'Just a suggested meeting? You didn't
mention the background details?'

'I didn't think background details were necessary.' Felix
paused. 'Or, in the circumstances, politic. If the sale turned
out not to be wholly above board after all then the time for that
fact to come out was when the two of us were face to face.'

'And you arranged the meeting for Mounychia, right?'

'Correct.'

'Why Mounychia? That's out in the sticks even by Piraeus
standards, Felix. At night, especially.'

'A combination of business with pleasure, sir,' he said stiffly.
'There was a full moon that night, and I wanted to see the Shrine
of Bendis by moonlight. It was most impressive, and well worth
the effort.'

'Uh, yeah.' Gods alive! Well, the little guy was entitled to his
idiosyncrasies, I supposed, but that was pushing it. 'Still, you told
me earlier you'd never met Argaius.'

'I didn't meet him, Corvinus. He didn't turn up. Of course,
now I realise why.'

'Yeah.' I swallowed a reflective mouthful of Caecuban. 'Had
you, uh, told Smaragdus about this meeting beforehand, by any
chance?'

Felix was no fool. There was a long silence before he answered.

'Yes, sir, as a matter of fact I had. When I brought up with
him the subject of his partner's existence. Naturally I asked him
to pass the message on, although for obvious reasons I informed
Argaius independently.'

'Uh-huh. What did Smaragdus say when you told him you
knew about Argaius?'

'That he was fully empowered to conduct negotiations on
behalf of his partner. He hadn't thought Argaius's direct involvement was necessary.'

And I thought that I'd been stupid! 'Jupiter, Felix! And you
believed him?'

'Let's say I found it . . . politic, again, not to comment. But it did make a meeting between the three of us more imperative. Remember, as far as I was concerned the deal was already concluded.'

'And Argaius didn't come. For obvious reasons. What about Smaragdus?'

'No. I never saw him again.'

The timing fitted. Sure it did. If his landlady was to be trusted Smaragdus had already packed his bags and lit out for the beach hut.

We looked at each other. It was Felix who put the shared thought into words.

'Smaragdus knew his partner was going to die, didn't he, sir?'

I nodded slowly. 'Yeah. He knew, all right. He set it up.' Good sweet Jupiter! And I'd felt sorry for the murdering bastard!

'There was one thing that puzzled me, even at the time.' Felix shifted in his chair. 'Smaragdus's desire to avoid Argaius I can understand. But why me? I was a committed purchaser, his best and only option, and as I said the bargain was made. Wouldn't it have been more sensible for Smaragdus to have come to the meeting, professed surprise at his partner's absence or made some excuse for it and brazened the matter out?'

'Felix, pal.' I managed to keep my face straight, although it wasn't easy. 'You mean you wouldn't, honest citizen that you are, have called off the deal, at least temporarily while you checked with the authorities?'

Felix smiled. 'Oh, I don't believe that would have been necessary, sir. After all, as the single surviving partner Smaragdus would have had a perfect right to make the sale, wouldn't he?'

'Yeah,' I said drily. 'In that case I see your point. Gaius must want the Baker pretty badly.'

'It is a unique piece, Valerius Corvinus. And we had already gone to considerable trouble and expense to acquire it.'

I took another swallow of wine. Well, I wouldn't really have expected anything else from that pair: Gaius was no Priscus, and although I was willing to stretch things I wouldn't put myself on a par with Felix, either. I reached for the wine jug . . .

The itch at the back of my brain came back in full force.

• David Wishart

Only this time, suddenly, I knew what I'd been trying to tell myself ever since Felix had mentioned the cave. *His best and only option* . . .

'Oh, gods alive,' I murmured. 'It's beautiful.'

'Sir?' Felix gave me a sharp look. I waved him down and sat back as the pieces of the puzzle slipped smoothly into place.

'"His best and only option",' I said. 'Best maybe, but not only.'

'You mean he considered selling the statue to you?'

I shook my head. 'No, not to me. He had his chance to do that when we met, and he still took me to the wrong cave. I was the one prospect who was out of the running, because I'd have scruples. He could afford to drop me without a qualm because he still had two customers left.'

'Two?'

'Yeah.' I felt very tired; and, unaccountably, very sorry for Harpalus: the poor bastard hadn't known what he was in on, and it had killed him. 'You were one, potentially at least.'

'And the other?'

'The other was a guy called Demetriacus.'

32 ∫

He'd had to be involved somewhere, sure, but I hadn't worked out where until now. However, with Smaragdus's scam clear in my mind for the first time – or at least reasonably clear in what passed for my mind – this was the only way that made sense.

'Demetriacus?' Felix said.

'You don't know about him?'

'No, sir. A recent discovery of your own, I assume.'

'I thought your guy Memnon was tailing me.'

'Not lately, sir. I'd decided that the time had come for us to meet direct. I instructed Memnon to – shall we say – make himself obvious in the hope that you would find him at second-hand, and so me. As indeed you did.'

'This was part of the game, was it?'

'Yes, sir. Of course.'

Jupiter! 'You couldn't just have sent the guy round to introduce himself, I suppose?'

'That would not be in accordance with the rules I'd set myself,' Felix said primly. 'I told you about the master's instructions regarding anonymity.'

'Yeah. Okay. Forget I asked.' I'd never understand Felix. The guy's thought processes were so convoluted he was lucky he didn't strangle himself going to the bathroom. 'Demetriacus is a local businessman. Among other pies he has his finger into is a brothel called Aphrodite's Scallop.'

'Ah, yes. That name is certainly familiar from Memnon's reports.'

A thought struck me. 'By the way. The cellar your gorilla pulled me out of. Was that the Scallop or not?'

'No, sir. It belonged to a house not far from here. The owner is abroad and the property is empty at present. That I did discover.'

'Uh-huh.' Well, that made sense, although I'd bet a jar of Falernian to a pickled walnut Demetriacus had charge of the keys. 'You have the address?'

'It's in Collytus, near the Temple of Zeus Phratrios. The owner's name is Polyhymnius.'

'Thanks.' I made a mental note. Callippus would be able to check it back, and it might give us another strand to the rope he was plaiting to hang the bastard. 'Memnon didn't think to follow Prince Charming when he left me tied up at all? Or did he?'

Felix sighed. 'Memnon may be willing, but he is not unduly burdened with brains. His instructions were to follow you and watch your back. He interpreted them literally.'

'A pity he didn't interpret them literally when the guy slugged me in the first place, pal.'

'That is a sore point, I'm afraid. No pun intended.' I grinned. 'He did, I understand, witness the attack, although he was too late to prevent it. He considered that his priority thereafter was to follow and release you when opportunity offered.'

Yeah. There were holes in that one as well, but I didn't have either the time or the energy to bother with them now. 'Okay. It's done. Leave it. Let's talk about Demetriacus.'

'By all means.' I noted with interest that Felix seemed relieved.

'So.' I topped up my wine cup. 'Background. Up to now Smaragdus has managed to keep you and Argaius apart, but just when he's ready to do the trade you hit him with the news that you've found he's got a partner and you want to meet the guy. Smaragdus is caught, and he knows it. He's got two options. One: he forgets the scam, goes to Argaius, tells him he's negotiated a sale, and takes his legitimate cut. The problem with that is that it comes too late. Argaius has set up a deal already, and he's going to be pretty surprised to find out he's suddenly got two customers ready to buy instead of one; also, pretty suspicious that Smaragdus hasn't told him about this second prospect before. And finally he's positively going to hit the roof when the three of you get together and he finds out you'd never heard of him.'

Felix nodded. 'A fair assessment, sir. The second option?'

'Smaragdus solves the problem by murdering Argaius. On the face of it, this is attractive because when the sale goes through he ends up with the whole amount, which was his plan to begin with. The trouble is that option's too risky, because Argaius's death puts the deal into a whole new league, one that needs either total imbecility or total complicity on the part of his customer. Scratch imbecility: no one's that stupid. As for complicity, well, you and I may know Gaius wouldn't care a pickled anchovy about Argaius so long as he got the Baker, but Smaragdus can't be certain. Added to which now murder's involved our pal the Crown Prince would expect him to drop the price in exchange for a bit of imperial strabismus.'

Felix was smiling. 'Oh, Corvinus! You wrong the master, you really do!'

'Is that so, now?' I said drily. Like hell I did: where his own interests were concerned, Gaius was as single-minded as a fox in a chicken-run, and Felix would be on his side all the way. 'On the other hand, if you don't turn out to be an idiot or a crook after all' – Felix's smile widened – 'then the authorities are going to be involved. In which case Smaragdus will be asked questions he'd prefer not to answer.'

'But Argaius needn't actually be *found* murdered, sir. He could simply disappear. At least until the sale was made.'

'Exactly. That'd be sensible, and it would certainly grease the wheels because it would provide a moral let-out clause for a customer not unduly burdened with scruples.' Another smile. 'The only thing is, it didn't happen. Argaius's body was dumped the night after he went missing, in the most public place in Athens. Common sense says if Smaragdus had killed him or arranged his death he wouldn't have played it that way.'

'Unless he wanted to stage a bluff, perhaps? If Argaius were killed between his house and Mounychia Smaragdus would naturally be a prime suspect. However, if the body were found elsewhere and exhibited signs of torture – as it was and did – the implication would be that others were responsible who knew of the Baker's existence but not its whereabouts. With the man demonstrably dead by hands unknown and the body quickly recovered there might be no obstacle to finalising an unrelated business deal.' Felix smiled brightly. 'I'm speaking theoretically, sir, of course.'

Jupiter with little bells on! The guy had a nastier imagination than I had! 'You think Smaragdus was capable of that degree of sophistication?'

'Perhaps not. But it is a suggestion.'

'Sure. Only it doesn't explain why Smaragdus kept his head down even after he knew Argaius was gone.'

'Very well.' Felix nodded. 'Accepted.'

'And given that fact, the next question's obvious: if the guy was in hiding, really in hiding, then who and what was he afraid of?'

'You have the ball, Valerius Corvinus.' Felix sat back. 'Carry on. This is fascinating.'

'Okay.' I sank another mouthful of the Caecuban. 'A scenario. Let's say Smaragdus has a third option. He approaches – or is approached by, or maybe he already has been approached by – another potential customer who we'll call for sake of argument Demetriacus and who is unquestionably as crooked as a snake's backbone. They talk and come to an arrangement. Smaragdus will sell Demetriacus the Baker at a bargain price. Say two-thirds of what he and Argaius were asking together.'

Felix's eyes narrowed. 'That's quite a drop, sir. And one – if I've followed you correctly – that Smaragdus was unwilling to make. Why should he do so now?'

'Wait. There's another side to the deal, and that's the clincher. In exchange, Demetriacus undertakes to murder Argaius in a way that'll leave Smaragdus in the clear and provide a red herring or two in the process.'

'Ah!' A nod. 'Oh, I see.'

'Only then comes the twist, because remember we're talking about crooks here. After the agreement's been reached both guys independent of each other proceed to go back on it. Sure, Demetriacus kills Argaius as per contract, but before he does he persuades the guy to tell him where the Baker is; the idea being, of course, to heist the statue under Smaragdus's nose and leave him high and dry with no comeback. Meanwhile, however, Smaragdus has staged his own heist and moved the gold elsewhere. And when Demetriacus finds Argaius's cave empty and realises he's been outmanoeuvred he is not a happy little criminal.'

'Hence Smaragdus's continued disappearance and Demetriacus's attempts to trace the statue before and after his partner's death.' Felix was beaming. 'Beautiful, sir. My congratulations.'

'Yeah, well. It explains the facts, anyway.' I paused. 'Or all of them apart from one, rather.'

'And that is?'

'Smaragdus is sitting pretty. Argaius is dead and he has the Baker to himself. His only problem is that now he has no one to sell to.'

Felix's smile froze. 'Yes. Yes, I suppose that's true.'

'He's shafted Demetriacus, and the guy may still want the statue but only with Smaragdus's giblets hung round its neck. Me, I'm out: like I said, Smaragdus had his chance to make a proper pitch when we met and he blew it, intentionally, by taking me to the wrong cave.' I paused, and then said slowly: 'So, pal, you were the only one left.'

Felix's smile was still there, but it was false as an octogenarian's curls. 'But I told you, Valerius Corvinus,' he said. 'I didn't see Smaragdus after our last encounter several days before his partner's death. And I certainly did not know where he was hiding.'

'Yeah. Maybe not. But when I went to see his boyfriend Harpalus to arrange the meeting Harpalus assumed I'd come from you. The implication is that Smaragdus was expecting some sort of contact to be made. If he wasn't in touch already.'

'Harpalus needn't have been aware that our relationship had ended.'

'That wasn't the impression I got. Another thing. When I talked to Harpalus after I'd found Smaragdus's body he said he hadn't described me to his friend, he'd just said I was a Roman. That seemed to be enough for Smaragdus.'

'But I'm not a Roman, sir. I was born in Corinth.'

'Come on, Felix! You know what I mean! I don't care if your mother had bandy legs and drank mare's milk. Smaragdus knew who you worked for. The day I met him he was expecting a Roman, sure. I just wasn't the one he had in mind.'

'Sir.' Felix faced me levelly. 'I give you my bonded word that I had no other dealings with Smaragdus than those of which I've informed you.'

We stared at each other. He was lying, we both knew that. Proving it on my side was another matter, and we knew that too. The silence lengthened . . .

Ah, hell; right or not, I was in a no-win situation here, and it probably didn't matter anyway because that particular deal had never gone through. I shrugged my shoulders and sank a bit more of the Caecuban. 'Fine, fine. Okay, we'll leave that as it stands.'

Felix gave a small grunt. Maybe it was indigestion, not relief, but I wouldn't've laid any bets.

'So, sir,' he said, and his voice was cheerful again. 'What happens now?'

'I carry on trying to find the statue. Plus Callippus and me do our best to nail Demetriacus.'

'I see.' He paused and then said tentatively: 'Perhaps then, sir, we can work together on your first objective.'

'Gee, that'd be nice, Felix, but somehow I don't think it would be a terribly good idea.'

He looked pained. 'Valerius Corvinus! Our interests coincide here! And if we do find the Baker I'm sure we can come to some amicable arrangement as to its disposal.'

I hesitated; I didn't trust Felix above half, but he was smart, too smart to antagonise and too dangerous to ignore. Also if you made certain allowances – considerable allowances – he was straight enough to rank with the good guys, if only just. Lastly, I needed the help. Sure I did.

'Maybe,' I said finally. 'Give me a day or so to think it over.'

'If that's the way you feel, sir' – he drew himself up with great dignity – 'then there's no more to be said.'

Huff, huff, pout, pout. I grinned. 'Okay. So how does this sound? If I find the Baker I hand it over to the public auctioneer and we bid for it fair and square. Agreed?'

'Ah.' Felix's eyes glazed. 'You . . . ah . . . think that's necessary under the circumstances? After all this was a private arrangement, and with both principals dead we are the only two parties involved.'

Oh, no: I wasn't going to let the bastard wriggle out that easy!

'That's the deal, pal, take it or leave it. Argaius and Smaragdus may be dead, but Argaius left a wife in Crete. I'd like her to get what's coming to her. And if you do outbid me in the end I'm sure Priscus won't be too disappointed to have lost out to an imperial.'

'It might be advisable for him to do so in any case, sir.' Felix didn't smile. 'If you take my meaning.'

Jupiter! That was something I hadn't thought of. Maybe we were lucky to be living under the Wart after all; and in five years' time we wouldn't be. Gaius would be emperor, and he was the sort who'd bear a grudge until hell froze over.

'Yeah,' I said carefully. 'Yeah, I take your meaning, pal. I'll bear that in mind. So. Do we have a deal or not?'

'We have a deal, sir.' Felix stood up. 'But I mustn't keep you. No doubt you have more important things to do. It's been a delight to see you again, Valerius Corvinus, and, as always, extremely stimulating. Please do keep in touch.' He held out his hand.

'I mean to.' Sure I did, if only to make sure the bastard didn't throw me a wobbler the first chance he got. We shook. 'My regards to Memnon, by the way. He isn't around?'

Felix didn't hesitate. 'I gave him the day off, sir. Knowing that we would be talking. It's his choir evening at the local men's club, and he always likes to attend if he can.'

'Yeah.' Gods alive! 'A choir evening. Right. You ... uh ... intend suspending him from duty altogether, by the way?'

'That,' Felix said primly, 'very much depends on you, sir. And on your decision re locating the statue.'

Well, I couldn't expect anything different, I supposed. But it did mean that I'd have to be extra-specially careful over Tiny. Felix might be okay at base, but his loyalties were fixed. If he got a crack at the Baker without me holding his lead Chrysoulla had as much chance of getting her money as paddling back from Crete on a washboard. Still, it had been good talking to the little guy again.

Besides, now I had something to take back to Callippus.

Dida was still waiting outside with the Twins.

'You find the man, lord?'

'Yeah,' I said. 'In a manner of speaking.' I took out my purse and held out a gold piece. 'Thanks, pal. Split this with your friends. Don't spend it all in the one shop.'

He grinned and pocketed the money. Gods alive, I was keeping the whole carriage-drivers' union in funds here! Or rather Priscus was. Still, it was worth it, and next time they might find Prince Charming for me.

'Where to now?' Dida said.

'Home, Dida.' I got in. 'That's enough for one day.'

We started off. The Twins weren't looking as happy as they had when we'd set out, but that was their worry. Well, maybe between here and the Lyceum Road we'd get hit by a gang of marauding Scythians who'd zigged instead of zagged at the Black Sea and they could try out their shiny new clubs. Meanwhile I closed my eyes and did my best to block out the smell of oil-jar-shifters' armpits.

That little conversation had been interesting, in more ways than one. Sure, finding out that Eutyches was my old pal Felix closed off one avenue of enquiry, but it raised the fresh question of how far I could trust the little weasel. Not that the answer was all that difficult: judging by both past and present acquaintance I'd put the distance at about half as far as I could spit. Felix had lied about his later contacts with Smaragdus, that was certain: there was no way Smaragdus would've painted himself into a corner over customers, and the fact that he'd taken me to the wrong cave instead of welcoming me with open arms, scruples or not, was a clincher. Shafting Demetriacus argued for a connection, too: I doubted if Smaragdus would've been brave enough or stupid enough to double-cross a guy like that unless he was pretty certain he had a fall-back, and a fall-back with clout, what was more. Felix's boss had that in spades; and remembering what Harpalus had said about Pergamum and Alexandria I'd bet good money that the little guy had sweetened the prospective deal with the offer of an anonymous place on the first ship out and guaranteed protection the other end.

Yeah. If I hadn't been quite so certain Demetriacus was our man I'd be having grave doubts about Felix . . .

The driver's flap rattled. I opened my eyes.

'Lord?'

'Yeah, Dida.'

'I thought I'd tell you. Your Ethiopian. He's tailing us again. Plainer tunic but it's the same man.'

Uh-huh. So much for the choir at-home: the guy had probably been feeding his face in the kitchen all the time. Jupiter! That little bastard would lie on principle if you asked him what direction the sun rose! He must get some perverse kick out of it, like he did playing these damned games of his.

'You want to stop?' Dida said.

'No. That's okay. It isn't worth the effort. Just ignore him.'

'You're the boss.' I heard the shrug in Dida's voice and the flap closed.

I frowned as I settled back against the cushions. Yeah. I wondered about Felix. I wondered about him a lot.

33

Next morning I had Lysias drive me down early to Watch headquarters.

'You want me to wait this time, sir?' he said when we pulled up outside.

'No, that's okay.' I shook my head: a tail would be easier to spot – and lose, if I wanted to – on foot than in a carriage, and besides I was getting a definite case of coach traveller's gut. 'Just go straight back, pal.'

Callippus hadn't shown up yet, but I was in no particular hurry: his secretary Critias was an okay guy when he didn't have to be monosyllabic, and he was good company. We chatted about the comedy that had been packing in the punters at Dionysus Theatre recently. I'd enjoyed it, Perilla hadn't: she likes plays with depth. Me, I've always thought that bastard Agamemnon had it coming.

Finally, around noon, the boss rolled in with a tall thin guy who could've stood in for Charon the Ferryman on a bad day. Callippus didn't look too cheerful either. Maybe it was catching.

'Hello, Corvinus,' he growled as he pushed past me into his office. 'Join us, will you? Critias, we'll need you too. Bring your pad.'

'Yes, sir.'

Ah, well, back to the monosyllables. I gave the guy a quick wink and followed him in. Callippus had ensconced himself behind his desk. The Laughing Skeleton and I took a chair each while Critias, as befitted a mere clerk, stood by the door, stylus poised.

'There've been further developments.' Callippus fixed me with a glare.

Uh-oh. Something told me I wasn't going to like this one bit. 'Is that so, now?' I said carefully.

'This gentleman' – he indicated the Gravedigger – 'is Lysimachus. He's a doctor, and he's here to make a formal statement.'

A doctor, eh? Well, I hadn't been far out with Charon at that. If his bedside manner wasn't cheerier than this I'd bet his patients died just to get rid of him.

Callippus's glare shifted to his new pal. 'Go ahead, sir,' he said. 'Critias, take this down.'

The guy cleared his throat with a sound like ashes shifting in an urn. 'Watch Commander Callippus approached me today with an enquiry concerning the condition of health of my patient Demetriacus son of Demetrius, citizen of this city, in the period from a date two days before the last of Elaphebolion to the third of Munychion, with special reference to the latter of those dates aforementioned. Said period being of this current year. Mmmum.'

I stared at him. Jupiter! The guy was worse than Priscus! And I'd never got the hang of the Athenian calendar. A lunar year that staggers around like a drunk in a gale is bad enough, but any society that counts forwards *and* backwards depending what third of the month you're in needs its communal head examining.

'Uh . . . what does that work out to in Roman, pal?' I said.

The guy gave me a look like he was weighing me up for a suppository.

Callippus sighed. 'The third of Munychion was the day Melanthus disappeared, Corvinus,' he said. 'And two days before the end of Elaphebolion was five days previous to that. March 30th, in case you'd forgotten. Happy?'

Juno's knickers, the guy was a real grouch this afternoon! 'Yeah,' I said. 'Sorry. Just checking.'

'Fine.' He turned back to Laughing Boy. 'Go on, sir.'

'Demetriacus has the misfortune to suffer from a chronic stomach ailment which is more severe at some times than others and gives him great pain. The period in question lay in such a time. I was able to inform the Watch Commander that my patient was confined to bed on my orders throughout said period, and it was only on the fifth of Munychion – that is two days after the third, Lord Corvinus, and so four days ago . . .'

'Yeah, I'd worked that out for myself, friend. Thanks anyway.'

'. . . that he was recovered sufficiently to rise, and then only for part of the day.'

I frowned as I worked out what all that came to. Hell. I'd been right in thinking I wasn't going to like this. Lysimachus might've put it in a less fancy way, but the message was clear enough: the night Demetriacus was supposed to be having his friendly chat with Melanthus prior to slitting his throat the guy was bed-bound a mile off with a serious gut ache.

There went the case. No wonder Callippus was peeved.

'Ah . . . you're sure about this?' I said.

That got me another terminal glare. 'Quite sure.'

'Hundred-per-cent spit on your grandmother's grave and cross-your-heart sure? I mean, he couldn't've been putting it on?'

The glare went critical. 'Are you impugning my professional diagnosis of the patient's condition, sir? Or perhaps it is my veracity that is in question?'

Callippus had closed his eyes and his lips were moving like he was praying. Finally, he opened them again. 'Corvinus, just shut up, will you, please?' he said mildly. 'Have you got all that, Critias?'

'Yes, sir.'

'Good.' He turned to the doctor. 'Lysimachus, I don't think we need detain you. If I have any further questions I'll be in touch. My thanks for your trouble.'

'No trouble at all.' The guy stood up. He was still glaring at me. 'Mmmum!'

'See the doctor to his carriage, Critias,' Callippus said. He waited until the door had closed and then rounded on me. 'Corvinus . . . !'

'Yeah, yeah, I know.' I held up a hand. 'I'm sorry. But the bastard's lying. Demetriacus must've bribed him.'

Callippus went through his praying routine again. 'Lysimachus of Cos is one of the best doctors in Athens, not to mention the richest. He does not lie. And he has no need for bribes.'

'That's all you know, pal.' Jupiter, I felt sick: if you believed Corpse-face the theory was well on its way right down the tube. I was almost sure he'd thrown us a wobbler, but still . . .

'Look, I'm as disappointed as you are,' Callippus was saying. 'But you cannot argue with the facts.'

If I had to go, I'd go fighting. 'What facts? The only "fact" here is that that po-faced quack has taken a backhander big enough to buy him another block in Cydathenaeum.'

Callippus paused. 'How did you know Lysimachus speculated in property?' he said.

'I didn't, pal, but it doesn't surprise me. Scratch a doctor and you get a compulsive property developer. Back in Rome my father's freedman Sarpedon might own half the Velabrum and be able to buy me out twice over but the bastard still sucks up to patients with a spare acre or two.'

'Well.' Callippus rubbed his jaw. 'You may be right. Although if you remember when we talked to him Demetriacus did say that he'd been ill.'

'Sure he did. But what he didn't say was that the evening Melanthus did his disappearing act he'd been at home rolling around hugging his guts; in fact, he didn't say anything much at all apart from deny that he'd met the guy full stop. Because at that point he didn't know we had no real proof.'

'And he does now?'

'He's still walking free, isn't he?'

'Yes.' Callippus frowned at his desk. 'Yes, I suppose you're right.'

'Never mind, pal.' I forced a grin, even if with my theory threatening to collapse round my ears I felt more like howling. 'Asking the doctor was a good idea, it just backfired, that's all. If Demetriacus is lying we'll nail him eventually. He's human, like the rest of us, and he must've slipped up somewhere.'

'Indeed.' Callippus didn't grin back, but his mood lifted a little. 'So. Any news your end?'

'Yeah. You could say that.' I told him about Felix. 'You know him, by the way? Professionally, I mean?'

'No. He's certainly not here in any sort of official capacity, which is understandable from what you tell me. You say your paths have crossed before?'

'Yeah.' I didn't elaborate: Prince Gaius's involvement in the Sejanus affair wasn't exactly public knowledge, and besides as a Greek Callippus had about as much interest in backstairs Roman politics as he had in sexing chickens. Less.

'And you believe his involvement and that of his principal is limited to a legitimate interest in the statue?'

He sounded hopeful, but not too confident. I grinned. 'You seen any flying pigs recently? "Legitimate" isn't a word I'd use of Felix. Or Prince Gaius. In either of its meanings.'

'Ah.' Callippus didn't smile; if anything, he looked sadder than ever. 'I see.'

'Felix isn't a murderer, though. At least I don't think he is.' I hesitated. 'At least . . .'

'You mean he has scruples?'

'Scruples?' I laughed. 'Felix?'

'I take it that means no.'

'In spades. Felix has as many scruples as a snake has toenails. Especially where his boss's interests are concerned.'

'His boss's interests. Exactly.' Callippus moved a pen from one side of the desk to the other. 'Corvinus, we have to go carefully here. Very soon, perhaps before the year is out, Gaius will be emperor.' I kept my face expressionless. 'If his agent is involved – criminally involved – in this affair then whatever the consequences I will do my duty and arrest him; however if there is any doubt – *any* doubt – then he has the private right of any citizen to be free from molestation.'

'Felix isn't a citizen, Callippus. He's a slave. Or at most a freedman.'

'That's beside the point and you know it. I don't care if the man's a bloody female contortionist in disguise' – I blinked: I'd never heard Callippus swear, ever – 'I won't touch him with gloves and a ten-foot pole, for you or for anyone. Not without solid proof. Now is that clear?'

'Yeah. Yeah, it's clear.' Jupiter! 'Calm down, Callippus, no sweat, okay?'

'I am calm. I'm also being very, very serious. Never more so. As such my advice to you is to stop all this silly theorising before it lands you in real trouble. Or if you can't help yourself don't involve me until you've got some hard facts to back you.' Callippus stood up. 'Now I've got other things to do this afternoon, like looking after the rest of the City's population. You'll excuse me?'

'Sure.' I swallowed.

Well, that was that. End of ball-game. I might as well pack up and go home.

34

The first thing I saw as I left the building was Memnon lounging on the back steps of the Town Hall and looking about as inconspicuous as a tap-dancing rhino. Jupiter knew how he'd picked me up again, but personally at that moment I couldn't have cared a penny toss. I gave him the big wave just to show him he'd been spotted, then headed up the Panathenaia towards the Rock. Let the guy get blisters, I thought sourly. They'd be about all he did get from me today. Whether Demetriacus's tame pill-pusher was bent or not, all I wanted now was to go home and spend the rest of the afternoon and evening getting quietly stewed.

'Bent or not.' Yeah, well, if Corpse-face was telling the truth then maybe I should think a little more deeply about Felix. Sure, if you took the current theory he didn't fit. He had no connection with Melanthus, as far as I knew, and Melanthus was crucial. The same went for Demetriacus . . .

Or did it?

I stopped. A bald-head behind me in a sharp mantle gave me a glare as he pushed past; judging from the hurry he was in he was headed for the public latrine at the corner of Attalus Porch and doubted if he'd make it.

Okay. Maybe I'd been guilty of too many assumptions here. Stripped of its incidentals, the plot was pretty straightforward. Argaius had done a deal with Priscus to sell him the statue. His partner Smaragdus had done his own deal, unbeknownst to Argaius, and tried to con him. Then Argaius had been murdered and his body dumped by the Founders' Statue of Ptolemy on Market Way . . .

Hold on. Stop there. Sure, Perilla had thought dumping Argaius at the Ptolemy statue was a chichi egghead clue, but maybe she was wrong. Or rather she'd been clever in the wrong direction, which was par for the course. The Scallop was near Ptolemy's Gym, and if Felix had wanted to point a finger at Demetriacus that was just the cryptic way of doing it that might appeal to the cerebral little bastard.

This needed thinking about.

I was level with Phoenix's wineshop now, opposite the Temple of the Two Goddesses. There were a couple of empty tables – rare for Phoenix's – and I was tempted to go in and order up a jug. Being just round the corner from the Roman Market, Phoenix's catered more for western taste than most City wineshops; which meant they served Falernian. Real Falernian, too, not the fake stuff you saw sometimes masquerading under a whacky label. It cost an arm and a leg, though, and after my contribution to the carriage-drivers' benevolent fund my purse was pretty light. Too light. I sighed, and went on past.

So. If we were thinking laterally then what about Felix's own theory of the Argaius murder? That Smaragdus had done it himself to take the heat off? That fitted, too, if for Smaragdus you read Felix. More, handing me the real solution on a plate – letting me think it was a throwaway idea when it was the truth all along – was just the sort of twisted intellectual game the devious bugger enjoyed. Felix could've set Argaius's death up with Smaragdus as easy as Demetriacus could. And a double bluff would be just his style.

Right, so let's follow that through with a scenario. Felix and Smaragdus acting together have got rid of Argaius. Smaragdus stays in hiding while keeping in touch with Felix. So far, so good: the sale's finalised, Felix is just waiting until the dust settles and it's safe to move the statue, or maybe he's arranging a transfer of funds from Rome and generally fixing things up for Smaragdus and his boyfriend to split for quieter climes. Trouble is, at that point Valerius Corvinus sticks his nose in. He traces Harpalus who in all good faith reports back to Smaragdus that one of Felix's agents wants to get in touch. Before Smaragdus can check if the guy's legit or not the Roman's knocking on the door of his shack. Smaragdus realises there's been a mistake, only it's too late to remedy. So he takes the nosey Roman to the original cave – now empty – and fobs the sucker off with a sob story of theft and grim deception.

Then Smaragdus dies . . .

Smaragdus dies. I frowned. This was the tricky bit, the part that didn't fit. Smaragdus's death had been an accident, sure, but the guy had been running scared at the time, I'd bet my last obol on that. With Demetriacus out of the picture what reason would he have? Who was there to run from? Not Memnon: if Felix knew where the guy was hiding already he wouldn't have needed me to lead him to the beach hut, and why should Smaragdus be afraid of Felix's agent? Besides, I knew already who'd chased Smaragdus because he'd admitted it himself, as well as to killing Argaius. The visitor must have been Prince Charming; and Prince Charming didn't fit into this set-up at all. Not nowhere, not never . . .

Unless he was Felix's second-string.

The back of my neck prickled. Wait a minute. Wait a minute. The idea had come, but I didn't know why yet. I'd have to work this one out.

Okay. PC is working for Felix, along with Memnon, and both of them are tailing Corvinus. As such, they witness the meeting on the beach and suspect that Smaragdus might be throwing another wobbler by showing me the real cave. That would fit; the guys couldn't be sure where we went, because we took the *Alcyone* and they couldn't follow. I'd know PC from Argaius's place, sure, but the first time I'd seen Memnon was at the Aphrodisian Gate, when he must have tailed Lysias with the coach. So the pair come to an agreement. As the unknown tail Memnon goes after me while PC waits for Smaragdus to get back. He doesn't make his move straight away; he stays hidden and watches to see what Smaragdus will do next. And what the guy does is pack. Misunderstanding on both sides. As far as Smaragdus is concerned, he's moving to the second hideout up in Acte to avoid future contact with the nosey Roman, but PC doesn't know that. He thinks the bastard is staging yet another double-cross, and he moves in fast. Smaragdus has never seen PC before, his nerves are shot to hell, and he runs. PC makes the reasonable assumption that he's suffering from a bad case of conscience and gives chase to ask him why. Misunderstanding perpetuated, Smaragdus zeroed . . .

Yeah. That would work. Sure it would. Maybe I was on to something here.

The crowd had begun to thin a little when I turned left at the Eleusinion on to the main drag round the north face of the Rock. I glanced back. Memnon was still with me. Just for the hell of it I waited to see if he'd catch up, but he didn't. Suit yourself, pal, I thought, and carried on walking.

So. With Smaragdus dead Felix is stymied. He has to work on two contradictory assumptions at the same time: one – less likely, but still a possibility – that the sneaky Roman bastard knows where the Baker is; two, that he doesn't, but being a sneaky Roman bastard he'll move heaven and earth to find out. So he has PC slug me outside the Scallop and cart me down to a handy cellar where he endeavours to scare the wollocks off me in the hopes that I'll spill any beans I've got just to avoid ending up like Argaius. In the process – for the sake of future security, because killing me is not an option – PC encourages any half-arsed theories I might have as to who's behind the scam. That part was true, at least: if I'd misjudged anyone in the course of this business, it'd been PC. Whatever else he was, PC was no dumbo, that was sure: he'd told me just what he wanted me to know, or think I knew, no more and no less. Okay. So when the strong-arm approach doesn't work and I insist on meeting his boss PC takes the second option. He leaves the cellar and his mate Memnon takes over. Memnon stages a phoney rescue and I'm restored to the bosom of my caring family, full of gratitude and with an idea of the set-up as valid as a radish's views on cosmic order.

Yeah. It held together, and it might even be true. The problem was, there were loose ends. I couldn't just dismiss Melanthus and Demetriacus as irrelevant because that would involve more coincidences than even one of Perilla's favourite dramatists allowed: Melanthus was my professional contact over the Baker, he was definitely involved with Demetriacus, and for him to get himself killed just at the most convenient moment was too pat by half.

Unless, of course, Felix had lifted him himself to provide

his own authentication of the Baker. And the only reason Demetriacus fitted into all this was his connection with Melanthus. But then if Felix didn't have the statue he'd still need Melanthus; so why get rid of the guy before he'd had a chance to use him? Unless he already had used him. But then why should Felix . . . ?

Ah, hell, there were problems whichever way you played it, and I was giving myself a headache here. Theorising isn't easy when you're sober; maybe I should've stopped at Phoenix's and got expensively smashed after all. Now it was too late to turn back, and home and a jug of my own Setinian was still a long way away.

Time for a change of plan. Up ahead of me a chubby guy was paying off his litter. I broke into a run and grabbed it a yard in front of an Egyptian tourist who'd evidently decided his gilded papyrus sandals wouldn't last out the trip back into town. I was grinning as I settled down among the cushions: Egyptian curses are pretty hot stuff, and this guy was clearly an expert. I'd have to remember that one if Perilla and I ever did the pyramid tour.

Memnon wasn't too pleased either. Especially when I waved goodbye.

35

Forget the quiet afternoon. When I got back it was to find
Bessus the Piraeus stevedore waiting for me in the hall where
Bathyllus had left him sitting on the door slave's bench and
kicking his plebeian heels. Jupiter! Things were moving now
with a vengeance!

'You've found Tiny, pal?' I said.

He nodded. 'He showed up first thing this morning, lord.
Another loading job. We finished early and I followed him
home.'

'Uh-huh.' As I picked up the regulation wine jug and cup from
the hall table and led the way through to the atrium I should've
been crowing, but I wasn't. I had a nasty feeling about this. Sure,
Bessus couldn't have done it any other way, but I suspected that
Tiny was a man who valued his privacy. 'He see you, by any
chance?'

The guy looked uncomfortable. 'He may have done, lord,' he
said at last. 'I didn't think it mattered.'

I groaned. He didn't think it mattered! Oh, great. Fantastic.
That put the lid on. Well, it was my own fault. I should have
warned him, and there wasn't anything I could do about it now.
At least he'd found where the guy lived. I poured and drank.

'You want some wine?' I said.

'Sure.' The stevedore grinned; probably surprised I hadn't
chewed his balls off.

I turned to Bathyllus, who'd padded in on my blind side and
was pointedly ignoring Bessus. 'Bring us another cup, little guy.
And tell Lysias to bring the coach round.'

'Yes, sir. At once, sir.' Stiff as hell: Bathyllus's standards don't allow for serving Setinian to dockhands. Still, from Zea to the Hippades Gate was quite a walk, unless he'd hitched a lift on a wagon, and the guy's tongue would be trailing the marble. 'Do I take it, then, sir, that you'll be going straight out again?'

'Got it in one, Bathyllus. You win the nuts.' I sank another quarter pint: if I had to go all the way to the Piraeus and back, even by carriage, I needed to get tanked up first. Especially if I was meeting Tiny. 'Is the mistress around, by the way?'

'No, sir. She's visiting her friend Euelpida, as I understand.'

Nestor's latest victim. I grinned, wondering if she'd taken the ivory plaque with her. I hoped so: Euelpida needed as much fun out of life as she could get. 'Okay. Just say to her when she gets back not to hold dinner.'

'Very well, sir.' Bathyllus oiled out. I'd been counting those 'sirs' and I made it five. The little guy was seriously miffed.

'Now.' I waved Bessus to a chair. 'Tell me.'

'He's camping out in one of the old trireme sheds, lord.'

'Yeah?' That made sense. The Zea sheds might've been out of commission for the past two hundred years, but they were a dosser's dream. If he could get into them, that was. 'I thought these places were kept locked up, pal. They're still government-owned, aren't they?'

'Sure.' Bessus shrugged. 'But he'd broken off the padlock. And who cares, these days? Most of the sheds are empty.'

Yeah, that was true. Ninety per cent of the Piraeus trade went through the main harbour on the other side of the peninsula. Even let out as warehouses the sheds wouldn't be at a premium.

Bathyllus came with the extra cup and I filled it. Bessus downed the Setinian in one while the little guy fizzed.

'Lysias says he's ready when you are, sir,' he said.

'That's good.' I poured out two more belts and gave Bathyllus the jug. 'Put that into a travelling flask, would you, sunshine? And wrap up a sausage or two and a bit of bread while you're at it. We may get peckish on the way.'

'Peckish, sir. Indeed, sir.'

That made it eight. A record. He left, radiating disapproval, while I went through to the study to restock my purse. First the carriage drivers, now the stevedores' guild. This was getting serious: if I wasn't careful the Roman aristocracy would lose their reputation for exploiting the provincials.

We set off for the Piraeus.

Even if I'd known Tiny was living in one of the trireme sheds finding him wouldn't have been easy, because there were a good two hundred of the buggers, stretching all the way round the harbour. Bessus led me to one of the last in the line, not far from the harbour gates. It was big – it would have to be, to take four warships plus their tackle – and access from the land side was by a heavy wooden door fastened with iron bolts and a padlock. Or rather, the door should've been fastened; the padlock was missing and the bolts were drawn. Uh-huh. So either Tiny was in residence or he hadn't bothered to lock up when he left.

I looked round carefully before we went in. The harbour area wasn't exactly deserted, but as far as I could see there was no obvious candidate for a tail. Which didn't mean much. Sure, we'd probably given Memnon the slip with our fast turnaround, but that didn't mean to say we were running free: Felix would've had the house watched as well, and by a face I didn't know. Maybe Demetriacus, too, if his alibi was pure moonshine and he was our villain after all.

The big guy wasn't at home. Oh, we'd got the right place, that was sure: almost immediately behind the door in the space reserved for tackle was a home-made brazier and a truckle bed with a rough blanket on top. Two earthenware bowls stood on the floor beside the bed, one filled with water, one with scraps of meat. Of course: Tiny had had a dog. I remembered the dog. There was nothing else, not so much as a spare undershirt.

'Lord, I'm sorry.' Bessus was frowning. 'He must've spotted me after all.'

'Yeah.' A pity, but like I said it couldn't be helped. He'd be back.

Those drawn bolts, though . . .

Maybe the cupboard was bare, but I had the feeling we were being watched. Not a pleasant feeling, either. I peered into the shadowy interior of the shed where the triremes themselves had been. Enough light was coming in through the gaps the builders had left between the roof joists to see by, but he could've been

hiding anywhere; behind a pillar, maybe, or in one of the niches
that lined the walls. Or just lying flat and motionless on one of the
quays. Empty though it was, the place was big enough for even
Tiny to hide in. Not that I was going to go looking for him. No
way. I hated hide and seek even as a kid, and just the thought of
that huge mad guy jumping out on me gave me goosebumps.

'Hey, Tiny!' I shouted. 'You there?'

I waited until the echoes died away. Finally. I felt the hairs
crawl on my scalp. Something was listening, sure, I knew that
in my gut. The problem was, in that place it could've been just
that: some*thing*. I found myself hoping the silence wouldn't be
broken by the splash of oars . . .

Shit, this was silly. I was being too imaginative for my own
good. I tried again.

'Tiny! Remember me? The Roman in the cookshop? I want to
talk to you. About a statue you moved for your pal Smaragdus.'
Again I waited. Nothing but echoes, and the feeling of eyes.
Beads of sweat broke out on my forehead. 'Hey, Tiny! There's
no need to be frightened, pal! No hassle, I promise!'

Still nothing, but the echoes whispered. My throat constricted.
Okay, I was spooking myself here unnecessarily, I knew that, it
wasn't rational . . .

What the hell. Suddenly I knew that Baker or not, pride or
not, I had to get out.

'You . . . uh . . . want to call it a day, Bessus?' I said as casually
as I could manage.

He gave me a sharp look and shrugged his shoulders. 'Your
decision, lord.'

I swallowed. 'Fine. We'll give it just one more try, okay?' I
owed that, at least, to my self-respect, especially since it seemed
I was the only one doing the sweating. This time I had to work
to keep my voice from cracking.

'Tiny! You know Bessus here! If you don't want to talk with
me now then that's fine, that's okay, just fix a meeting up with
him. Any time, any place, I'll be there.' Jupiter! I was babbling.
Fix up a meeting, nothing: from what I'd seen of the guy I'd
back his dog against him intellectually any day. Still, what else
could I do?

Get out, that was what. Before the echoes had properly died

down I was moving towards the door, trying to keep from running. Telling myself I was acting like a five-year-old didn't help, either.

I made it without a whimper. Just. Fresh air had never tasted sweeter. I leaned against the door jamp and breathed deeply.

Bessus was behind me. He was still looking at me like I'd turned purple and sprouted feathers.

'You okay, lord?' he said.

'Yeah. Yeah, I'm fine.' I wondered what he was seeing in my face. Ah, the hell with it: madness I just couldn't take, especially when it was hiding in the dark. Fumbling in my purse, I took a gold piece out and handed it to him. 'Here. With my thanks.'

He stared at it. 'That's too much,' he said. 'Far too much. Tiny wasn't there.'

'Sure he was.' I was breathing easier now, but I still wouldn't've gone back inside that shed for a dozen jars of Caecuban. 'And you'll earn it. Or at least I hope you will. I want this place watched, day and night, until the guy comes out. And if you can get him to me or me to him, then the pay's doubled. You understand?'

'Sure.' He looked uncomfortable. 'But I told you before. Tiny doesn't do nothing he doesn't want to.'

'That's your problem, pal. Even so, I have to see him and I'm not going inside there again. Keep in touch, okay?'

I left him standing and walked back to where Lysias had parked the carriage. I wasn't feeling too proud of myself, and the trip had been less than satisfactory all round, but I didn't see how else I could've played things. If Tiny had been there – and even now when I was out and halfway rational again I'd bet he had been, and heard every word – I'd at least left a message. Now it was up to him and Bessus.

And to Argaius's killer, whoever he was. We could've been seen going in to that shed, sure we could; there were enough places for a watcher to hide round about the harbour, especially if the watcher wasn't a familiar face. Beggars can't be choosers but I just hoped I hadn't made a mistake.

I was shattered when I got back. Reaction, probably. Perilla was in, but I skipped dinner and went straight to bed. I didn't even stop for a cup of wine, which shows you how far gone I was.

I woke up early the next morning feeling great and slipped downstairs without disturbing Perilla: a sweet lady she may be in many ways, but morning person she isn't, and if she doesn't get her eight hours and wake natural the whole world suffers.

Bathyllus was up and around, though, and I got him to bring me breakfast in the garden. While I mopped up olive oil with my bread I ran over the current state of the case. For what it was worth.

First, the Baker itself. That we'd only have one crack at. I was pretty sure Tiny knew where it was hidden, but he was the only one left alive who did and I hoped to hell the next time I saw him wouldn't be as a stiff on the boat-shed floor. Baker aside, any more corpses I could do without.

Who our villain was was less clear-cut. Alibi or not, my money was still on Demetriacus, however much of a shining light of his profession the guy's doctor was. He was the only candidate who accounted for all the facts, and a six-figure-value block of property would be a pretty good exchange for one little lie. Fortunately, that was one avenue I could check: Demetriacus might have Lysimachus in his pocket, but he'd also have slaves who'd know damn well where their master had been on the night in question. What was more, they'd be willing to tell me for less than the price of a City tenement.

On the other hand, if you took things differently and allowed for a few ragged edges (which might not even *be* ragged edges) then my pal Felix made a good second runner. Maybe even a scrape-home first. The guy was devious as a Market Square lawyer, he'd been after the Baker from the start, and he was totally devoted to his boss's interests. Yeah, I could believe in Felix. Except that his way of getting the statue wouldn't've included murder, especially multiple murder: one death Felix might regard as unavoidable, but three he'd see as downright sloppy workmanship. Felix was a con artist, not a killer. Demetriacus was different. That bastard was capable of killing, although when he did it'd be a carefully chosen means to a definite end with all sorts of back-ups in place.

Yeah. Judging purely by temperament, even from what I'd seen of him I'd go for Demetriacus over Felix every time.

Maybe.

I sighed. What I wanted was both Felix and Demetriacus together, and that I couldn't have . . .

Or could I?

I stopped, an olive halfway to my mouth. Okay. So let's let that one go and see how it runs. Demetriacus wouldn't want the statue for himself: he was a businessman, not an end-user, and he'd still need a customer. Felix was a natural. Say that Demetriacus approaches Felix, who he knows from any of a dozen different sources is interested in the statue. Or no, scrub 'interested': desperate. And as such not too choosey how he gets it. Yeah, that might fit, just. So when Smaragdus stages his double-cross the two join forces. Felix pretends to Smaragdus that he's on his side and . . .

Wait a minute. That wouldn't do. For a start it only avoided Felix being involved in one of the murders, Argaius's, and I was still left with the problem of the doctor. Anyway, why should Felix 'pretend' anything?

Unless he was staging his own double-cross. Of Demetriacus this time. Only Demetriacus was wise to it and sent his agent Prince Charming to cut the corner. But then . . .

'Good morning, Marcus. Are you intending to eat that olive or just stare it to death?'

'Uh . . . morning, Perilla.' I put the olive down guiltily. 'Sorry, I was thinking. Neither. Maybe I'll just let it live.'

'Fine.' She kissed me. 'I take it you slept well.'

'Like a log.'

'So I noticed.' She sat down and reached for the rolls and honey. 'If logs snore. How's the investigation proceeding?'

'It isn't.'

'Nonsense.'

'Believe it, lady. I've got two suspects and they're going round each other like a pair of kids' tops. That's to say if they aren't both part of the same top to begin with.'

'Now that really is nonsense!'

I helped myself to a roll. 'The killer has to be Demetriacus. Only it can't be if you believe his doctor Lysimachus because he wasn't at the Scallop to talk to Melanthus who's his only link with the Baker and who ends up that same evening with his throat slit by Prince Charming.'

'Pardon?'

'Or alternatively the villain's our old pal Felix aka Eutyches, working for Gaius in Rome. Only it can't be him either, because when push comes to shove, twisted as the little bastard is, I can't believe he'd stoop to murder. Not the Argaius kind, anyway. Nor Harpalus's. Let alone cutting that poor bastard Melanthus's throat, which makes no fucking sense at all.'

'Don't swear. There's no excuse for it even if you do feel frustrated.'

'I'll swear if I like, lady. And that was mild.'

'I'm also not particularly taken with snarling at breakfast, Marcus.' Perilla dipped her roll in the honey. 'If there are difficulties with both then why need it be either? It could be someone else entirely.'

Oh, great! Marvellous! Just the help I needed! 'Jupiter, Perilla, there *is* no one else! Unless you think old Alciphron up at the Academy killed them all because their library books were overdue. Or maybe Melanthus didn't talk to Demetriacus after all. Maybe he popped out for a chat with Tiny and they fell out over a definition of beauty and the nature of the fucking soul.' I sat back and balled up my napkin ready to throw it into the rose bed . . .

I didn't do it. I didn't do it because suddenly everything shifted sideways, the sun came out and I knew beyond a doubt who the killer was.

Somewhere, somebody coughed. I looked up.

'I'm sorry to disturb you, sir.' Bathyllus. And he had on his peeved prude look.

'Uh, yeah. Yeah, little guy,' I murmured. Gods! What an idiot! The answer was obvious! 'What is it?'

'You have a visitor.'

'A visitor?' I tried to get my brain back into kilter. What passed for my brain. 'At this hour of the morning?'

'Yes, sir. He sends his apologies, but he says it's important and he must see you.'

'Okay. So are you going to divulge the guy's name or do we get three guesses?'

'That won't be necessary, sir.' A sniff. 'The gentleman's name is Demetriacus.'

Perilla said something, but it didn't register. Demetriacus. Sure it was, it couldn't be anyone else. And if I was right then his business was important as hell; though why he'd decided to come now, and to me rather than Callippus, I didn't know . . .

'Marcus?'

'Hmm?'

'I asked if you were all right.' Perilla was staring at me, and she looked worried.

'Yeah, lady. Yeah, I'm fine. More than fine. Excuse me a minute, will you?'

I got up and followed Bathyllus inside.

Demetriacus was sitting in the guest chair. He wasn't alone. Behind him stood Antaeus, glaring at me like Megaera the Fury watching Orestes put on his running shoes. Uh-oh. This might be tricky.

'Corvinus.' Demetriacus was looking grey. 'I'm sorry to disturb you so early, but since our talk I've been doing a lot of thinking.'

I nodded. 'And you've decided to come clean after all.'

He gave me a sharp look. Antaeus rippled.

'I told no lies!'

'I never said you did, friend.' I took the chair opposite. Slowly, and with both eyes on Antaeus. I'd have felt happier if I'd had my knife in its wrist sheath, but you don't expect to need that kind of insurance in your own home, especially over the breakfast porridge. 'All you're guilty of is being economical with the truth and trusting your staff too much.'

Antaeus shifted again. He was the one I had to watch: one word from his boss and, own home or not, I'd be dead meat before I could whistle.

Demetriacus was silent for a long time. Then he said quietly: 'You know what I came to say already, don't you?'

'Yeah, I know.'

'But not quite everything, I think. Hermippe isn't "staff", Corvinus. She's my sister. Stepsister, rather. We had different mothers.'

I sat back as the last piece slid into place. Sister. That explained a lot. Come to that, it explained the whole bag. 'I didn't get that impression when we talked at the Scallop.'

'And I didn't intend that you should. I told you before, I don't like needless complications. Our relationship isn't common knowledge outwith the family; not even the girls know. Nor is it relevant to anything.' He paused. 'Or hasn't been, up to now. Which is why I am giving you the information.'

Bathyllus was hovering. I sent him for a jug of wine. 'You're partners? In the Scallop?'

'Yes. We always have been, since Melanthus sold it to us. And equal partners in all other respects as far as business is concerned.' Demetriacus paused again. 'Unofficially, of course. Hermippe's name doesn't appear on any deeds. It's unfortunate that our society won't tolerate a woman in business. Not in the higher reaches, that is; which was another reason for not making the relationship widely known.'

'You mean she's the brains and you're the front?'

'I wouldn't put it quite so crudely. We have our different strengths and weaknesses, and they balance each other. Hence our success. But Hermippe is certainly the driving force. The ruthless one, the risk-taker. My role is to implement her recommendations and follow them through. To be her public persona, if you like to call it that.'

'Uh-huh.' Check. That fitted in with what Callippus had told me. 'She certainly struck me as . . . full-blooded, shall we say.'

'Why not? It's a good phrase.' Demetriacus looked down at his carefully manicured fingernails. 'Hermippe has always had greater appetites than I. In every way. Also she's much more intelligent.'

Yeah, well, maybe. Or it could be her intelligence just took a different slant. Certainly she had a high opinion of her own cleverness: one got you ten Perilla had been right about the Ptolemy statue.

'Don't put yourself down too much, friend,' I said. 'It's bad for the male image.'

He smiled. 'I'm a realist, Corvinus. If a thing is obvious I state it. That is one of *my* strengths.'

I thought of the Scallop's decor, and the way Hermippe had picked me up when I looked at the painting in the hall. 'She's interested in art, too, isn't she?'

'Very. It's one of her passions. And Hermippe has passions rather than interests. That was what first attracted Melanthus.'

I nodded: there had to be something like that going on. 'They were lovers?'

'Yes. From the first days of the Scallop. Before, even. Until my sister tired of him.'

Bathyllus tiptoed in with the wine. I didn't take my eyes off Demetriacus while he poured. 'Not the other way round?'

'No. They stayed friends afterwards, but Melanthus was by far the more constant of the two. He continued to use the Scallop because it was congenial and satisfied him physically, but I suspect he always hankered after a re-establishment of the old footing.'

That made sense too. I held out my hand for the wine cup. Bathyllus offered one to Demetriacus, but he shook his head. Yeah. I'd forgotten. Maybe I should've offered the guy some warm milk.

'So,' I said. 'Melanthus got into the habit of dropping in for what he hoped might turn out to be more than a chat after he'd finished upstairs.'

Demetriacus's lips pursed. 'Again I wouldn't put it so crudely, young man. If I have my weaknesses then so do you, and I'm afraid crudity is one of them. I told you, Hermippe is intelligent. Very intelligent. Melanthus enjoyed talking with her. And when I was on the premises – which I was careful to be if possible when Melanthus visited – then we all talked together. For me it was an education, which is something I feel I have always lacked.'

Sure. And for Melanthus I'd bet it was one almighty pain in the rectum. Still, it takes two to make the third a gooseberry, so maybe I was being too hard on him. 'The staff – I mean the girls – knew about these little get-togethers, right?'

'Naturally. Although we encouraged the assumption that Melanthus was my particular visitor. That was Hermippe's idea, to avoid gossip. And our private quarters are out of bounds, so they wouldn't know whether I was there or not.' He gave a wintry smile. 'Mind you, being unaware of the true relationship between Hermippe and myself I believe the girls thought her already spoken for.'

That added up. A brothel's like any other small closed community: the inmates live on gossip. And even if there was nothing in it Hermippe wouldn't be too keen on the rumour getting around that she was sweet on one of the customers and vice versa. Bad for discipline. It explained why Cotile hadn't made the link, too. Demetriacus wouldn't have objected, either: commercial big wheel or not, the guy obviously preened himself on his relationship with a top-notch philosopher, even if it did have to be kept private.

'Okay.' I took a swallow of wine. 'Let's summarise. Stop me if I go wrong. Melanthus regularly came round for a chat with your sister even when you were away.' Especially when the poor bugger was away; but there was no sense in labouring the point. 'They talked about high-powered stuff like philosophy and art. Then one day when you're bed-bound with your chronic gut ache Melanthus happens to mention to her that he's acting as quality control in negotiations for a certain unique statue. The buyer's a Roman, and Melanthus, being a good Greek, says he thinks it's a shame it should go abroad.'

'I'm sorry, Corvinus, but there I can't help you. If that is how things happened then as you say I wasn't present. And I knew nothing about this affair until after Watch Commander Callippus's visit, because Hermippe never mentioned the Baker.'

'Yeah. I'm coming to that, and it's important. Okay. Knowing that Hermippe is a rich woman in her own right as well as a culture buff Melanthus suggests they cut the Roman out in the interests of Greek solidarity. Maybe he also suggests – tactfully – that it would be good for the family and open a few closed doors, because gifting the Baker to the city would send her brother's street cred sky-high.'

'That is certainly a possibility,' Demetriacus said gravely. 'We'd talked about it often before in different terms. I had thought of building a porch, perhaps, or even a theatre.'

'Uh-huh.' A theatre, eh? Jupiter, the guy must be loaded! 'Only by telling Hermippe he made a bad mistake. As far as she was concerned the city fathers could go hang: she wanted the statue, sure, but she wanted it for herself, either to look at or to sell. And she'd no intention of paying for it if she could avoid it. Right?'

Demetriacus nodded slowly. 'Again, I can't speak from knowledge. But it fits Hermippe's character, certainly. As I told you, she has the ruthless streak in the family. And she has always found it hard to spend money when it isn't necessary.'

'The problem is, she can't afford to let things slide. You're out of the picture but it won't be for ever. Sooner or later you'll be back at the Scallop and the first thing Melanthus will talk about when he calls in for his cosy post-coital chat will be the Baker.'

'Indeed. So she had him killed to stop me finding out.'

'She had him killed.' I swallowed the last of the wine in my cup and poured myself another belt. Maybe I should've offered Antaeus some, but I didn't know exactly what footing we were on here yet. 'Speaking of which, who's Prince Charming?'

Demetriacus looked blank. 'I'm sorry?'

'The heavy who did the actual killing. Must've done it. Callippus described him to you the last time we talked.'

'Glycus?' Jupiter! Pure accident, but I'd been close: the name means 'Sweetie'. 'He was the murderer?'

'Three times over, pal. And that's not counting Smaragdus.'

'Who?'

'It doesn't matter.' I waved the question away: I kept forgetting Demetriacus was an innocent after all. 'One of the owners of the statue. So who is this Glycus?'

'I mentioned my sister's appetites.' Demetriacus was frowning. 'Glycus is a freedman of hers, a slave she bought in Paphos before we left and manumitted last year. They have a . . . relationship.'

'Postdating Melanthus's?'

'Correct. Or so I believe.' The frown deepened. 'Corvinus, would you mind if we didn't go into that aspect of things? I find it very distasteful.'

Yeah, I'd believe it; I'd met the guy. And having your sister jump into bed with one of her slaves, manumitted or not, wasn't likely to go down a bundle with someone who hoped to be one of Athens's top Five Hundred one day either. 'No hassle, pal. There's one in every family. All I want to know is where I can find the bastard.'

'At the Scallop, of course. He has a room next to Hermippe's. But he won't be there at the moment.'

Something cold touched my spine. 'He won't?'

'No. I called round this morning to collect Antaeus: a precaution which I hope you don't resent, young man. Glycus had already gone.'

'So where is he?'

Demetriacus looked up at his bodyguard. The big guy spoke for the first time. 'The Lady Hermippe sent him on an errand at first light, sir. To the Piraeus, I understand.'

I stared at him. Oh, Jupiter! Jupiter best and greatest! 'You happen to know where to in the Piraeus exactly?'

'No, sir.'

Shit! Tiny! It had to be Tiny! We'd been shadowed right enough. And first light meant that Glycus had at least a two-hour start . . .

I put down my cup hard and yelled for Bathyllus.

'Yes, sir.' The little guy must've been hanging around outside.

'Tell Lysias I want the coach now.' I was on my feet. 'Make that as of ten minutes ago.'

'Of course.' He paused. 'Your mantle, sir?'

'Screw the mantle, get the coach!'

'Is something wrong, Corvinus?' Demetriacus's eyes were wide.

The understatement of the century; but then he didn't know the details. 'Yeah. Your Glycus is just about to raise his total to four. Plus maybe one solid gold statue.' The little guy was still hovering. Gods alive! 'Bathyllus, will you get the fucking coach!'

'Take mine. It's waiting outside.' Demetriacus turned to Antaeus. 'Go with him.'

I hesitated, then decided: if I had Prince Charming to face then Antaeus would be useful to have along. 'Okay, sunshine,' I said. 'You're on the team. Give me a minute to get my knife.'

We set off for the Piraeus at a speed that nearly knocked my teeth loose. All the way I was praying to every god I knew that Tiny would still be breathing when we got there; but we were two hours behind, and I wouldn't've risked any bets.

37

We were too late. The boat shed door was wide open, and there was a crowd outside. I took the last stretch at a run and pushed my way through. Inside, two men were standing over the huddled body of a third. I stopped and stared . . .

The third was Glycus, and he was dead. Very dead; like he'd tried to stop a charging rhino with his bare hands and hadn't half made it.

'What happened?' I asked Bessus. No point in asking the last member of our little group; Tiny couldn't've answered.

Bessus's face was grey. 'He arrived half an hour ago, lord. There wasn't anything I could do alone, so I went for help. When I got back Tiny here had him in a bear hug and it was all over bar the screams.'

Holy gods. I looked at the big guy in awe: he was crying. Bessus had said before that Tiny wouldn't hurt a fly. Well, maybe flies were safe but he'd done a fair enough job on Glycus. We could've slid what he'd left of the bastard under the shed door and not worried about the clearance.

'Why?' I said simply.

Tiny didn't answer. He just held out something he'd been holding. Cradling. A small fat dog with a severed throat.

I swallowed. Good sweet Jupiter. Yeah, that would do it, okay, and with a bit left over: Glycus had signed his own death warrant and never known it. 'He wanted you to take him to the statue, right? And when you wouldn't he killed your dog to persuade you to change your mind.'

Tiny gibbered something at me. The tears were streaming down his cheeks, and I didn't think they were for Prince Charming.

'You know the man, lord?' Bessus said.

I nodded. Antaeus had come in behind me. He was looking down at the corpse, his face expressionless.

'That's Glycus, all right,' he said at last. 'It seems, sir, that you were worried about the wrong person.'

'Yeah.' I'd seen enough, more than enough; I turned away. 'Let's get some fresh air, okay?'

We went outside. So. Exit Prince Charming. I wasn't sorry. It couldn't've happened to a nicer killer.

The crowd of gawpers shuffled aside to let us through. Gods, I hate these ghouls.

'Somebody go for the Watch,' I said. 'Otherwise the show's over.'

The crowd dispersed, slowly and reluctantly. Bessus was heaving the door to behind us. 'It wasn't Tiny's fault, lord,' he said softly.

'No.' I shook my head and tried to ignore the buzzing in my ears: reaction was setting in. 'No. I know that. Don't worry, I'll explain.'

'If you don't need me now, Valerius Corvinus, then I'll be getting back to the master,' Antaeus said. His face was stiff, but he still had the air of a perfect butler. 'I'll leave that . . . carrion for you to dispose of.'

'Sure. Go ahead.' I sat down on a bollard and took a deep breath. 'Tell him thanks, okay?'

'Of course.' Antaeus gave me his best butler's bow and walked back to the coach.

We waited in silence for the local Watch officers to turn up. Tiny didn't join us. He sat apart, still cradling his dog. Every now and again he stroked it. Finally I went over to him.

'You want us to bury her for you, pal?' I said quietly.

He looked at me. One big hand touched my cheek. Then he shook his head, got up and shambled towards the harbour gates. I didn't try to stop him. I doubt if I could've, anyway.

It took half an hour for the Watch rep to arrive: not the boss, of course, just a young squaddie barely out of his teens. I led him inside, showed him Glycus and watched him lose his breakfast.

'Send a message to Callippus at Watch headquarters in the

City,' I said when we were outside again and he'd asked Bessus and me all the usual questions. 'He'll want to know.'

'Yes, lord.' The kid hesitated. 'And the man responsible? This Tiny? We'll need to talk to him. Purely a formality.'

'Sure.' I felt tired; well, they could try, anyway. 'Talk to him all you like when he gets back. He's off burying a dog.'

'A dog?' The squaddie's eyes widened, and he glanced quickly at the boat-shed door. 'Zeus in glory! He squeezes someone to death then goes off to bury a dog?'

'Believe it.'

The guy obviously didn't, but he straightened. 'Very well, lord. If you'll take the responsibility.'

'Yeah. No hassle.'

'Fine. I'll send a cart for the remains. It shouldn't take long.' He looked again at the boat shed. 'You say he was a freedman. His ex-master will have to be informed, too.'

'Make that ex-mistress, friend. In both senses of the word. And frankly I don't think she'll want to know.' He was staring at me. 'Her name's Hermippe. Tell that to Callippus as well. He knows where to find her.'

There was a question in the squaddie's eyes, but he didn't ask it. He just gave me a salute, turned and left.

Tiny must've been lying low somewhere watching for him to go. He'd evidently buried the dog because when he came along the quayside towards us his hands were empty.

'You okay, pal?' I said.

He didn't answer, not even a grunt. He didn't stop, either. His right hand reached out in mid-stride and gripped my wrist. Hard. My spine turned to ice. I tugged. Nothing. I might as well have tried shifting the boat shed.

'Tiny!' Bessus had been kicking his heels a few yards off. Now he rushed over, but he stopped short before he reached us. A wise move: the big guy could've swatted him away with his free hand as easily as an over-troublesome gnat.

I looked down at Tiny's hand. Jupiter, he was strong! The fingers were wrapped all the way round. I knew I couldn't pull free, and if I was stupid enough to try I'd probably dislocate something. 'Uh . . . you care to let go, maybe?' I said, fighting to keep the panic out of my voice. Blank eyes stared back at me out of a dough-white face, and I felt the sweat break out on my forehead. 'Bessus! Do something, will you? I can't take this!'

'Let the Roman go, Tiny.' Bessus's voice was shaking. 'He's a friend. And you've got yourself into enough trouble for one day.'

The grip didn't slacken. Tiny gibbered a word or two and walked off towards the gates, dragging me along behind like a dog on a short lead.

'I think he wants you to go somewhere with him, lord,' Bessus said.

'Yeah.' I tried to keep my voice level. 'I'd sort of worked that out for myself, pal. But there isn't a lot I can do about it at the moment.' I hadn't been kidding about not being able to take this, either: being hauled along to the gods knew where by a madman three times as strong as I was was worse than my worst nightmare, and I was close to yammering already.

'You want me to get help?' Bessus was almost running to keep up with us, and for all the attention Tiny was paying either of us we could've been talking Parthian.

'Uh-uh.' My voice shook; help, nothing: it would've been like trying to hold back an elephant with a cobweb. I was on my own here, and what nerve I had was just about all used up. I gave it one last shot before I went over the edge of sanity into a screaming fit. 'Okay, Tiny,' I said carefully. 'I'll come. Just let go of me, will you? I'm a big boy now, I can walk on my own.'

Mercifully, the fingers opened. I fell back, breathing hard and clutching my wrist. Tiny stood waiting while I rubbed the numbness away.

'You feel like tagging along?' I said to Bessus. I tried to make it sound casual but my voice was shaking too much to be convincing.

'Perhaps I'd better.' Bessus's face was the colour of whey. 'He's never done this before, lord. And after what's happened . . .'

He didn't finish, because Tiny had reached over and gently pushed him away. The message was clear enough: three was a crowd. Sweet gods. I didn't like this, I didn't like it at all, even though I thought I knew where the big guy wanted to take me. Climax to the case or not, at that precise moment given the choice between finally getting my hands on the Baker and walking home barefoot I'd've opted for the hike.

Given the choice. But then I didn't have a choice. All I could do was hang in and make the best of things.

'Okay, pal,' I said, and prayed I didn't sound as scared as I felt. 'Message understood. So let's go.'

Bessus stood aside. 'You want me to tell the Watch, lord?' he murmured.

'No.' I shook my head. If the kid I'd just met was an example of the Piraeus's finest then there wasn't a lot of point. And I'd be safe enough physically; at least I thought I would, and for sanity's sake I had to keep on thinking so. 'I'll see you around, friend.'

He didn't look convinced. That made two of us.

We left the harbour precinct and headed off in the direction of Zea Theatre. Tiny kept a pace or two in front, looking back over his shoulder to make sure I was still following. Then he took a left towards the high ground of Acte. We hit the lower slopes and Tiny suddenly veered east towards the coast. Uh-huh, so we weren't headed for Smaragdus's back-up cave after all, which would've been one possibility; he was taking me to the beach hut. It still had to be the Baker, though, because there wasn't anything else out this way, and I began to feel the first prickles of excitement as we left the road and crossed the broken ground leading to the shore.

The *Alcyone* was still beached in the cove: Jupiter knew why it hadn't been stolen, but maybe no one had noticed it yet. Tiny didn't even break stride. He hauled it down to the water easy as a kid launching a toy yacht, got aboard and sat down.

Journey's end, evidently. Or the first part of the journey, at least. I stopped, and swallowed. Hell. I'd been afraid this might happen. The trip across the gulf with Smaragdus had been bad enough, but taking to the open sea alone with a mad gorilla who'd just popped a guy's ribs for him was the stuff bad dreams are made of.

'Uh . . . can you handle one of these things, pal?' I said. 'Only I'm telling you now that I don't know a lee shore from a hawser, and I swim like a ton of concrete. These may be problems.'

Tiny gibbered and beckoned. Yeah, well, there went the excuse. I gritted my teeth and started to wade through the shallows . . .

'Corvinus! Valerius Corvinus! Sir!'

I spun round. A figure had just breasted the skyline, holding its side like it had a stitch. Oh, good sweet Jupiter, I didn't believe it!

The little guy in the emerald green tunic waved and came closer.

'Felix!' I only hoped I didn't sound as glad to see him as I felt. A swelled ego in that direction I could do without. 'What the hell are you doing here?'

'I followed you, naturally.' He was gasping. 'All the way from Zea.'

'*Zea*! You were at the boat shed?'

'Since last night.' His hand kneaded a spot just left of his liver. 'A moment . . . please . . . to catch my breath. I'm not used to running, and your friend sets quite a pace.'

'So choke, you bastard.' Nerves or not, I couldn't help grinning. Not just out of relief, either: for the first time since I'd met Felix I could be sure that what I was getting was the plain unvarnished truth. The guy was unquestionably, undeniably knackered. My grin widened. 'You spent the night at the harbour?'

He coughed and straightened. 'Yes, sir. It was most . . . uncomfortable. But after my colleague reported that you had paid an abortive visit to one of the trireme sheds I put two and two together and decided my personal presence was necessary.' Gasp.

Jupiter on a tightrope! Forget just one tail, it seemed we'd been heading a procession. Maybe I should've hired a trumpeter and thrown nuts to the crowds.

'You had my house staked?' I said.

'Only slightly, sir. And in your own best interests.'

'Sure. Which, oddly enough, happened to coincide exactly with yours.' Ah, well, it was done and I had to admit I was glad of it. I looked across at Tiny. He hadn't moved; hadn't so much as acknowledged Felix's presence. 'Okay, Felix, we're going for the Baker. As if you didn't know. Since you're here you can tag along if the big guy agrees. But we have a deal, remember?'

'The statue sold at open auction with the money going to the widow,' Felix said primly. I grinned again: the degree of concern for the maintenance of fundamental principles like honesty, openness and fair play that shone through every word could've powered a major political campaign. I'd have voted for the oily little fraud myself. 'Yes, of course I remember, sir. The agreement stands, naturally.'

'Fine.' I turned to Tiny. 'Hey, Tiny! This is Smaragdus's other customer and an old friend of mine. He'd like to see the statue as well. You have any objection?'

The pear head swung towards Felix. I waited, and prayed to every god in the pantheon I knew. The guy might have his faults, and despite what I'd said he wasn't exactly a friend, but at least he'd be human company.

Finally, the head nodded.

'Great.' I let out the breath I'd been holding. 'So. Let's go for it.'

We waded across to the boat.

38

Tiny set the sail and we were off. No, I didn't throw up. Maybe it was the excitement, but I felt great. Not so Felix: forget human company, the little guy began to change colour as soon as the first wave hit us. Then we were out in the gulf proper where we hit a smacker of a wind that had him half over the side losing his breakfast in earnest. I watched benignly. That would teach the sod to tail me.

We were headed for the same stretch of coast Smaragdus had taken me to last time, but Tiny was bearing further right, closer to Eetioneia. Yeah. That fitted. The signs I'd seen on the path showed that the statue had been carried down to the beach, so Smaragdus and Tiny must have ferried it round to another cove. Sensible: sure, there would've been places nearer by where they could've taken it instead, but in the process they'd have left tracks a blind man could follow. This way it could be anywhere.

While Felix was doing his best to turn himself inside out I looked ahead; and what I saw made me wish I hadn't. We were making for the dead centre of a line of cliffs; no beaches, no inlets, and from the looks of the cliffs themselves only a mountain goat tired of life on the hoof would risk climbing them. Added to which the chain of rocks stretching a good hundred yards out from the shore would gut us before you could say Ulysses. I glanced up at Tiny. He was holding the steering oar firm as Plato's famous helmsman.

'Uh . . . you sure you know what you're doing here, pal?' I said. Philosophical metaphors are okay in their place, but I'd bet one look at Tiny would've had Plato reaching for his pumice stone.

No answer: the guy might as well have been deaf. We got closer. Tiny turned a fraction out of the wind and the boat lost speed. We were coming in at a slant now, but the rocks were so close I could've reached out and picked off the clams. Shit. Baker or not, I must have been mad to agree to this. I should've made a dash for freedom back on the beach while I had the chance.

And then I saw it: a hollow at the base of the cliffs with a scrap of pebbly beach that looked just about big enough to spread a mantle over. If the mantle happened to belong to a midget. I looked back at Tiny.

'That's it?' I said. 'That's where we're going?'

He grinned and gibbered, nodding his head. Oh, hell. When the first rock scraped the side I closed my eyes and offered up a prayer to Neptune and the anonymous god who protects pointy-skulled gorillas and non-swimming Roman smartasses . . .

Two minutes later, incredibly, I was still breathing air. I opened my eyes. We were past the rocks and into deep water, and Tiny was grinning like he'd performed a minor miracle. Maybe he had.

'Nice work, friend,' I said. I meant it, and it was the under-statement of the year: mad gorilla or not, the guy could handle a boat. Maybe Plato wasn't so far out after all.

We nosed into the cove. Tiny lowered the sail, beached us gently on the pebbles, and threw out the anchor-stone. Then he jumped out and waded ashore.

Felix was still slumped against the side with his eyes closed, like he'd been the whole trip. Shame. All that excitement and he'd missed it. Well, some people have all the luck.

'Hey.' I dug him in the ribs. 'Show a leg, pal. We're there.'

The eyelids didn't flicker.

'I think, sir,' he said, 'I'll just die here quietly, if you don't mind.'

'Death isn't an option.' I grinned: the bastard was human after all. 'By the way, you know your face is the exact colour of a slice of Rhaetian cheese?'

He belched. 'Corvinus, please. No references to food. Cheese especially.'

'It's the truth.' I pulled him upright and his eyes opened. Now he looked like a slice of Rhaetian cheese with two poached eggs on top. I almost felt sorry for him. Almost. 'Don't worry, you'll be okay soon.'

'You mean I can die after all?'

I glanced over at Tiny, gibbering on the beach. He looked like he was getting anxious, and that we didn't want. I heaved Felix to his feet and propped him on the edge of the boat.

'Right,' I said. 'Break's over, sunshine. Back to work. Just knuckle down and think of Gaius.'

'Fuck Gaius,' Felix muttered; at least that's what I thought he said but I must've misheard. The guy wasn't that human.

Well, no point in pussy-footing around here. And he had insisted on coming . . .

'Hold your nose,' I said; and pushed.

He went in like a sack of carrots. I'd checked, of course: there was a good three feet of water to break his fall. And a pint or so of sea water taken internally is a good cure for seasickness. So I'm told, anyway.

Besides, he still owed me.

I had to hand it to Smaragdus; he'd hidden the Baker somewhere no one would think of looking in a million years. Even from this close up the place was a dead end: no obvious caves, no holes in the rock, nothing but cliff and a lot of scattered boulders. And only accessible from the sea. If you could call what we'd come through an access.

We waded ashore. At least, I waded while Felix dripped.

'You're sure this is the right place, Corvinus?' he said. The guy's impromptu bath seemed to have done him good once he'd coughed up half the gulf, even if he had come up in a foul temper. 'Because if it isn't then you owe me for a new tunic. That was *not* necessary.'

Tart as hell. I grinned. 'Put it on expenses, chum. Gaius can afford it more than I can. And this is the place all right. You have my personal guarantee.'

Tiny was standing beside the biggest pile of rocks, waiting for us to catch up. When we did he stepped aside to let us past, and I saw it.

Tucked away behind the boulders, and invisible until you were right on top of it, was a cave, the entrance wide as I could stretch both arms but no more than waist high.

Felix drew in a breath and let it out slowly. 'My apologies, sir,' he said. 'You can forget about the tunic.'

I nodded: I was feeling pretty overawed, too.

Tiny reached inside the cave and pulled out a lamp and strike-light. Once the wick was going he ducked down under the lintel and disappeared. I followed with Felix at my heels.

Even with the lamp and what little light there was coming through the entrance it was pretty dark. I stood up cautiously, but I needn't have worried: the ceiling was at least three feet above my head.

Then my eyes adjusted, and I saw the gold.

There wasn't much of it, but what there was was impressive as hell: gold dishes, gold figurines, even a gold tripod. I reached over and picked up one of the figurines, a Hunting Artemis complete with bow and quiver. It reminded me of a statuette I'd seen once in Argyrio's shop in the Saepta. That had been bronze, and the price still overran the tag. If this was just the scrag end of the Tolosan treasure then no wonder the two families had spent the best part of a hundred years looking for it.

'Sir?' Felix had moved past me into a darker part of the cave. I looked up. He was pointing to a bundle wrapped in an old blanket. A bundle the size and shape of a standing woman . . .

I unwrapped her carefully. She stood on a small pedestal, one foot pushing out from under the fringed hem of her mantle. Both her hands were extended, palm out. The right held an ear of corn so real I could count the grains, the left a flat loaf. Her hair was braided and her eyes looked into mine across six hundred years. A golden, smiling woman who stood in the lamplight and shone from the crown of her beautiful head to the toenails of her sandalled feet.

'Jupiter!' I murmured. 'Dear holy Jupiter!'

Felix was checking the inscription on the pedestal. That guy has no poetry in his soul.

'"Croesus King of Lydia to Apollo of the Delphians",' he read. "Far-shooter, the Slayer of Pytho". Sir, my heartfelt congratulations.'

'I can understand Hermippe now,' I said. The almond-shaped

eyes and enigmatic smile still held me. 'This lady is something else.'

Felix looked at me sideways. 'Worth killing for, Valerius Corvinus?' he said softly.

'No, not that. But she comes close.'

'Oh, dear. Then we had better wrap her up again, sir.' Felix reached for the blanket. 'Before either of us gets any ideas.'

I grinned and tore my eyes away. Gods, that smile . . . 'Fair point, pal. And we'd better think about how to get her home, too. Maybe if we came round by land we could rig up a crane. Hoist her up the cliff and use a stretcher. It won't be easy, though.'

We'd forgotten about Tiny. He'd been standing to one side watching us and holding the lamp. Now he set it down, put his huge hands under the Baker's armpits and lifted. The pedestal grated against the rock floor and swung free. Jupiter, this I didn't believe! No one was that strong! Maybe old Croesus had pulled a fast one on Apollo and the statue was hollow after all.

On the other hand, remembering the cement bags and what the guy had done to Glycus I wouldn't like to place any large bets. And he must've done it before.

Felix and I looked at each other in silence.

'I think, sir,' Felix said quietly, 'that your friend has plans of his own.'

'Yeah.' I swallowed, and watched.

The veins on Tiny's neck were standing out like ropes, but his expression didn't change. Slowly, very slowly, he carried the Baker over to the entrance and laid her down on her back with the blanket beneath her. Then he went outside and pulled her through.

Scratch the crane: it would appear that we were taking the Baker back with us. Ah, well, I wasn't going to argue with someone capable of lugging four-and-a-half-foot solid gold statues around.

'What about the rest of the stuff?' I said.

Felix was picking up the lamp. 'We leave it here for the moment, sir,' he said. 'If you agree, of course. The Baker's what is important, and now we know where the cave is there's no hurry.'

'Right.' I paused. 'Uh . . . how's your stomach holding out, by the way?'

That got me Felix's best glare. 'Perfectly well, sir,' he said primly. 'Besides, I have my master's statue to consider now.'

'Is that right?' I grinned. 'Remember you said it, then, pal. It's a long rough way back.'

Felix didn't answer.

39

When we came out of the cave Tiny had loaded the Baker on to the boat and was waiting for us. I didn't like the way things were going here, not above half: the *Alcyone* was pretty small to begin with, and although Felix didn't take up much room Tiny and me together would just about fill all the available space. Also, there were these wormholes in the planking to think about. Personally I'd still have gone for the land option: left the Baker where she was, sailed round Eetioneia into the main harbour and fixed things up in town. The trouble was, Tiny was still calling the shots and, peabrain or not, he obviously liked doing things his own way. Which meant going back the way we'd come . . .

Rowing back the way we'd come, because this time the wind was against us. That was one difficulty I hadn't even considered, obvious though it was. And it *was* obvious, even to a non-sailor like me. I looked at Felix.

'Uh . . . how are you with an oar?' I said.

'I would imagine about as handy as you are, sir.' The guy sounded as cheerful as I felt.

'That bad, eh?' Hell. Purple-stripers didn't row; it was written into the Law of the Twelve Tables. Well, there was nothing else for it, and we needed Tiny at the steering oar. 'Okay. So let's get it over with.'

We waded out and pulled ourselves aboard. Tiny sat impassively in the stern as I picked up the oars.

'You want left or right?' I said to Felix.

'Your choice, sir.' I could hear the guy's teeth gritting. 'Frankly, I don't think it matters much.'

'Yeah. Okay. I'll take the left.' I picked up the oar and pushed it through the leather strap. 'Just close your eyes and think of Gaius.'

Mumble, mumble, curse, curse. I grinned despite myself. They say travel broadens the mind. True. I was finding out a lot about Felix this trip.

We lifted the anchor-stone and shoved off. Forget your gentlemanly paddle on Lake Como while the reeds whisper in the scented breeze; this was hard work, and as much fun as an abscess. Dangerous, too: Felix hadn't been kidding, and he caught more crabs than I did which meant more often than not we were drifting side on at right angles to where we wanted to go or lurching about like a one-legged duck with a hangover. Jupiter knew how we made it through the rocks, but it was more by good luck than good judgment. Even Tiny was sweating.

With the Baker aboard the *Alcyone* moved like a pregnant heifer. What felt like hours passed before I saw the break in the shoreline over to our left. Enough was enough. I stopped rowing.

'Hey, pal,' I said to Tiny. 'That's the harbour mouth over there. You want to call it a day and turn left?'

Beside me Felix lifted his head. If he'd been knackered before he was completely on his uppers now. Well, at least neither of us had been sick. We didn't have the energy.

'I think . . . sir,' he gasped, 'that the wind . . . is shifting.'

He was right: it'd swung from head-on to landwards, and it was coming in gusts. 'Hey, great!' I said. 'Maybe we can . . .'

Which was when I saw the clouds. Big fat black ones, rolling up the gulf towards us and trailing a curtain of grey beneath them like a shroud. Something cold touched my spine.

'Oh, shit!' I murmured. 'Oh, holy Jupiter! Tiny . . .'

He'd seen them too, obviously. He put the steering oar over and the stem of the boat edged sluggishly towards the land, following the wind.

Felix picked up his oar again. 'Sir . . . we need more . . . way. Perhaps you could . . . help, please?'

'Uh, yeah. Yeah, sure.' I might be no seaman, but I saw the problem. We needed to turn far enough round to be able to use the sail; that way we might make the safety of the harbour before the storm hit. The problem was, with the Baker aboard we were too low in the water, and if we turned too suddenly we ran the risk of being swamped. So the turn had to be gradual: a wide circle that would finally bring our nose to the harbour mouth and put the wind square behind us. That would take time we didn't have; which meant, of course, that we had to increase our forward speed.

We almost made it. Almost. Felix and I rowed like madmen while Tiny worked the oar. Jupiter knew how long it took, and how close the storm was, but finally I could see the harbour entrance straight ahead and the wind was at the nape of my neck. Tiny got up to set the sail . . .

Which was when the wave came. It came from nowhere and slammed into us broadside on like a kick from a mule, canting the *Alcyone* sideways and flooding her. Tiny made a grab for the mast and went arse over tip as the Baker shifted and slid beneath him, smashing through the wormed planking like a battering-ram. Sky and sea changed places, and suddenly I was trying to breathe air that wasn't there any more. I had one glimpse of the golden woman sinking beneath me, blanket flapping and both hands held out towards me before something slammed into the back of my head and all the lights in the world went out.

I woke up stretched halfway across a rock, vomiting and with a splitting headache. Some evil-minded sod was digging the heels of his hands into my back just above the kidneys. I retched, bringing up another straight pint of Greek seawater . . .

'That's it, sir. Go ahead, better out than in.' Squeeze. Retch. 'You'll be all right shortly.'

Oh, Jupiter! Oh, Poseidon! 'Felix, you ham-fisted, overcheerful bastard . . . !'

'Just think of it as a permanent cure for seasickness.'

I retched again. This time I only managed a dribble. Then the coughing started.

Never cough ribs-down on a boulder. I turned over and sat back to do it in comfort. Relative comfort.

'What happened?' I said when I'd finished.

Felix sniffed. 'We sank, sir.'

Neptune and all his tritons! 'Yeah. I'd sort of gathered that, pal.'

'Well, you did ask.'

I looked around. We were on a beach somewhere and it was throwing it down like there was no tomorrow. Otherwise there wasn't all that much to go on. 'I was thinking more in terms of the fine detail,' I said.

'Indeed. Before or after you tried to dive for the statue?'

'I didn't . . .' I started coughing again. Pain stabbed the back of my head. 'Ah, forget it. Where's Tiny?'

Felix hesitated. 'I'm afraid I haven't seen him. Not since he went overboard.'

'Oh.' I stared at him. 'Oh, shit.'

'Quite, sir. But then again we're lucky to be alive ourselves.'

'Yeah.' That was true enough, especially since I couldn't swim a stroke. I was sorry for Tiny, though. 'By the way, Felix. How the hell did I get ashore?'

'I pulled you, sir. Draped very artistically over an oar.'

'Is that so, now?' Jupiter! That was all I needed: my life saved by Felix. It was mortifying. 'In that case . . . uh . . . maybe I should say thanks. I'm very grateful.'

'Don't mention it, sir. A pleasure. Certainly undeserving of such effusiveness.'

'Right. Right.' I had another look round. 'You know where we are?'

'Somewhere near the point of Eetioneia, I'd imagine. Not far from civilisation. If you can call the Piraeus civilised.'

'Uh, yeah.' Well, that was something. We could follow the coast and pick up a carriage or a chair at the Aphrodisian Gate. If they weren't all taken in this rain. I felt empty, and not because I'd tossed up the contents of my stomach, either. 'The Baker's gone for good, isn't it?'

Felix was quiet for a long time. 'Yes, Valerius Corvinus,' he said finally. 'I'm afraid so. Even if we knew exactly where she was when she went down, the water's too deep. And a statue that heavy would have buried itself in the mud.'

'Uh-huh.' Yeah, well, some you win, some you lose. 'So. We may as well go home.'

'There's always the treasure in the cave.'

I nodded. It wouldn't be the same, though. Not without the Baker. She'd been some lady. I stood up.

'Okay, pal,' I said. 'Game over. At least we're alive. Let's walk.'

It took us two sodden, mud-sucking hours. Neither of us felt particularly like conversation.

40

We picked up some spiced wine and dry clothes at a cookshop near the harbour and found a coach to take us back to Athens. I dropped Felix off in Colonus and went straight home. Bathyllus took one horrified look at what the wineshop owner had thought the well-dressed Roman noble should be wearing that year, paid off the carriage and hustled me into the baths.

I sat there for an hour sweating what I'd brought back with me of the Saronic Gulf out of my pores and thinking about things. Jupiter, what a mess! Another death and the Baker gone for good, too deep even for a gang of Arabian pearl-divers to reach. Nice going, Corvinus!

Ah, well, maybe it was for the best: Gaius would've got the statue for sure, one way or the other. We still had the rest of the treasure, and if I managed to get him the little Artemis figurine then Priscus needn't be too disappointed. Besides, Harpalus had been right about one thing: the golden lady had caused too many deaths to be chancy. First Argaius's, then Smaragdus, Harpalus himself, Melanthus, and now Tiny. Not to mention the nameless crew who'd brought her to the Piraeus in the first place and the gods knew how many more prior to that. I wasn't superstitious, or no more than the next man, but just the thought of seeing that lovely bland face smiling at me across Priscus's dining-room gave me goosebumps. When you reckoned it all up then maybe she was better off staying where she'd cause no more trouble ever again.

Which brought me to Hermippe. That was none of my concern, but I'd hate to see the bitch escape scot-free. Sure, I'd no worries about Callippus: when he got my message he'd've put two and two together and come up with five. However, we were back to the original problem: simply knowing that Hermippe had been ultimately responsible for the killings might not be enough, especially since she was a woman. Callippus would have his work cut out to screw even a majority verdict from an all-male Athenian jury, and I'd bet a mouldy sprat against a barrel of Baian oysters that she'd only have to bat her beautiful eyes at the jurors and blame it all on Glycus to have them bring in a not-guilty verdict *nem. con.* And Glycus was already dead.

Hell, the whole thing had turned into a pig's breakfast. Yet again. Once, just once, I'd like to come out of an investigation knowing that it had done some good and the world was a better place as a result, with virtue rewarded and evil sent down the tube. It didn't look like that was going to happen this time, either. Maybe there was some mean-minded god up there who had it in for interfering smartasses. If so then he was really working his butt off.

I sighed and nodded to the slave with the oil and scraper. Bath over, time to face my public. Life might seem more cheerful once I had a good dinner and a pint or two of wine inside me, but I doubted it.

In the atrium, waiting for me, I found Callippus.

'Corvinus.' He was looking grave. 'I thought it best to come straight round and tell you the news myself.'

'Yeah?' I filled a wine cup from the jug on the table. 'What news might that be?'

'I've just been at the Scallop. Hermippe's dead.'

I stared at him, the cup halfway to my lips. 'What?'

'An accident.' His face was unreadable. 'She fell downstairs and broke her neck.'

'Is that so, now?' Carefully, I filled another cup and handed it to him, waving him on to the guest couch. 'When did this happen, do you know?'

'Early this afternoon. Not long before I arrived, as a matter of fact.' He studied his wine. 'I'd received your message regarding . . . Glycus, was it?' – I nodded – 'from my Piraeus colleagues, and I thought a visit was in order. Demetriacus had just had her body carried to her room.'

'Demetriacus was there?'

'Yes. We had quite an interesting talk.'

'How about Antaeus?'

Callippus's eyes came up to meet mine. They were calm and level. 'Yes, Corvinus, Antaeus was there too. Freshly back from your Zea boat shed, I understand. He witnessed the accident, as did Demetriacus. There was nothing they could do.'

'Uh-huh.' I drank my wine. 'Convenient, right?'

'There will be no investigation.'

'That wasn't what I meant.'

'No, I do realise that, Corvinus.' He frowned and twisted the stem of the wine cup in his hand. 'Hermippe died from natural causes. If you can call falling down a flight of stairs natural. Personally I'm willing to leave the matter there.'

'She died easy.'

'Perhaps. Let's be charitable and hope so. More easily than Glycus, and certainly much more easily than Argaius. Anyway, as of today the case is officially closed.' He set the wine down untasted. 'Now. Did you find the Baker?'

'Yes and no.' I told him what had happened. 'We'll take up the rest of the treasure in a day or so. By land, this time. No more risks.'

'Very wise.' He nodded. 'There's the question of legal ownership, of course, but I'm sure the authorities will take an enlightened view. Especially since you're willing to bid for the goods at public auction and give the City their percentage. And especially since your friend Felix is so . . . well-connected.'

'Yeah.' I downed a swallow of Setinian. 'Mind you, I'd hate to be in that bastard's shoes when he tells his boss. When Gaius gets the news he is not going to be a happy little Caesar.'

The front door banged. 'Marcus!' Perilla's voice.

'In here,' I shouted.

She came straight across the room, ignoring Callippus, and hugged me tightly. 'Marcus, I've been so worried!'

'It's okay, lady. It's finished. We won, sort of. If you can call it winning.' I kissed her.

'You found the statue?'

'Yeah. For what it's worth.'

'Marcus . . .'

I put a finger to her lips. 'I'll tell you later. You know Callippus?'

'Yes, of course.' She smiled at him. 'How is Damoclea?' Damoclea was Callippus's wife.

'She's well, Lady Perilla.' Callippus was on his feet. 'Corvinus, I'm sorry to rush off but I must be going. We'll meet again soon. For dinner, perhaps?'

'Yeah, that'd be great.'

I saw him out. Not a bad guy, Callippus, and he'd been right not to push things over Hermippe's death. Sometimes these things were best left to the family to settle.

Perilla was on the couch when I came back. I lay down beside her and put my arm round her shoulders.

'So.' She snuggled in. 'What happened?'

I told her. About the Baker, and about Hermippe.

'He killed her?' She stared at me incredulously. 'Her own brother?'

'Sure. Or had Antaeus do it for him.'

'But that's terrible!'

'It was the only way. And I always knew Demetriacus had a killing streak in him, where he had reason enough. Don't waste any tears on that lady, Perilla. She had it coming, and considering how Smaragdus died maybe it was poetic justice.'

Bathyllus soft-shoed in to say dinner was ready. About time: I was starved.

'Also, sir,' he coughed, 'I'm afraid we've received a formal complaint from our neighbours.'

I sat up. This was serious: Diomea was a high-class area that kept itself to itself, and a formal complaint from a neighbour was tantamount to a major border incident. 'Yeah?'

Perilla put her hand to her mouth. 'Oh, Marcus, I forgot to tell you! Nestor got loose this morning and strayed into next door's garden.'

Jupiter! 'The brute's wings are clipped. How the hell can he "stray"?'

'He climbed up the fig tree on the back wall, sir, using his claws and beak.' That was Bathyllus, stiff as hell. 'It was quite an achievement.'

'I'll bet!' So. Strayed, nothing. I should've known better: the cunning bastard had planned the whole thing. 'Okay. So tell me what happened.'

'You know Leonidas's sister, sir? The maiden lady?'

'Melpomene?'

'Yes, sir.'

I groaned. Shit, no! Not that! Leonidas, of course, was our neighbour, something big on the local council. His sister Melpomene was a prim spinster of about fifty-five, over on a visit from Corinth. I closed my eyes. 'Go on, Bathyllus. Tell me the worst.'

'The lady was sunning herself in the garden at the time, so I understand, sir. The parrot walked up to her and told her to . . .' Bathyllus stopped with a glance at Perilla, then leaned down and whispered the rest in my ear.

My eyes widened. Jupiter on wheels! There were a couple of words in there even I didn't know, but they were pretty clear from the context. I wasn't sure if what Nestor had suggested was anatomically possible but if Melpomene had been silly enough to try it and been caught she'd be on the first boat out.

'The lady had hysterics,' Bathyllus said, 'although unfortunately for us she was lucid enough to recall the bird's message and repeat it to her brother verbatim.' Oh, gods! 'Leonidas, I'm afraid, was not amused. Hence the complaint.'

'It's the last straw, Corvinus.' Perilla wasn't smiling much either. 'The parrot will have to go now. He's a positive liability.'

'Yeah. I know.' I sighed. Well, the bastard had had his chances, and he'd systematically and with malice aforethought blown every last one of them. A pity in a way, because he was a real character. However, enough was enough, and when he got chopped he'd only have himself to blame. 'Okay, little guy, tell Alexis to . . .' I stopped.

'Sir?' Bathyllus gave me a puzzled look.

Jupiter! It was beautiful! And it solved everything! 'Tell Alexis to take him round to a guy called Felix in Colonus, with my compliments. A thank-you present for services rendered.'

Yeah. Maybe I'd come out ahead this time after all; or at least not too far behind. Priscus would have his statue; if not *the* statue at least something he could show off to his pals. Hermippe had her come-uppance, thanks to her brother's sense of justice. And

Felix would get, free, gratis and for nothing, a very expensive and most individual parrot. And if I was very, very lucky the little bugger might even send it, sight unheard, to his boss in Rome as a peace offering . . .

Life wasn't all that bad, really, once you thought about it. I was grinning as I picked up the wine jug and went through to dinner.

AUTHOR'S NOTE ∫

Croesus's Baker statue, and the story of Caepio and the Tolosan treasure, are factual. The first I knew about, and it provided the original idea for the book; for the second (and for much of what follows here) I am indebted to Professor Christopher Smith of St Andrews University's Ancient History Department.

Herodotus, writing in the fifth century BC, mentions the Baker as part of the rich offerings made at Delphi by King Croesus of Lydia over a hundred years previously. However, by the time Pausanias wrote his *Guide to Greece* in the second century AD the Baker had vanished, along with all the other Lydian dedications except for a single piece of ironmongery.

So where, during the intervening six hundred years, had the statue gone?

My explanation, unfortunately, is almost certainly historically false. Although Brennus's Gauls did reach Delphi in 279 BC they did little or no damage to the sanctuaries, and those responsible for the theft were probably Greeks from Phocis some seventy-five years earlier. However, Caepio and the Tolosan treasure existed and remain an outside chance good enough for my purposes, especially since the historian Dio Cassius specifically identifies the latter as part of Brennus's Delphic loot removed (as I have it) to Gaul. Another interesting quote, which I also made marginal use of at the end of the story, comes from a second Roman writer, Aulus Gellius, who claimed that whoever touched a piece of the plundered gold 'was doomed to a wretched and agonising death'; and indeed the phrase *aurum Tolosanum* (Tolosan gold) became proverbial in Latin for something that always brought bad luck.

• David Wishart

My thanks, as always, to my wife Rona; to Roy Pinkerton of the University of Edinburgh; and to Ann Buchanan ex-RNR who relieved my anxiety over the likelihood in Roman times of recovering a statue lost off the coast of the Piraeus. Any faults and errors in the book (and I'm sure they exist) are wholly my own.

Ovid
DAVID WISHART

Marcus Corvinus is a young man who likes to have a good time and enjoy wine, women and laughter far more than a hard day's work. He also happens to be the grandson of Ovid's former patron.

So when Ovid's stepdaughter, the luscious Perilla begs him to recover Ovid's ashes and bring them back to Rome, how can Marcus refuse? Not that the task turns out to be easy: official permission is abruptly denied. And as Marcus starts asking questions in the higher echelons of Roman society, he finds himself drawn deeper and deeper into a web of secrecy, treachery and deceit.

Comic, bawdy and extremely engrossing, OVID is an intriguing tale of mystery and suspense. Wearing his classical scholarship lightly, David Wishart gives us an up to the minute thriller and a unique insight into Roman life.

David Wishart's first novel *I, Virgil* is a Sceptre paperback:

'An interesting imaginative leap and a thoughtful account of the difficulties of keeping a grip on personal and artistic integrity' *Scotland on Sunday*

∫

SCEPTRE

A selection of bestsellers from
David Wishart and Hodder and Stoughton

Sejanus	David Wishart	0 340 68447 X	£6.99	☐
Germanicus	David Wishart	0 340 68445 3	£6.99	☐
Ovid	David Wishart	0 340 64683 7	£5.99	☐
Nero	David Wishart	0 340 66702 8	£6.99	☐
I, Virgil	David Wishart	0 340 63511 8	£5.99	☐

All Hodder & Stoughton books are available at your local bookshop or newsagent, or can be ordered direct from the publisher. Just tick the titles you want and fill in the form below. Prices and availability subject to change without notice.

Hodder & Stoughton Books, Cash Sales Department, Bookpoint, 39 Milton Park, Abingdon, OXON, OX14 4TD, UK. E-mail address: order@bookpoint.co.uk. If you have a credit card you may order by telephone – (01235) 400414.

Please enclose a cheque or postal order made payable to Bookpoint Ltd to the value of the cover price and allow the following for postage and packing:
UK & BFPO – £1.00 for the first book, 50p for the second book, and 30p for each additional book ordered up to a maximum charge of £3.00.
OVERSEAS & EIRE – £2.00 for the first book, £1.00 for the second book, and 50p for each additional book.

Name _____

Address_____

_____

_____

If you would prefer to pay by credit card, please complete:
Please debit my Visa/Access/Diner's Card/American Express (delete as applicable) card no:

Signature _____

Expiry Date_____

If you would NOT like to receive further information on our products please tick the box. ☐